The Island Sisters

The
Island
Sisters

a novel

MICKI BERTHELOT
MORENCY

bhc
press™

LIVONIA, MICHIGAN

The Island Sisters

Copyright © 2023 Micki Berthelot Morency

Published by BHC Press

Library of Congress Control Number: 2021945964

ISBN: 978-1-64397-330-2 (Hardcover)
ISBN: 978-1-64397-331-9 (Softcover)
ISBN: 978-1-64397-332-6 (Ebook)

For information, write:
BHC Press
885 Penniman #5505
Plymouth, MI 48170

Visit the publisher:
www.bhcpress.com

To Gabrielle Anne Berthelot,
my late maman from whom I drew strength and used it.

The Island Sisters

Part One

1
Monique

A faint sound intruded into her slumber. Monique blinked several times, shading her eyes with her hand from the early morning sunshine bursting through the open window. The warm breeze blew the sheer curtain, infusing the room with the smell of ylang-ylang and jasmine. She inhaled before reaching for the glass on the side table and swallowing a mouthful of water to moisten her mouth. She had drunk too much last night with that man. *What was his name again?* Well, she had done more than drink. She giggled. She had no interest in seeing him again. She stretched her body on her childhood bed, like a well-fed feline, and yawned. Her stomach growled.

The smell of smoked herring tickled her nose. She smiled. Maman always served her favorite breakfast when Monique came home. After washing up in the adjacent bathroom, she bounded down the stairs, tying the sash of her cotton robe over her nightgown. Hearing a loud knocking downstairs, she stopped in her tracks to listen. The knocks raining on the door now sounded urgent. At the foot of the staircase, Monique spied a blur of movement as the butler glided down the hall. She rushed into the dining room, kissing her parents' furrowed foreheads before taking a seat next to Maman. "Who's that?" Monique asked. Maman raised her shoulders almost to her ears and kept them there, waiting.

Soon, Pierre appeared inside the arched entryway to the formal dining room, dressed in a black three-piece suit, white shirt, and a black bow tie. Rivulets of sweat coursed down from his hairline to pool over his upper lip. Monique caught the butler's eyes and sighed, sensing his discomfort in the ridiculous uniform. A small crease between Pierre's eyebrows told Monique Papa would be unhappy with the visitor. Her heart thudded. *One more day.*

In Haitian Creole, Pierre announced, "Monsieur Julien Etienne is here to see Mademoiselle Monique." He looked at Papa with fear dancing in his eyes.

Sharp intakes of breath came from her parents. Monique sprang up from her chair, staring at them in confusion. *Julien! That was his name.*

"What—" Maman exhaled the word, her shoulders finally came down, and a soft cry left her lips as her hand came up to cover her mouth. Papa motioned with his head for Monique to sit back down and stomped out of the room. Instead, Monique walked toward the front door. The sound of tight voices coming from the vestibule stopped her. She looked at the scene through the half-open French doors. Papa's bulk, dressed in a pair of khaki shorts and a white linen shirt, filled the doorway. His knuckles were white as he held on to the doorknob.

"How may I be of assistance, Monsieur Etienne?" Papa said, his light tone failing to mask the tremor on the last word.

"Bonjour, Monsieur Magloire," Julien said. "Nice to see you again." He snorted. "I met your daughter last night at the party. I want to see her."

"What?" Papa staggered back as if he'd been punched. "I'm sorry, but... um...she went back to Miami early this morning."

Papa knows Julien? Monique closed her eyes and tried to clear her head. Julien had not mentioned it last night...or had he? He took a couple steps closer to the threshold as if to peek behind Papa. He looked rumpled, dressed in the same clothes he had worn last night. His shaved head glistened in the sun. His upper lip disappeared under his mustache, and his wide-set eyes narrowed to stare at Papa. In the light of day, Julien did not look as appetizing as he had the night before after the full bottle of Rhum Barbancourt. Monique pulled her head back to avoid being seen, her whole body alert. "But she told me she was leaving Sunday. That's tomorrow." Julien said as if Papa might be senile.

"I'm sorry. Something came up, and she had to go." Papa began to shut the door. "You care to leave a message?"

Julien's face gathered like a fist. "No!" He said with a sneer. "I'll give *her* the message myself." He left.

Papa bumped into Monique and Maman in the hallway. He grabbed Monique's arms, and dug his fingers into her flesh as he pushed her into his den and whispered, "Monique, you have never listened to me before; you better listen now." He pointed a shaking finger in the direction of the foyer. "That man out there is the son of *Hector Etienne*, Duvalier's henchman. I don't know why his son was standing on my doorstep, but he can never return. I hope it's not too late."

A shiver of fear caused goose bumps to form on her skin. "Too late for what?" Monique asked, rubbing her upper arms. "I met Julien at the party last night, and I stopped by his place for…um…a nightcap." She looked away. "He's a local businessman like you, Papa."

"Marcel, you're scaring the child," Maman said, following them into the office and sitting on the couch. "Let's talk about this with—"

"Shut up, Lucia," Papa said. "She better be scared."

"Don't talk to Maman like that." Monique glared at Papa as she lowered herself next to Maman on the sofa. "Why are you so scared of this man? We're not always what our fathers are." She snorted.

"You think you know Haiti, Monique?" Papa said. "You live in America, ignoring what's happening to families like *ours* here." He lowered his voice. "I have friends in prison for no other reason than having financial means and being *mulatre*. They resent *us*." He ran his fingers through his wavy hair as if to emphasize his pedigree.

"Here you go again, Papa. Why are there people like *us* and *them* here?" Monique said, looking at her parents and trying to understand the fear that braided them together the way love never could. "That's why you're afraid and I'm not."

"Well, for a so-called smart woman, you're naïve about life in Haiti," Papa said, standing in the doorway as if to keep something out.

"Well, my home is in Miami. I can't deal with this…this place." Monique threw her arms up in the air. "I came to see Maman for two days, and there's already drama." She shook her head.

"As always, you caused it," Papa said.

"What? Now I'm responsible for Duvalier's dictatorial regime and this man?"

"Obviously, he knows you," Papa said, leaning against his mahogany desk and facing Monique like a judge. "What happened last night with this man?" His voice rose. "Why was he at my house, Monique?"

"I don't owe you an explanation." Monique shifted on the couch next to Maman and leaned forward. "How does he know you, when clearly, he's not in *your* circle?"

Papa turned his head toward the single window. Purple bougainvillea had crept over the trellis, blocking the sun. A green lizard grabbed onto the window frame and bobbed its head as if waiting for an answer as well.

"A few years ago, before he became head of the militia, Julien's father barged into one of my factories and demanded jobs for some of his goons. I happened to be on site and explained I have a waiting list of applicants and I don't operate my business like that. He left." Papa slowly moved his gaze to Monique. "Now you have brought him back here."

"This has nothing to do with me. You had no right to lie and tell Julien I left. You want to run everyone's life. No more. I—"

In two strides, Papa towered over the women. Maman burrowed deeper into the cushion. "And who do you think you're talking to like that, Monique?"

"I'm talking to you." Monique started to get up.

"*Oh mon Dieu!*" Maman pulled Monique back down next to her. "Please stop fighting. That's all you two have ever done. Marcel, it's my fault. I shouldn't have left Moe alone at the party last night, but I had a migraine." Maman sobbed, wringing her hands until they turned red. "This…this man must have come after I left."

Monique hugged Maman's shoulders, running her palm over the beads of bone along Maman's spine. "It'll be okay, Maman, but I'm not a child." Monique cleared her throat. "I chose to stay. I've been keeping myself safe all these years." She cut her eyes at Papa. "Julien doesn't scare me. I—"

Papa grabbed Monique's upper arm and tried to pull her away from Maman. She shrugged his hand off. "Go get your bag," he ordered. "You're leaving. The thug might return later."

Monique jumped from the sofa and stood almost eye level with him. "Don't you *ever* lay your hands on me again." Her nostrils flared. "You can't order me around like that anymore. What the hell is really going on here?"

Papa blinked and stepped back. His steel-gray eyes bore into hers. She did not look away. "Please go, Monique!" he said.

Papa had never said please before. Maman stood, took Monique in her arms, and whispered, "Go, Moe. For my peace of mind, please go. This time he's right."

"Then come with me, Maman. You can attend my graduation," Monique said with hope coating her words.

"I'd love to, *bébé*"—Maman sniffled—"but my passport expired and I—"

"But…but I told you that I'd graduate in—"

"June 1980," Maman said, stopping her. "I'm sorry, *mon amour*. I promise to be there when you become *une avocate* in three years. *Oui!*"

Monique hid her disappointment behind a smile that quivered on her lips. "It's okay." She wiped the tears running down Maman's pinched face with the sash of her robe. "Law school graduation then." She kissed the top of Maman's head.

She scowled at Papa. "I'll go because I don't want to upset Maman, but you can no longer control my life," she said before sprinting up the stairs to pack.

Shortly after, Monique climbed into the back of the family's car and settled into her seat, looking out the window as the car made its way down the verdant hills of Montagne Noire where the houses hid behind high walls with tropical hedges. An occasional car passed them on its way up. Monique rolled down her window. The cool air carried the smell of money and indifference.

Minutes later, the car entered the commotion of Port-au-Prince. The city teemed with people. Monique inhaled the smell of burnt grease from the food vendors who spent their days jockeying for the best spot on the sidewalks. Buzzing flies and the pungent odor of overripe fruits mixed with dust crawled inside the car. She leaned on the open window and could have touched the pedestrians waltzing between the cars to cross the street to the sounds of angry horns. The women carried loads on their heads, on their backs, or in their hands while the men swung their arms with cigarettes dangling from their fingers or shoved into their pants pockets. She rolled up the window and closed her eyes. She hadn't gotten much sleep last night. What had she done? How was she supposed to know Julien was connected to Haitian politics? She had never seen Papa spooked like that before. Julien told Papa he would deliver his message to her. How? She needed a drink.

On the plane, Monique's eyes lingered on the familiar seats of the first-class section before she made her way to the back. She folded her body into an economy seat, her knees pushing the tray in front of her. She squirmed as she tried to get comfortable. Sacrifices came with independence. Once the plane was in the air, she reached inside her handbag for her pack of gum. Instead, her hand closed around the envelope addressed to Papa with the grievance letter she had written a year ago. She pulled it out and tore it up before shoving the pieces back into her satchel. She no longer needed it. Now, three days before her college graduation, she had achieved the means to gain her financial freedom from her father.

Over the years, Papa's iron fist had left its imprint on her skin and her soul. Red anger licked around the edge of her brain like tongues of flame as she blew a loud bubble of Juicy Fruit gum. She took a deep breath and let it go. Papa could never hurt her again. She closed her eyes and let the hum of the engine carry her back to Miami where she was safe. But Julien had known who she was when she'd met him at the party. Had he planned their encounter? If so, why?

Monique gripped the bangle bracelet around her wrist, and the warmth of the gold chased away some of the cold fear her parents had branded her with earlier. "*How much trouble can you get into in one night?*" Maman had asked yesterday before leaving her at the party.

Monique hoped to never find out.

2

Cecilia

A fter a ten-hour shift at the supermarket where Cecilia had worked since high school, she boarded the bus in front of the store and made her way to the back. She needed a nap. She closed her eyes, but sleep would not come. Instead, the excitement of her upcoming graduation needled her brain to remember the journey.

In the fall of 1976, Cecilia had opened her freshmen orientation packet, and a flyer had fallen out. She had picked it up and read: *Free counseling for students every Thursday in room C-100 at the Kalter Student Center from 6:00 p.m. to 8:00 p.m. Topics: Homesickness, anxiety, relationship issues, abuse, academic assistance, and…* Cecilia had stopped reading because her eyes kept going back to that word. *Abuse.* How many students would show up for abuse counseling? Would she be the only one? She could always lie and say she was there because she was homesick, but she had no home.

On the first Thursday, she'd peeked through the small square of glass in the door of room C-100 and saw five women including Ella, her roommate. Ella was a Haitian student with a thick accent, but she spoke such perfect English that she had yet to contract her verbs. Cecilia had smiled. *What is her issue?* she wondered. Surely not abuse. Not like Cecilia. She pushed the door open and walked in.

It was a small room off the student center with a couple dozen metal chairs arranged in four rows. An older woman in a burgundy blazer sat behind a gray desk, riffling through a manual. A young woman with short blonde hair huddled on a chair in the second row, sniffling into a crumpled tissue in her hand. Several of the recessed bulbs in the dropped ceiling were out, casting the back of the room in shadows. Ella stood with the other two attendees and waved to her. Cecilia halted her steps for a second and considered bolting out of the room.

"Cecilia," Ella had said, grabbing her hand, "this is Monique. She is from Haiti like me, but we might as well be from different continents." Ella laughed and asked the other student, "How do you say your name again?"

"It's *L a n e i*, pronounced Lah-knee. I'm from Guam." Lanei extended her hand. Cecilia noticed the thin silver band on her ring finger.

At five feet tall, Cecilia had stepped back to make eye contact with the three women. Monique towered over them. Lanei's long auburn hair seemed to glow in the dimness of the room. A tight French braid pulled Ella's thick hair from her narrow face. Cecilia patted her short afro, hoping her ebony skin hid her sudden envy deep in the fold of its darkness.

"Guys, meet my roommate, Cecilia," Ella said. "She is from Saint Thomas." She squinted at Cecilia from behind her thick glasses. "You did not tell me you were coming to counseling. Oh, she prefers Ceecee," Ella added.

Cecilia nodded at the women. *Ceecee.* The nickname her daddy had given her that made her feel special. The one her mother had never used because Cecilia wanted her to. "Nice to meet you, Monique, Lanei." Then she'd whispered, "So, what are you guys here for?"

The three women said almost at the same time, "Abuse." It was as if they had rehearsed it. They stared at each other with varying degrees of puzzlement before sitting next to each other in the third row. Cecilia had relaxed her spine against the back of the chair. She was not alone.

Now she smiled at the memory, reached over her head, and pulled the cord on the bus to signal her stop. She made her way toward the hissing door, carrying the bag with the groceries for their graduation dinner. She hoped she hadn't forgotten anything off the list Monique had given her before she'd left for Haiti. Cecilia couldn't find it this morning before leaving for work. She hefted the sack over her shoulder.

On the street, the warm June wind carried the smell of island spices, making her hungry. She strolled toward the corner. The houses in the lower-middle-class neighborhood of North Miami sat close to each other with small patches of brown grass on their front lawns. She waved to the neighbors sitting on plastic chairs on their one-car driveway, trying to catch a late afternoon breeze. They were islanders. The Americans barricaded themselves inside, inhaling the recycled air pumped in from their air conditioners. Cecilia soaked in the heat.

She stopped in front of the house that had been her family home before the accident took her daddy away. Hard to believe it had been four years. She wondered if the family who occupied the house now was happier than hers had been.

At the next block, she climbed the two steps of an identical house and inserted her key in the door. No one was home. Cecilia exhaled, grateful for some quiet time. After putting the perishables in the refrigerator, she made her way to a back bedroom. She stripped out of her uniform and tried on the blue cotton sundress she'd bought that afternoon. She knew it would be hidden under her graduation gown, but she wanted something pretty to wear for her mom. Surely, her mother would come. Cecilia had curbed the urge to call her all day, grateful the store was busy. She had four long years of stories to share with her mother.

She turned and opened the dresser drawer. She took out the business card the lady had passed out after the pre-graduation seminar last week. Cecilia read the inscription. *Freda Murphy, Crisis Counselor.* Most of the seniors had left the cards on the floor of the hall, but Cecilia had tucked hers in her purse. Most twenty-two-year-olds perhaps had never experienced a crisis. But she had lived through many. Cecilia stepped out of her graduation dress and hung it in the closet. She dressed in clean clothes and grabbed her purse as she walked to the front door.

She fished some coins from her purse and locked the door behind her. She jogged to the pay phone at the end of the street. She was about to hang up after the ninth ring when a voice said, "Hel...hello."

"Mom, it's me...um...Cee...Ceecee. I—"

"What the hell do you want calling me at this time, Cecilia?" She pulled the receiver away from her ear and held her breath as if she could smell the gin on her mother's loud words alone.

"I...I sent you a ticket." She molded her voice to hide her angry need. "Graduation is on Monday. Um...today is Friday—"

"I know what goddamn day it is. Should have sent the money instead." Her mother burped. "Leon had to go die, leaving me alone with the boys. You need to stop harassing me like this. You're grown now, Cecilia."

She bristled at the mention of her father's death, as if he'd died just to punish her mother. "But I'll help you once I start work, Mom." Cecilia heard the desperation in her voice and swallowed. "I'm graduating with honors. I'm going to be a high school teacher. Can you believe that?" Cecilia spoke fast, trying to get the words out before her mother could hang up the phone. She wanted to convince her to come to Miami. She needed her mother to tell her she was proud of her. That she loved her. "And I'm starting graduate school, too, in the evening."

"Good for you," Mom muttered. "You make up in brains what you ain't got in looks. Send some dough when you make it. Your brothers gotta eat."

"So…so, you're coming tomorrow, right?" Cecilia asked, holding her breath.

"I don't know…" Mom said. "You want me to come watch you? *Why?*" Cecilia touched her cheek as if she'd been slapped. Her mother cleared her throat and spat.

"Mom, I'm graduating with no student loans because I earned an academic scholarship all four years. My GPA is over—"

"Stop braggin'," Mom said, cutting her off. "Gotta take a piss." Her mother hung up.

Cecilia stayed in the booth and banged the receiver against the dial pad, screaming in anger. Once spent, she cradled the receiver until the dial tone died away like the little parts of her heart did every time her mother touched it.

She pulled the counselor's card from her back pocket and read it again. She raised her wrist to her cheek and rubbed the bangle bracelet over her face in a circular motion as if the beauty of the gold would penetrate her skin and make her pretty too. Like a thousand bee stings, Mom's words stung her skin, her brain, her soul, but Cecilia still needed her mommy on Monday. Surely her mother would come.

3

Lanei

Lanei woke up early on Saturday morning and fixed Kevin a breakfast fit for a king. She had learned in the past four years of marriage that keeping his stomach full kept his fists off her body sometimes. God had answered her prayers last night. Kevin was working overtime today. The less time she spent around him the greater her chance of making the flight to Miami the next day for Monique and Cecilia's graduation.

Kevin strutted out of the bedroom in his summer work uniform, an olive-green short-sleeve shirt and matching shorts. His biceps bulged as he fisted his hands, hard like the steel he shaped at the factory. His regimen at the boxing gym bulked his body into a deadly weapon. He stared at the table before raising his gaze to hers, his green eyes speaking words without opening his mouth. She shoved the book she was reading in the top drawer of the sideboard and poured him a cup of coffee. His wet close-cropped hair spiked like hackles. He pulled up a chair and sat down.

"Kev, I made you a Guamanian breakfast of fried rice and a sunny-side up egg. Oh, I even found some sausages that taste like the ones from home."

"Mmm," he grumbled, scraping the chair legs on the wooden floor. Lanei scampered to the kitchen and returned with a heaping plate. He shoved the fork into the food like a shovel filling a burial hole. Lanei sat across from him in the small kitchen and sipped her sweet black coffee, trying to appear calm.

"There's a program at the church tonight," she said. "I'd like to take Maria if she's having a good day. What time do you get off?"

"Don't know. They are busy this month so I'm puttin' in a lot of overtime. We gotta get our own pad soon."

Suddenly, the coffee pooled in her throat, choking her. She swallowed. Living with her mother-in-law, Peggy, since she'd left Miami with Kevin a couple years ago had made life bearable. The brutal winters in Chicago continued to challenge Lanei's genetic island makeup. This June was particularly hot, and she relished spending most of her time outside to enjoy the heat as if she could store it up for the next winter. A whimper from the room at the end of the hallway pulled her from her chair. "Maria's up," she said.

She picked up her daughter from the crib and carried her back to the kitchen. She brushed the damp curls from Maria's forehead and kissed it. Kevin pushed his chair away from the table and stood. "She wants to say hi to her daddy," Lanei said, smiling.

Maria struggled to get out of Lanei's arms, extended her arms to Kevin, and babbled, "Dada."

Kevin reached for his daughter and planted a loud kiss on her forehead before handing her back to Lanei. He palmed his keys from the table. "Gotta leave now, or I'll be late for work."

Halfway to the door, he walked back and grabbed Lanei's buttock from under her housedress and leered at her. "Be home when I get back," he said and left. She fought the urge to shower every time Kevin touched her.

Later that day, she scoured the house, did two loads of laundry, and started dinner before pulling the suitcase from under the bed to pack. She had wanted to remind Kevin of the trip after breakfast, but fear had paralyzed her. Lanei had never wanted to travel so bad, except for when she'd left Guam with Kevin four years ago, hoping the move would iron out the new wrinkles in her month-old marriage.

Lanei heard the front door open and stiffened. Had Kevin come back early? Instead, Peggy poked her head into the bedroom Lanei occupied with Kevin, her red hair plastered to her scalp from a passing summer shower. "Food smells good, Lan," she said, shaking her body like a wet dog. "I'm going to miss you. Kevin told me you guys plan to move out soon."

"Oh, Peg. If I had my choice, I'd stay here. Living with you has sheltered me from…" She stopped and smiled. "Let's go to the kitchen. I'll fix you a plate."

"Are you okay? Thought you'd be happy about your trip to Miami tomorrow."

"I am, but I need to remind Kevin to take me to the airport early. He hasn't mentioned it since I told him over a month ago that I was going."

"I'll take you. What time is your flight?"

"Oh, um…Kevin will want to do it. Thank you."

Later that afternoon, Lanei strapped Maria in her stroller, grabbed her copy of *Lady Susan*, and started toward the church. Less than one block from the house, the sleeveless cotton blouse stuck to her skin. The heat made her long to see her mama.

Four years ago, Lanei had left Guam for Miami with her goal of becoming a pharmacist packed in her heart like a tangible piece of something she owned. But at age eighteen, she'd also brought along a husband. Marrying Kevin was not a choice, but her previous actions had demanded it. At least that was what her priest had said.

Hours later, before heading home after the outdoor summer concert on the church lawn, she pushed the stroller into the open chapel and knelt in front of the statue of the Virgin Mary. She pulled her rosary from her skirt pocket and settled into praying for guidance and protection. On the third Hail Mary, the stroller shook, and Maria's arms shot out. Lanei jumped into action. She looked at her watch and noted the time. It was 7:12 p.m. She reached into the diaper bag on the pew and pulled out the small, quilted blanket and laid it on the floor. She unbuckled Maria from the stroller and put her down. She watched her daughter writhe in spasms as she stroked her hair. A hand touched her shoulder. She turned and stared at a man she'd seen at the concert earlier.

"Should I go find a phone and call for help?" the man asked.

"Thank you, but she'll be fine," Lanei said as Maria's body sagged into the quilt. "This is her third seizure today. I'll take her home now."

"I can drive you if you need a ride."

Lanei strapped Maria into the stroller. She shook the blanket and folded it before shoving it back inside the bag. Her movements were hurried and jerky as if Kevin could see her. "Thank you, sir, but I live nearby." She pushed the stroller until she turned the corner and sprinted all the way home.

When she saw the truck parked in front of the house, she looked for Peggy's car across the street. It wasn't there. She quickened her steps, but her heart wanted to take flight toward freedom. She put her key in the lock, and the force of the door being pulled open almost toppled her over the stroller.

"Where the hell have you been?" Kevin slapped her hard across the face. "Where is my goddamn dinner? I told you to be home early."

Lanei rushed to the stroller and unstrapped Maria. "Kevin, let me put her down. She had a seizure while—"

"Where's my food?" he screamed.

Lanei ran down the hall, placing her sleeping daughter in her crib. Her cheek throbbed. She hurried back to the kitchen. Her hands shook. Was it from anger or fear? She grabbed the plate with both hands, set it on the table in front of him, and stood like a soldier.

"Get me a beer," he said, chewing with his mouth open and spraying the table with specks of food.

She did.

After he finished eating, she washed the dinner plates. Kevin drank more beer. In silence, they watched television. Lanei kept looking at him from the corner of her swollen eye, gauging when it would be a good time to remind him about going to Miami the next day.

Then she knew. Her hand sought the rosary.

In the bed that night, she turned on her side and faced him. She forced her hand to move and touch his shoulder. "I'm...sorry I was late," Lanei whispered. "Kev...you remember I'm going with Maria to Miami tomorrow for Monique and Cecilia's graduation. The flight leaves at..."

He raised his torso from the bed and glared at her. "Remind me again where you find money to go on trips. Huh?" He kicked the sheet off his legs. He was naked underneath. Kevin resented the confinement of clothes on his body. He was a free, malevolent spirit. "We need money to move..."

Lanei steadied her hand to stroke his cheek. "My friends paid for the ticket. I did tell you. Remember?" She hated the plea in her voice, but she had to go on that trip. "I'll be back on Tuesday."

"Didn't Maria have a seizure tonight? She hasn't flown since her surgery. Is it safe?"

Kevin's concern for their daughter touched her in places Kevin had long been banished from. "I asked her pediatrician earlier this week." Lanei scooted closer to Kevin. "She said Maria's heart is fine. She only needs annual cardiac evaluation."

"Who else is gonna be there?" He snaked his fingers through her hair and tugged.

Lanei winced. Her hand moved down to Kevin's nipple. "It's going to be the four of us. Can't wait to see them. It's been almost two years since..."

"Well, now I'm horny, *baby girl*." He grabbed the back of her head and pushed her face down between his legs and said, "I'll think about it."

Lanei closed her eyes and opened her mouth. Father Abbott had said she had marital duties to her husband. She wanted to be a good wife. After Kevin groaned and released her head, Lanei waited until he started to snore and slid out of the bed. She closed the bathroom door behind her and threw up in the bowl. After rinsing her mouth, she sat on the floor, twisting the gold bangle bracelet around her wrist in an endless circle. The movement slowed down her heartbeat. She prayed she'd earned a trip to Miami.

4

Ella

E lla reached for Bernard in the dark. Her hand closed on the rumpled sheet. She sat up and put on her glasses after turning on the bedside lamp. His plumped-up pillow next to her pointed to his absence. Her eyes fell on the graduation invitation on the nightstand, and in the dim light of the bedroom, she could not hide her envy and her failures.

Four years earlier, she had arrived in Miami from her remote Haitian village on a student visa that had cost her family many heads of cattle and several fertile acres of land. She had come here to be a doctor. Now only Monique and Cecilia would get their degrees. The night they met at the student center they'd pledged to graduate together. Who could she blame now?

Cecilia had the privilege of being born an American citizen in Saint Thomas, giving her access to resources. Monique had all the money she needed to become whatever the hell she wanted to be. When Ella's family had cut her off financially for marrying Bernard, she'd had to drop out of school. The unplanned pregnancy had temporarily sealed her fate. If she'd had money like Monique, she'd be walking on Monday as well. Ella was happy for her friends, but what was that feeling choking her?

She slipped into her robe and walked into the common area of the one-bedroom apartment she had lived in since she'd married Bernard the summer of her freshman year. Alex, her three-year-old son, slept on a cot in a corner. She opened the cupboard for a tumbler and filled it up with wine from the fridge before sitting on the lumpy couch to stare at the bare walls. After her second drink, she strode back into the bedroom and unfolded the letter she kept on her bedside table as a talisman. She was going back to school in the fall. It said so there. She shook the sheet of paper. Bernard would support her; they were a team. She closed her eyes and let the alcohol smooth out the bumps in her life.

"Elle...*Ella*," Bernard said. "Why're you sleeping across the bed? Been drinking too much again?" He bent down to kiss her forehead.

"Hey, *mon amour*." Ella pulled him down on the bed. "Where have you been? It is...it is late."

"I told you I was going to a community meeting after work." He took her in his arms. "You know how those Haitians can talk." He kissed her lips and murmured, "I'm exhausted. I need sleep."

"Mmm." She nibbled on his bottom lip. "Not so fast."

Bernard peeled Ella's arms from around his neck and stood. She sat with her back against the headboard and watched him strip out of his clothes. His slight frame belied his physical strength. He hung his shirt on a metal hook on the wall before unbuckling his belt and pulling down his zipper. He turned to face Ella. The top of his white briefs peeked over the waist of his dress pants, and pubic hairs poked over the elastic around his trim waist. The bulge tenting the front of his slacks caught her attention and held it. His face opened in a smile, stretching his broad nose with each breath. She took off her glasses and placed them on the nightstand. She stuck her tongue out at him, pulled the sheet over her head, and giggled. His weight settled over her before his hand roamed under her cotton nightgown, his fingers plunging inside her.

"Someone's ready," he said, kissing the back of her neck.

She turned on her back and traced his wide lips with her thumb. He sucked it into his warm mouth. Bernard slithered down and took small bites of her skin along the length of her stomach and her legs. Her skin on fire, she gripped his head and pulled him up, taking him in. Ella sopped up the love and attention he offered.

Bernard fed her hungry heart, filling the holes left by the mother she'd never known and the father who blamed her for her mother's death. Her world at this moment narrowed to just this shabby apartment with her son and Bernard.

With their legs entwined under the sheet and her head on his chest, she listened to the humming of his heart as if it was singing to her. With her support, Bernard had obtained his degree in engineering in less than four years.

"I'm so proud of you, *chéri*, for graduating early and landing this great job. You should attend your graduation ceremony on Monday. You earned it," Ella said.

"I'd rather go to work." He massaged her scalp, and she moaned. "Besides, you get to be with your girlfriends without any distraction from me."

Ella's head popped up. "I hope Lanei will make it. With Kevin…" She shrugged. "Monique went to see her mother. I wish I had a mother or even a family who cares enough to see me."

Bernard kissed her nose. "*Mon amour,* you don't need those people in Haiti anymore. You have me and Alex. We're your family now."

"I know. But…once I have my medical degree, I am going back. You and I can do so much good in our village."

"Let's take it one day at a time, Elle."

"You are right as always." She kissed his chin. "Starting this fall, I will have almost seven more years before I finish medical school."

Bernard shifted his body, his fingers combing through her hair with urgency. "Ella, I'm starting graduate school in the fall." He teased her nipple with his other hand. "Let me finish school, then you can go without any interruption."

"What?" Ella pushed him away and reached for her glasses. She needed to see his eyes. "When did you decide that?" She sat up and peered down at him. "I am here for school too."

Bernard cleared his throat. "Sweetheart, think about it. With my master's degree, I'll earn more, and I'll be able to take care of everything when you go back to school."

Ella bristled. "I do not know, Bernard. That was not the plan. I want to go to school *now.*" She heard hysteria in her voice.

"Your turn will come, *ma belle.* You trust me, don't you?"

Ella did not answer. The last time Bernard had asked her that question, she'd ended up pregnant and had dropped out of school. She slid to the edge of the bed as if she needed space to process this new development. Bernard leaned over and kissed her quivering lips. "*Bonne nuit, chérie.*"

He turned his back and placed the pillow over his head. She turned off the lamp and listened to the whirring of the ceiling fan. What should she do? It sounded reasonable, but why was she making all the sacrifices? Would Bernard support her academic plan? She had been working a lot to save money, and she had student loans. She could not do it alone. Could she? Her doubt escalated in tempo with the crickets outside the window. In the dark, she twirled the bangle bracelet around her wrist, feeling the strength of the friendship that had sustained her with each breath, and a decision took shape.

She was going back to school as planned in the fall. Bernard would accept that and wait for graduate school. She would not let him convince her otherwise. She would be firm in her resolve. But doubt and fear had stolen away her sleep. Bernard always seemed to get what he wanted. What did he really want from her?

5
Monique

M onique rushed toward the stage, her heels click-clacking on the flag-stone ramp in rhythm with her heartbeat. When she reached the platform, she turned and faced the auditorium. She saw Cecilia in line against the back wall, a hibiscus sprouting from her afro. Then her gaze settled on Ella and Lanei in their seats next to each other, each holding her child on her lap. The tribe was here.

Four years earlier, the "island sisters," as they had dubbed themselves, had mapped a road to graduation. Today, the sadness in Ella's eyes had a green tinge to it even through her thick lenses. Lanei raised her hand midway and waved. Monique nodded and turned back to the stage, but she couldn't help noticing two tracks of tears frame Ella's face in a rictus halfway between a smile and a cry.

After the ceremony, Monique and Cecilia found their friends leaning against a tree in the parking lot, their children playing on the grass next to them. The women extended their arms toward each other and formed a circle, just like their identical bracelets that sparkled under the Miami sun, before climbing inside Monique's car.

"I'm so glad we're all here," Monique said, starting the car. "I'm sorry—"

"Not today, Moe," Lanei said. "It's happy time."

Monique drove through Coral Gables, the streets littered with a carpet of pink petals from the oleander hedges, orange flowers from the flame trees, and red bougainvillea. She wished Maman could hold her diploma, but she wouldn't go back to Haiti until Julien forgot about her. She sighed and rolled her neck to relieve tension. Lanei reached from the back seat to squeeze Monique's shoulders. "That was a beautiful ceremony," Lanei said. "God's good, Moe. Didn't I always say that?"

"Every chance you get, sister," Monique said, making eye contact with Lanei in the rearview mirror and smiling. "I'm thrilled you're here, Lan. I know it must have been a...challenge."

Lanei's grip pinched Monique's skin under the thin fabric of her blouse. "It's always a challenge," Lanei replied, "but I'm here."

Monique pulled into the driveway, and they walked into her family's vacation home that had been the sanctuary for their monthly gatherings in the early years. Alex stirred in Ella's arms and whined. "Hush, son," Ella whispered, handing him to Monique. Lanei followed with eleven-month-old Maria. They laid the sleeping children down in one of the bedrooms and left the door open.

The women scattered around the kitchen like choreographed dancers to gather the ingredients Cecilia had purchased on Saturday for their specialty dishes. Like the bracelets, the food had become more than corporal sustenance. It was a ritual that kept them tethered to each other wherever they happened to be on their journey.

Lids slapped the top of pots, and metal spoons scraped the bottom of glass bowls. Water splashed in the sink, while corks popped out of bottles. The familiar sounds relaxed hunched shoulders. They stared at each other and started a chorus of snorts that swelled into sidesplitting laughter.

"That's more like it," Monique said, wiping her eyes when she caught her breath. "We were beginning to look like goddamn funeral directors."

"Oh, that feels good," Ella said, blowing her nose on a paper napkin. "It is a happy day even for me and Lanei who did not make it to the podium today. Let us cook. I am hungry."

Monique pulled the cooked red beans from the fridge and fresh garlic and onions to make rice and beans the way Ella had taught her. Cecilia dusted the marble counter with flour, placed the dough down, and hefted the roller to work on the crust for her ginger-apple pie. Ella poured a generous amount of oil in a deep pot, turned on the vent over the stove, and dropped chunks of seasoned pork into the hot oil to make *griot*. Lanei lined the bottom of a baking pan with strips of bacon, sliced breadfruit, and coconut milk before placing it in the oven.

As the food cooked, they sat down around the table in the breakfast nook of the large kitchen. Lanei reached for a glass and poured wine from the open bottle. Three mouths dropped open.

"Okay, okay," Lanei said, a smile crinkling the corners of her deep brown eyes. "Who's going to say it?"

All eyes turned to Monique who slapped her thigh and let out her high-octane laugh. "I'll be damned. Lan, remember freshman year when you prayed over us for drinking underage. I—"

"Well, we're twenty-two, Moe," Lanei said in her soft-spoken voice, cutting Monique off. "I'm not breaking any laws *now*. I can't believe four years can go by so fast and leave such a trail of...defeat for some of us." She made eye contact with all of them, lingering on Ella who still hadn't put her glass down. Lanei raised hers. "To Moe and Ceecee! Your graduation today makes me believe that Elle and I will get there one day." Lanei smiled through the tears she mopped off her face with a wad of tissue. "Let's drink to your continued success. You two have earned your freedom today."

Ella stood, raising her glass. "Sisters, Lan is right," she said, the slurring of her words thickening her accent. Monique moved the bottle away from Ella's hand. *"Oui, oui!"* Ella continued, "Lanei and I will find a way to manage our families and achieve our professional goals. We will follow in your path."

"I'll drink to that," Monique said, taking a gulp of her red wine. "Ceecee and I are here for both of you always."

Cecilia nodded, pulling a cigarette from the pack on the table. She put it back when Lanei looked in the direction of the hallway.

"These things can kill you," Lanei said. "By the way, I was hoping to finally meet your mom today."

Cecilia's dimples disappeared as she filled her mouth with air and let it out with a whoosh. "My mother doesn't need a visa to come here from Saint Thomas," Cecilia said, "yet she never comes. I feel like an orphan today." She shrugged, placing both elbows on the table and dropping her face in her palms. "I miss my daddy."

Lanei reached across the table and touched Cecilia's arm. "I'm sorry about your mom, sweetie," Lanei said. "Look at me, Ceecee. Your father was a good man. He can see you today because he's in the kingdom of God."

"Oh, Lan! I don't know where he is." Cecilia shook her head. "I only know he's not here with me. I wish I had your faith."

"I wish you all did," Lanei said, staring at them with the same pained look that Monique had seen on the face of the Virgin Mary statue at church as a child. "My faith has seen me through some dark moments in my life."

Lanei's tears unmasked the bruise under her right eye that she'd covered with makeup. "Lan, what the hell? Kevin did that to you?" Monique pointed at Lanei's face, her hand shaking in anger. Ella and Cecilia leaned in. "What are you gonna do about this situation?" Monique asked.

"Moe," Lanei said. "I'm not talking about this."

The four women glared at each other. Monique swallowed the angry words she wanted to throw at Kevin like stones. Ella reached for the bottle and topped off their glasses. She raised hers to her mouth, and when she set it down, it was half empty. "No man should be allowed to do this, Lan. Do you understand?" Monique would not let it rest.

"I have lost my appetite," Ella said, trying to stand up from her seat and falling back into it. "I have not accomplished anything in my life that I am proud of."

Once again, Ella turned the attention back to herself. Monique shook her head in frustration. Lanei jumped up and stood behind Ella's chair, rubbing the back of her neck. "How can you say that, Elle?" Lanei asked. "What about your son? He's a gift from God."

"Oh, please," Monique said with a snort before she could stop herself. "Any woman can make a baby if all her parts work. She just needs a dick to—"

"Stop it, Moe," Cecilia said, in her moderator voice. "Let's talk about our true feelings without wisecracks or judgment." She threw a side-glance at Monique. "I also have truths I need to face. I think we made a mistake when we stopped going to counseling. We all should have continued with therapy somewhere. I plan to start again soon." Cecilia smiled at Ella and said, "Go ahead, Elle."

Ella cut her eyes at Monique. "Growing up without a mother left me feeling hollow and…guilty," she said, drying her eyes with a napkin.

"But your mother dying in childbirth isn't your fault, despite what your father wanted you to believe," Cecilia said.

"I know that Ceecee, but I still had such a big hole to fill. I married Bernard because I felt so…so empty."

"We all have holes to fill," Lanei added.

Laughter erupted from Monique, causing her to spit her wine back into her glass. The women stared at her. "What?" Monique said. "I'm sorry, Lan. The *hole* thing was funny."

"These *holes*," Lanei continued, "are our common threads besides our island connections."

"I'm sorry, guys," Monique said, swallowing the tail end of her laughter. "Let's eat." The aroma of the food filled the kitchen with memories. She inhaled and smiled. Nothing could stop her now.

They set the dishes on the counter, and each filled a plate. After the meal, Monique and Cecilia cleaned the kitchen while Ella and Lanei checked on their children. They moved to the family room, where they sat in their regular spots.

"Lan, do you have to go back to Chicago?" Monique asked, sipping her wine next to Cecilia on the couch. She was not willing to let this go. "You can stay here, you know. We have resources available at my job at the women's center. I—" She stopped as Lanei slid her hand into her skirt pocket. Monique could see her fingers rubbing her rosary beads the way she did when trying to control her panic.

"I can't just walk away from my marriage. God sanctioned it. I want my daughter to grow up with her father the way I was not able to," Lanei said, shifting her weight next to Ella on the love seat.

"Well, what good is a father who destroys his family with his actions?" Monique said, anger deepening her voice. She instinctively reached behind her neck and rubbed the ragged scar where her father's belt buckle had ripped the skin off years ago. Monique no longer remembered which rule she had broken. There were too many. "Does your God say you stay until you get killed?"

Ella jumped to her feet so fast she had to grab Lanei's shoulder to steady herself. "Leave her alone, Monique," Ella said, screeching in her high-pitched voice and pushing her glasses up her nose. "A marriage is not a one-night stand. See what happened to you in Haiti last weekend with that guy? It takes commitment and patience to make relationships work."

"Oh, yeah? How's yours working out, Elle?" Monique said, straightening the slack in her spine. "You should be starting medical school this fall. Instead—"

"Moe, honestly," Cecilia said. "Ella doesn't need to hear this today."

"When should we tell her then?" Monique said. "I thought we were speaking the truth today. If we've learned anything from going to counseling, it is to be open and talk about what hurts the most. Right?"

Ella stopped pacing and stood in front of Monique. "Well, what the hell is your truth then, Moe?" she asked. "You jump from one relationship to the next with no consequences except for phone calls from soppy guys crying for your love. You fight with your father because he has too much money, but you luxuriate in it. You are moving out of this mansion"—Ella waved her arm around the expanse of the family room that overlooked the screened pool and the Japanese gardens—"into a small apartment because you want to know what it feels like to live on less when the three of us here struggle for the basics!" Ella sucked her teeth so loudly, Monique wondered if she'd swallowed a few this time. "You do not know my truth, sister," Ella said, spitting the words out. "My husband is not perfect, but he loves me. If I had money like you—" She stopped and peered into her glass. "I am going to be a doctor even if I die trying."

Lanei pulled a bawling Ella back down onto the love seat. "Elle, you have had enough." Lanei took the glass from her hand. "We're celebrating Moe and Ceecee's big day. I'll get you some water."

"Oh, Moe, I am…I am so…so sorry," Ella stammered. "I did not mean—"

"It's all right, Elle." Monique smiled, squatting down in front of the coffee table. She opened her hands, palms facing up. The three women joined her on the floor and held hands in the silence of the house that had witnessed their tears, their joy, and their victories. "Don't apologize," Monique continued. "Everything you said is true, Elle, except… You all know Papa beat me…a lot when I was a kid. I don't want to stay in this house, because it's his and I need to find my own way." Monique squeezed Ella's and Lanei's hands in hers. "Like soldiers on the battlefield, no one here will be left behind."

Monique felt the tension of the day ebb from the tips of their joined fingers with every breath they exhaled. She stood. "I'll put some music on, and we'll dance to celebrate being together."

The phone rang as Monique made her way to the stereo. She reached for the receiver on the side table. "Hello?" she said, smiling. "Maman?"

"Monique Magloire, you think you can get away from me," the voice said. "*Think again.*"

In a flash the smile vanished from Monique's lips. She dropped the receiver and closed her eyes. Fear tapped at her chest to be let in. When she opened her eyes, she was standing in the middle of a circle as if her friends wanted to keep her happiness from evaporating on the breath of her angry sobs.

"It was Julien," she whispered as if he could hear the panic in her voice.

The circle shrank until her friends' bodies anchored her in place, keeping her standing tall and strong.

6
Cecilia

C ecilia yawned and turned on her back, placing her hands behind her
head. She stared at the blurring ceiling fan in one of the guest rooms in
Monique's family home. For a homeless woman, Cecilia had many rooms, but
she would have been happier living with her mother and her brothers under
a bridge if only her mother had wanted her. The euphoria of her graduation
yesterday had waned. She had never doubted that she could do the work to
accomplish her dream of becoming a teacher, but every time she had reached
out to become the daughter and the sister she was born to be, she had failed.

Last night she'd missed another opportunity to tell her friends the truth
about what had happened to her ten years ago. Cecilia still believed they would
not understand. How could they? They each had someone in their lives who
loved them. Ella and Lanei had created their own families, and with her looks,
Monique could have whatever or whomever she wanted. The jealousy she felt
toward her friends shamed her. She pulled her arms from behind her head and
ran her thumb over the smoothness of her gold bangle. From the very first
night they had slipped them on, their bracelets had connected them like
unbreakable links.

It was their freshman year, and they were spending their first Christmas together even though they had all wanted to go home. Instead, they had
settled at Monique's place to celebrate the end of their first semester. After
their traditional dinner, Monique had picked up the packages she'd placed
under the tree earlier and handed one to each of them with a *ho ho ho*. Cecilia
ripped her box open and said, "You shouldn't have, Moe. I don't have anything
for you. I saved every penny in case Mom still wants me...you know...to
come home for the holidays."

Inside each bag was a bracelet identical to the one Monique wore all the time. "Oh, Moe! I'll never take it off." Lanei and Ella had slipped theirs on and nodded in agreement.

Cecilia had raised her beer bottle in a toast, and the three women had joined in with Lanei lifting her can of ginger ale. "Here's to the 'island sisters,' class of 1980," Cecilia said, christening them that day. They entwined their arms and the bracelets jingled.

Maria's soft cry from the next room pulled Cecilia back from the past and reminded her why they hadn't all graduated yesterday. She heard footsteps going toward the kitchen. She rolled off the bed and made her way next door. Maria lay on her back with a thumb in her pink mouth. Her green eyes swam with unshed tears, making them glow like wet marbles. Cecilia picked her up and buried her face in Maria's soft hair, the same deep auburn as Lanei's. Her baby smell stoked a hunger in Cecilia's belly. She sat with Maria on her lap in the wing chair and rocked her body back-and-forth.

"Oh, Ceecee, did Maria wake you?" Lanei asked, walking into the room and shaking a bottle of milk, her fingers pinching the nipple.

"I was awake." Cecilia reached for the bottle. "Let me feed her."

Maria latched onto the nipple, and her small hand left the bottle and grasped Cecilia's thumb. Cecilia's hardened heart melted from the baby's touch. She blinked several times to stop the tears. "You're a natural, Ceecee. Maria doesn't do well with strangers, but they say babies can tell good people from bad."

"She's so beautiful, Lan. I hope she overcomes her seizures soon, so you can resume your studies. But she's…worth it. I have no doubt."

"Well, now that you've reached your academic goal, you can have a family too," Lanei said. "Mama loves me more than she should, but being a mother now, I understand the depth—" Lanei stopped. "Oh! I'm so sorry, Ceecee."

Cecilia placed the bottle on the side table and raised Maria to her shoulder. She ran her palm over the baby's back. "It's okay, Lan. My daddy loved me a lot, too. I guess he needed to make up for Mom's…neglect."

"It's her loss." Lanei sat at the foot of the bed and touched Cecilia's knee. "One day you'll meet the man who will be worthy of your beauty, your brains, and your goodness." Lanei's face clouded over. "Did we hurt each other yester-day by speaking the truth, Ceecee?"

"Truth said among the four of us should never hurt." Maria burped loudly. "We'll be all right." Cecilia winked.

"My marriage has...issues," Lanei said. "I talk to my priest. Who do you talk to?"

"I met Freda recently when she gave a one-day seminar at school before graduation. She's a crisis counselor."

"Good. I wish you'd go to church." Lanei paused. "Please talk to some-body if you need to."

"I did call Freda after talking to my mother Saturday. I made an appoint-ment, but I'm doing okay. I have everything I need for now." The lump in Cecilia's throat reminded her that she couldn't lie to herself.

She placed a sleeping Maria back on the bed and hugged Lanei, inhaling the rose-scented shampoo her friend liked. Lanei leaned her head back, looked at Cecilia, and said, "At least you haven't been...hurt by a man."

"Lan, it's never okay for a man to abuse you in any way." Cecilia touched the bruise under Lanei's eye. "Remember how we learned in freshmen year about all the different ways women can be abused?"

Lanei nodded, squeezing Cecilia tight. When she let her go, Lanei picked baby items off the bed and threw them in the open suitcase on the floor. "My flight is in a couple hours, Ceecee. I have to get ready."

Cecilia walked back to her room and locked the door. Staring into the dresser mirror, she saw her mother, the men from under the stairs in Boston, her prom date, all the bad people who had battered her body, and her soul etched on her skin like glyphs. She needed to tell someone what she had endured.

Cecilia never wanted to be a victim again.

7

Lanei

Lanei zipped her suitcase and waited in the family room for her friends to drive her to the airport. She looked around the room, trying to imprint the joy she felt here into her heart. In the past this house had provided her with respite from the onslaught of Kevin's rage. Being here with her island sisters had always made her feel like the teen she was instead of the married woman she had become at eighteen.

On their way to the airport, they picked up Ella from her apartment. The love in the car buzzed louder than the hurtful words they had flung at each other the day before. It showed in the way they squeezed shoulders, held on to hands too long, and gazed into each other's faces with wet eyes. At the airport Lanei hugged her friends so tightly that their heartbeats thrummed through her body where they touched. They wound their wrists together and clinked their bracelets, rubbing their palms together. People stared and smiled.

"I believe God will bring me back to Miami," Lanei said. "I appreciate your concern." She touched the tender bruise on her face. "I'll be okay."

She watched Monique's lips move. Lanei pushed the stroller through the automatic door, and with tears streaming down her face, she turned back and flapped her hands like wings. *Hafa Adai*, she mouthed. The women smiled and yelled the Guamanian words back to her. "*Hafa Adai.*"

She walked to the pay phone in the terminal, dug into her purse, fed coins into the slot, and dialed. The line connected, and she heard Kevin grunt. "Hi, Kevin. I'm sorry I couldn't call yesterday. It was a busy day. Oh, Maria did well. She—"

"Good. You on your way?"

"Yes. I'm at the airport."

"I'll pick you up." He hung up.

Lanei's stomach roiled. What if she'd listened to her friends and stayed in Miami? Would God forgive her for walking out on her marriage? But if she followed Kevin's rules, everything would be fine. She needed to be more obedient. He loved his daughter, and Maria deserved to grow up with her father. Lanei sighed, dropped more coins into the slot, and dialed again.

"Hey. Are you busy?" she asked, wiping her sweaty palm on her denim skirt.

"Hi, Lane," Nate said, using his special name for her. "Never too busy for my favorite friend. Is Maria okay? I've been worried. Oh, how was the graduation? Did—"

Lanei smiled, feeling the tension leave her body. "Maria is well. No seizures since we got here." She inhaled and released the breath to slow her heart. "The ceremony was beautiful. I wanted to be up there receiving my diploma yesterday too. Why can't I just be happy for Moe and Ceecee?" Lanei asked as if she were talking to herself.

"Guess what? You're human, not a saint...*yet*." Nate laughed. "You will... graduate, I mean."

She blew into the receiver. "It was emotionally...intense after...when we got to Moe's, but I'm glad I came."

"I'm glad you went too. You needed it. Should I pick you up?" Nate asked. "There's another pharmacist on duty today, so I can leave for a—"

"Oh, no!" she said too loudly. Maria stirred in the stroller next to her and opened her eyes. "Kevin is coming to get us. I just wanted to hear your...to say hi."

"Have a safe trip." His words tunneled through the wires to touch her. "See you soon."

She left the stroller at the gate and carried her daughter onto the plane, her heart breaking in two pieces. One piece wanted to stay in Miami, to finish college, to be with her friends, and to be free. The other piece needed Nate in Chicago to give her hope that life could be more than fearing God and surviving Kevin's fury. Maria raised her hand and touched Lanei's face as if she knew her mother needed comfort. She looked into her daughter's green eyes and frowned. Kevin had left his imprint all over her body like his signature of ownership.

She opened her book, unfolding the dog-eared page of *Love and Friendship*. Lanei mused about how she had plenty of both, yet was forbidden from one and isolated from the other. She wondered what additional price Kevin would extort from her for this escapade. Lanei fingered her rosary and braced herself.

8
Ella

E lla tied a bath towel around her wet hair and peered into the mirror, her nose touching the glass. She wiped the condensation off her glasses before slipping them on. The pregnancy with Alex had rounded the sharp angles of her lean body into soft curves. She looked away from the mirror.

Her envy yesterday at Monique and Cecilia's graduation had no place in their friendship. Yet she doubted Monique even knew how much her education had cost. Her father always took care of the unpleasant issue of money in Monique's life. Blessed with a high IQ, Cecilia breezed through college with ease and an unwavering focus. Ella's family had made great financial sacrifices to send her to college in Miami. After four years, all she had to show for their investment was her son and Bernard, the husband they had not wanted for her. But now she was going back to school, and she would pay them back one day.

Her job as a nurse aide on the maternity floor had cemented her goal of becoming an obstetrician. Would her life have turned out differently if her mother hadn't died in childbirth with her? Her father had ignored her existence but had given her the opportunity of a lifetime to study abroad. What had she done with it? Could she face the truth without falling apart?

She plugged in the hair dryer and started on her hair. Tonight, she would meet the people who had helped her husband secure an engineering position with a local plant in town and permanent visas for them both. They had paved her return to school with the documents she needed to be able to apply for student loans.

Ella needed her tribe for support but watching Lanei leave this morning had shaken the foundation where her strength to succeed dwelled. She pulled the two pressing combs from the kitchen drawer just as the doorbell rang. She let Cecilia in, hunching down to hug her friend tight. Cecilia's spongy afro brushed against Ella's cheek, releasing the sulfur odor of her pomade. Ella turned the burner under the combs.

"Ceecee, thanks for coming over to press this unruly mess." She ran her fingers through her thick hair. "I want to look fabulous tonight. Let us do some magic, sister."

"No magic needed, honey. You're beautiful. Let's get started. Your hair takes a long time to press."

Ella flipped the switch to turn on the overhead light in the tiny kitchen. The hair sizzled under the hot comb and smelled like popcorn before the butter is added. "Ceecee, I can press your hair if you want," Ella said, folding the top of her ear down away from the tip of the comb. "It would look nice on you. You want a beer? It is so hot."

"No thanks to both," Cecilia said. "When I was four, my mom sent me to this evil woman to press the kinks out of my hair, because she didn't know what to do with it. You can't see them, but I bet I still have scars on my ears, my forehead, and the back of my neck from hot combs. My hair texture, unlike yours, needs a lot of heat to submit to the run of a brush." Cecilia patted her hair and sighed. "I love my afro."

"You are beautiful, Ceecee." Ella stared into the hand mirror, admiring the way her pressed hair fell straight below her ears. She met Cecilia's eyes in the mirror. "I was mean to Moe yesterday. I really am happy for the two of you. I hope she forgives me *again*."

"Come on. You know Moe doesn't hold grudges, secrets, or her tongue." They laughed. "She probably already forgot about it. You know, this morning Lanei was concerned about our...talk as well."

"I admire Moe's determination to be self-sufficient when she does not ever have to work, Ceecee." Ella twisted the gold bracelet on her wrist and swallowed her guilt with a gulp of her beer. "You are right. I hope the situation with this Julien guy is not too serious."

"I hope not. Moe was spooked last night."

"Maybe it will teach her to stop sleeping around."

"Come on, Elle. Moe doesn't sleep around the way you make it sound."

Ella shrugged.

A few minutes later, she handed the pink sponge rollers to Cecilia. "Flip the hair up in the back when you roll it. In Haiti, we call that style *queue de canard*, which means 'duck's tail.'"

"Cute," Cecilia said, patting her afro. "My hair is too short for that."

They hung around the apartment all afternoon watching TV, eating Haitian stew, and talking. When it was time to get ready for the evening, Cecilia helped her with her makeup. Ella's skin glowed under a light coat of sparkly powder. She ran the tube of red lipstick over her thin lips several times to give them a fuller look. Feeling like Cinderella, she twirled around. Alex dropped his Lego pieces on the shaggy brown carpet and clapped his hands. "I wish I could afford contact lenses," Ella said. "I hate these glasses."

"You still look gorgeous, Elle. And smart," Cecilia said, putting the makeup back into the zippered bag.

They all turned to the front door as it banged against the wall. Bernard stood in the doorway with his navy-blue suit jacket draped over his arms. The shoe lift and his erect posture added an extra inch to his height. His fleshy lips narrowed in annoyance that he tried to pass off as a smile, but Ella knew better. He didn't care much for her friends. He believed they had influenced her decision to stay on her academic path.

Two days ago, he had shrugged and said nothing when she had told him that he needed to put his graduate plan on hold, because she was going back to school this fall.

"Good. You're almost ready," he said in greeting. He waved his hand at Cecilia, but it seemed more like a goodbye than a hello. "Elle, we don't want to be late."

"Hello, Bernard," Cecilia said. "I was just leaving." Ella hugged her, and Cecilia kissed Alex on her way out. "You're so handsome, Alex. You look just like your mommy."

After he'd had a few minutes to clean up from work, Bernard stepped out of the bathroom dressed in his new black suit and a starched white shirt Ella had spent a whole hour pressing earlier. He looked as if he had shaved off years along with the stubble on his angular face.

"Help me with this," he said, fussing with his green paisley tie.

Ella smiled at her husband and her son, staring at them. She knew she had made the right decision three years ago when she had put them first. At twenty-two, she had time to start over. She stood over Bernard in her silver sandals with three-inch heels and bent down to brush his cheek with her lips.

Bernard narrowed his eyes. "You know I prefer it when you wear flats."

"Well, I want to wear heels today. I do not have a problem being taller than you, so you should not either."

He snorted. "If I ever have a problem with anything, Ella, I take care of it. Besides, we're the same height."

"No. I am taller." She ran her hand over his short, pebbly hair. "You look handsome, *Monsieur* Engineer."

"One day, it will be *Doctor* Engineer."

"But not before I am *Mrs. Medical Doctor*, right?" she asked, waiting for the assurance.

He snatched his keys off the table. "Let's go. It's getting late."

"Bernard—"

He kissed her forehead. "*Tu es élegante, ma belle.*"

She beamed. Her cranberry-red, V-necked sheath dress showed a hint of cleavage and accentuated her long neck. Her hair was parted on the side and sprayed stiffly in place so it covered her right eye. Ella twirled around for her husband.

After dropping off a sleeping Alex at the babysitter's, Ella sang along to Les Ambassadeurs, her favorite Haitian band, as one of their songs played on the car stereo. Bernard squeezed her thigh and smiled. "Do I make you happy, Elle?"

"Always!" she said, laughing. "Okay, almost always, my love."

When they arrived at their destination, Bernard opened the car door and helped her out. The house sat back from an expansive front lawn with tropical trees and bushes. Colored light beams splashed across the landscape, making everything look festive. The June night enveloped Ella in its warm breeze, and the starry sky twinkled over the multiple water fountains.

Bernard walked toward a short older man with a white beard. "Elle, I'd like you to meet Professor Griffin, my mentor. His recommendations landed me the job."

The professor kissed the back of Ella's hand. "Nice to meet you, young lady." He released her hand. "You got that job on your own merit, young man." The professor smiled at Ella. "Keep an eye on him. He's sly. He'd run for president of the US if he could."

Ella smiled back. "My husband has big dreams for us, sir."

Bernard took her hand and said, "Let's go meet the rest of the department staff, sweetheart."

Ella sipped champagne all night and talked to strangers about her scholastic dreams, her obstacles, and her hopes. Alcohol peeled off her inhibitions and loosened her tongue. Coming from the powder room, she came face-to-face with a tall man in a striped suit.

"Hello, gorgeous," he said. "I'm Mr. Taylor, the dean of the engineering school."

Before she could answer, Bernard cut the distance between them with long strides and held her elbow.

"Dean Taylor, this is Ella, my wife."

"You're a lucky man, Bernard," the dean said, bowing to Ella. "Your wife looks like a model."

Someone called to Bernard across the room. He squeezed her arm and left.

"Thank you," Ella said to the dean, smiling. She extended her hand. "Happy to make your acquaintance, sir." He took it and held on a bit too long.

"*Enchanté.* Please call me Arthur," he said, winking. "Bernard has great taste." He licked his lips, leaned over Ella's ear, and whispered, "Your accent feels like sex on my skin."

She pulled her hand away and wiped it on the back of her dress as if to erase a stain. "Dean Taylor, you—" A blue-haired woman in a loud print dress walked up to the dean and looped her arm through his.

"I'm *Doctor* Taylor," the woman said to Ella. The tip of her nose almost pointed to the sky. "I'm the head of the Psychology Department. What did you graduate with yesterday, *dear?*"

Ella stared at her. "I did not, ma'am...um...Dr. Taylor. I completed one year of premed three years ago and then had a child. I am going back this fall. My husband graduated yesterday though."

The woman turned to her husband. "Arthur, this gathering was strictly for graduates with honors." She yanked her arm from his, sloshing his drink over his hand, and walked away, leaving behind a whiff of expensive perfume and sudden shame. Ella stared into the empty glass in her hand. Bernard appeared next to her as if she had summoned him from the last melting ice cube at the bottom of the glass. "Thank you for the invitation, Dean Taylor," Bernard said. "We have to pick up our son."

"But Alex is spending the night at the sitter's," Ella said, staring at the dean with what she hoped was naked fury. "I would like to—"

Bernard squeezed her fingers. Her wedding band bit into her flesh. "We're leaving now," he said, smiling and nodding at people as they made their way to the door.

They reached the car and climbed in. After they had been driving for a while, she said, "You missed the turn to get Alex."

He kept driving. Before Bernard had even locked the apartment door from the inside, he pulled her against his chest and kissed her hard. Her lips hurt.

"You're drunk, and you were flirting with the dean." He pressed his erection against her thighs. "Your so-called 'island sisters' make you drink too damn much."

"I am not drunk. The dean was inappropriate." Ella tried to push him away. "I wanted to set him straight."

"Well, don't let all the attention tonight go to your head. You're my wife, and I don't like to see any man leering at you."

"Oh, honey, you do not need to worry about that. I love only *you*." She threw her arms around his neck.

He pulled her down on the couch and kissed her exposed skin everywhere. They slid down to the floor. Bernard stretched the length of his body over her back, his weight flattening her into the shaggy carpet like a bug. He unzipped her dress and pulled it off over her legs while running his fingers under the elastic waist of her silk panties. A moan escaped her lips. She buried her face deeper, inhaling the dust and loose fibers. When he pulled her panties down with his teeth and straddled her back, she tried to form words. "Honey, you remember…my doctor had me stop taking the pill because…because—"

"*Mon amour*, you're ruining the mood," he whispered, sucking her earlobe. "Don't worry. I know what to do."

He snaked his arm under her belly and spread her legs with his knee. When he entered her, she stopped thinking. Her orgasm was slow and long. Bernard eased her flat on the rug. When his semen flowed between her legs, he growled like a lion marking his territory.

As she drifted to sleep, her fuzzy brain registered he had not used a condom, and he had not pulled out before he came.

9
Monique

Monique gulped straight Haitian rum, but the phone call from Julien had spread terror so deep throughout her body that even the alcohol could not dilute it. Had it not been for the fear that palpitated between her parents about Julien, she would not have remembered the sex. It was forgettable. Papa had rushed her out of the country like a fugitive, making her miss her rendez-vous with Tina. Now she needed to tell Tina about this situation. Her island sisters could not understand the potential for trouble from Julien, but Tina would. Monique had made a promise to her childhood friend the first day of secondary school at the prestigious Sacré Coeur Académie.

Fourteen-year-old Monique had sat next to the shy girl sitting alone in the back of the classroom. "Hi, I'm Moe."

The girl's eyes had opened wide. "Saintina. My friends call me Tina. But—" She'd shrugged.

"Nice to meet you, *Tina.*"

Monique had glared at the girls she'd met at previous schools, debutante balls, ballet classes, and the airport lounge. One girl crinkled her nose and said, "Monique, she's on scholarship," as if it was a contagious disease.

"Shut the fuck up," Monique had yelled at her. "You're an insensitive cow."

Tina had whispered, "Thank you, Moe. Will you still be my friend tomorrow?"

"Always, *mon amie,*" Monique had replied, squeezing Tina's fingers.

Monique smiled at the memory of that day so many years ago. Tina had taught her about the side of Haiti she had never known before. She stretched her arms over her head and turned to look at the bedside clock. "*O merde!* I'm going to be late." She sprinted to the bathroom. She'd taken a longer nap than planned after dropping Lanei at the airport. "Ceecee will have my head."

They were signing the lease for their new apartment this afternoon.

Of her three friends, she was glad to share a place with rational, calm, and responsible Cecilia. Ella's thinly veiled jealousy and Lanei's religious crusade would drive Monique nuts. She rolled her eyes in the bathroom mirror and laughed. The apartment, law school, student loans, and her part-time job would provide the physical and financial freedom she sought as she became the attorney she had always wanted to be.

She picked up the phone in the kitchen and dialed, pulling the long cord to the sink so she could start the coffee.

"Hey, Tina," Monique said. "Graduation went well yesterday but wait till I tell you what happened Friday night in Haiti and why I didn't come see you."

"Hey, Moe," Tina whispered. "I thought you were calling because you had heard."

"Heard what?" Monique turned off the faucet and sat on a stool.

Halfway through Tina's story, the call got disconnected. After several attempts to call back, Monique gave up. But she had heard enough through Tina's sobs. She slammed the receiver down. She needed to see her friend. But what about Julien? He couldn't know Monique was back in Haiti.

She had an idea.

10
Cecilia

Cecilia splashed cold water on her face after picking her afro with her fingers. She ran her palms over the light wrinkles on her cotton sundress. It was a blazing summer day in Miami. Why her childhood friend Mel had chosen to get married in the summer, Cecilia would never know. She had gone to all the bridal shops in south Florida with Mel months ago and had seen so many pretty gowns she would've picked for herself if only she had a man who would ask. All her friends had somebody. Monique even had a man she didn't want. Cecilia's shoulders slumped. She turned away from the bathroom mirror.

She had met Melissa Walker on the school bus shortly after her family had moved from Boston to Miami. They were sixth graders and neighbors, but Cecilia needed a friend. Mel's southern charm and her popularity as a cheerleader buffered Cecilia from the bullies who fed on self-pity. After what had happened to her in Boston, Cecilia wallowed in it.

Mel was the reverse of everything Cecilia saw in the mirror. Their friendship had protected her through high school, and Mel had delivered her to her island sisters in college. When her mother abandoned her in Miami after high school, Mel's home became Cecilia's. She'd stuffed her friendships with these women in cubbyholes in her heart, always leaving the biggest spot for her mother's love.

Mel poked her head into the bedroom. "Ceecee, darlin', remember we're going shopping for accessories for the bridesmaids later."

Cecilia tucked a red hibiscus in her hair and secured the stem with a hairpin. "Don't worry. I'm seeing the therapist first, then Monique and I are signing the lease. After that I'll be all yours. Oh boy! I'm so excited. I hope you'll have time to visit my place after you're married."

Mel walked into the room and pulled Cecilia down on the bed. "Ceecee, I want you to know that my being married will never affect our friendship. Mike adores you. I wouldn't marry him otherwise." Mel tickled her until tears flowed from their eyes.

"Aren't we too old for this?" Cecilia hiccupped. "We've been doing this since the sixth grade."

"Never, *sistah*!"

"I love Michael." Cecilia turned serious. "He adores you. Every woman should have a Michael."

"On that note, I know I vowed to never try to set you up again, but"— Mel grinned, rolling off the bed—"wait till you meet the best man. He's cute and *single*."

Cecilia resented the fact that all her friends felt the need to find her a mate as if she could not do it on the merit of her looks. "Stop!" Cecilia said, shaking her head as if to erase the painful image. "We agreed you'd never set me up again after prom night."

The smile disappeared from Mel's face. "I'm sorry. I—"

"I'll be back soon." Cecilia stood from the bed, fixing her clothes and her hair in the full-length mirror in the corner before slamming the bedroom door behind her. She plucked a fresh hibiscus from the front yard and slid it behind her ear.

The appointment she'd scheduled with Freda had weighed her down with anxiety all night. She stood on the threshold of the room in the back of the hospital where Freda met with women in crisis. But was Cecilia in crisis now? She appeared to have it all together from the outside, but inside a storm brewed. Folding chairs lined the back of the room. Fluorescent light flooded the wall decorated with crayon artwork from clients' children. A scuffed track on the linoleum floor led to the chair next to the desk.

"Come on in, Cecilia," the woman said with an undetectable accent. Her salt-and-pepper afro framed her round face. "Congratulations on your graduation."

"Please call me Ceecee," she said, smiling as she walked into the room and sat next to the desk.

Freda pushed a box of tissues closer to Cecilia. "Whatever you say here will stay here."

Cecilia grabbed a handful of tissue. "Thank you." She dabbed at her eyes. "My mother didn't come to my graduation. I'm angry. I refuse to cry, but I feel like I might drown from the tears inside."

"Tears scour the soul clean and prepare it to receive self-love."

"I don't love myself...much. My own mother doesn't love me." Cecilia swallowed a shameful sob as if she were responsible for this fact.

"Let's talk about your mother." Freda patted Cecilia's hand across the desk.

Cecilia pulled her hands away and placed them in her lap. "I'm not strong enough today."

Freda nodded. "You have to love, respect, and value your own self before you can offer it to be loved by others, especially a partner."

She blew her nose. "My experience with men, if you can even call it that, has been disastrous." She pushed her mother back inside a compartment for another day. "I just got mad at my friend Mel for trying to set me up again because of what happened on prom night."

"Maybe we can start there, Ceecee?"

She nodded.

⟡⟋⟍⟍

Prom fever had been abuzz on their high school campus, but Cecilia knew she wouldn't catch it because no one would ask her. So when Elliot had asked her the week before, Cecilia's gaze had stopped on the jock's broad shoulders, unable to make it to his face, and she'd said, "Um...I'll let you know tomorrow." She ran to find Mel at her locker.

"Ceecee, you gotta say yes," Mel said. "He's Garth's best friend. We'll double date."

Cecilia had splurged and bought a blue organza gown and white platform sandals that added four inches to her height. On prom day, her round face glowed like freshly pressed satin under Mel's ministrations with a makeup palette. She stared in the mirror and for the first time she saw a glimmer of the pretty girl her daddy had bragged about. The silver headband with the glitzy silver flowers looked like a tiara. Daddy's black princess. Seated in one of the wing chairs in Mel's living room, Cecilia barely breathed so as not to disturb anything.

"Ceecee, you look beautiful!" Mel squeezed her bare shoulder. "I swear I'm gonna steal your dimples."

Soon they heard knocking at the front door. When Mel let Garth into the house, the girls looked behind him. "Where's Elliot?" Mel asked.

"I don't know," Garth said. "I haven't seen him all day."

They sat down and waited for Elliot to arrive. An hour later Cecilia looked down at her lap and saw mascara-stained tears falling on her blue dress; she'd been unaware she was crying.

"I'm sorry, Cecilia," Garth said. "I knew nothing about Elliot's intention, but there's this dare going around school to ask…um…girls from this list and get them to say yes. I never thought Elliot would do that to you, seeing as you're Mel's best friend and all."

"Garth, get out!" Mel had screamed, pushing him toward the door. "Don't ever come near me again. Men are disgusting."

Cecilia and Mel had changed into jeans and T-shirts and gone to a late movie. But the rejection had covered her with another layer of self-loathing.

Cecilia could not look at Freda. She dried her tears and stared at her pink toes in the taupe slide-in shoes she had stepped into that morning. Her size-four jeans stopped at her slim ankles which were crossed in front of her. She had taken a critical look at herself in the full-length mirror at Mel's house and had liked the image of the woman staring back at her. Why did she need her mother to accept her? Would that complete her? She should be proud of surviving without it her whole life. She raised her eyes to Freda's as if the woman would have all the answers.

"You made a success of your professional life, because you believed in your abilities and set high expectations for yourself," Freda said. "It's no different for love. But it begins with you loving yourself fully, warts and all."

Cecilia nodded. "I'm going home for Christmas. I miss Grandma Agnes. She's my most precious link to my late dad. Maybe Mom and I will connect. I still need that, Freda." Cecilia shrugged, letting her shoulders fall.

They were still talking when a horn blared outside just as loud as Monique herself. "It's my friend Moe." Cecilia stood. "You remind me of my second grade teacher back home. I loved her. She inspired me to become a teacher."

Freda smiled and said, "I look like all the second grade teachers from all the islands. I'm from Barbados." They laughed, but Freda turned serious. "Go see your mother, so you can move on with your life."

"I'll see you next week." Cecilia kissed the older woman's cheek, grabbed her macramé bag off the floor, and hurried outside. She had a plan. She'd go see her mother in December. She skipped down the last step to Monique's car, feeling a sliver of light enter her dark heart.

11

Lanei

In her junior year of college in Miami, Lanei had seen a future where she would no longer rely on Kevin for her financial freedom. Her part-time job at the local drugstore had stoked her passion for her chosen profession, but it had also brought her in contact with her coworker Nate. Nate, a senior in pharmacy school, had mentored her and encouraged Lanei to persevere.

Seated in a corner of the library, Lanei had spied Nate's arrival while she studied for her midterm. His face opened in a wide smile under his cornrowed hair. Tight jeans framed his slightly bowed legs. He touched the back of her left hand where the silver band Kevin had placed there two years before rested. "Hey, Lane," Nate said. Sensation coursed through her body.

"Hi, Nate," she said, looking down at her chemistry book. "Thanks for coming to help. I appreciate it."

Nate sat in the chair next to her, his thigh touching hers. She pulled her legs together. "You know I'll do anything for you. You need only ask."

Lanei opened her notebook, and they worked in silence as they solved chemistry problems. But her feelings required weekly confessions to absolve her of impure thoughts.

Later that afternoon, dressed in her drugstore uniform, Lanei had rushed out of the bedroom when she saw the time on the clock radio on the nightstand.

"Oh, Kev, let's go to Moe's Halloween party tonight," she said, stopping at the front door. "They're a lot of fun. I'll be off at eight. We can go after?"

Kevin looked up from his boxing magazine at the dinette table. "Gotta work at the stockyard tonight. Won't be home till way after midnight. Besides I've got a raging headache."

She turned from the door. "Maybe you should make an appointment to see a doctor at the VA hospital. After all, you drive vets almost every week, and you've been having these headaches a lot."

He threw the magazine on the table and stood. "I don't mind helpin' the vets, but that place is depressing as hell. Reminds me too much of—" He stopped.

She waited. Kevin never talked about his experience in Vietnam, but she knew it might have changed him into the angry man he was most of the time. "Of what, Kev?"

He shook his head. "Never mind."

"But…" Lanei gulped down the rest of the words. Kevin's face had closed like the sun hiding behind stormy clouds. "Okay. See you later then." She opened the door.

"Be back before midnight," Kevin shouted at her.

She nodded and left to walk to work. The late October breeze lifted her mood. Three more semesters till graduation.

Lanei stood in the doorway of Monique's house that evening in a gray smock with *PHILIPS DRUGSTORE* embroidered on the left pocket and matching pants. She knew Monique would either send her away or dress her up in an appropriate Halloween costume for her *Madame Monique Boudoir* theme.

As predicted, Monique pulled her into a bedroom and dressed Lanei in Daisy Duke shorts and a red tube top. She slipped her feet into Monique's red pumps and felt sexy. Her watch said it was a few minutes after nine. Plenty of time to change back into her uniform and make it home before midnight. Packed with college students, the house buzzed with cheers. The smell of cigarettes, pot, alcohol, and hormones filled Lanei's senses with a longing to enjoy her youth. What would it hurt if she took a sip of beer? She grabbed a cold can of soda and made her way to the pool area in search of a familiar face, wishing she had worked up the nerve to invite Nate to the party.

"Look at you!" Cecilia said. She was dressed in a black satin negligee under a matching short robe with fringe above her knees. Red feathers swayed from her afro. "Nate is in there." Cecilia pointed toward the garden. "He asked about you."

"Oh…um… Who invited him?" Lanei asked, her armpits suddenly moist.

"Moe saw him on campus today. You know how she is; the more the merrier." They giggled.

When Lanei found Nate, his eyes widened. She crossed her arms over her chest, feeling exposed. She shivered.

"Are you cold?" he asked. "I'll give you my smoking jacket. I'm a *pimp*." He smiled.

"Thank you. But I have my work smock if I need…something." She shook the plastic bag in her hand.

Nate led her to the dance floor after securing her bag under a chair. Careful not to touch each other, they danced to the fast beat of a Haitian song neither of them knew, but it didn't matter. Nate would not let her look away. His gaze sought to pierce her heart and see her secrets. She allowed the music to enter her body, and it chased away her fears. Arms raised above her head, she hummed, swaying her hips side to side. Monique and Cecilia found her on the dance floor. "Where's Elle?" Lanei yelled over the din.

"She was here," Cecilia yelled back. "Alex is sick. Bernard called her home."

"As if he can't take care of his own son," Monique said, rolling her eyes.

A slow song started, and Nate offered his hand. Eyes closed, she let him pull her to him. She inhaled his male scent mixed with his lemony aftershave. The muscles in her bare midriff spasmed as she became aware of his erection, and her yearnings pulled her like a rope to the other side of happiness. Her confession this week would be a long one. She leaned into him. Time stopped.

A jab on her shoulder made her jerk her face away from Nate's neck, and Lanei stared into the squinting eyes of her husband. She gasped and bit into her bottom lip to stifle a scream. She let go of Nate and grabbed her bag from under the chair. "I'll go change, Kevin. These…these are Monique's clothes."

"We're leavin'," Kevin said, his lips barely moving.

"Hi, I'm Nate." Nate extended his hand, looking up at Kevin. "May I get you a drink, sir?" His eyes sought Lanei's, but she looked away.

"No! You may not get me a drink, college boy," Kevin said, the words coming out slowly, "but you may stay away from my wife. *Capisce?*" He poked Nate's chest with his middle finger. Nate reared back, raising his fists. Lanei snatched Kevin's hand and pulled him toward the door, hoping to avoid a scene that might involve Monique.

"Lane," Nate said, "will you be okay?"

She pulled the door closed behind them. They climbed into the car, and she crossed her legs tight to stop the trembling. Kevin whistled along with a song on the car radio. When they reached the parking lot in front of their building, she walked quickly ahead of him, making her way to the emotional prison Kevin called home. He caught up with her and gripped the waist of her shorts, pushing her down the corridor toward their first-floor unit. Lanei scraped her elbow on the row of mailboxes on the wall. Bugs sizzled on the naked bulbs on the low ceiling. Two wilted plants stood like tired sentries next to her neighbor's door. They walked into the apartment, and Kevin turned on the television, looked at her, and said, "Where is my dinner?"

She hurried to the kitchen, pulling the red tube top up to her armpits. When she heard the television's volume go up, she tensed. She smelled Kevin's Old Spice mixed with sweat before he grabbed a handful of her hair and yanked her around to face him. The punch to her stomach threw her across the small kitchen. Her head slammed into the refrigerator. Dazed, she stayed on the floor.

"Look at you, dressed like a two-dollar hooker. I saw the way that boy Nate was squeezing your ass. Did you like that, *Lane*?"

The television drowned his rants and her screams. "Kevin, please stop! I didn't do anything wrong." She managed to sit up, hoping to break through his fury and stop the kicks.

"Don't talk back to me, girl!" He ripped the tube top down over her hips, stripping off her shorts in the same motion. She scrambled backward to get away from him but hit the wall. *My obituary will say that I was only twenty years old, and that I wanted to be a pharmacist,* she thought. *I haven't seen Mama in two years.* She felt herself being pulled across the linoleum floor. "You think I'm old? I'm gonna show you what this old man can do."

Kevin pushed into her. Hard. A piece of raised linoleum dug into her back. She bit her tongue and tasted blood. She closed her eyes and prayed for it to end.

When he was done, he stood over her and yelled, "Shit, you made me break the goddamn condom. You better get on the pill like I told you, Lanei. I don't want any goddamn kids. You hear me?"

She raised her torso off the floor and stared at him. Her faith in her merciful God unwavering, she said, "Kevin, as a Catholic, I wanted to use the rhythm method in my marriage. But you strike like the serpent in the Garden of Eden."

His demonic laugh followed her as she limped to the bathroom. She filled up the tub with hot soapy water and stepped in, hoping to wash Kevin's seed away before it took root.

But it had been too late. He'd left a permanent mark this time.

Now sitting on the plane with her daughter sleeping in her arms, Lanei rolled her rosary beads between her thumb and index fingers, repeating the words of solace. She would not let the fear of going back to Chicago intrude into the thread of hope she was taking back with her from Monique and Cecilia's graduation. Maria stirred in her arms just as the pilot announced they were preparing for landing.

Kevin would be waiting.

12
Ella

Ella stretched her body to remove the kinks from her joints. Bernard had let her spend the night on the shaggy rug in the living room. Turning on her side, she patted the carpet around her until her hand landed on her glasses. She slipped them on, and she could see her new dress under the coffee table where Bernard had thrown it after the party. She touched the wetness between her legs, counted the number of weeks since her last period, and relaxed. Last night had felt like a fairy tale. Now that Bernard had been appointed Community Liaison for the Haitian Business District, she hoped they'd attend more social functions. Ella loved to dress up. She smiled when she remembered what the professor had said about Bernard's slyness. "He would make me the First Lady of the United States if he could," she said aloud and laughed. Bernard always got what he wanted.

Three and a half years ago, he had called Ella from Haiti to discuss his plan to join her in Miami. He had needed her to help him get the admission information from the school.

"Bernard, do you have any idea how expensive it is to live and to go to school here?" she'd said.

"Don't worry about the money. I'll get it. I just need to get in."

Now they were a family with a son and many dreams. She picked her dress up off the floor and threw it on the couch before running to the bathroom to empty her bladder. There was a note on the toilet seat. She smiled.

Elle, I have a community meeting after work today. Enjoy your day off.
Love you. B.

After a cup of coffee and some toast, she tidied up the apartment before heading out to pick up Alex. On a whim Ella got off at the bus stop in Little Haiti, a neighborhood of Miami that is home to thousands of Haitians. The squat cinder block homes painted in fuchsia pink, sunny yellow, sky blue, and pea green shared chain-link fences between their small yards. People ambled around in pairs and groups as if they had no specific destination. Ella entered every store, admiring the arts and crafts and inhaling the smell of cinnamon, smoked herring, and dried mushrooms. The smell of home. The Meridien Supermarket was owned by the richest Haitian family in the area and occupied a city block. Bright murals depicted scenes of slaughtered animals amid blue water and palm trees on a pink wall. She stepped into the air-conditioned store and stopped in front of a life-size poster of Bernard smiling next to a light-skinned woman with golden hair and the whitest teeth Ella had ever seen. The caption read: *HAITIAN COMMUNITY LEADERS*. She frowned.

A saleswoman walked up to her and followed her gaze. "That is Monsieur Bernard Antoine and Mademoiselle Yolaine Meridien. Her family owns a whole lot of Little Haiti," the saleswoman said, flattening her lips into a thin line. "Monsieur Antoine works on her campaign. She'll win. She gets whatever she wants." The saleswoman shrugged.

The red tips of the woman's—*Yolaine's*—fingernails poked behind Bernard's waist in the picture. "Campaign for what?" Ella asked.

The saleswoman moved away from the poster as if she'd said too much. "Can I help you find something in the store, madame?" she said in Creole.

On the bus back home, Ella peered through the window while bouncing Alex on her lap. She marveled at how in less than four years Bernard had obtained his college degree, found a good-paying job, and immersed himself in local politics such that he had literally become a poster child in the Haitian community. What had she done with her life so far besides giving birth to a child and supporting her husband's dreams?

That night Bernard breezed into the bedroom, pulling his tie out of his shirt collar. She placed the copy of *Vogue* facedown on the bed and pushed her glasses up her nose. His trim body showed the discipline of a healthy eater and a jogger. He leaned over and kissed her lips. She sniffed.

"I thought you'd be asleep by now," he said. "Did you get some rest today?"

"Not really. I cleaned, cooked, and went to Little Haiti to buy some groceries. I went to *le Meridien*."

Bernard stopped on his way to the bathroom. "Oh, I thought you didn't like that area. Too Haitian for you." He snickered.

"I saw the poster, Bernard. You never told me you were helping with this...Ms. Meridien's campaign. What is she running for? Who is she?"

"Well, in case you haven't figured it out yet, Ella, the right connection gives you *leverage*. Now that's a word you need to look up." He sat on his side of the bed and looked at her like a stranger. "Why do you suppose I've been volunteering at the community center since I got here? I'm building leverage like a bridge that will carry me from the disadvantage of my birth to a place of power. People here already know who I am. In a few years, you'll see how far this village boy will go. I will *run* this place."

"I do not want to live here permanently, Bernard. I want to practice medicine in Rosale. Do you understand that? You promised we would go back home."

He made a face. "You would take our children to *Rosale*? I thought you had a brain, Ella."

"Our child, not children," Ella said, correcting him. "And I do have a brain."

"How about your island sisters? You'd leave them behind?" He made a sad face. "Oh, wait, your bracelets are magical, right?"

"Why are you being so obnoxious tonight, Bernard? You do not have friends. You collect people. Like Professor Griffin, Dean Taylor, and now Yolaine Meridien. Why?"

"Oh, you're a psychiatrist now." He laughed and walked toward the bathroom. Before closing the door, he turned and said, "My dear, you'd make one hell of a cute nurse. *Maybe!*"

"What!" she yelled to his back, jumping off the bed. "Bernard, I'm going to be a doctor. No *maybe* about it."

But self-doubt had already wiped the sleep clean out of her body.

13
Monique

Monique spun in the middle of the small living room, dancing to a song in her head. "This is going to be our new den, Ceecee." She stopped in front of the wall of windows overlooking the garden from their third-floor apartment. "I wish Lanei was here for our monthly gatherings. I'm worried about the bruises we don't see."

Cecilia turned from the window with the unspooled measuring tape in her hands. "I know. I'm concerned as well. Ella may have some pushback from Bernard about her academic plan, but she says he never hits her, and we haven't seen marks on her either." She tapped the floor with her toes, and they sat down. "I've never been in a relationship, Moe, so I don't know what makes women stay in bad ones. I hope Lan will come to Mel's wedding in a couple months. We'll help her when she's ready."

"Kevin's a bruiser, and Lanei is obsessed with her religious crap." Monique shook her head. "I don't know. Maybe we need to talk to her priest and get him to absolve her or whatever the hell he does, so she can leave without surrendering herself to damnation." Monique said.

"Well, I'm not going to pretend like I understand Lan's religious belief. We'll try again when she comes back." Cecilia narrowed her eyes. "So what was the news about Tina?"

"I have to go to Haiti." Monique sighed. "Something happened to her mom. She needs me."

"But what about that Julien guy? Can't you just call Tina?"

Monique snorted. "Few Haitians have phones, and Tina's not one of them. We can only talk when she's at work, and the reception was shitty last time." She slapped Cecilia's thigh. "I'll be fine. I'll only be there overnight."

"I know I can't talk you out of it, Moe. When a friend needs you, you're always there."

After signing the lease, Monique dropped Cecilia back at Mel's. "You're sure you don't want to come to Chantal's birthday party tonight?"

"No, I wish I could though. You know I love your cousin, but I need to help Mel with some more wedding stuff. Give Chantal my love."

Monique and her cousin Chantal had spent all their summers together in Miami since Monique was eight. She'd managed to escape Papa's fists for three months out of the year.

She drove back home after a trip to the hair salon for a trim and a shampoo. She dug her wallet from her purse and stared at the empty cavity where the credit cards used to be. She had saved her money from her part-time job for the past four years in preparation for this day.

By the time she arrived at Chantal's fifteenth-floor apartment that evening, Monique had lost her lust to party.

"Why the long face?" Chantal asked as they hugged. "Where's your posse?"

Someone called Chantal from across the room. "Go take care of your guests," Monique said. "We'll talk later."

She plucked a bottle of rum and a can of soda from the table and slipped into her cousin's bedroom, trying to muster up the courage to make the trip back to Haiti. When Monique finally decided to leave the bedroom, a tall, lanky man with rimless glasses and dreadlocks tied under a blue bandana bumped into her at the door.

"I'm sorry," he said, extending his hand while staring into her eyes with his large tamarind-brown ones. Monique took it and fought the urge to sweep back a lock of hair that had escaped for a better look. Something fluttered in her stomach. Was it gas? She hadn't eaten much tonight. "I'm Brian Collins. Nice to meet you, Miss—"

"Monique…Magloire." The words came out breathy, and she remembered saying them to Julien only a few days ago. She pulled her hand away.

The heat from his long fingers traveled through her. "I hope you weren't leaving," he said, cocking his head. "*Magloire*. You and Chantal must be kin. I see the strong resemblance."

Monique did not remember what they talked about the rest of the evening, nor did she care. She only knew that she wanted to talk to him again. After seeing her guests off, Chantal made coffee, and the cousins sat in the kitchen. The strobe lights from an ambulance splashed against the picture window, bathing them in red. "Ooh! I think *Doctor* Brian digs you. He quizzed me about you when you went to the bathroom earlier."

"Really? What did he want to know?" Monique asked, holding her breath like a teenager.

"Brian's a really nice guy and a good friend. Moe, I wouldn't want you to...toy with him if—"

"He looks like he can take care of himself," Monique said, stopping her cousin's preaching. "So he's a surgical resident too?"

"Yeah, he's a year ahead of me."

"Well, where have you been hiding him? He's handsome and he must be smart. They don't let dummies into medical school, right? Except you?"

Chantal chased Monique to the door, laughing. "Very funny, Moe."

"He promised to call when I return from Haiti."

"You're such a puzzle, cousin. Hard on the outside and all gooey inside. I hope Tina's okay. Please be careful in Haiti."

"I will." Monique shuddered. "You know Maman and Tina make Haiti relevant in my life. Otherwise, I'd never go back there, at least not until this oppressive regime is gone."

That night she packed an overnight bag and laid out the clothes and the wig she had bought at a thrift store earlier for a disguise. No one in Haiti would recognize her.

After an uneventful flight, she took a taxi from the airport in Haiti and directed the driver to Tina's neighborhood in Croix Bossale. When the car pulled over on the dirt road, she jumped out. Vendors across the street called their wares to prospective buyers, trying to outdo the competition in octave. A swarm of blowflies flew off, revealing a pile of rotted fruit peels and a skinny dead dog. Monique sneezed. The flies buzzed their discontent and circled the mounds before diving back again. She entered the corridor flanked on both sides by huts, mud houses, and wooden shacks. Smelly water filled muddy holes as it trickled its way toward the market below.

She moved the printed sheet flowing in the breeze from the doorway and walked inside the small house. She found Tina sitting on a cot in the back.

"Moe, is that you?" Tina squinted, trying to get a good look at her visitor.

Monique pulled off the wig and the shades. "I have to be careful. What happened, *mon amie?*" Monique asked.

She sat on the cot next to Tina and put her arms around her shoulders. Tina blew air between her clenched teeth and whispered, "My mother is dead."

Monique gasped. "Oh no, Tina. What—"

"She was run over by a car driven by a militia man. It took over three hours for her to die on the street like a dog." Tina's face crumpled. "I was at work."

"Do you know the driver?"

Tina nodded. "Yet I can't do anything about it except bury her."

Monique pulled Tina closer as if to protect her from further harm. "Oh, Tina. Why didn't you call me before?" Rage synchronized their heartbeats. "I will help... It's a crime." Monique stood, pacing in a circle.

"They were *Tonton Macoutes*, Moe. Nobody can help me. I didn't expect you to come back to Haiti after Julien. My uncle took her body to Gonaives where my family is from. I'm leaving tomorrow, and you should too."

Monique sat down on the cot and reached for her friend again. "Do you have enough money? I don't have a lot, but I can help."

"I'll be okay." Tina squeezed her hand. "You know your father pays me well because you drove him crazy about giving me the job after high school. Guess he didn't want to hear your mouth on a loop."

They talked and cried until Tina said, "You should leave before it gets too dark."

"Will you be okay? I feel like I should be doing something," Monique said, hating the helplessness of the situation.

"I'll be fine. We learned at a young age to keep our mouths shut. You have done a lot by being here. I love you, *mon amie*. I owe you big."

Monique kissed her forehead and whispered, "You owe me nothing. We're friends."

Sitting in the back of another taxi, Monique watched the women and the young girls crossing the streets in the dark and wondered what horrors they hid within their quick steps as they went to wherever they might feel safe in Haiti. The taxi left the bustle of the inner city and climbed the hill of Montagne Noire, the affluent neighborhood where Monique had grown up. It stopped in front of the gate in the ten-foot wall topped with broken glass that surrounded the Magloire residence. The wall kept intruders away, but inside, its female residents had no hiding place from her father's tyranny. Monique hoped to spend a quiet evening with her mother and leave on her afternoon flight the next day. She banged on the gate for a long time before the footman opened it. When she saw the cars in the driveway, she considered going back to Tina's for the night. She wasn't in the mood to deal with her sisters.

Maman stood so fast from the dining room chair that it fell backward. "*Bébé*...are you okay? Why are you dressed like—"

"I'm fine. I flew in today to see Tina." As was customary, she walked around the table and kissed every member of her family before telling them what happened to Tina's mother.

Esther stood and hugged Monique. "I'm so sorry, Moe. Poor Tina."

Solange pointed to her clothes and laughed. "You look like a *vagabonde*. What are you doing here? Papa told me and Esther what happened last weekend. You need to keep your *college-educated* ass in Miami."

Monique counted to five in her head and breathed, ignoring Solange who was clearly drunk. "Papa, there must be something you can do to help," Monique said. "They can't get away with this shit."

Papa narrowed his eyes. "Why did you come here, Monique? Julien—"

"Marcel," Maman said, "the child should be able to come home."

"Did anyone ask you a question, Lucia?" Papa said.

"Show her respect," Monique yelled. "She has a voice. Are you that different from them?" Monique fisted her hands.

Solange grabbed her Louis Vuitton handbag. Halfway to the door, she turned and said, "Who gives a shit about your friend Tina anyway?"

Monique sprang from her chair. Maman grabbed her arm. Monique rocked on the balls of her feet, fuming.

"I've helped Tina plenty," Papa said. "You made me give her a job and help her get into university. This is not our fight. Leave it alone."

"What?" Monique shouted. "There shouldn't be their fight and ours. We're one people." Monique slammed her fist on the table. The utensils bounced and settled back. Water spilled from glasses. Her gaze circled around the table, landing on each face. She shook her head, puckering her lips in disgust before sprinting upstairs and locking herself in her old bedroom. Lying on the bed, she looked out the window until the sun pushed through the dawn.

The following day, dressed in her disguise, Monique picked at her lunch while she listened to the rain pelting the dining room window. Thunder growled, followed by streaks of lightning. She hoped her flight would leave on schedule. She pushed her plate away.

"Why does Solange hate me so much?" Monique asked.

Maman patted her hand on the table. "*Bébé*, Solange doesn't hate you. She's angry that she didn't get to live her life on her terms. Sol always wanted to study in France but—" Maman shrugged. "She and Esther got married because that's what Papa thought was best. As the middle child, I think Sol felt... unseen. You on the other hand pushed and fought your way out and made it."

Monique nodded with new understanding. "I never knew much about Solange. Esther was like my second mother. Remember?" Monique smiled. "They're my sisters. I love them, but it's hard to like Solange."

On her way to the airport, Monique peered through the sheet of rain before glancing at her watch. She had plenty of time. She relaxed. Exiting the car, she fought with the umbrella as she pulled her carry-on toward the terminal door. A car screeched behind her. Before she could turn to see what was going on, a voice called, "Monique Magloire, I've been waiting for you to contact me since you landed yesterday."

She spun on her heels and saw Julien leaning against a silver Mercedes, dressed in khaki shorts and a black polo shirt. His teeth gleamed in a snarl. Raindrops bounced off his shaved head like an obsidian ball. People stopped long enough to stare at him before they hurried to get inside. Monique stood less than ten feet away from him. "What? Why would I call you?" she said, her heart beating like a drum. "Wait a minute. How did you know I was here? I don't even remember your last name."

"*Etienne*," he said. "And it will be yours soon."

Her skin prickling with nervous sweat, Monique dashed into the terminal like she was being chased by a *loup-garou* from her childhood stories, hoping the bad spirit would not get on the plane with her to Miami.

14
Cecilia

C ecilia ran from the bus stop to the back room in the hospital. She hugged the therapist and sat in the chair. She wondered suddenly if she could speak the ugly words of what had happened to her a decade ago. The pain still smarted like a fresh wound.

"You don't have to talk about anything you're not ready to face yet," Freda said. "Therapy may take a long time. Sometimes a lifetime."

"But I need to tell you everything that happened to me that has pushed me into this shell I'm trying to emerge from."

Freda nodded and pushed the tissue box to the middle of the desk. Cecilia pulled out a handful of tissues as if to build a nest to protect her fragile self and began.

When ten-year-old Cecilia had arrived in Massachusetts with her family, she had left more than Grandma Agnes and Friendy, her little dog, behind in Saint Thomas. She'd left the blue sky, the salty air, and the little pink house with the fenced-in backyard that had provided refuge from her mother's abuse. Now their fourth-floor apartment in the HUD-subsidized building in Roxbury looked out on an empty lot surrounded by broken barbed wire. The tenants ignored the giant dumpsters and threw their trash on the ground. Roaches outnumbered residents by a hundredfold. The teenagers loitering around the yard yelled insults at her when she took the trash out.

"What's your name, darky?"
"Where you from, shorty?"
"Burn them clothes, clown!"

Cecilia pretended the words did not hurt. One night she waited up for her father to come home from driving a rig around the country for three weeks out of the month. Daddy made everything better.

"Princess," he whispered, brushing her face with the back of his warm hand. "You fell asleep with the book on your pretty face again."

She rubbed her eyes with both fists and whispered back, "I miss you Daddy, and I miss Grandma and Friendy and—" A sob escaped her pressed lips. She threw her arms around his neck. Cradled in Daddy's arms, she whimpered. "I really don't like it here. I want to go home." She moved her lips close to his ear. Both of them were afraid of waking up Mom in the next bedroom. "I'm scared of the kids outside. They call me names when I take the trash out."

"I don't want you taking the trash out, baby. We'll go home for a visit one day, but I have to get us out of this neighborhood first." He tickled her neck. Cecilia giggled in her throat.

She put the pillow over her head a few minutes later, but she could not block the voices coming from her parents' bedroom. "Anna, honey, don't let Ceecee go outside alone. It's not safe," Daddy said.

"I'm scared of these people around here too. They look at me with hate, Leon," Mom said. "A boy called me a 'yellow monkey' the other day. I want to move to Miami. It's already getting cold, and it's not even winter yet. I hate Boston."

Cecilia squeezed the pillow harder. Those mean boys had called her beautiful mother mean names. Cecilia longed for the pale yellow skin and the long, wavy hair her mother was blessed with. Maybe the kids were nicer in Miami. While Daddy waited for his job transfer, her mother drank with the neighbor next door. As the months piled up like the snow outside, Cecilia took full responsibility for the household and her two younger brothers.

One late spring day, Daddy came home with great news. "Ceecee, we're moving to Miami when school gets out in a month. I'm getting us a house. You'll have your own room. Miami is like home with coconut and palm trees, the ocean close by, and plenty of heat." He smiled.

"Oh, Daddy! I'm happy to get mommy away from…drinking. She's meaner when she's drunk."

"What do you mean?" he asked, his forehead pleated in his tired face.

"N-Nothing. Tell me about the move. I got straight As again. Can we go home this summer? It's been two years—" Cecilia always had so much to share with Daddy, and the time was always too short.

He kissed the top of her head. "Sweetheart, we can't afford a house and a trip home. We'll go back one day. I promise."

One week before her father's return to pick up the family for the move to Miami, the boxes he left were still empty. Mom binged daily with her drinking buddy. Cecilia packed their belongings. When she had no room to maneuver with the three bags of trash in the middle of the living room, she started taking them to the dumpsters. There were a couple of little kids playing in the yard, and it was still early for the bullies. She hurried. On her third trip, thick clouds rolled in and covered the setting sun. It smelled like rain.

As she placed a foot on the first step to her building, strong hands yanked her by the collar of her blouse. She heard the rip of the fabric before she fell backward. The rag shoved into her mouth cut the scream bubbling in her throat. Arms dragged her to the back of the building and over the gravel that dug into her bare back as her blouse rode up to her shoulders. Hands pawed at her clothes. With her arms pinned down above her head, she kicked, but failed to make contact. Her muffled screams threatened to choke her.

When her vision cleared, she saw three of them. The pain between her legs connected her to the assailant on top of her. It seemed like an eternity before another one took his place. She blacked out. When she came to, an older man was putting her torn underwear and shorts back on as they soaked up the blood flowing from her. "I'm calling the police," he said. "What's your unit number?"

Cecilia stood on rubbery legs, shaking her head from side to side. She crawled up the stairs while holding her tattered top over her chest. She only wanted to tell her mommy. Cecilia stepped into the apartment. Mom raised her head from the dinette table, sneered at her, and said, "Why is the food not ready, Cecilia? Where have you been?"

Cecilia let the blouse fall to the floor. "Mommy...they hurt me."

Her mother squinted as she walked toward Cecilia. The girl opened her arms. Instead, the slap sent her reeling against the entry wall. "Didn't I tell you to never leave your brothers alone in here?" her mother yelled, coming out of her drunken stupor. Cecilia stepped back, hugging the wall behind her and hoping to make it to the bathroom door before the next hit came. "Girl, you can't do nothing I tell you to do right."

Cecilia had locked herself in the bathroom and proceeded to try to wash the shame from her skin, but it was already burrowing into her marrow.

Silence filled the room. Freda reached for her hand as if she knew Cecilia could not continue the story. "How do you feel now?" Freda whispered.

Cecilia wiped her face dry. "I was twelve. Now I know they took away my self-esteem. How do I feel now?" She paused. "A bit lighter! I've been trying to make my mother love me."

"Let's talk about how to address that need."

Cecilia sat up straighter in the chair. Over the years she had cried for her mother's love as if it was the key to unlock her happiness. She had called and had sent letters, airline tickets, and special occasion cards. But was it her job to do all that?

"My mother has hurt me more than those savages in Boston because she stole my childhood innocence, making room for mistrust and self-hatred to take root. Even all the love I got from Daddy could not protect me from the pain she inflicted on my soul."

"Seeking therapy is an important tool toward building self-awareness. What do you want to achieve here?"

"Self-love," Cecilia whispered, raising her hand to her lips and kissing her skin.

"Just like that." Freda nodded. "But start from within."

Cecilia hugged the woman who smelled like toasted Palma Christi oil, like Grandma Agnes. She pulled the door closed behind her, raised her face to the July sun, and smiled. She might have a long way to go, but Cecilia could see the beginning of the road out of victimhood and into self-acceptance.

15
Lanei

L anei dried her hands on her skirt and ran for the phone in the living room. She had been waiting for their scheduled weekly call, but nature had called first. "Lan, we're getting you a ticket to come to Mel's wedding. We really need to talk to you about your safety," Monique said.

No greetings. Monique wasted no energy on unnecessary words or gestures. Everything she did left an impact. Maybe not always warm and fuzzy but honest. Lanei smiled.

"Moe, come on," Ella said. "Why do you always have to give orders?" She sucked her teeth. "How are you, Lan, and how is Maria? It has only been a week since we saw you, but it feels like too long already."

Lanei could almost see Monique sprawled on the bed in her bedroom. Cecilia would be on the extension in the kitchen, and Ella on the family room sofa with a drink. Lanei clinked her bracelet against the phone and the other three women did the same and fell silent. The sound echoed deep inside Lanei, softening life's many blows. "I'm fine, Elle, but Maria is still battling her seizures. I'm forever hopeful that she will outgrow this. The doctors say so, and God will ordain it," Lanei said. "Don't make that face, Moe."

"Hey!" Monique yelled into the phone. "I didn't make a face. So last week you said you'd ask your master if you could come to the wedding. I—"

"Hi, Lan," Cecilia said, cutting in. "Moe, give a sister a chance to breathe. Geez!"

"Hey, Ceecee," Lanei said. "Yesterday wasn't...um...a good day. Kevin works late tonight, but I'll ask...I mean I'll tell him soon. I promise. Moe, have you heard anything else from the man you had the...encounter with? The one who spooked you at the airport."

Ella snickered, then cleared her throat. "Is that what we call sex with strangers now? *Encounters?*"

"Shut up, Ella," Monique said. "Maybe you and Lan should have had some *encounters* before you two married the first man who ever looked at your panties."

Lanei stroked her bracelet. She let out her breath through her nose, refusing to acknowledge the truth of Monique's statement. Not the part about sleeping with strangers, but perhaps waiting for the heart instead of relying on the flesh to recognize its true-life companion had some merit.

Ella shrieked. "Monique, you know—"

"Stop, you two," Lanei said, raising her voice.

Silence rang out until they all started talking at the same time. Lanei smiled. "Call us soon," Ella said before they hung up. Lanei pictured the argument happening now in the house and wished she was there.

She slung the diaper bag over her shoulder and, holding a fidgety Maria in her arms, walked to the bus stop. A short ride later, she stepped off the bus in front of the library, taking the sunbonnet off Maria's head inside the cool building. She had not had a seizure yet that day. Lanei feared that the stress of living with Kevin during her pregnancy might have caused Maria's heart defect and plaguing seizures. Before the move to Chicago, Kevin had beaten her for refusing to have an abortion. Lanei believed he had moved them here to take her away from her friends. Her priest said that sometimes God would send the devil into your path to test your faith. Kevin was her test.

Tonight she'd tell him about her plan to attend Mel's wedding the following month. Her friends had left no room for debate during their phone call. Lanei headed to the playroom in the back of the library where an excited Maria would play with the other children, and she would wait to see Nate.

16
Ella

Ella stepped into the bank lobby and reached for her wallet from the bottom of her bag. The envelope with the student loan application was tucked under her armpit. She had been away from school for three years, but the excitement of going back to the campus lifted her spirit and energized her tired body. She had worked many extra shifts to fatten up their nest egg since she had started planning to be a full-time student again. She walked to the teller window and slid her picture identification under the glass panel.

"Good morning, sir," Ella said. "I do not have the passbook. Um… my husband handles—" She lowered her voice when the woman at the next window turned and stared at her. "The account is under Mr. and Mrs. Bernard Antoine."

"Good morning," the teller said, taking her ID.

He turned and pulled open a drawer, looking for a card with her signature on it that he could compare with Ella's state ID. Holding two cards, the man hit several keys on the machine, looked at Ella, and frowned.

"Mrs. Antoine, Mr. Antoine had two accounts with our bank. He closed them a while back, but your name was never on either one."

Ella blinked several times behind the glasses that had slid down her sweaty nose and talked slower, enunciating each word to smooth out her accent. "There must be a mistake. I asked him…um…my husband last week if we still bank with you…and he said yes. Can you check again? Please."

"Mrs. Antoine, there's no other place to look. I'm sorry." The teller leaned his head to the side and waved at the customer behind Ella.

She stumbled out of the bank not quite understanding what this meant. Bernard probably had changed banks and forgotten to tell her. But she had asked him. He had lied. Why? Where was her hard-earned money? Her stomach churned. She walked back to the bus stop, and before she made it to the bench, she threw up on the side of the road, heaving until her chest ached. When she arrived at Janet's, she kept her finger on the doorbell, so she could stay upright.

Janet had been the mother Ella never had. She'd met the cantankerous woman three years ago after completing her freshman year of college. Janet had worked at the hospital cafeteria, and Ella was a volunteer. The first day she'd walked into the cafeteria, the plump woman had served out plenty of opinions along with heaping scoops of mashed potatoes.

"Oh, I cannot eat all that, ma'am," Ella had said. "Um...how much is it anyway?"

"Child, didn't the folks upstairs tell you? You get free food as a volunteer," the woman said with an unmistakable Jamaican accent. "You need to fill up them long legs."

When she went back for seconds, Janet had smiled and joined her at the table with two cups of steamy Jamaican coffee. "Thank you, ma'am."

"Call me Jan, child. Ma'am makes me feel old." Her laughter had revealed two missing teeth on each side of her mouth.

Now Ella pulled her finger off the doorbell lest she sour Janet's mood more than necessary. "Child! Are you okay?" Janet said, grabbing Ella and pulling her to a chair in her kitchen. "You look as pale as a ghost."

Lois, who had been washing dishes in the sink, placed a glass of water in front of her. "Thank you, Lois," Ella said. "Glad to see you here."

"I stop by to check on Mom's medications," Lois said, hitching her chin toward Janet. "You know how she can be."

"Oh, you two." Janet slapped the air with her palm. "Elle, what's wrong?"

"I just came from the bank. My name was never on our accounts, and Bernard closed them months ago. I trusted him with my weekly checks. He takes care of the bills and such—" Ella put her head down on the table, too embarrassed to look at Janet's face.

"Lois, take Alex to the back porch with a Popsicle," Janet said before turning to Ella. "I know he's your husband, but that boy is a weasel, Ella. I should know." Janet clucked her tongue. "Had me a couple of 'em. I busted the last one's head open with my cast-iron skillet for putting his hand on me and stealing my money."

"Bernard never hits me," Ella said, thinking of Lanei. Her anger toward Bernard faded. "He would *never* do that."

"Just the same. Taking your money is wrong. Child, open your eyes. A man can keep you underfoot in so many ways that you don't recognize till you can't take the next breath. They use words and deeds instead of their fists, but they hurt just as hard."

"You know the other night he told me I should be a nurse. It is as if he does not want me to be a doctor."

"So you give him your check." Janet shook her head so hard, her headscarf moved sideways. "And he gives you…what? An allowance?"

"Bernard takes care of me and Alex. He—" Ella stopped, realizing how needy she sounded when she worked so hard to contribute to the finances of her household.

She stood. "Jan, I have to get home. I do not know what I would do without you and Lois. I am very grateful."

"I want you in school where you belong. Don't be trusting people blindly like that, child. Especially men."

Ella opened her mouth to defend her trust in Bernard, but then she realized how his actions would adversely impact her plan to return to school and closed it.

With Alex trotting behind her, she trudged to the bus stop to go home to get some answers.

17
Monique

M onique hated that Julien could reach all the way to Miami and torment her soul with his threat. His vile words stuck in her mind like a stain she could not scrub away. "*Etienne*," she muttered and wanted to brush her teeth to get rid of the nasty taste the name left in her mouth. It had been three days since her trip to Haiti, and fear kept her company at home and at work. She wondered if she should call Maman to warn her family, but of what? How had Julien known she was in Haiti? Tina almost had not recognized her in her disguise. What did it all mean? At least she was safe here.

The two messages left on the answering machine from Brian told her he'd been thinking about her as much as she'd been dreaming about him. Was this what love at first sight felt like? She kicked her shoes off and stripped out of her work clothes. Her job at the women's center delivered a daily dose of distress from the plight of other women. After her shower she paged Brian. She pulled leftover food from the fridge for dinner. It was several minutes before the phone rang.

"Hey," she said, sighing. "I heard your messages. Still coming over after work? I could use some company."

He groaned. "There was a multicar accident on 95 a while ago. We're swamped. But I want to see you. The night I was free you were in Haiti. It's beginning to look like a conspiracy to keep you away from me."

"Won't work. I'm looking forward to getting to know you better."

"It's as if you were a mirage the night I saw you over at Chantal's. I want to see more," he whispered.

Something fluttered in her stomach. "I'll be here when they let you out." She laughed.

Monique heard a siren in the background.

"Oops, gotta go. I'll call you tomorrow."

She pirouetted around the kitchen like a ballerina. Brian might be the one. Her heart told her so. After dinner she grabbed her car keys and headed out. She needed respite from her battling emotions and knew exactly who could set her straight.

18
Cecilia

Cecilia punched out at nine in the evening. She had put in twelve hours on that shift. She almost had enough money to buy the car she wanted before starting her teaching job next month. As she shook the coins for the bus like dice in her closed fist, a car horn boomed in the night. Cecilia smiled. Monique seemed to take the air with her when she was away from them and bring it back with a whoosh. She climbed into the car and hugged her friend, kissing her cheek. "Hey, I thought Brian was coming over tonight to *talk*," Cecilia said, cocking her brow. "What happened?"

"A multicar accident. But work was…depressing today. One of our clients is in a coma. Her boyfriend beat her up really bad." Monique hit the steering wheel, and the horn screamed again. Cecilia placed a hand over hers to stop her.

"How awful. Is she gonna be okay?"

Monique shrugged. "Hope so."

Cecilia leaned her head back and closed her eyes. Wasn't it a good time to tell Monique what had happened to her in Boston? But she was too tired to put her experiences into words. "I'm glad you're back."

"Let's go to my house," Monique said. "I told Mel's mom you were staying with me when I went by her house earlier. I have more to tell you."

She sprawled on the love seat across from Monique. They drank beer and smoked Cecilia's menthol cigarettes. Cecilia looked at Monique through the smoke haze.

"What color are you going to paint your room? Mine will be blue. That was my daddy's favorite color too."

"Right now, Ceecee, I need to focus on moving out of here. I wish we didn't have to wait till the end of August. I'm scared to be here alone sometimes."

Cecilia put the bottle down and moved to the couch, throwing her arm around Monique's neck. "I'll stay here with you until we move except for when Mel needs me. You know I have maid of honor duties."

The ringing phone broke through Cecilia's thoughts of being there for her friends, and she wished she could clone herself and be with Lanei in Chicago as well. "Ceecee, it's for you," Monique said, handing the receiver to her. Cecilia frowned.

"Hello? Uncle Paul?" She sat up, her head clearing as if someone had doused her with a bucket of ice water.

"Ceecee, I called you at Mel's, and she gave me Monique's number. I'm sorry but Mama died tonight in her sleep."

"No, no, no," Cecilia screamed. "Uncle Paul...I haven't seen Grandma in years. I was planning to come for Christmas to see her and—" She stopped and listened.

After she hung up the phone, Cecilia fell into Monique's open arms and cried about her many losses.

"I'm so sorry, Ceecee. I know how much you love your grandma," Monique said, making circles on Cecilia's back with her fingers.

The sobs turned to dry hiccups scraping her throat. "Moe, Grandma Agnes was the closest family I had after Daddy died. I live with the guilt that I forced him to go to Saint Thomas that summer after my high school graduation." Cecilia closed her eyes against the pain. "Daddy took me home to spend a month with Grandma and Friendy, my dog, then he died in a car accident on the island. Mom came to bury him and stayed there with the boys."

"Oh, Ceecee," Monique said, pulling her closer. "But you made it. You have us. You'll never be alone."

Now she had to go back to bury her grandmother. She'd planned to go in December, because she needed the time and space to find her own beauty before she could face her mother. The love she'd seen in Grandma's face when she'd twirl Cecilia in front of the mirror every Saturday after braiding her hair in cornrows and rubbing lotion on her skin until she gleamed like polished ebony had kept her going. But life had a different plan. Could she suddenly put her grievances aside and forgive her mother for her neglect? For her abuse? She still wanted to reconnect with her family.

These strangers were her blood. Death had a way of bringing family together. What did she need a mom for at twenty-two? She could not make a list, but was it wrong to want to mend the relationship with her own mother? Self-love and loving her family were not mutually exclusive. Maybe her mother would open the door to her heart. Cecilia was now strong enough to try one last time.

19
Lanei

A s Lanei wiped bacon grease from the stove, she threw side-glances at Kevin, who was reading a magazine at the kitchen table. Why was he still home? She prayed he had not been fired again. An unemployed Kevin was a volatile missile. She needed to leave with Maria for her library playgroup and hoped Nate would show up today. Twice a week he stopped by the library on his lunch hour to visit with her and Maria. He hadn't come last week. She'd picked up the phone a couple times to call him but set it back down instead. Maybe Nate was pulling away from her, knowing that she couldn't give him what he wanted. She placed a cup of fresh coffee in front of Kevin, swallowed to wash any trace of unease from her voice, and said, "Kev…are you off today?"

"I go in at noon," he said, folding the magazine. "I almost got the dough for our own place, baby girl."

Lanei bristled. "Please…um…don't call me that. Now that I have a *baby girl*, it makes me feel…uncomfortable."

"Don't care what you say." He reached under her skirt. Lanei scissored her legs and stopped the progress of his hand. He looked at his watch, and she looked at the clock on the wall. It was ten minutes before noon. Even for Kevin that was a stretch. "You will always be my baby girl. I'll make you happy later." He winked, squeezing her buttocks on his way to the door.

Lanei forced her body to relax into him and said, "Oh, um…I'd like to go to Miami for Mel's wedding. My friends—"

She stopped when he frowned. "Woman, I'm workin' like a fuckin' donkey so we can move. You just went to their graduation." He glared at her. "You ain't goin'," he yelled, tugging hard on her ponytail. "You hear me?"

She nodded slowly to stop the twisting of her neck. She closed her hand around the cross on the rosary in her pocket, and the metal dug into her palm, not unlike the nails in Jesus's hands. God would protect her. But her tribe offered an escape. Was that God's way of sending the help she'd been praying for? How could she tell?

As soon as Kevin left the house, Lanei applied a touch of rouge on her cheeks and dabbed lip gloss on her plump lips. She pulled the rubber band from her ponytail and brushed her hair until it fell in loose curls down her back and around her face, the way Nate loved. Nate, who had not given her a choice but had followed her from Miami over a year ago. Lanei still lived in fear that Kevin would find out that Nate lived in Chicago. Nate would meet someone one day. He could not possibly spend his life waiting for her to choose between God and him. But for now she enjoyed his presence, knowing how selfish and sinful her feelings were.

She filled three sandwich bags with snacks for Maria and placed them in the diaper bag on the table. She didn't want to miss the bus and lose precious time with Nate if he came. With the bag slung over her shoulder, Lanei suppressed the panic rising in her chest at the thought of moving by tightening her grip on Maria with one hand and fingering the rosary in her pocket with the other.

She sat on the alphabet rug at the library, trying to read while Maria played with some blocks. A few minutes later, Nate breezed through the door and pecked Lanei's forehead. The heat of his breath on her skin traveled to places in her body she'd been taught by her parochial school nuns to despise. He scooped Maria up and spun her around. She giggled.

"Not too much, Nate. She had a seizure early this morning. Put her down on her feet. Let her show you what she can do." Lanei smiled.

Maria took three fast steps before tumbling forward on the rug. Nate clapped. Maria turned, started clapping, and smiled, showing her eight teeth. "She walks! She walks!" Nate exclaimed. "When did that happen?"

"Last week. It's as though she wants to talk, walk, and run all at the same time to make up for being so frail. Why didn't you come last week?"

"I was sent to cover another pharmacy. I wanted to call you." Longing snaked around the words Nate had said and twisted through Lanei's stomach. "But you warned me not to ever call your house. I don't understand—"

Lanei reached over and touched his face, running her palm down to his neck below his shirt collar. Nate stopped talking and looked at her as he raised his hand to cover hers. The hunger in his eyes filled her belly. She pulled her hand away as if she'd done something bad. "Oh, um—" Lanei looked away, waiting for her face to cool off. "Nate, never call the house or come by."

He shook his head. "I know, I know." He pouted like a little boy. "So are you going to Mel's wedding?"

"No. We're moving out. We need to buy furniture and—"

"Didn't your friends pay for your ticket? I remember how happy you always were around them."

"I'm going to miss all the fun. Moe will be outrageous in some kind of way. Ella will be jealous because she didn't have a *wedding*, and Ceecee's looking forward to meeting the best man. 'He's cute and single,' Mel said." Lanei smiled, feeling a warm spot in her heart for these women. "The best time I've had in my life was when the four of us went on spring break our freshman year."

Lanei closed her eyes to bring back the memory of a time long gone. Yet it felt like yesterday that she was eighteen and in Key West with her island sisters.

Nate broke into her reverie. "Do tell, Lane. Now I want to know."

And she began to tell him.

20

Ella

Despite the two strong cups of Haitian coffee Ella had drunk the night before, she had succumbed to sleep. She'd worked a double shift yesterday, still trying to save money to prepare for school in less than six months. She needed to know what had happened to her money. There ought to be a reasonable explanation for never putting her name on the accounts and moving the funds without telling her. She opened her eyes and blinked against the sunlight streaming into the small bedroom she had shared with Bernard since they'd married four years ago.

As a little girl, Ella had envisioned an elaborate wedding where everyone in the room would focus on her. Her whole life she had felt invisible. Her father had never seen her. Her six siblings tended to her like the cattle on the family farm. Then Bernard had come along. He had wanted her, and she never could say no to him.

After a particularly long night of lovemaking in the summer of her freshman year, Bernard had flipped Ella on her back and stared into her eyes. "I have an idea, Elle. Don't go to Haiti for the summer. We'll cash your ticket out and use the money to get married. I love you so much. I want to be yours."

She thought of how marriage hadn't stopped Lanei from going to school, and Ella had said, "Um…I have to tell my tribe."

"Let's surprise them, *mon amour.*" He'd kissed her all over.

She'd married Bernard at City Hall two days later with two clerks serving as witnesses. The following day a loud knock on the door had pulled her off the lumpy couch. Monique and Cecilia had barged inside.

"We saw Bernard at the supermarket today, and he said you didn't go home as planned for the summer," Cecilia said. "What happened?"

Ella suddenly felt boxed in. "Um…did he tell you?" she asked, displaying her left hand with the thin silver band Bernard had bought at a pawn shop. "We got married."

"*O merde!*" Monique said, pulling up one of the mismatched chairs from the tiny kitchen and sitting. "You're joking, right?"

The look of horror on her friends' faces flooded Ella's stomach with doubt. "*Non.* We did. Bernard wanted me to surprise you. We are having a party soon to celebrate. Come on, it will not change anything. He loves me so much. And he wants me to volunteer at the hospital for the summer instead of going home. After all, I am going to be a doctor. Right?" Ella raised her eyebrows.

"I hope he loves you enough to let you be *you*." Because Monique was not one to hold her opinions, she added, "I think you made a big mistake. Well, don't get knocked up."

"No! Bernard uses condoms. He said other methods would make me…fat and cause terrible side effects."

"Sister-friend," Monique said, shaking her head, "you need to be in control of your reproductive choice. Do you understand?"

Two months later, Ella was pregnant with Alex.

Now she wiped her glasses with the bedsheet. The clock told her she was going to be late for her morning shift. Bernard had come home so late last night she had passed out waiting for him, and this morning he had left early. It was as if he knew she needed to confront him. She hustled Alex out of bed and somehow managed to make it out the door in under half an hour. Janet would feed Alex.

Standing at the bus stop, Ella looked around and longed for the green, open spaces of her village. The apartment buildings felt like they were closing in on her, keeping her confined within their concrete walls.

On her lunch break, she called Bernard at work. "You need to come home after work today," Ella said. "I went to the bank yesterday. We need to talk."

"Why did you go to the bank? Don't I take care of the family? I have a community meeting later."

"I do not want to talk about this over the phone, Bernard. Be home." She hung up. Ella was going home with her medical degree one day to save women's lives. Nothing would stop her now.

21
Monique

Monique pulled out the small suitcase she had just emptied from her trip to Haiti and started packing for Saint Thomas. She wished it was a more joyous occasion, but she couldn't let Cecilia make this trip alone. Besides, it would take her mind off the creepiness of Julien's remark at the airport in Haiti. She zipped the luggage closed, and the phone rang.

She grabbed the receiver on the nightstand. "Hello."

"I wonder if you'd mind having dinner with me on Saturday," Brian said. "I actually have an afternoon off."

"I'll be in Saint Thomas with Ceecee." She kicked the base of the nightstand in frustration. "I told you about my college friends the night we met at Chantal's. Remember?"

"Yes. Your island sisters?"

She raised her eyes heavenward and mouthed, *he listens.* "Well, we're part of a tribe. We share island bonds."

"What are those bonds?" She could hear laughter in his voice. "I'm from Tennessee. How do I become part of *your* tribe?"

"Wrong gender. Wrong country. Wrong history." Monique laughed. "Sorry, pal."

"You don't mince words, do you?"

"Nope. It gets me in trouble a lot, but that's me."

"I like that."

"You're sure you don't like docile females? I'm definitely not one of those."

"Well, I grew up with three bossy older sisters and a mother who marched for civil rights in the *South*," Brian said. "Yes, I'm sure. I love my women tough."

Her thunderous laugh boomed through the room. "I'll call you when I get back."

"Promise?" he whispered.

"Promise," she whispered back. Gas gurgled in her stomach again. Maybe it was butterflies. A smile spread over her face as she hung up the phone.

She whistled a tune on her way to the kitchen. She loved that Brian liked his women tough. No man had ever said that to her before. "*Mmm*," she muttered. She recalled his boyish grin when he'd held her hand that night at Chantal's. Even in her high heels she'd had to look up into his brown eyes. She touched her chest as if her heart could communicate its secrets to her brain. Halfway to the kitchen, the phone rang again.

"Hello, brown eyes," Monique sang, laughing. "I'm going to starve if you keep calling—"

"Mine are black," the caller said.

Monique swallowed the laughter so fast it became a rock in her throat. "Who's this?" But she knew.

"Your lover, *Julien Etienne*," he said, stretching the syllables.

"Julien! How…how did you get my number?"

"Everything is for sale in Haiti if you have the money, Monique. I have the money."

"We're not lovers. We had a one-night stand. Don't ever call me again."

"It's all right, *chérie*. I wanted to tell you how much I miss you. See you soon."

The wet sounds of Julien kissing the phone coated her skin and made her want to jump in the shower. She listened to the loud dial tone until it stopped. She turned around in a circle in the kitchen as if searching for an evil presence in the house. Fear replaced hunger in the pit of her stomach. Julien was not going away as fast as she had hoped. What did he want from her? Monique was afraid of the answer.

22

Cecilia

Cecilia soaked in the sights from her window seat as the plane began its descent to the Harry S. Truman Airport in Saint Thomas. She pointed to the beautiful mountains ringing Charlotte Amalie—the capital. Boats floated on the water like colorful dots on a blue canvas. She closed her eyes when the plane touched down, hoping to slow her heart back to its normal rhythm.

"Guys, I'm so glad you came with me," she said, squeezing the hands of her friends seated on either side of her on a bench outside the airport terminal as they waited for her uncle.

"You couldn't keep me away," Monique said.

"Me either," Mel drawled.

After a short wait, Uncle Paul arrived, and they climbed inside his car. When he turned onto Highway 30, the road that led to the center of town, Mel yelled, "*Sweet Jesus,* he's driving on the wrong side of the road!"

Cecilia laughed. "Here we drive on the left—a remnant of our British colonization."

The car made its way slowly through traffic. Tourists braved the July sun with wide-brimmed hats and gobs of sunscreen. The natives went about soaking in the heat and enjoying the sea air coming from the ocean. Cecilia rolled down the window and inhaled the smell of her childhood. Cruise ships docked along the shore, flooding the city with people in search of adventure. She pointed to her right and turned to look at her friends. "That is Fort Christian. I spent a lot of time there with my dad. I was once into pirates." She smiled.

Leaving the center of town behind, the car entered the Tutu Valley where Cecilia had lived the first decade of her life. Uncle Paul slowed in front of the small house where her family had lived, now painted yellow and blue. Cecilia remembered the fenced yard where she played with Friendy to escape her mother. They drove another two blocks and stopped in front of Uncle Paul's: a white, wood-framed house with blue shutters and a front porch.

"Your mother lives on the next street," Uncle Paul said, "but we never see the boys. I've tried."

Cecilia hugged him. The airy living room was painted a soft pink and was furnished with natural wicker furniture covered in pastel blues and greens. A ceiling fan helped the window unit chase away the midday heat. Cecilia kicked off her sandals and stepped onto the cool cement floor. Monique and Mel did the same and moaned in relief.

"Auntie went to the food store, and the kids are at summer camp," Uncle Paul said. "Make yourself comfortable. Ceecee, you know where the kitchen is. Get a snack. We'll have dinner later." He took their luggage, and they followed him to a bedroom in the back with two twin beds. "The sofa in the living room opens into a bed too. I have to go to the funeral home for some final details."

"Don't worry," Cecilia said. "We'll be fine. Thank you for everything."

A framed picture of her father on the sofa table against the wall drew Cecilia's gaze, and she walked over to the table to get a better look. Cecilia ran her palm over the glass, wishing she could crawl into his arms once more. Tears flowed like a geyser for her many losses. Monique and Mel stood next to her with hands on her shoulders.

"You've got his dimples," Monique whispered. Cecilia sniffed.

After a dinner of callaloo, roti, and pâté with her uncle's family in the late afternoon, Cecilia and her friends headed out. She waved to neighbors sweeping their front yards. Squealing kids chased each other between the houses, raising fine dust behind them. Dogs barked and followed the kids with wagging tails.

Cecilia knocked on the red door at the address Uncle Paul had given her. The door opened and Mom stared at her, squinting. She walked slowly toward her mother as if Cecilia's presence might frighten her away. When she got too close, Mom stepped back, holding the top of the faded robe with the missing button with her hand. Her once high-yellow skin was sallow and wrinkled like tissue paper. A string of gray hair stuck in the corner of her mouth, and she spat it out. "Mom, you know Mel," Cecilia said. "And this is my friend Monique."

The two women stood on the first step and waved. With the closed drapes and a ceiling light fixture with only one burning bulb, Cecilia held her breath and waited for her vision to adjust before she started picking up dirty cups, food wrappers, and empty alcohol bottles off the floor. "Mom, where are the boys? Why's this place so...untidy? What—"

"Stop!" Mom screamed. "What are you doing here?"

Cecilia stopped, her hands full of trash. "Grandma died. You didn't hear the news?"

"Why would I know that? That old witch. She—"

"The funeral service is at ten tomorrow morning at Holy Family," Cecilia said. "Be there with the boys...*Mom*. Please."

"Okay, okay. But...I have no money to give them."

"What did you do with all the money you collected after Daddy's death four years ago? His life insurance from his employer, the proceeds from the sale of the house in Miami, the settlement from the truck company—" Cecilia stopped, immediately wishing she could take the words back.

"Oh, that's why you're here. Get the hell away from me, Cecilia." Mom threw one of her slippers at her while trying to get up. Cecilia pulled the door closed behind her. On the walk back to Uncle Paul's with her friends, she was silent. She did not care about the money. She no longer needed it, so why had she brought it up, antagonizing her mother when she had agreed to coming to the funeral? They would go someplace quiet to talk after the service tomorrow. Cecilia would apologize.

The space she saved in the pew for her mother and brothers remained empty. Her anger and embarrassment mounted. As soon as the last guest left the reception hall, she collapsed into a chair. Monique sat next to her and massaged her neck. "I'm sorry, but your mother is a bitch. I bet she was mean before she started drinking."

Cecilia stood. "I'll be back."

The drizzling rain became a downpour and mixed with her tears. She welcomed the cleansing, hoping to leave her anguish in the puddles at her feet. She didn't remember the long walk from the reception hall to the park. She sat on the same bench near Tillet Gardens where she and Daddy had stood, pretending to fly. At the cemetery she brushed wet leaves from her dad's tombstone and sat. Grandma Agnes now rested next to him.

"I miss you, Daddy. Every day. I graduated college last month, but you're not here to share that with me. I was raped." Cecilia wailed. "I'm sorry

I couldn't tell you. I still feel pain when I think about it. I'm twenty-two, and I'm now working on healing and loving myself. Why did you give me a mother who can't love me? I need you." Cecilia beat the cement slab until her palms throbbed. "Why did you leave me, Daddy?" She put her head down and sobbed. The rain beat down hard on her back. Thunder growled while lightning flashed around her.

When her sorrow was spent, anger took over. She plucked the red hibiscus from her hair and placed it on her father's tombstone. The long walk from the cemetery failed to dilute her rage. She banged on the red door until her knuckles turned purple. Shuffled steps grew louder.

"Oh, it's you. I'm sor…ry 'bout missing the service," Mom said, her voice slurred. "Your brother…Emilio's in jail…my poor son—"

"Stop, Anna!" Cecilia screamed. She could no longer call her mom. Anna had never mothered her. "You are *evil*. I know you never liked Grandma, but you could have made the effort to show up at her funeral to honor Dad's memory."

"You're dripping water on my floor," Anna said, taking a long pull from the cigarette between her gnarly fingers. "That ugly old bitch never liked me anyway."

"No, you never liked her, you *racist* drunk," Cecilia yelled. "You think your looks make you special? I have news for you, Anna. You're a *black* woman. You treat me like dirt because I look like Daddy. You can't even be a mother to the sons you love for favoring you." Cecilia exhaled and glared at Anna. "Why did you marry my father? I need to know."

Spittle flying from her twisted lips, Anna screeched and said, "I married him 'cause I was twenty-eight and single, and he had a good job." She spat out the words. They were laced with poison. "You'll have a career soon. Maybe you'll find a man who might need your paycheck too."

Cecilia stumbled backward to put distance between herself and the painful words. "I hate you. You should have been the one to die in that car crash." She slammed the door and sat on the front stoop, unable to make her legs carry her away from the woman who had given her life and had done everything to destroy it. She stopped crying as if she'd turned off a faucet. She stood.

Death sometimes birthed life. Her heart was open for love. Self-love. Cecilia would never let anyone hurt her so deeply again. What did she need Anna for? She couldn't say. She hoped the answer would soon be *nothing*.

23

Lanei

Excitement for their freshman year spring break traveled through them like a virus. Lanei ran outside, dragging her suitcase behind her, when she heard the honk. She placed her bag in the back of the Oldsmobile station wagon Monique had rented for the trip and climbed in the back to sit next to Ella. They'd planned for weeks, but as always, they had all prayed Kevin would allow Lanei to go.

Monique turned the car toward the highway and found a radio station playing the latest hits. The singing began.

"Lan, I'm so happy you could come," Cecilia said during a commercial. "Moe was planning a kidnapping if necessary."

Their laughter filled the car. "Oh, Kevin wanted me to go. In fact, he's taking me away at the end of the month for my birthday. Can you believe we're turning nineteen this year?"

"I am already nineteen," Ella said. "I will always be the oldest of the group—having been born on New Year's Day." She shook her head and sighed. "No wonder my father has never forgiven me. When my mother died that day, 1958 must have been the worst year of his life."

"Let's all pledge to not talk about anything unpleasant on this trip," Monique said. "We're going to have fun and nothing less."

Lanei ran her thumb and index fingers over her lips like a zipper. Monique belted out Diana Ross's "Love Hangover," and they all joined in, singing, talking, and laughing for four hours while they crossed over the many bridges toward Key West.

Halfway to their destination, they pulled over in the parking lot of a wooden shack that advertised the best seafood in Marathon, Florida. It looked like every college student in America had stopped to eat here too, based on how busy the place was. They ordered pink lemonade while they waited for a table.

The smell of fresh-baked bread made Lanei swallow her saliva several times to keep from drooling. A bunch of boys made their way to the group of girls. They were from Pennsylvania, and even the two black ones needed a tan. The tallest one smiled at Monique and said, "Where are you ladies headed?"

"Key West. Just stopping for a bite," Monique said, batting her eyelashes. Lanei tried hard not to laugh.

"Our final destination as well," the tall boy said. "Hope to see you ladies there. We're seniors. We can buy booze."

"Great," Ella said. "We are freshmen."

The shortest of the group scribbled his name and his hotel on a napkin and slid it toward Cecilia. "You're a perfect plum, my favorite fruit. Don't hide from me in Key West."

Cecilia crumpled the paper and left it on the bar when the hostess took them to a booth.

"Good," Monique said. "It's too early to start taking names. There'll be hundreds, thousands even."

"Ella and I need no names," Lanei said. "I have a husband, and Ella has Bernard."

"Too bad," Monique muttered, clearing her throat. Lanei elbowed her ribs.

They gorged on crab cakes, corn chowder, and fish and chips. When the waitress brought the check, Lanei asked for some extra rolls. She returned with two bags of bread and said,

"Go give the boys hell. Y'all are gorgeous."

After the waitress left, Cecilia said, "Damn, I wish I could leave her a very generous tip. She put me in the gorgeous category."

"You are gorgeous, Ceecee," Ella said. "Why do you always question that?"

Cecilia shrugged and said, "Can I drive the rest of the way, Moe?"

"Sure," Monique said. "We'll drive to many more places in the future. This is a big country, you know."

"Well, not all of us have the privilege to travel all over the world," Ella said, rolling her eyes.

Monique's face gathered like a storm. "Ella, why do you always have to bring that up?"

"Let's go," Cecilia said, pushing Ella inside the car.

It started to drizzle when they left the restaurant. Lanei looked up at the giant gray ball of cloud hovering over the area. Ahead she could see blue sky. Cecilia flipped the wipers on and changed the station to classical music.

"Hey, Ceecee, you are putting us to sleep," Ella said. "I need drums."

Cecilia shook her head, put the car in reverse, and backed out of the parking lot. Ahead a rainbow splashed the sky with buckets of color. Lanei cranked her window down when the rain stopped, and suddenly, they were driving under the bluest sky. She stuck her arm out and waved her fingers, feeling the breeze run through them.

A giant sign tied to lampposts spanned the width of the street. Lanei pointed to it and read out loud: WELCOME TO KEY WEST SPRING BREAK 1977. "We're here, guys," she screamed with unusual exuberance.

After Monique checked them into the hotel using the credit cards her father had given her for emergencies, she said, "In my book, this *is* an emergency." Monique made a sad face. "We couldn't possibly not go away for our first spring break. I would have gone mad." Her deep laughter followed them to the banks of elevators.

When they reached their room, Monique and Cecilia dove onto one of the two double beds and started a pillow fight. Lanei and Ella opened their luggage on the other bed and reached for hangers for their clothes. Monique jumped off the bed after a while and snatched Lanei's book. "You brought Jane Austen along on spring break?" she said, throwing the library's copy of *Emma* back in the suitcase. "How boring."

Lanei placed the book on the night table. "Because you don't like to read, Moe," Lanei said. "Books are my escape, and I adore Jane's writing. It's as though she's a friend. Besides I can't sleep until I've read at least one chapter. That's my drug."

"Booze works just as well," Monique said with a roar. "Let's go to the beach for a swim, and then we'll come back and dress for the night."

In the bathroom, Lanei stripped out of her blue jeans and white T-shirt, grateful the bruise on her stomach would remain covered. She slipped into a mustard-yellow one-piece bathing suit that blended into her skin and tied her hair in a loose bun on top of her head. Wrapping the beach towel around her waist, she stepped out and said, "I'm ready to have some fun." She stared at the thin band on her finger and twisted it around. It crossed her mind that she could take it off, just so she wouldn't have to talk about it, but she couldn't. Kevin had put it on her finger in the presence of God.

"Wow! Look at you, Lan," Ella said. "Exotic! That is the word."

"Look at you, Elle," Lanei replied, taking in Ella's light brown two-piece suit that made her look almost nude.

Monique stripped naked in the middle of the room and slipped into a fiery red one-piece with deep cutouts on the sides and the back. "Ceecee, come out already," Monique yelled.

Lanei's eyes grew wide when Cecilia glided out of the bathroom in a shimmery white one-piece that seemed to push her dark skin deeper within shadows. Her white teeth shone bright in her dimpled face. "Ta-da," Cecilia said, turning around in a circle.

"What a sight," Lanei said. "Ceecee, you look like an African goddess."

Their giddiness connected them like magnets. Whistling sounds from a group of frat boys followed them into the cool water. They splashed each other until Lanei hiccupped with laughter and dove underneath a big wave. She opened her eyes briefly as if she could see her future at the bottom of the ocean.

They watched the sunset dance on the surface of the water like a light show before disappearing within it like a magic trick. They bought hot dogs from a street vendor for dinner. Monique took her hot dog from the bun and shoved half of it inside her mouth, pulling it in and out and moaning. The young vendor dropped the next hot dog on the ground as his jaw followed. Their laughter cascaded behind them all the way back to the hotel.

"Monique Magloire, you are incorrigible," Cecilia said.

Back in the room, Ella brandished a bottle of Haitian rum from her handbag. She mixed some with soda in a plastic cup and sipped as she made her way to the bathroom to shower. "Help yourselves, ladies," she said. "Lan, I brought ginger ale for you."

Monique snuck into the bathroom and took Ella's glasses. "Wait for it," she said to the other girls.

"Moe," Cecilia said, "go put her glasses back. That girl is liable to hurt herself, she's so near-sighted."

Lanei heard the shower turn off, and Ella screamed, "Goddamn it! Monique, bring me my glasses." They laughed at Ella standing in the bathroom doorway, water dripping from her hair and her arms extended in front of her like a blind person. "You need to grow up, Moe. Seriously."

A few hours later, just before Monique closed the door to the room, Lanei said, "Um…I need to call Kevin before we go. I imagine it might be too late when we come back."

Monique pulled her through the door and locked it. "We just got here today, honey. You can call the warden tomorrow."

Lanei opened her mouth. Ella pulled her toward the elevators.

The pulse of the club sucked them in like a vacuum. A man whispered something in Cecilia's ear, and she followed him to the dance floor. Surrounded by three men vying for her attention, Monique danced in the middle of the circle, her winding waist keeping them in place as if they were bolted to the floor. Ella flirted with a man who'd followed her all night. Lanei closed her eyes and let the music wash over her. She felt bodies bump into her but did not mind. This was her night. She wanted the music to smooth out all the wrinkles of her complicated life.

By the end of the weekend, none of them had taken names, but they had taken many memories. In the car on the way home, Lanei said, "I can honor my marriage without sacrificing my youth and my happiness."

"I want to share my life with Bernard one day, but I will never let him control it," Ella vowed and looked at Cecilia.

"I can put small cracks in the shield I built around myself, so I can see myself with my own eyes," Cecilia whispered.

"I want to be free to do whatever the hell I want," Monique stated. "Just like any man."

Lanei had recognized Monique as the leader of their tribe. She smiled at Nate.

"Whoa!" Nate said, when Lanei finished the tale. "That was a fun time."

Lanei nodded, stretching her legs on the library rug. "I think I deserve more."

24

Ella

A few days after her trip to the bank, Ella opened the door and let Janet and Alex into the apartment. "Jan, thank you for bringing him home. I am so tired lately. I do not know what is wrong with me."

"It ain't no trouble at all," Janet said. "I brought you some fried fish. At least you won't have to cook dinner."

Ella smiled before the smell of the food wafting out of the plastic bag shot her out of the chair like a cannon. She ran to the bathroom, almost missing the bowl. Janet rushed in behind her.

"You okay, baby?"

"I am not sure. I threw up this morning at work too. Oh no. I cannot be—" Ella stopped.

She remembered the night after Bernard's graduation party almost eight weeks ago.

"Can't be what?" Janet helped her into a chair in the kitchen.

"Pregnant," she whispered. "The only thing to stop me from going to school in January is money or—"

"A baby." Janet finished the sentence, her upper lip almost touching her nose. "I thought you were trying a new pill."

"I hemorrhaged with that one too. My gynecologist recommended I stay away from the pill. That was the fourth brand she had prescribed." Ella's stomach churned with fear or nausea. She was not sure. "But I have an appointment to be fitted with an IUD. Jan, why is God punishing me so?" She had tried to tell Bernard that night. He had failed to protect her.

"God is not evil. It seems like your husband doesn't want you in school. You need to find out why."

"But why would he not want me to go to school? I am happy for him that he graduated. He promised to support me. We are a team."

Janet snorted. "I don't know much about books and such, but I know you gotta be in school to be a doctor."

Ella waited for Bernard by the front door and pounced when he walked in. He stepped back, and she thought she saw glee in his eyes. He had said he knew what to do that night, but he had done nothing.

"Bernard, I believe I am pregnant, and it would have happened that night after your graduation party. I have been careful since. Did you plan this?" Ella took off her glasses to wipe her eyes before putting them back on to look at her husband.

Bernard placed his right palm on his chest like he was about to testify. "Elle, you don't even know that you're pregnant for certain."

In their small kitchen, he tried to take her in his arms. She pushed him away, using her hand as a shield on her thumping heart. "I threw up twice today, and my period is late." Ella gripped the back of a chair to keep her body from shaking. "How can you do this to me? Where have you been the past couple of nights? Lately you sneak in after I fall asleep. What is going—"

He waved his hand like he was swatting a pesky mosquito. "Elle, stop." He opened his arms, but she stayed behind the chair. "I'll buy us a house before the baby comes—if there *is* a baby. I met this Haitian broker last week at a community meeting. He'll help us."

Ella looked around the one-bedroom apartment with the shaggy brown carpet and the threadbare brown couch and had the urge to bolt. To leave Bernard with Alex sleeping on the cot in the living room. Two of the mismatched chairs around the dinette table were broken. Ella kept the light on during the day to chase away the darkness. Bernard removed his jacket and held it over his shoulder with his index finger like he was preparing for a photo shoot. Even his Pierre Cardin cologne still wafted off his body after a long day. Ella ran her hand through her uncombed hair, stared at the bleach stain on her wrinkled housedress, and wanted to run into the bedroom and hide.

"Where is my money, Bernard?" she said a bit too loudly. "What am I going to do if I am pregnant?" It all seemed to be too much.

He tsk-tsked like she was a petulant child or an idiot. "If you'd told me your plans, I would have saved you a trip to the bank. I invested our money with a financial planner at work. Don't worry your pretty head. I'll always take care of you."

Ella bristled. "But I want to take care of myself. I am capable of that. I want to see the statements."

"No problem, love," Bernard said with a smile meant to melt the outer crust of her icy heart. "I have nothing to hide from you. I should have told you. I'm sorry."

"What are you sorry for, Bernard? That I found out about the money? That you did not consult with me before you made decisions concerning our family? That I may be pregnant—"

Ella ran to the bathroom and vomited into the toilet until Bernard walked in and helped her up from the floor. He washed her face with cold water. In the pitted mirror over the sink, they stared at each other. Ella could not decipher any emotion on Bernard's blank face.

Two days later, the positive pregnancy test crushed her. She called her tribe. Ella waited at the hospital cafeteria after her shift. Monique breezed in like a storm, disturbing the air around her just as Cecilia seemed to put things back into place with her measured movements. They hugged before clinking their bracelets together. A long sigh escaped Ella's pressed lips.

"Hey, what's the matter?" Monique said, looking at Ella.

"Moe, sit down," Cecilia said, taking Ella's hand.

"*Miss Peterson*, I'm not your student," Monique said, sticking her tongue out at Cecilia. She pulled out a chair and sat backward, leaning on the backrest. They stared at Ella, expectant looks creasing their brows.

"I am not going to school in January as planned, because I am pregnant. Bernard moved our money. I do not know where it is exactly." Ella raised her palm and glared at Monique. "I cannot have an abortion, Moe."

"What— " Monique raised her hands in surrender. "Okay, I was thinking you ought to."

"I'm trapped. It's as though Bernard planned my pregnancies to keep me from school. But…but that's absurd. That's why we're both here."

Ella needed to believe that. She looked everywhere except at her success-ful friends. The ones who had graduated college because their lives weren't tied to a man. Monique patted her hand and said, "Whoa! Ceecee, Ella contracted a few verbs. It's serious."

Cecilia shook her head, squinted at Monique, and said, "Elle, I thought you were going to be fitted with an IUD?"

"I am…I was. I have been working so much that I kept rescheduling," she said, mopping up her tears with a fistful of napkins from the dispenser on the table.

"How can we help?" Cecilia asked, stroking her arms. "Bernard is your husband. You need to understand his motivation. I have to admit that he seems—what's the word?"

"Conniving," Monique offered.

"Opaque," Cecilia said. "With Kevin, you know you're looking at a bully, but with Bernard… I don't know, Elle. Keep your eyes open."

"Here is my plan, ladies. I'm having tubal ligation after this baby and going back to school full-time in the fall instead. Baby is due in April." Ella blew her nose and smiled. "I feel better already. I talked to Lanei this morning. Oh, Ceecee, I did not even ask about the trip. I'm sorry again about your grandma. Did you see your mother?"

"I did," Cecilia said. "For the last time." Ella saw something hard and feral replace the compassion in Cecilia's eyes.

When Cecilia didn't say anything else, Ella looked at Monique who shook her head without moving a single hair. "So, Moe, have you seen Ryan…Brian— you know, the guy you met at Chantal's?" Ella asked, changing the subject.

"It's Brian," Monique said. "We finally have a date tomorrow."

"And how about Julien? No more threats?"

"I think the creep got the message that I'm not interested," Monique said. "Haven't heard from him since his last call."

After putting her son to bed, Ella sat on the couch and waited for Bernard to come home from a community meeting. Janet and the girls had urged her to keep her eyes open. What should she be looking for? Her sister Therese had alluded to a secret regarding Bernard when Ella had told her she had married him. Did she want to know? They were a couple now, and she was having his children. She would go back to school next year. Bernard loved her and had followed her twice since they had met in high school. Her friends meant well, but they didn't know the history and the emotions that tied lovers together.

Ella walked into the bedroom to wait for her husband.

25

Monique

After a long day of work at the women's center where Monique scheduled appointments for callers with legal aid attorneys, social workers, or psychiatrists, she was restless. One day she would be the lawyer giving them a voice and finding them justice. The meeting with Ella yesterday at the cafeteria had done nothing to improve her mood about what women endured in the name of love.

When she got home, she packed some more of her belongings into boxes, glanced at the clock in the hallway, and wished she didn't have to wait twenty-four hours for her dinner date with Brian. Her heart jiggled like Jell-O at the thought of seeing him. She wondered what was happening to her. Whatever it was, she liked it. It felt good. She gulped a lungful of air, feeling as if the house was closing in on her. She picked up the receiver and dialed. "Good evening, Mrs. Walker," Monique said to Mel's mother. "Is Ceecee there?"

When Cecilia answered the phone, Monique said, "Hey, let's go to a movie. I need to get out of this house."

"I can't. Mel has the wedding party here, and we're rehearsing. I can call you after and come over, but it might be late."

"Okay. We'll talk tomorrow." They tapped the receiver with their bracelets.

Grabbing her keys, she headed to the garage. This was what physical, financial, and mental freedom felt like. She wanted to be the woman her mother and her sisters were not allowed to be in Haiti.

After enjoying a quiet dinner and a funny movie, she turned the car in the direction of the house. Whoever said you needed a man to have fun? Monique belted out a song and tapped the steering wheel. A black car parked at the curb, mere feet from the driveway, made her stop singing. It was past midnight. She sat up straighter in the driver's seat. As she got closer to the lamppost, she noticed a shape in the vehicle. She checked that her car doors were locked.

Once past the parked car, she looked in the rearview mirror and saw the dome light come on inside the black car. She parked her car and ran to the side door to the garage, her heart racing. She fumbled with the key. Once inside, she leaned against the locked door and breathed. When the doorbell rang, she held her breath again. It rang twice more as she tiptoed into the kitchen and reached for the telephone on the wall. When she heard the lock turn, she stopped. Was it Papa? He had finally learned to knock first. She placed the phone back in its holder and walked to the foyer. The door banged against the wall. Monique stared at the man and screamed.

"*O merde*! Wh…what are you doing here? How did you know… Oh my God, my lost keys." Monique closed her eyes and opened them, hoping Julien would disappear.

"May I come in?" he asked, stepping inside and closing the door behind him. "I came a long way to see you, *mon amour*."

"You're already in my house *without* an invitation." Monique glared at him. Anger battled fear. "You stole the keys from my purse when I was at your house?" she said, fighting her flight instinct. "What the hell do you want from me, Julien?"

"I've been waiting for over three hours." He walked slowly toward her. "This is what I get for wanting to surprise you." He took her hand. She yanked it away.

"We need to talk. Then you leave." Monique walked into the family room and pointed to the couch. "I'm not in love with you, Julien. In fact, I'm in a relationship with somebody."

"I don't like the sound of that, Monique." Hardness crept into his voice. "And did this *relationship* happen before or after you fucked me a few weeks ago?"

Monique recoiled with disgust. "You're a sick bastard."

"But I love you." Julien's voice was whiny now. "I want you to be with me in Haiti. We'll be happy there."

She tapped her feet on the tile floor to disguise the shaking of her body. She scooted away until the armrest of the couch stopped her. "Julien, my life is here. I'm starting law school in a couple weeks. I don't ever want to live in Haiti." She faked a yawn. "You need to go."

"May I stay here? It's just for a couple hours. I have an early flight."

"No! I can direct you to a hotel near the airport." She stood.

"Go to your room." He smiled. "I'm terribly sorry. I had no right to barge into your home like this. I took the key because…I wanted something of yours to hold. I'm glad we talked." Julien pushed her lightly toward the hallway. He pulled the afghan from the back of the couch and lay down, placing a throw pillow under his head.

Monique walked into her room and locked the door. She reached for the phone to call the police when she heard two tentative knocks.

"Monique, I want to say goodbye. I'm going to the airport now." The doorknob rattled. "Why did you lock the door? I won't hurt you."

"Okay. Goodbye. We have nothing more to say to each other. Please lock the front door behind you," Monique said in a voice she hoped conveyed her anger and concealed her panic.

The bedroom door flew inward, knocking a painting off the wall. Wood splinters rained on the tile floor. Monique's hand shook as she dialed the number nine on the rotary telephone. Julien lunged and ripped the receiver from her hand. He pushed her backward toward the bed.

"How about a second-night stand for my trouble?" His voice trembled. "I came a long way to go back empty-handed."

"Let go of me, *cochon!*" she screamed. She swung her fists at his face, but she could not hit him as hard as she wanted. He held her tight against his chest before throwing her on the bed and straddling her thighs.

"Monique, I love you. The idea of another man touching you drives me crazy." He punched the pillow next to her head. She flinched. "What's your boyfriend's name? Does he make your toes curl? Huh!"

He brushed the hair out of her eyes and bent over her closed lips. She bit his tongue and tasted blood before his fist came down, and she blacked out.

When she came to, she was alone. She got up from the bed and inspected the house. Her body felt sore, as if she had been in a boxing match. She called Chantal.

"Don't take a shower," Chantal said. "Call the police. I'm on my way. That scumbag can't come and do this shit here."

Monique came home from the hospital after her encounter with law enforcement, a rape kit, and a handful of pamphlets about how to survive after a rape from the hospital social worker. She stood in the shower until the only hot water left was the tears coursing down her cheeks. She toweled off, fixed herself a drink, and called her tribe.

26
Cecilia

C ecilia walked into the familiar room, plucked the tissue box from the desk, and sat across from Freda. She stared at the counselor. The painful words stuck in her throat like a heaping spoon of peanut butter. She swallowed to moisten them. She needed to speak these words. To birth them, then kill them. Losing her grandmother should have stripped her of the emotional connection to home. She knew nothing about her two younger brothers. In fact, their births had banished Cecilia from whatever small spot she might have occupied in their mother's heart. Tears ran down her face and dripped into the ball of tissue in her hands. She lifted her head and nodded at Freda. "I'll be okay. I know that now. I no longer need a mommy; I never had one. But I need to talk about her. It would clear space in my heart to be able to love myself, and maybe one day I can let a man love me, not because of my paycheck, but—" Cecilia stopped. Freda frowned. "It's something my mother said to me this week that hurts as much as her kicks, but the words will keep me alert."

"Ceecee"—Freda leaned forward in her chair—"it may have been painful to see your mother again, especially after losing your grandma, but I hope the experience will help you to decide how to be the daughter you want to be. Or if you want to be a daughter. You've kept a lot inside but talking about the past, whether it's good or bad, helps us plan the future."

Cecilia was ready to bury her grievances against her mother. She no longer needed to be a daughter. She needed to be enough. She touched her forehead as if the many bumps from her mother's slaps and punches were still there.

She shifted in her seat. "You know, Freda, sometimes I'm jealous of my friends. They seem to have everything I want. Beauty, love, marriage, mothers—" She stopped. Freda waited.

"Ceecee, don't you think your friends wish they had something you have?"

"Like what?"

"That's for you to find out. You do have *everything*."

Cecilia hung on to these words and hurried back to Mel's, ready to help her childhood friend make her wedding as beautiful as she could.

When Monique called that evening for dinner and a movie, she would have preferred to go out with her than be stuck with Mel's clueless friends with their gaudy engagement rings, their bouncy hair, and their concern about the zits that might ruin their complexions mere days before the wedding. Sitting in a corner of the living room, Cecilia looked at the six women. *What do I have that they might want?* Her mother's idea of beauty had been drilled into her since birth, and no matter how pretty her daddy claimed she was, she could never see it.

Late in the night, someone shook her awake. "Ceecee...*Ceecee*," Mrs. Walker said. "Monique is on the phone for you."

Cecilia blinked and looked at the bedside clock. She picked the receiver up off the nightstand. "Moe, what—"

"Ceecee, Julien was here. I need you," Monique said, her ragged breath placing spaces between each word.

Cecilia blew air out of her mouth. Maybe she did possess attributes her friends needed. Loyalty, calmness, responsibility, thoughtfulness...

Sleep left her body like a thief.

27

Lanei

L anei massaged her legs to release the cramps from her lotus position on the library floor. Nate smiled along with her about Monique's stunt with the hot dog. The fond memories of that spring break made Lanei long to escape her life, even for a few days.

"I didn't know you had a wild side," Nate said, teasing her with his eyes. "I have to go back to work." He stood. His white coat reached below his waist, leaving his bowed legs clad in khaki pants next to her face. Lanei fought the urge to wrap her arms around them and let Nate drag her away. Her faith would not allow her.

Till death do us part.

She packed Maria's bag with more books and set out toward home. A home she had not chosen. A husband she feared. A future she could not see. For her whole life, choices had been made for her. She had learned to live with the consequences.

In her mother-in-law's kitchen, Lanei lifted the lid off the pot of stew on the stove and stared into it, lost in thought. The phone rang, sounding loud in the quiet house. She snatched it before it woke Maria from her nap.

"Hello…oh, Hafa Adai, Mama," Lanei said. "How is everything?"

"God is good, Lan," Mama said. "I can't complain. Father Arnoldo sends his blessings. How is my beautiful grandbaby? Thank you for the pictures."

"We hope to see you someday. I tell Maria stories about Guam. I know she's only a year old, but it's her heritage." Lanei walked around the kitchen counter and sat on a stool. "I'm sorry, Mama. I didn't listen to you about…not giving myself to a man until I was married. I believe I should have waited until I was *sure* he was the right man."

"Well, I couldn't have been any surer about your father, yet he married someone else."

Lanei had never questioned her mother about her father for fear of hurting her feelings, but she *had* brought it up. "I remember watching my father climb the church steps on his wedding day. I was eight. You took me there to witness it, Mama. Why?"

Mama sniffed. "At least Kevin made an honest woman out of you. You can receive communion. When you give yourself to a man before marriage, you commit a sin. I had to pay for my weakness."

"But why did he marry the other woman and leave us behind? I need to know. I'm not a child anymore."

After a long pause, Mama said, "His mother made him choose between us and his inheritance. I'm from the wrong side of the tracks. He made a choice that day, baby."

Lanei tightened her grip on the phone and stared out the window. How much of herself had she wanted to give Kevin in the beginning before he took it all? She needed to keep some for herself. For Maria. For—

"Lan," Mama said, breaking into her thoughts. "Let's pray."

"Yes, Mama." Lanei closed her eyes.

Long after she hung up, Lanei sat in the kitchen, praying the rosary. Kevin hadn't made an honest woman out of her. She lied to her friends, to Nate, and to herself about her true feelings. But she never lied to God.

Maria let out a wail, and Lanei ran to the bedroom. Her daughter appeared to have stretched to twice her length. Before she could pick her up, Kevin, who had just walked in from work, reached for Maria. He cradled his daughter in his arms, murmuring, "It's okay. Daddy is here. Daddy is here." He turned to Lanei. "You all right? You didn't hear me come in."

"You're home early. Don't you take Fred to dialysis every Wednesday?"

"He's in the hospital. Poor guy. I'll go see him tomorrow. He has no one."

"He has you, Kev. That's a very Christian thing to do."

"I'm lucky to have you and Maria in my life. I don't ever want to lose you, Lan."

Lanei watched as Maria's body sagged against Kevin's chest. She opened her clenched hand and touched her daddy's face. On her way back to the kitchen, the phone rang again. She picked it up. "*Hafa Adai*," Ella said.

"*Sak pasé*," Lanei replied, remembering the Creole greeting her friend had taught her. "How—" She stopped to listen.

"Did I not always say Moe would get in trouble with the way she plays with men's feelings?" Ella waited. Lanei said nothing. "Well, Julien came to Miami last night."

"Oh, no! What happened?" Lanei looked at Kevin, sitting in one of the dinette chairs and cooing to Maria, and her free hand touched the fading bruise on her upper arm.

"He raped her. That's what happened. I feel bad for her," Ella said in an "I told you so" tone that irritated Lanei instinctively, "but Monique acts like she is an *American* because she has lived here a long time. You can't mess with these regime thugs like that. She thinks—"

Lanei looked at the gleaming bracelet on her wrist and banged it hard on the phone. Ella stopped talking and after a beat clinked hers. Lanei knew Ella was dealing with her second unplanned pregnancy, Bernard's lack of support, and the estrangement from her family back home. But none of those things justified her judgmental tone. Ella had a healthy son and a husband who never hit her. She needed to be more grateful for God's blessings.

"You know, Elle, men of all creeds play with *our* feelings without consequences. Why shouldn't Moe have a fling with a man?"

"Wait…who are you? Did you go to Mass today?"

"Did you? Jesus loves us, sins and all, and asks us to withhold judgment. I love you. Now I have to call Moe."

"I am sorry." Ella sounded contrite. "I am not mad at Moe. It's just that I wanted her to be our hero. The one who survived unscathed. You understand."

"I do. But like all of us, Moe is human."

Lanei could not help the feeling of defeat and fear that filled her as well. She had been naïve to think that success would protect a woman from abuse. She turned to Kevin, who was humming to their sleeping daughter. She wished she had run away the first day she'd met Kevin on that beach in Guam. Now her life was tied to his by her wedding vows and the child they would always share.

28
Ella

Ella shoved clothes, linens, and kitchenware into boxes scattered in the middle of the living room, at times pretending a pot or a bowl was Bernard's head. Still her anger would not be denied. He had bought a house without showing it to her as if he was picking up a gallon of milk on his way home. The physical stress of working full-time while caring for her son, dealing with morning sickness, and getting ready to move into the new house was turning Ella into a person she did not like at all.

Bernard had come home last week and handed her a set of keys. "What are these for?" she'd asked.

He'd kissed her lips. "We did it, Elle. We're homeowners. I'm so proud of you."

"*Ki sa?*" she'd said, staring at him as if he was speaking gibberish. "You bought a house?" She'd thrown the dishrag on the floor and stomped on it. "You had no right to do that. When you asked me to get my employment verification, you said it was to start the process, but you knew all along that you weren't going to ask for my input in choosing *our* home." Ella's eyes opened wide with incredulity. "*Oh mon Dieu,* so my name is not on the house?"

"It is," he said. "You signed the papers."

"I do not believe you. Why do you need to lie when the truth would do, Bernard?" She stood so close to him that his breath fogged her glasses. "You didn't give me a chance to weigh my options. I would've rather used the house money for my education. And where are the bank statements? Huh?"

The smile on his lips did not reach his eyes, making him look like he was in pain. "Elle, I wanted to surprise you. Please forgive me. And you will go back to school. Be patient, my love." He reached for her chin.

"You can surprise your wife by taking her on a vacation or buying her a piece of jewelry"—Ella pulled her face away—"but not by buying a house."

Ella crossed her arms over her chest. "I'm still waiting for statements about our money."

"I bought us a house, didn't I? Besides the statement comes quarterly. I told you. Did you forget?"

Ella had frowned, wondering if she was losing her mind at twenty-two. She couldn't recall that conversation, but Bernard had looked so sincere.

Now she closed the box in the kitchen with the pots and pans and labeled it. She stood and massaged her lower back. She held on to the shame she felt from Lanei's rebuke on the phone earlier. What had happened to Monique was horrible, and Lanei was right about the double standard women lived with. Of all the sisters, Ella valued Lanei the most because she was genuinely good. Lanei never maligned anybody the way Monique did at times. Lanei did more than pay lip service to Jesus—she lived his truth. Lanei understood the choices Ella had made in her life, because she had faced the same obstacles. How could Monique and Cecilia understand their lives? The two graduates were free to do and be whatever they wanted. Ella's marriage demanded that she give up a part of herself to Bernard to make a unit. She loved Bernard, but somehow, she had a lot more skin in the game than he did. It would just take her longer to present her medical diploma to her father for the sacrifices he had made to send her here. She would honor the silent promise she had made to him back in Haiti. To make him proud in their village. Her father's words were stamped on her brain. *All Ella does is take away everything I love. What is she going to give me in return?* The wind had carried the regret in his words that day in Rosale and deposited them on fourteen-year-old Ella's skin like an insect bite.

"I will bring you a medical degree, Papa," Ella said to herself as she tore the packing tape with her teeth to close the box. "I promised."

"Mommy, Mommy," Alex yelled as he pulled on the bottom of her muumuu. She looked down at her son. "You have a boo-boo? You're crying."

Ella touched her wet cheeks and tried to smile. "Mommy just misses her daddy, sweetheart." She sat back down and put the boy on her lap, kissing his chubby face and inhaling his scent of talcum powder and innocence.

"You have a daddy? Where is he?"

"He is in Haiti where Mommy and Daddy were born. One day I'll take you and your little brother or sister who's in here"—she patted her stomach—"to meet your grandpa."

"Daddy has a daddy too," Alex said.

Ella did not know much of anything about Bernard's family. He never talked about them. Maybe she needed to find out why? What could she glean from Bernard's childhood to help her understand what drove him to excel at any cost? Ella remembered Cecilia referring to Bernard as opaque. Janet had called him evil. Ella did not believe that, but she could not see anything beyond what Bernard chose to show her and the world. Maybe she needed to find out why her family was so opposed to him. It couldn't possibly be because he was too poor. There ought to be more to their objections than that. Ella would find out the truth, so their marriage could sit on a truthful foundation that would allow them both to reach their goals without competition.

She needed to talk to her sister Therese.

29

Monique

The smell of bacon reminded Monique that she was hungry. Her battered body complained when she swung her legs off the bed. But the hurt in her soul filled her with anger. It was painful to move, but after washing up in the bathroom, she made her way to Cecilia in the kitchen by sheer force of will. She didn't want to be broken. She would not give Julien that power.

Monique ate scrambled eggs, three dinner-plate-sized pancakes, and many strips of bacon. She drank two cups of coffee to wash it all down past the lump in her throat. Cecilia, on the other hand, picked at her food. "Ceecee, I'm going to be okay. You know that, right?" Monique covered Cecilia's hand with hers on the table.

"That's what you think, Moe. But rape leaves its stamp on your soul…I heard."

"What do you know about it?" Monique asked, squinting at her friend.

"We're here to deal with your…situation," Cecilia said. "We need to change the lock today. I'll call to see if we can move into our apartment any sooner."

"Chantal called a twenty-four-hour locksmith last night, but the asshole won't come back. He's a coward. He knows I'd call the authorities, *and* this is not Haiti."

"Good. Now you definitely can't go back there anytime soon. How would you protect yourself?" Cecilia shook her head.

"My uncle gave me a number for an immigration lawyer. I'm filing for American citizenship. I should have done it long ago. The American Embassy in Haiti protects its citizens—even the dark ones."

Cecilia rolled her eyes. Monique reddened under her not-so-dark skin. "You told your uncle about, you know…what happened last night?" Cecilia asked.

"Damn right! I'll tell everybody. I'm not ashamed; I'm mad. I did nothing wrong. You understand."

"We're going to Freda's program, Women Talk. She's helped me a lot. I've been telling you guys to talk to her. Now you have…issues."

"I've always had issues. Not unlike yours. Your mother doesn't like you. My papa hates me. Now this asshole came here and raped me. I hope you never have to face that, my friend."

"Moe, our issues are similar but never the same. It's all about how you experience them. You seem to be able to react fast, but some of us need a lot of prodding to leave the past behind, focus on the present, and plan the future."

Monique stood on the threshold of the room in the back of the hospital. She looked around the room and thought about leaving. As if she could read her mind, the counselor smiled and motioned her in with a nod. Monique sat and listened. Cecilia held her hand.

"Welcome to Women Talk," Freda said to the group. "This is a forum to talk about personal experiences. Nothing leaves this room. We use first names only. We go around the room, and you can either share or pass."

For over an hour Monique listened as women talked about the abuse they'd suffered at the hands of men they had loved and trusted—and complete strangers in some cases. After everyone had been given a chance to share, Freda said, "When a man rapes you, he takes from you what you did not offer. Don't give him more by letting him invade your daily life and your spirit with guilt and shame. You come here because you want to take your physical and emotional freedom back from your abuser. Rape demoralizes the woman and turns her aura as dark as the nights she comes to fear. It turns her into a *victim*. Rape replaces beauty with self-hatred that no amount of scrubbing can remove or makeup can cover. Unless you stop its progress. In your packet is information about housing, financial, educational, and childcare programs to help you when you are ready to act."

Freda hugged every woman before they left, whispering to each in a soothing tone, before turning to Monique. "Have a seat." Freda pointed to the chair next to her desk after the last woman closed the door behind her.

Monique wiped her eyes with the crumpled tissue in her hand, surprised to find herself crying. "Julien, my rapist, is a guy I chose to have sex with one time a couple months ago. Then he came here and... I know I didn't do anything wrong but...I should have known better."

Freda said, "How could you say that after hearing the stories today, Monique? Let's talk about this."

Monique squared her shoulders and felt a loosening. A shift. It allowed her to breathe out an ounce of anger and breathe in a teaspoon of hope.

On their way home, Monique turned from the driver's seat to face Cecilia and said, "Thank you for bringing me here. I like Freda."

Cecilia lit a cigarette and offered the pack to Monique, who shook her head. "I know. I'm working on quitting," Cecilia said, closing her eyes. "Something horrible happened to me too. It was when I lived in Boston. I was twelve. I've never told a soul. But I told Freda. Now I'll tell you."

When Cecilia finished her story, Monique reached across the passenger seat and hugged her. Together, they cried. "Ceecee, you're always there for us but never seek our help. I can't believe you've never even told Mel all these years."

"Now, you understand"—Cecilia threw the cigarette butt out the window—"but I don't think Mel could. I never wanted to burden her with this...or shatter her illusion that life is perfect. Her life *is* perfect."

"I know what you mean. But...but is anybody's life truly perfect?"

Cecilia shrugged. "I know mine isn't. I'm working on it every day. Don't tell Ella and Lanei. They have enough to worry about. Promise!"

"I promise. But I hope you'll tell them one day. Happiness and sadness should be shared equally in friendship. I wish I had your quiet strength, my friend."

"I had to be strong, Moe. You met my mother. Now you understand why I haven't dated. I'm scared."

"We're on the right track by seeking therapy again. Remember how abuse connected us the very first day we met?"

"I suppose we thought we were cured." Cecilia snorted.

Monique thought about how much she had looked forward to seeing Brian before her attack. Now maybe they could talk over a meal. The idea of a man touching her body sent waves of nausea up her throat.

"Let's go home," Monique said. "Brian is coming for dinner tomorrow. I need to talk to him about why I can't see him right now. Please stay with me tonight."

"Of course. I wouldn't dream of leaving you alone."

Before she climbed into bed that night, Monique took the telephone off the hook. She needed to get a good night's sleep. She clutched the extra pillow for comfort. She woke up screaming from a nightmare. Julien was chasing her with a fishnet. She changed her sweat-soaked nightgown and climbed into bed with Cecilia in the next room.

What if Julien wanted more from her than what he had already taken?

Now sleep eluded her.

30
Cecilia

ecilia woke up with her arms wrapped around a sleeping Monique. Sharing her secret with her friend last night had stripped away another layer of shame. Freda had helped her see that she was a victim of vicious crimes, but she had not been able to form scabs over the many wounds that had penetrated her on the inside. In therapy she was learning to heal.

After they had finished breakfast, Monique headed to the market, and Cecilia needed to help Mel with the final wedding program. But she stopped at the phone booth to call Lanei first. They all needed to talk to someone. Cecilia believed that. She was a crusader.

"Ceecee, I'm so glad you're there for Moe," Lanei said. "Ella called to tell me what happened, and now she may be upset with me. I love Moe; I love *all* of us. But Moe's honesty is brutal sometimes, and I think some people may misinterpret it. She may be a bit...unconventional, but she's loyal to her friends and her causes. And what she just experienced will sharpen her tools to fight."

"Sharpening tools. I like that. I love all of us too, Lan. We all have our shortcomings," Cecilia said, thinking of Ella. "By the way, Moe started therapy with Freda. Are you still talking to your priest?"

"Yes, but it's...different. I've thought about therapy. There are so many conflicts between my faith and my heart."

"Remember to take care of yourself too. That's what therapy does. It heals your inner wounds. The ones you can't see but that hurt like they've been rubbed raw. How's my pretty girl?"

"She's still having episodes, so I have to be home with her."

"Are things okay...at home? We're so sorry you're not coming to the wedding, but we can still help you."

Lanei sighed so loudly that Cecilia pulled the receiver away from her ear briefly. "It's complicated. Here in Chicago, I have my church, Maria, Peggy, Nate—"

"That man will follow you to the end of the earth. It's too bad you didn't meet him first," Cecilia said, pausing when she realized what she'd said. "I'm sorry, Lan. I shouldn't have said that."

"Don't apologize. I've felt the same way, but my lot is cast. Listen, I can try to come in October for Monique's birthday since she's the last birthday in the tribe. We can celebrate all of us at the same time."

"That sounds like a great idea. We'll have a birthday bash just for the four of us, and we'll christen the apartment as our new den."

"In that case, I'll move heaven and earth to be there," Lanei said.

"I can help with your airfare. I'll be a full-fledged teacher by then."

"You guys paid for my ticket to come to the graduation in June. I believe God will make a way."

The Miami heat bore into Cecilia's pores inside the booth. "Lan, nobody has a right to your body without your consent, not even your husband. You understand?"

"Ceecee, I gave into temptation at age sixteen, and now I have to uphold my marriage vows. My lot is cast."

A woman outside the phone booth bounced a fistful of coins from one hand to the other and glared at Cecilia. "I have to go. We'll talk soon on *my* house phone." Cecilia tapped the mouthpiece with her bracelet, and Lanei did the same at her end.

She climbed inside the used Nissan Sentra she'd bought the week before. Pride filled her. This car represented the extra hours she had worked because she had set a goal. She started the car and headed in the direction of the mall. She had a list of last-minute items she needed to complete her outfit for the wedding. She was no longer concerned about competing or pleasing anybody but herself. But if the good-looking, single best man was interested, what would be the harm? For the first time, her budding confidence sprouted a desire for adventure.

31

Lanei

Lanei had learned early on that God had his hands in everything. So the day she met Kevin on a beach in Guam had to be God's will. Clad in a forest green bikini that hugged her lanky frame, sixteen-year-old Lanei had sauntered down the beach, looking for her cousin Carlina in the throng of people. Instead she'd come face-to-face with a fierce-looking man. She locked eyes with the stranger. Neither moved. His shirtless reddish-brown torso glistened with sweat, and his muscles twitched when he breathed.

"Can you kick the ball this way, gorgeous?" the man said, pointing to the volleyball resting at her foot.

She picked up the ball and carried it to him. "I don't want to ruin my pedicure." Her eyes never left his green ones. They were hypnotic.

"Nice toes. Nice everything… I'm Kevin." He winked. "My friends call me Kev. Hope you will too."

Her temperature spiked, causing a blush to rise on her skin. "My friends call me Lan, short for Lanei," she said, looking at her toes. "You must be from the base?"

He smiled. "You must be the most beautiful girl on this enchanted island. Is it your birthday?" He pointed to the balloons around the picnic tables.

"No, it's my cousin's sweet sixteenth. Mine was in March, except I didn't have a party because—"

"Well, go back to the party, *baby girl*," he said, cutting her off. "Thanks for bringing me the ball." He turned to leave.

"I'm not a baby. I'm interning at the university this summer because I'm going to be a pharmacist," she said with pride. "Besides how old are you?" She didn't want him to leave, but she wasn't sure why.

"Thirty-two. Old enough to be your daddy."

"I don't have a daddy, nor do I need one." Lanei kicked the sand.

Kevin rejoined his friends.

On Monday afternoon, he showed up at the university. "Is it safe to get in a car with you?" Lanei asked, leaning on the car door. "I don't really know you."

"Ah!" Kevin pulled his passport from his pocket and handed it to her. "I knew you'd say that. I'm from the base. Remember?"

She leafed through it and shrugged. They drove to the beach where they had met on Saturday. Kevin showed up every day that week. He brought soft drinks for her and beer for himself, a blanket, a transistor radio, and board games. Lanei talked about her dream of becoming a pharmacist, her late father's rejection, and her desire to leave Guam to explore the world. Kevin listened, interrupting her periodically to ask questions.

"Oh! What time is it?" She jumped up one evening. The white sand had cooled off under her bare feet, and the turquoise water had turned ink-blue on the horizon. A warm breeze whistled through the palm fronds in the park across the street, battling the humidity and failing.

"It's only 7:30," Kevin said. "It's still early."

"Mama worries about me all the time. It's the curse of being an only child."

Kevin stopped his Jeep at the entrance to the unpaved courtyard in the village of Dededo, where her extended maternal family had lived for generations. Lanei shared the smallest two-bedroom house with the faded green paint and the broken front window with Mama. Her cousin Carlina lived next door with her parents and siblings. "Good night, Lan," Kevin said.

She leapt out of the Jeep and skipped into the house. Mama was waiting behind the door. "Where have you been?" Mama said. "Carlina came looking for you."

"I was with my new friend Kevin from the base. We met at the beach Saturday. Remember, Mama?" Lanei knitted her brows. "He's from Chicago but lives in Miami. Oh, and he's an only child on his mom's side, just like me. He didn't see his father much growing up either—"

Her mother smiled. "You two were sharing life stories. Did he just graduate high school?"

"No. He's a bit older."

"How much older, Lan?"

Lanei kissed the frown on her mother's forehead. "I'll go see what Carlina wanted." She ran out the door.

For over two months, they were inseparable. At the end of her summer vacation, he said, "Lan, can we spend the day together tomorrow? It's the last Saturday before you start school." He raised himself on his elbow off the beach towel and brushed strands of wet hair from her eyes.

Lanei inhaled. "I don't know if it's a good idea, Kev. I mean spending the whole day—"

"Have I done something wrong?" His voice broke.

"No. No—" She sat up next to him. "It's just that I don't want you to get the wrong message. I just want to be friends. I'm not ready for anything more than that."

"I'll pick you up at ten. Bring your swimwear." He kissed her lips for the first time. Confused, her hands shook as she nearly grabbed the back of his neck before she put them back down on the towel.

The following day they drove with the top down to Talofofo Falls. The breeze fought the humidity that blanketed the island. They drove through the main village before Kevin steered the car below the hills to the coastal community of Ipan. It seemed as though Lanei had stepped into a new country. He stopped at a small bungalow, fished a key from his pocket, and opened the door.

"What's this place?" she asked, taking a couple steps back as if the devil himself was waiting behind the door. "I thought we were going to the beach."

Kevin took her hand, and she crossed the threshold. Her eyes took in the couch in the entry room facing the console television set. Through the glass door, she saw the beach beyond the back porch.

"This cabin belongs to a friend." Kevin grazed her cheek with a kiss. "I love you," he whispered in her ear. "Let's go get the food from the car. I have a basket."

What did he mean? She was too young to be in love, but why had she followed him all summer? Lanei was confused and afraid. She should go home. Kevin brought fried parrotfish, red rice, and a green salad for lunch and a big bag of her favorite chocolate chip cookies for dessert. Lanei picked at her food.

When they were done eating, she stepped out of her shorts and T-shirt, wearing the same green bikini she'd worn when they'd met, and ran into the water. "Come on, Kev. Get in." She giggled.

His black Speedo gave Lanei a lesson in male anatomy. His muscles wrapped around his body like ropes. The turquoise water danced in his blazing green eyes. Lanei beat the water and splashed him. When he encircled her waist, he bent down and kissed her, pushing his tongue inside her mouth. She experienced a mélange of emotions, but the predominant one was fear.

When they got back to the cabin, she took her bag and locked the bathroom door behind her. She reached behind her neck to unclasp her top, but she could not. She pulled the hair trapped in the metal clasp until her scalp was sore. She looked for a pair of scissors in the drawers. Frustrated, she unlocked the door.

"Kev, I need help. You'll need scissors to cut my hair."

Standing behind her, he freed each strand of hair. Body heat flowed between them in the small space. His heavy breathing on her neck raised bumps on her flushed skin. He kissed the back of her ears.

She turned and threw her arms around his neck. His face was wet with tears. "Why are you crying? Are you okay?"

"No. Yes! I love you so much, Lan. You're only sixteen. I'm scared... I don't wanna hurt you, but I can't let you go. I wanna marry you. You should run away from me. I don't know what I'm saying. I—"

"Shh, shh. Kev, I'll wait for you. I want you to take me away from here after high school. I want to go to pharmacy school in Miami. Can we take Mama?"

"Of course! Whatever you want, baby girl. I want to make you happy." He kissed her parted lips.

Kevin scooped her up. "What...where are we going?" she said.

He deposited her on the bed, his crushing weight pressing her into the mattress. He kissed her as if he was trying to swallow her doubt. He reached behind her back and unhooked her top.

"Kev...please don't," she said with her eyes closed. He took her nipples in his mouth. She jerked upward, her back arching and her breath shallow. "I can't...have...sex. I—"

"We're not having sex. We're making love," he whispered. "There's a big difference."

"There is?" She opened her eyes and stared into Kevin's. "I'm scared. Please stop. I want to go home." She tried to slide out from under him.

He invaded her virgin body like a pirate plundering a laden ship. He'd used three condoms by the time they left the cabin after sunset.

"Lan. Lanei!" She stared straight ahead, unable to look at him. Kevin put the keys in the ignition but did not start the car. "*Lanei!*" he yelled.

"Yes?" she mumbled. The pain in her groin was a reminder of her carnal sin. He turned her face toward his with his index finger. "Baby girl, you can't tell anyone. You understand? I'll get in trouble. But once we're married, everything will be fine. I promise. I'm going to take care of you, Lan."

"Can we get married now so I can receive communion?"

"Baby, you ain't listening to me. You can't live on the base with me till you're eighteen. You know I love you, Lan…but you can't tell nobody about today. Please."

"I have to confess to Father Arnoldo," she said matter-of-factly.

"Fuck," he muttered, starting the car and backing out of the driveway.

"Let's go to church tomorrow, Kev. Please."

On that fateful day, Lanei had entwined her life with his, but she would bring him to Jesus who would cover them with his blood and wash them clean of sins. Her lot was cast.

32
Ella

The spacious one-story house on the cul-de-sac in the suburb was a major improvement from the dingy apartment Ella had lived in the past four years. The houses on her street looked alike. Neighbors brought casseroles, pies, and fruit baskets to welcome her family to the neighborhood. The sidewalks stretched for miles. Tall pine trees fenced the houses like green curtains. Ella sang the beautiful French love songs of her youth while cleaning the bathroom mirrors. Sometimes she found an unexpected smile on her face.

The fenced yard offered the possibility of a garden, a place for her children to play, and room to entertain her friends. She thought of how Bernard had never brought a friend home. Now he could invite the Haitian diaspora he'd been rubbing elbows with since he'd come to Miami. Ella had yet to meet Yolaine Meridien or attend any political functions with her husband. When the doorbell rang, she dropped the dust rag and walked to the door.

"What a surprise," Ella said, opening her arms wide to embrace Monique and Cecilia. "Moe, honey, I didn't expect you today. I'm sorry I haven't been able to see you since the…incident. This pregnancy saps my energy. I still work every day, take care of my family, and now…this house." She ushered them to the carpeted living room, and they sat on the floor around dozens of unopened boxes. "Our new furniture is coming tomorrow. At least I got to pick it out." She turned to Monique. "How's it going, sister?"

Monique cocked one eyebrow and said, "Okay, Elle, now you're speaking like the average American." She slid down to sit on the floor. "How 'bout that?"

Ella shook her head. Nothing could dampen that woman's spirit. "Moe, I'm too tired and busy now for extra words. American English is faster." The three women laughed until Ella said, "But how are you doing really?"

Monique stretched her legs in front of her on the floor and leaned her head back against the pink wall and sighed. "You know me, Elle. I don't dwell, but I'm having trouble sleeping. Ceecee has been staying with me. Can't wait to move out." In one fluid movement, Monique stood and pulled Cecilia to her feet. "Come on, let's attack these boxes. We're here to work."

"I can't tell you how much I appreciate it. I'm so tired." Ella groaned. "The sight of all these boxes makes me want to weep."

For a couple of hours, they worked in silence except for the French songs coming from the stereo on the floor. Ella had done a good job labeling everything, so Monique and Cecilia knew where to place things. "You guys should stay for dinner," Ella said. "I'm making rice with mixed vegetables and grilled goat."

"Girl, I can go get pizza," Monique said. "You look exhausted. No need to cook."

"You're kidding, right?" Ella tilted her head to one side. "Bernard likes home-cooked meals."

"Oh yeah, does he cook?" Monique asked. "How are you gonna handle that and two kids when you *do* go back to school? Something is gonna have to give, Elle."

Ella shook her head. "You're from Haiti, Monique, and you act like you know Haitian men who cook. *I* taught you to cook here because you grew up with maids and cooks and—"

"Ella, why do you always have to bust my—" Monique said.

Cecilia banged her bracelet on an aluminum cup on the kitchen counter. Ella and Monique turned toward the sound. Cecilia raised her hand, her fingers opened in the peace sign. Ella exhaled, walked up to Monique, and hugged her. "I'm sorry, Moe."

"My dad was a good husband and a super father, yet he did not cook either," Cecilia said. "Our culture designates these roles for us, but I have noticed that here roles can change. Women can be professionals; men can cook. Both parties have to be open to switching things around a bit. Come on, we'll help you with dinner, Elle."

"Thank you, Ceecee," Ella said. "You know, Bernard acts as if his eight hours at work are longer and more important than mine. And I come home to do another shift. After I give birth, things will change. You'll see."

"Remember I offered to teach you to drive," Monique said. "I think you need a car more than before. It's going to be a long commute to the city from here. We can start this week before school starts."

At the mention of school, Ella felt resentment replace the compassion she had experienced for Monique, who still had a fading bruise on her left cheek from Julien's attack. And what made Monique think Ella could afford a car right after they'd just bought a house? With the mortgage, Bernard's new car note, and higher utility bills, Ella was worried about how this new child and all their expenses were going to affect her return to school.

"Thanks for the offer," Ella said instead, "but I can't afford a car right now, so what would be the point?" She tried to keep the smile from slipping off her face.

"For one thing, you can drive the car when Bernard's not using it." Monique ticked her index finger. "Two, it's something new to learn. Practical skills that will serve you—"

Ella swallowed her bubbling anger. "All I want to learn is how to be a doctor, Monique. Can you and Cecilia help me with that?" Ella asked, her voice rising.

"What…how—" Monique stopped and turned to Cecilia, raising her shoulders.

"I didn't think so," Ella said, taking off her glasses to wipe her face before putting them back on. She saw the hurt on her friend's face. "Let's cook. My husband will be home soon from the office."

"Elle, you're not being fair," Cecilia said, following her to the kitchen. "We're here to help and want nothing more than to see you back in school. But you made your choices, and there are consequences for everything we do."

The three friends stood in the middle of the kitchen like gladiators in an arena. Ella plastered a smile on her face, stroked her belly, and said, "These hormones wreak havoc on my personality. Forgive me, sisters. I love you."

She walked toward them with open arms, wondering why she'd gotten angry with her friends when deep down she knew exactly who her enemy was in the fight to reach her professional goal.

33

Monique

Monique chased sleep all night after helping Ella unpack. The two drinks had failed to douse her fire. Embers smoldered. The resentment Ella harbored about Monique's graduation and her privilege of birth did not bother her as much as Ella's blindness when it came to Bernard's manipulation. If that was unconditional love, Monique wanted none of it. In fact, later today she would tell Brian to keep his distance for now. She needed to sort out her jumbled feelings about him, her anger toward Julien, and her fear of what this rape would do to her.

In the morning she took her cup of coffee into the bathroom and peered into the mirror. The bruise under her left eye had faded to a light yellow. She refused to let the bruise in her heart find a home there. She didn't know how, but she would make Julien pay for what he'd done to her. Her father had used her body like a drum to shape her into submission. She would die before she'd let another man abuse her. She looked at the time and called Tina at her office in Haiti.

"*O mon Dieu*, I can't believe this evil followed you all the way to Miami," Tina said after Monique told her what happened. "These people are ruthless. I heard Julien's father would kill husbands when he wanted their wives. Are you...okay?"

"Therapy gave me insights." Monique sighed, sipping her cool coffee in the kitchen. She pinched the skin between her eyes to stop the tears. She hated crying. "A road map. To help me heal."

"Oh, *mon amie*, I wish I could be there for you the way you were here for me. I'm glad you have your island sisters."

"Tina, is Francois still teaching self-defense classes to women in your neighborhood?"

"*Mais oui!* We have a big group. Women have to be prepared to defend themselves here…everywhere so it seems."

"I've signed up for a self-defense class here too. It's all part of my plan. We'll talk soon. Love you."

Armed with her shopping list, Monique dropped Cecilia at Mel's and drove to Little Haiti for the supplies she needed to fix dinner for Brian. She didn't want to go out on a date, but they could talk in private at the house. The smell of fried pork, Haitian pâté, and rice and beans made Monique smack her lips. Loud Haitian music spilled from mom-and-pop stores, and she quickened her steps to the beat of the *Konpa* rhythm. She bowed to two older men playing dominoes on the sidewalk.

"*Bonjour, Messieurs,*" she called out.

They waved to her and smiled. "*Bonjour, belle mademoiselle.*"

Monique mingled with people on the streets in *Ti Maché*, and she haggled over prices like a true Haitian. When she turned onto her street after her shopping trip, she noticed a blue car parked in her driveway. Her hands closed into fists. A haggard Brian dressed in scrubs and a wrinkled white coat climbed out of the driver's seat. His long braids were stuffed under a surgical cap.

She rolled down her window. "Is everything okay? What…I—"

"Let's go inside. I'll explain," he said.

She dropped her bag on the kitchen counter and turned to face him. "I'm sorry about what happened, Moe. I've been worried sick about you." He ran the pad of his thumb down the bruise on her cheek. "Where's Ceecee?"

"I'm okay, Brian. I really am." She stepped away from him. "She's coming back later."

"I have to cover for my friend tonight. His son was admitted today. I wanted to check on you. My life is crazy and will be for another three years of residency. I—"

Monique pushed him gently toward the door and said, "It's all right. We can have dinner another time. I'm in no rush. Go."

He looked at her. "How about tomorrow? I think I can squeeze a couple of hours out of my schedule."

She shrugged. "Maybe."

After Brian left, she locked the door, checked all the windows, put the groceries in the fridge, and lay down on the family room couch for a nap. The shrill of the telephone jolted her awake a few minutes later. She blinked several times and stared at the muted picture on the television screen before sitting up.

"Hello," she said, rubbing sleep from her eyes.

"Papa is in prison," Solange screamed. "They arrested him on his way to one of our stores this morning. We finally saw him an hour ago. They hurt him. A man just called the house and said, 'Only Monique can get him out.' What the hell is going on? Is there something you're not telling us? Monique... Mo—"

"Stop!" Monique yelled, grabbing her forehead. The room was spinning. "I need to think, Solange."

"There's no time to think. Get your *liberal, feminist, educated* ass back here today. Papa won't last long in prison." She hung up.

"Julien!" Monique hissed. "*The son of a bitch.*" She smashed the telephone on the tile floor.

She always thought Maman and Tina would be the reason she'd return to the belly of the beast. Now she had to go back to rescue Papa. But at what price?

34
Cecilia

W hen Michael showed up without the best man, Cecilia hid her disappointment behind a smile that never left her face all night. She hugged him and looked at the entrance of the restaurant, expecting what? Who? She chastised herself for being so eager to meet a total stranger. As if Michael could read her mind, he said, "John had a family emergency. He can't make it tonight, but he'll be there for the wedding on Saturday."

"He better," Mel said. "Ceecee and I have worked too hard to make everything perfect." She leaned into her husband-to-be, and he put both arms around her as if to protect her from harm. Mel kissed his lips and turned inside the circle of his arms so her back was against his front, her hands lost inside his. "Besides, Ceecee can't wait to meet John. Honey, you said he's single right?" Mel asked.

Heat rose to Cecilia's face. "Mel—" she mumbled.

"It's all right, Ceecee," Michael said. "John quizzed me about you when I showed him that picture of you and Mel in my office. He thinks you're beautiful, and I concur."

Cecilia wanted to clone Michael right this instant, so she could feel loving arms around her as well. All her life arms had hit and pulled at her. But John thought she was beautiful after only seeing her picture. She couldn't wait to meet him and see what might develop. It was as though Cecilia needed to try out her newfound self-awareness. John could be the guinea pig. She smiled, feeling confident in her skin. She felt no pressure to tangle her life with a man in order to be complete. She should be enough. But was she?

Back at Mel's house Cecilia closed the bedroom door behind her, trying to block out the senseless chatter from Mel's friends. As soon as she pulled the pillow over her head, there was a knock on the door, and Mel entered the room. Cecilia opened her eyes.

"Ceecee, honey," Mel said, "thank you for taking care of everything. It was a beautiful affair. You're the best maid of honor a bride can have."

"And you'll be the most beautiful bride."

Cecilia stood and threw her arms around her friend. The first friend who had stood up for her against the bullies in grade school. "I'm truly happy for you, Mel. No one deserves happiness more than you."

"Your happiness is around the corner," Mel said.

"But I'm happy *now*," Cecilia said, feeling the total weight of her accomplishments. "My happiness comes from within. I only want someone to share it with one day. I can wait, for now. I'm working on being enough."

Freda would be proud of her at this moment. But all the same, Cecilia was looking forward to meeting John.

35

Lanei

anei remembered the many times she had asked Kevin to stop that afternoon in Guam. She had meant it. Cecilia had said something that nagged at her brain. When a man used your body without your consent, it was a crime. It was rape. Her priests told her that certain duties came with being a married woman. Lanei cooked, cleaned, did the laundry, fixed Kevin's lunch, and mended his clothes, but was Kevin taking her body whenever he wanted it part of her marital duties? And what was she entitled to as compensation? She should have been able to afford a ticket and have the freedom to go to Mel's wedding. She had earned it.

Lanei folded one of Kevin's shirts and threw it on top of the pile on the couch. She kicked the overflowing basket to the side and stood. She paced the length of the two-bedroom apartment they had moved into a couple of weeks ago. Like a caged lion, she longed to be free. To run. To leave it all behind. She stared at the door and stopped pacing.

She picked up the phone and dialed. "Hi, Peg," she said. "Can I leave Maria with you for an hour or so? I need...I need to run some errands." She listened. "You sound congested."

"Oh, my allergies are acting up, but I'm okay. You know I love to spend time with my grandbaby."

Lanei changed into a white sundress and yellow espadrille sandals. She brushed her hair loose, patting her new bangs. Kevin hadn't noticed them yesterday when he came home from work. She picked up her daughter from her crib and locked the apartment door behind them. She hailed a cab. When she got to Peggy's, she opened the door using the key her mother-in-law had wanted her to keep. She walked into the bedroom and placed her daughter in the bed with Peggy.

"Hey, Lan," Peggy said, her eyes and nose red and puffy. "You look pretty. Where are you going?"

"I'm meeting one of the mothers from the library group." Lanei broke eye contact with Peggy, shifting her feet. "Maybe I should cancel. You don't look so good."

Peggy waved her away. "Go. I'm fine. It's allergies. I'm glad you're making friends here."

Lanei took another cab and gave the driver the Oak Park address she'd memorized. She fluffed her new bangs with nervous fingers and applied more lip gloss to her lips. She closed her eyes and prayed while the taxi carried her away. When she opened them, they were driving on a quiet street full of single homes with expansive front lawns shaded by giant trees. The cab stopped. She paid the fare and stepped out in front of a two-story redbrick house. Before her brain could chastise her heart, she rang the doorbell. *I should leave.* But her feet did not move.

Nate opened the door, trying to button his denim shorts. His bare chest was covered with curly hair. "La...Lane, is everything okay?" he asked, staring into her eyes. "What are you doing here?"

She walked closer to him and smiled. "Surprise. I wanted to check on you. Maria and I missed you the past two weeks. I—"

"Nate, who is it?" a female voice asked.

Lanei stopped and leaned to look over Nate's shoulder, inhaling the smell of fresh intimacy on his skin. The light from the TV beamed on a woman with chestnut-colored hair wrapped in a bedsheet on the sofa.

Lanei touched her face, feeling the fire under her skin. "Um...I'm sorry, Nate." She backed away from him, staring into his eyes that remained mute. He touched his forehead and mouthed, *I like the bangs.*

In the cab, she sobbed. She wanted Nate now more than ever because he was gone. What had she been planning to do in his house? They'd never been alone before. Maybe God placed that woman in Lanei's sinful path today. She had lied to Peggy but never to God. *He sees everything.*

She wanted the ride to never end. To take her far away. But a half-hour later, Lanei closed the front door and called, "I'm back." Peggy's thunderous snore answered her. She rushed into the bedroom. Maria was on her back. Her body limp; her chest still. A blue tint ringed her lips. Lanei grabbed the phone by the bedside and dialed 911.

Then she started CPR on her daughter.

36
Ella

Ella dropped her bulk into a dining room chair, once more wondering if she was carrying twins. She had put on so much weight already with this pregnancy, and she was only in her first trimester. She opened the envelopes addressed to her and Bernard that she had brought inside from the mailbox, throwing the junk mail on the kitchen floor. She opened the last one and read.

> *The transfer you made to Haiti last week to Martha Antoine could not be disbursed this time, because she was unable to produce an ID. Please come to our office to make other arrangements.*
>
> *Western Union.*

Ella couldn't move from the chair. It was as if her physical body was as stuck as her professional dreams. Who was Martha? Was she Bernard's mother? His sister? Why hadn't he told her that he was financially supporting his family in Haiti? That would explain why he kept such close control of their finances. But Ella would not have objected to helping his family. Grateful she'd bought dinner at a Haitian restaurant on her way home, Ella ate more than she needed and drank two cans of Cola Couronne. But she wanted a real drink.

Bernard waltzed through the front door a few minutes later. She turned to him with the letter clasped in her shaking hand. Alex left his toy trucks on the floor and ran to his father. He wrapped his arms around Bernard's gray pleated pants. The sharp crease pointed to the tip of his shiny black Stacy Adams shoes. Bernard spent money and time to look good. "Daddy, come see what I made."

Bernard shook him off like an insect. "Don't touch my pants, boy. Your hands are dirty." He placed his briefcase on a chair and stared at the pile of paper on the floor. He stood behind one of the dinette chairs, his hands resting on the back.

"Uh-uh, they're not." Alex cried, running to Ella. She kissed his forehead.

"What's wrong with you?" Ella said. "You've been gone all day, and now you can't play with your son." She cut her eyes at him and tried to stand up. Her back hurt. She sat back down. He reached for his tie and turned toward the hallway. "Bernard, who's Martha Antoine?" she asked, shaking the letter. This time she leaned on the table and stood.

Bernard halted his steps and lunged at her, grabbing the sheet of paper. He glanced at it, and his face gathered like a knot. "Didn't I tell you not to open the mail? What were you looking at it for?"

"This is my house, and the mail I opened had my name on it as well." Ella glared at him. "I inadvertently opened the Western Union envelope. But I need to know the truth."

A smile spread on his face. "It must be a mistake. Antoine is a common name in Haiti. I'll go to the office tomorrow and let them know." He bent down to kiss her lips. She turned her head away.

"I don't believe you. I'm going to find out the truth."

"You're calling me a liar. What's wrong with you anyway? You look like you lost your best friend." He snorted. "Oh, but you have three of them."

"They arrested Monique's papa in Haiti. Julien is behind it."

"Really!" A smile flitted across his face. "Monique is a cockteaser. That's what happens to women like her. She can't come here anymore. You know the *regime* has eyes everywhere."

Ella bristled. "You can't mean that. Moe is my friend. She'll come here as long as this is my home. I don't give a damn who's watching."

"So now you think your measly checks can buy a house?" His nose flared, stretching wider over his fleshy lips. "I make the money, so we can live in comfort."

"My measly checks took care of us before you start making the big bucks with your college degree that I supported, Bernard. Who do you have in Haiti? I need to know. You never talk about—"

"Don't you ever ask me about my family!" His mouth twitched like he was having a seizure. "I don't give a shit about yours. You can do me the same favor."

"What…what do you mean?" She faced him. "Why can't we talk about it? I'm your wife."

"Then get my food." He walked down the hallway. Ella followed him into their bedroom.

"If you're going to ask me like that, you can get your own goddamn food with your own two hands. I'm your wife. Not your slave."

She slammed the door. A sharp pain ran across her lower abdomen. She rubbed it, feeling the energy of the life growing in there. She sat on the couch and took some deep breaths. Bernard paid the bills, and Ella had what she needed for herself and her son. But was that enough? She was too tired to stay in the fight tonight. But why had he gotten so mad when she had asked about his family? Ella needed to find out. It might explain why her family exiled her twice to keep her away from him.

But what if the truth destroyed the family she had created here with Bernard?

37

Monique

A fter calling her tribe, Monique took a cab to the Miami airport where Solange had bought her a one-way ticket to Haiti on Air France. It was a hot August day when she arrived in Port-au-Prince to rescue her father from Julien's clutches. She directed the chauffeur to his house. It had been less than two months since she'd been there with Julien. Before the car fully stopped, she opened the door and jumped out. She banged once on the door with her fist. Julien opened it as if he had been waiting for her.

"Julien!" she yelled. "What the fuck is going on? You arrested Papa to get me here. Why? What the hell—" Her heart pounded so loud she could not hear Julien, but she saw his lips move. "What did you say?"

"I asked if I may put a word in." He repeated his words with an irritating politeness.

"What do you have to say?" Monique balled her hands to control the shaking, surprised to feel something akin to love for her father. "We're wasting precious time."

"I didn't have Monsieur Magloire arrested." He looked away. "In a moment of weakness, I told my father about my feelings for you and… Anyway, I'm glad you're here."

"Don't insult me." She reined in the urge to slap him. "You're worse than the illiterate *Tonton Macoutes*. You should know better."

He pulled his car keys from his pocket. "Let's get your father out of prison before I change my mind." A vein throbbed in Julien's forehead.

At the front office of the police building, Monique sat on a bench against the mustard-colored wall with giant framed pictures of the Duvaliers. A faded wing chair swallowed the skinny guard behind a metal desk. She took deep breaths to slow her heart, hoping Papa would forgive her. A door opened. She closed her eyes and blinked. Papa shuffled behind Julien as if he was on a leash. "May I take you home, Monsieur Magloire?" Julien asked.

"I'll call the house to send our chauffeur," Monique said, running to her father. "Papa, I'm sorry. Are you—"

"Make the call," Papa said, pulling away from her arms.

She lifted the phone on the desk and dialed. The skinny gendarme with the oversized cap sat up straighter in the chair and started to open his mouth.

"It's all right," Julien said. He touched her arm. She willed herself to take a deep breath. "Monique, I'll see you later."

Papa did not say a word in the car. When they got to the house, he stood erect at the head of the table. His beige seersucker suit was wrinkled and muddy. His wide shoulders caved slightly forward. "Oh my God, Marcel," Maman said, bursting into tears. "What have they done to you? Your eye—" Monique's sisters started speaking at the same time.

"Did you sleep with that goon last time you were here?" Solange asked, squinting at Monique. "What? He wants more? Papa gave you the freedom to go to school abroad while me and Esther had to marry—"

"Shut up, Solange," Monique screamed, grabbing her pounding head. "I don't—"

Papa slammed his hand on the table, rattling her frayed nerves along with the glass bowl filled with fruit. "Stop, all of you." He looked around the table. His eyes stopped on Monique. "What have you done to bring this malevolence to our family? I knew your rebellious streak would get us in trouble one day. What does Julien Etienne want?"

Monique swallowed. "Nothing…Papa. It won't happen again." She wanted to believe her own words. "But—"

"This *cannot* happen again," he ordered. "You hear me, Monique?"

"But…can you all leave the country for a couple months and let this blow over?" Monique said, staring at her family. "Please."

Papa turned and left the room. Esther and Maman looked confused. Solange slung her purse over her shoulder and said, "Why should we run from them? It's all your fault." She slammed the front door.

The following day Monique managed to doze off on the flight back to Miami. Tentacles of exhaustion and fear spread through her body like spilled ink.

She barely touched the dinner Cecilia prepared that evening. She seemed to have lost her appetite for everything. She could never tell her family that Julien had raped her, but she knew. She would always know. "Let's go to bed, Moe," Cecilia said. "You look beat."

"I am." They hugged in the hallway, Cecilia's strength recharging Monique's drained body. "I'll shower and crash."

The phone rang before Monique could close the bathroom door. Her mouth became dry. She dashed to the bedroom phone.

"Hello," she said, adrenaline flooding her body.

"You think you can escape."

"*Oh, non, non, non.* For Christ's sake." She hated the fear trilling her voice. "What do you want, man?"

"I helped you, and once again, you just used me," Julien said.

"Are you listening to yourself?" Her words were tinged with rage and incredulity. "I guess you showed me how powerful you are, Julien. Now please stop. You can't make someone love you. There are plenty of women in Haiti who would fight for your attention."

She hung up, fixed herself a potent drink, and sat in the family room. Cecilia poked her head out. "Who was that?"

"Julien," Monique said, her voice sounding flat in her ears.

She kept drinking, hoping the alcohol would induce sleep. When the phone rang again, the jingle was like a punch. Her hand hovered over the receiver for several seconds.

"Let me answer it," Cecilia said.

Monique shook her head and squared her shoulders. She'd created the nightmare; she had to end it. "Hey," Brian said, "Chantal told me. Is your dad okay? How may I help? I'm—"

She mouthed to Cecilia, *It's Brian.* Cecilia left the room. Monique exhaled and felt her body relax into the cushion. "Papa is okay. Ceecee is here, and we're moving out next week. Thank you for calling."

"May I see you tomorrow? Don't cook; I'll bring the food. We can talk."

"Maybe one day, Brian. Not now. Good night."

She limped to the bathroom, feeling defeated. Julien had tainted her body and now her heart. The night she'd met Brian at Chantal's, she had felt something. She had wanted to explore it, but now she would need to take the time to make herself whole again and learn how to piece together the fragments of her life after rape had shattered it. She climbed into bed after a long shower, and her body succumbed to the exhaustion of the long day.

The phone rang again, waking Monique up. She reached for the receiver, dropping it twice. The alarm clock read 2:38 a.m. She sat up in the bed and clenched the phone tight in her sweaty palm.

"Hello?" She swallowed to moisten her mouth.

"They took Papa *and* Maman an hour ago," Esther said, weeping. "The commandant will only talk to *you*. They've accused Papa of plotting to overthrow the Duvalier regime, Moe. I'm sorry, but there's a ticket on Air France for you to come back today."

Monique hollered and ran to the kitchen, pulling plates, cups, and glasses from the draining basket and smashing them against the kitchen wall. At some point Cecilia said, "Okay, that's enough." She pushed Monique into a chair. "Destroying the house will not solve this problem."

"What will, Ceecee? Julien has something to prove, and he's using me and my family to do it." She banged her fist on the counter and winced.

At daybreak Cecilia drove her to the airport. "No need to alarm the others," Monique said. "I'll be back tomorrow." Monique had never wanted anything to be so true in her life.

"Moe, I don't understand what goes on in Haiti. Please be careful and come back to us." Monique hugged her friend like a soldier heading to war.

She closed her eyes on the plane, hoping to sleep during the ninety-minute flight to Port-au-Prince. But the image of Maman in prison prodded her like a hot iron.

She sat in the same police building as before guarded by a different skinny guard. Her previous defiance was replaced by unadulterated fear.

"Mademoiselle Magloire, I'm sorry you had to wait so long. I'm Hector Etienne, Julien's father," a short man said, puffing his chest like a peacock. "Julien tells me you two are—"

"*Hector!*" Monique stood, towering over him. He was dressed in the navy blue uniform of the militia and a pair of dark glasses covered his eyes. "There's no 'we.' Your son and I are *nothing*. I'm here because I love my parents."

A quivering smile lifted the corner of Hector's mouth. Monique controlled her desire to flee. "I'll get them out this time," Hector said, leering at her. "Let's go."

Monique followed Hector through the labyrinth of the barrack. Screams and the smell of human waste filled the air. Something ran over her foot and screeched. She bit her lips to stifle the scream rising in her throat. She wouldn't give Hector the satisfaction.

Flashlight in hand, he stopped in front of a cell, opened it, and let Papa out. "Let's go get your maman," Hector said, jingling the keys in his hands. Barefoot and wearing a pair of blue pajamas, Papa followed them. Monique blinked to make the image disappear, but the sight of Maman huddled in the corner of a smelly cell sobered her at once. Maman had barely had time to shove her feet into a pair of slippers. Her hands covered her breasts under her thin cotton nightwear. Monique broke down. She now understood why Hector had wanted her to see her parents through the bars. That image nudged her to a vulnerable place. "I'll get the paperwork," Hector said and left.

"We're going home, Maman," Monique whispered. "Please don't cry. I promise it won't happen again."

"That's what you said yesterday," Papa said between gritted teeth. "They confiscated our passports. We can't leave this—"

"Marcel," Maman said and Papa stopped. "*Bébé*, you should have stayed in Miami. We would have managed somehow... *Oh mon Dieu! Quel désastre!*" Maman whimpered.

Hector returned. "Glad I could help." He winked at Monique. "See you around!"

She shuddered as she linked arms with her parents and walked out of the prison. Leaning on a red BMW, Julien grinned and said, "I'll take you home."

Monique halted her steps and opened her mouth. Hector coughed loudly from the front door behind them. They piled into Julien's car. No one said a word. When they reached their house, Julien stopped in front of the gate. Her parents stepped out of the back seat. Julien squeezed Monique's arm lightly. "We need to talk." He rolled down his window and called out to her parents. "Have a good day, *Monsieur and Madame Magloire*."

Monique looked through the back window of the car and saw Maman swat at a fly that had landed in her open mouth. Julien hummed a tune.

When they arrived at his house, he introduced his staff of four. Monique noted the woman named Anita, who seemed to be in charge. "We'll eat dinner soon," Julien said. "Mademoiselle is tired. Prepare a bath for her."

"*Oui, Monsieur.*" Anita left.

Standing behind her chair, Julien massaged her shoulders, his hands snaking into her blouse. As she stroked her bracelet, Monique counted in her head the way she used to do when she was little to calm herself when Papa hit her. "Julien, I want you to know that I didn't set out to hurt you. I just want my family to be safe here, and I want to go back to Miami." She waited. Silence. "I'd like to go to my parents' house now. Please." She held her breath. Julien's hands delivered a different pressure around her neck.

That night Monique fought the urge to fight back when Julien sexually assaulted her. But the image of her parents behind bars floated behind her closed lids, freezing her hands.

In the morning she sat on the bathroom floor and retched in the bowl. She grabbed her knees and rocked until someone knocked on the door. "Monique, come down for breakfast," Julien ordered.

She made her way downstairs after a shower to relieve the kinks in her body from tensing so much. The smell of fresh Haitian bread reminded her she had not eaten the day before. When she saw the jar of *konfiti po chadek*, grapefruit marmalade, she hastened her steps. Fresh papayas, mangoes, and pineapples filled a bowl on the table like a colorful painting.

"Anita," Julien called out. The woman appeared in the doorway. "Mademoiselle is ready for breakfast."

Anita placed a cup of steaming black coffee and a plate of fried eggs in front of Monique and stood at attention, waiting. "*Merci beaucoup*, Anita," Monique said. "That's all for me." She nodded at the woman. Their eyes locked for a fleeting second. Monique could have sworn Anita winked.

"*De rien, mademoiselle*," Anita said, walking backward out of the room.

Monique drank the coffee and picked at her food. Julien stared at her like a hungry snake.

"Let's go to the living room," he said after breakfast. "I'm working from home this week even though I'm expecting a large shipment. I can't get enough of you."

Fear turned the coffee in her stomach into a vat of acid. She stood. "Julien, let's think this through."

He narrowed his perpetually hooded dark eyes. Beads of sweat sprouted on his bald head. "Monique, don't push too hard. I'm in a good mood today." He stood and walked down the hall.

With Julien in the house, the only time Monique was alone was in the bathroom. When her period came three days later, relief flooded her. Maybe there was a God in Haiti. She had not seen nor talked to her family and friends since Julien had locked the door behind her. On the fifth day of her captivity, he said, "We're going out today. We need to be there before noon."

"Where are we going?"

He clucked his tongue. "You ask too many questions. Just do what I ask you today and everything will be fine." An edge crept into his voice. He turned to leave the room, and for the first time she saw a gun tucked in his waistband.

After the magistrate pronounced them man and wife at the tribunal, she followed Julien to the car. "*Felicitations! Madame Etienne*," Julien said, taking his eyes off the road to look at her. "My father will be proud of me today. It's a special day!"

"For who, Julien? *I will never love you.*" She threw the words like a punch.

Julien whistled as if she had not spoken. As the car reached the center of town, people milled about. Julien stopped to let a group of pedestrians cross the street. Monique could not breathe. She opened her mouth, but something seemed to be blocking her airway. Sweat coursed down her face and her back. Her heart kicked against her rib cage. Her vision blurred. She opened the car door and dashed into a narrow corridor. Julien's car horn blared, pushing her deep inside the dark alley and away from her nightmare.

She ran.

38
Cecilia

C ecilia leaned into the mirror and brushed mascara onto her short lashes while she tried to hold back the tears threatening to ruin her makeup. She wanted to be there fully for Mel on her big day, but she felt as if she had been split in two. One part was at Mel's house getting dressed for the wedding, and the other was in the void Monique had fallen into. Nobody seemed to know where she was.

She'd dropped Monique off at the airport four days ago, expecting her to return the next day. No one had heard from her since. Not even her cousin Chantal. Cecilia splashed cold water on her face and started over. No more crying. Mel needed her today, and Cecilia didn't want puffy eyes when she met the best man. Maybe he would be the clone of Michael she wanted, not needed. She snorted.

"Are you almost ready?" asked one of the bridesmaids as she poked her head in the door. "The limo is here. Oh, your hair is cute, sugar." Her southern accent sounded like syrup running through her words. Cecilia stood in front of the full-length mirror in the bedroom and adjusted the crown of baby's breath around her afro. The pea green chiffon one-shoulder gown dusted the floor, making her look taller.

At the bridal shop last year, Cecilia had thought the color gaudy, but now it looked festive with a childish flair just like Mel. When Monique had seen the swath, she had pumped her middle finger in her mouth and said, "Ceecee, this is *Carrie* color." They had laughed at the reference to the movie they'd seen too many times when it had come out their freshman year.

The limo smelled like the perfume counter at Burdines. Cecilia sneezed a couple of times. Mel reached for her hand, and they stared at each other. "Melissa Anne Walker, you are the most beautiful bride I've ever seen," Cecilia said.

Mel smiled. "You are the most beautiful maid of honor. Your friendship over the past decade has enriched my life, Ceecee. You pushed me to go to college when, truth be told, I really didn't care to. But now my education has given me confidence in myself. And speaking of confidence, you seem… content since you've been seeing Freda."

"I had to go to counseling to find my strength, to find *me*," Cecilia said, stroking Mel's hand. She stared out the window but saw nothing, her mind on Monique. When Mel touched her shoulder, she turned and realized the limo had stopped in front of the church.

"I'm nervous, Ceecee," Mel whispered.

"Don't be, sweetie. I'm with you all the way," Cecilia said, shaking her head as if to put Monique in a separate compartment. "Well, except for the honeymoon. You're on your own there."

Their laughter carried her inside the church. Cecilia couldn't find Ella in the audience as she strolled to the altar. Where was her tribe? Monique had disappeared. Lanei was grounded. Now Ella was late?

After the ceremony, the best man never left Cecilia's side. They danced, and he fetched her drinks all evening. "You look beautiful, Cecilia," John said. "Michael told me you and Melissa have been friends since grade school."

"Yep! Mel is the sister I always wanted, and she came into my life at a time when I really needed a friend. She became both. I love her and would do anything to protect her." Cecilia looked at Mel slow dancing with her new husband. "Tell your buddy to watch out with my sistah," she said in a mock-southern accent.

"Oh, Michael adores Mel," John said. "Great guy. I met him at work recently, and he asked me to stand in because his best friend had emergency surgery. I suppose you know that."

Cecilia nodded. "What kind of law do you practice?" she asked, for once feeling comfortable talking to a man.

"Boring." He smiled. "So Michael tells me you're not dating anyone."

"Um…not at this time." She smiled up at him as if she had dumped a boyfriend recently. "So how about you?" She giggled.

"Free as a bird and hoping to get caught." He raised her hand to his lips. She looked into his blue eyes and took in his chiseled face under a shock of red curls. She almost raised her hand to dust off the freckles on his nose. Who would it hurt if she took him to bed tonight? A one-night stand here shouldn't land her in the kind of trouble Monique had found in Haiti. As he pulled her closer for a slow song, he asked, "May I have your company for a nightcap at my place later? We can continue…our conversation."

She tilted her head back and opened her mouth to respond when a tap on his shoulder made him stop dancing and turn to one of the groomsmen who said, "Hey, John, you have a call in the lobby. Your fiancée is in labor."

Cecilia closed her mouth and pushed him away. She ran into the darkness outside and blended into it. She'd been about to say yes to the nightcap. She sat in her car and cried, more angry than hurt, but the sutures had loosened around her tightly dressed wounds.

39
Lanei

Four sleepless nights at the hospital had stripped Lanei of more than physical energy. Her brain cried for rest from the fear and the guilt that wouldn't let her leave her daughter's side except when nature called. Maria's frail body disappeared within the bed, but Lanei trained her ears on the beeping sounds of the machines and her eyes on the beautiful zigzag line of the monitor that spoke its secret language of life.

She had almost lost her daughter because of her own sinful needs. But how could she have known that Peggy would react that way to her allergy medication? Every day after work, Kevin sat with her, watching their daughter in silence. Lanei caught him sometimes staring at her as if searching for something.

Yesterday, Kevin had pushed Fred's wheelchair into the room after taking him to his appointment at the VA clinic. "Fred wants to meet you and Maria," he'd said, smiling.

Lanei had reached for the older man's hand and shook it. "Nice to finally meet you, sir."

"Pleasure is all mine, ma'am. I pray for your daughter," Fred said.

"Thank you. I appreciate it," Lanei said.

"It's the least I can do after everything Kevin has done for me. He's my angel."

She'd looked at Kevin, searching for the person Fred was talking about and praying he would show up in her life as well.

Nate brought lunch every day to feed her body, but her soul still hungered for more. She learned that he'd met Edith through a friend and that they'd been dating for a couple weeks before she had showed up at his door.

"You barely touch your food, Lane," Nate had said the day before. "You did nothing wrong."

"You don't know what I had in mind to do," she'd snapped at him. "I was selfish, but…but you could have told me you were seeing someone."

The smile had disappeared from his face. "Why? You have a husband, a family, and your beliefs. I knew I loved you the first day I saw you on campus four years ago. But life is not always fair, Lanei. Is it?"

"I never asked you to wait or to follow me, did I?"

He'd only nodded and said, "What do you want me to bring tomorrow? How about some corn chowder?"

Lanei loved the way Nate cared for her and Maria, unlike Kevin who saw his daughter as an obstacle to his plan. Kevin's inability to keep a job had caused the family to suffer financially, and Lanei had paid for his frustrations with her body.

A few weeks ago, Kevin had beaten her because Maria had been sick all day and dinner was late. He had brought home a bag of medications from the local VA pharmacy the next day.

"I'm sorry, Lan," he'd said. "I should have stayed on my meds, but I hated the way they… I'll never hurt you again. I saw a psychiatrist today at the VA, and I'm going back to therapy too. I didn't mean what I said about Maria. I love my little girl."

The coldness inside Lanei had seeped into her voice. "Four years of marriage and now you're telling me that you needed to be on medication? What's wrong with you exactly, Kevin?"

He'd clenched his teeth, his jaw sliding back-and-forth. "Vietnam," he'd said, walking into the bedroom with the medications.

Now she bent over the hospital bed and kissed her daughter's cheek, inhaling the antiseptic odor of the hospital, but underneath that, the baby powder smell on Maria's warm skin. The clock on the wall told her Nate would be there soon with lunch. She washed her face in the bathroom sink and ran a brush through her hair. She dipped her finger into the jar of Vaseline and rubbed it on her lips. She kept looking at the clock. A nurse walked into the room and said, "Nate called to say for you to go ahead and get some lunch. He had to cover at another pharmacy today. He'll bring dinner instead."

Lanei stood up so fast the book on her lap fell on the floor. "Did he by any chance say which store he was at? I need to call him."

"No, he didn't." The nurse proceeded to take Maria's vital signs, while a storm raged inside Lanei. Since Nate had moved to Chicago from Miami over a year ago, she had managed to keep his presence a secret from Kevin.

After Kevin started taking his medications, life at home had been relatively peaceful. They'd shared laughs and he'd talked about their future, but the most important change had been the way he embraced his daughter and how Maria had bonded with her daddy.

After reading the same page in her book three times, Lanei closed it and paced for several minutes within the confines of the hospital room. She sat back down when she remembered that Kevin usually came after going home for a shower and dinner somewhere. She would send Nate away as soon as he arrived.

But when Kevin showed up early that afternoon, Lanei stood from the chair and threw her arms around his neck, craning hers to look behind him. "You… It's only four. What happened at work today?" she said, praying he hadn't gotten fired again.

"Work is slow, so I left early. Hey, why are you so jumpy? Is Maria all right?" Kevin disengaged from her and turned to the bed. Maria opened her arms and smiled at her daddy. He picked her up from the bed, swaddled her in a blanket, and sat on the recliner with his daughter on his chest.

"She had another great day today," Lanei said. "The neurologist said she might be discharged tomorrow."

"Good." He smiled at Lanei. "I miss you. The apartment is not a home without you…and Maria, of course. By the way, there were some messages on the recorder. Your mom left one. Cecilia and Ella left several messages about your other friend."

Lanei frowned, tapping her nails on the bracelet around her wrist as if she was typing in Morse code to her friends. "What did Cecilia and Ella say about Monique?"

"Don't remember. You can call them." He pointed to the bedside phone.

But she needed to intercept Nate at the elevators first. Her eyes flew to the clock. "Kev, I'll be back. I need coffee." She skipped to the half-open door.

She bumped into Nate. The yellow roses in his hand smacked her forehead and some fell inside the room. "Are you all right?" Nate asked, almost pushing her back inside the room. "Is Maria—"

She was so relieved the truth was out, she almost didn't care about the consequences. She was tired of confessing to this sin weekly. She backed into the room afraid to look at Kevin, but a force greater than her pulled her gaze to his face.

In his grin she saw hurt, doubt, and red anger.

40
Ella

⌐~⌐

Ella carried Alex and two shopping bags from the bus stop to the house. The commute had been taking a physical toll on her since they'd moved to the suburbs. When she put her son down to open the door, she could barely straighten her back. The boy was too heavy, but she'd needed to get home fast to get ready for Mel's wedding. She had reminded Bernard yesterday, but this morning he'd claimed he needed to go to work for a few hours. He had promised to be back in plenty of time. She wished she had taken Monique up on the offer to teach her to drive. She needed a car and a driver's license before starting school in the fall.

She put the groceries away and fed Alex a snack. It was now past two. She called Bernard's office. She was about to hang up when someone answered. "Hi, this is Mrs. Antoine, Bernard's wife. Is he still there?"

"Sorry, ma'am. No one worked today. It's Saturday," a man said.

"I know what day it is. I asked to speak with my husband," she repeated slowly.

"No one came into work today." The man spoke loudly like people did when speaking with someone with a foreign accent. "We're putting new flooring down, ma'am. No one is here."

"You don't need to yell. I'm not deaf. *Imbécile!*"

She threw the receiver down. Where was Bernard? Why had he lied about going to work? She had pretended not to notice his unpredictable schedule, his frequent out-of-town business trips, and his choice to not make love because she was pregnant. She should confront him after the wedding tonight, but she was afraid of the truth. What if he left her? How would she manage to go to school and care for two children on her own?

She clipped her hair on top of her head with a pin and shoved the shower cap over it. She shaved her legs and her armpits in the shower. She rubbed her jasmine-scented lotion onto her skin until it glowed like raw honey before getting dressed. She followed the tips from the counter girl and applied her makeup in a way that isolated each feature. Her eyes shone behind her glasses under a generous layer of mascara and pastel eye shadow. She stepped into a pair of white slide-in shoes, and her pink dress showed the allure of her pregnancy.

Alex's overnight bag sat by the door. Ella paced the length of the living room until her sandals got too snug. She kicked them off her feet, sat on the couch, and cried, messing up her makeup. The phone rang. "You're still home," Janet said. "I made macaroni and cheese for my boy. Ain't the wedding at four? It's almost five."

"Bernard is not home yet." Ella hiccupped through her sobs. "I called his job. He never went there. Where is he? How can he do this to me?"

"Ella, listen to me and listen good. This man treats you like you ain't got no sense," Janet expelled noisy air. "He took your voice, your money, your dreams." Jan paused as if waiting for an answer. "What are you gonna do?"

"What can I do? I'm pregnant. I don't make a lot of money. My family has shunned me." A sob escaped her lips. "I'm confused. I love Bernard. I do. *We have a plan.*"

"Your plan ain't the same as his plan." Janet snorted. "Open your eyes, woman."

Ella changed into a cotton housedress, scrubbed her face, and cooked dinner for Alex. She'd lost her appetite for everything. Even fighting with Bernard. She doubted the man ever listened to a word she said anyway.

When he finally came home after midnight, he stood in the doorway with the hallway light behind him. His gaze stopped on the dress on the floor at the foot of the bed and said, "Oh, Elle, I'm sorry. I was busy at work, then I went to a fundraising meeting. We're having a gala in December at the Haitian—" Bernard stopped when she groaned. The pain in her head threatened to poke her eyes out of her skull.

Ella flipped the switch next to the bed, and the ceiling light shone through the room as if to show her the truth in his lies. "Bernard, you are inconsiderate and chauvinistic. So now you're cheating on me?" She swallowed. She didn't want to give him the satisfaction of her tears. "I called your office. You never went to work today. *You are a liar.* What have I done to you to deserve this treatment?"

A smile broke on his face. His tight-fitting shirt clung to his toned stomach muscles and disappeared into the waistband of his slacks. He walked toward the bed, his arms outstretched. Ella scooted away. "Elle, why would I cheat on you? I simply forgot about the wedding. Can you forgive me? When I realized the office was under maintenance, I went to the library to start a research project I'm working on. I should have called you. We'll go pay Mel and…a visit at some point. *Oui?*"

"Bernard, don't come any closer." Her voice shook with uncertainty, and at this moment she hated herself for being weak and indecisive.

"Elle, come on," he said in French. Ella felt the loosening. He knew it too. "We're a team, *ma belle femme*. We're just on different schedules. That's all. Come here, *ma chérie*."

"If you touch me, I…I'll scream," Ella said with no conviction. "I need to think."

The smile never leaving his face, Bernard crawled from the bottom of the bed toward her like the giant spiders that tormented her as a child in her village. Ella opened her mouth and closed it.

She needed professional help.

41
Monique

Julien's car horn faded away. Monique took off her high-heeled sandals and kept running until she had to stop to ease the pain in her side. When she reached Rue du Centre, she flagged a taxi. The cab pulled up in front of Magloire Entreprise, a three-story building that housed the administrative offices for the many factories her family owned throughout the country. She walked into the lobby and told the receptionist to take care of the fare. People stared at her dusty feet and her mud-stained dress and looked away. Typewriter keys clicked like a symphony. Employees scurried by with stacks of papers in their arms. Heels echoed on the beige tile at a fast clip. Monique hurried to Tina's office on the second floor, hoping she wouldn't run into Papa.

Tina squinted. "What happened? Why are you in Haiti?"

Monique made a keening sound and doubled over in the chair next to the desk. Tina got up and locked her office door. She knelt in front of Monique and took her hands away from her wet face.

"Shh. Shh. What's going on?" Tina whispered.

Monique lifted her head, sat ramrod straight, and told her friend everything. "*O merde!*" Tina said, wringing her hands. "You married him? Moe, I told you these people were bad. *O bondie!*"

"They took my parents' passports. Julien threatened to kill Maman if I didn't sign the marriage papers. You know, I swallowed the curses for Julien burning my throat the past few days. But the Duvalier regime is my enemy here." Monique sobbed, putting her head in her hands. "How do I fight it?"

Tina kneaded the muscles of her neck and whispered, "What are you going to do, Moe?"

Monique shifted in the chair, lifted her head, and stared at the closed door. "For the first time in my life, Tina, I'm really scared," she whispered back. "I have no idea what to do. I'm trapped. Utterly trapped."

Monique had never cried so hard in her life, and the tears did not wash away the despair. With some money from Tina, she stopped at a pharmacy and bought six packs of contraceptive pills, no prescription needed in Haiti. Next, she directed the taxi to her sister Esther's house.

Stepping out of the cab, Monique looked at the gold wedding band Julien had slipped on her finger earlier, and she instinctively touched her neck, as if a noose encircled it. Solange was here. With their husbands at work, their children in school, and their households managed by underpaid and over-worked servants, the women had nothing to do. Monique told Esther what had happened since she arrived in Haiti a week ago. Esther guided Monique to a chair on the balcony and poured her a glass of cold lemonade.

"Well, well. *Princess* is back in Haiti for good," Solange said, chuckling. "Maybe we'll have some peace in our family now. You fucked the wrong man and thought you could waltz back to university." She snorted.

"Stop it, Solange," Esther said. "Can't you see Moe is upset?"

"What the hell is she so upset about?" Solange cut her eyes at them. "I wanted to study abroad, but Papa picked a husband for me instead. Now you've had your fun; it's time to settle down, *petite soeur.*"

Monique glared at Solange who moved away from her. "Esther, I need to use your phone, please."

Monique closed Esther's bedroom door behind her and called her cousin Chantal. "Oh my God, Moe. What's going on over there? When are you coming back home? I called Esther and could not get through. Brian has been driving me insane. He wants—"

"Chantal! Just listen. No questions, please," Monique whispered, holding her head to rein in the hammering migraine.

"Okay," Chantal whispered back.

"I married Julien today. I had no choice. And tell Brian...to forget about me."

"What kind of fucking backward animals are these shits? The man raped you, so you had to marry him. There must be recourse. You need an attorney, a hit man, something!"

Monique shook her head. Chantal was her kin. "I don't know when, but I'll come back to Miami. That I promise you."

Then she called each member of her tribe. Her ears still ringing from the symphony of the bracelets, Monique walked into Julien's house. He looked at his gold watch and said, "You made the deadline by three minutes. My father is on his way to celebrate with us."

She walked upstairs and closed the bedroom door. Monique opened the twenty-one-day pack of pills and swallowed one. She wrote the date on the outer box to stay on schedule: *August 28, 1980*. Then she hid the boxes in the makeup bag in her nightstand drawer. She might be physically restrained by Julien, but he would never control her will.

Part Two

42

Cecilia

In the past two and a half years, therapy had shown Cecilia the inner beauty that now spilled onto her face, through her relationships with her girlfriends, and in the way she carried herself with self-confidence and pride. Dressed in a powder-blue pantsuit and four-inch heels, Cecilia walked into the classroom to prepare for her workday. She stashed her Gucci purse in her desk drawer, turned to the blackboard, and wrote the date. Friday, February 11, 1983. It was Valentine's Day weekend. Cecilia had her first date the following day.

After the fiasco at Mel's wedding with John, she'd turned down dates from coworkers, men she met at the grocery store, and even blind dates arranged by friends. She had taken the time to know and love herself first.

The high school sophomores filed into the room, and the loud chatter and pushing stopped. They got into their seats, opened their math books, and faced her with their full attention. One of the girls in her math club said, "You look beautiful, Miss Peterson. Nice suit."

"Thank you, Marsha," Cecilia said. Then she clapped her hands with their red-painted nails and said, "Let's get to work."

The admiration and respect of the students from the very high school where she had experienced such pain and insecurity fueled her love for her profession. The math and science club she'd founded for girls attracted students who admitted to having never liked those subjects before. Cecilia sowed seeds of dreams in her young students the way Freda had done over the years to help her build the foundation of her self-esteem.

At the end of the period, Marsha stayed behind and stopped by her desk. "Miss Peterson, I look forward to your classes every day. I thought I wanted to just graduate high school. Now I want to go to college. Maybe I'll be a teacher like you."

Cecilia smiled. "My second grade teacher inspired me," she said with deep fondness in her heart for the woman who'd showed her love when she needed it. "See you Monday, Marsha."

The girl nodded and left. Cecilia waited for her second period class as she opened her own book to finish her homework for her evening graduate class. Her life as a twenty-four-year-old was too structured. Up at six in the morning to get ready for work and back to the empty apartment most nights after school. She sometimes hung out with Ella or Mel and their children in the evenings.

After her graduate class that evening, Larry, a PhD candidate who Cecilia had met in group discussion, changed her flat tire in the university's parking lot. He had a broad physique, deep-set brown eyes, and wore a wedding band. He seemed to bump into her a lot in the hallway lately and always had a haggard look on his face. She tried to be civil to him but was losing her patience.

"Thank you, Larry," she said, opening her car door to get in. "You're a life saver."

He pulled his folded shirtsleeves down over his wrists and said, "I wish I could save real lives." In the cone of light from the streetlamp, his eyes misted.

Cecilia stopped with one leg inside the car. "Are you all right?" she asked despite her desire to get in her car and go. It had been a busy week, and she wanted to get to bed.

"I'm fine," he said with a sigh. "It's my wife. She has cancer, and I can't... I wish I could save her life."

Cecilia got out of her car and leaned on the door. "I'm so sorry, Larry."

"I'm taking a sabbatical to take care of her. I'm so distracted I keep bumping into things and people. We have five-year-old twin boys... Life is so unfair."

Leaning against her car, they talked about loss, life, and hope late into the night before exchanging phone numbers.

❧

After a good night's rest, Cecilia turned over on her side on the queen-sized bed that swallowed her. She peeked out from under her light blanket at the clock on her night table and settled back into her down pillow. She looked forward to her weekly Saturday lunch with Mel when Cecilia could bask in her friend's happiness in her marriage. Sundays were reserved for Ella's food and the heavy dose of suspicion and fear that radiated from her. Maybe Bernard had never really loved Ella. Cecilia had accepted that fact about her mother and was stronger for it. The cool February air blew through the screen of her open bedroom window, moving the filmy white drape toward her like a hand fan.

When she finally emerged from her bed, she went to the bathroom for a shower. She let the water beat down on her tight muscles, adjusting the flow to the highest pressure. Her soapy hands traveled over every inch of her skin, igniting the nerves underneath before stopping between her legs. She closed her eyes tight, hoping to banish the image from under the stairs, but just like before, disgust replaced the warm feelings that began in her center. She never made it to the point where they would bring her release. She pulled her hands away and washed them for a long time. Maybe next time?

For once, Mel was there before her and made a show of looking at her Rolex watch, which had been a gift from Michael for giving birth to a perfect baby girl two years ago. "You're late, sistah," Mel teased. "I hope it was a busy night with a knight?" She laughed at her own silly joke.

Cecilia made a face and slid into the booth at their favorite diner in Aventura. The waitress came with two cups of regular coffee with cream and sugar. "Hey guys. The usual?" she asked.

The women nodded. After telling Mel about Larry from the night before, Cecilia said, "I could see the pain he's feeling. That's what true love is. Someone who's there for the good and the bad times. Someone who will love your damaged body no matter what."

"You're so right, Ceecee. Love is more about what's inside than outside. It's a great feeling knowing someone cares about your whole being so deeply."

Cecilia sipped her coffee to hide her envy. As if Mel could see the jealousy written across Cecilia's face, Mel added, "Ceecee, I don't understand why you haven't dated in all the years I've known you. What happened with prom was… cruel, but it was a long time ago. So, you're a twenty-four-year-old virgin?" She narrowed her eyes at the impossibility of such a fact.

Cecilia stiffened but smiled at her friend. "Mel, there's nothing wrong with waiting until you know for sure. Didn't you know when you met Mike?"

"I did. But I had tried a few, so that's how I knew." Mel leaned toward her. "You need a yardstick if you will." They laughed so loudly that the other patrons turned to stare.

"First of all, I don't want to date anyone from work or school. If things don't work out, it'll make life…uncomfortable."

"That's your problem," Mel exclaimed. "You think too damn much. Just live, girl. I wish Monique was here to take you out of that apartment on weekends. You heard from her?"

Cecilia blew air out along with a flash of anger. "We talk, but I sense it's painful for her to interact with us here when she hates it over there. I wanted to go see her last Christmas, but she said she didn't want me to see her like *that*."

"Like what?" Mel asked in her innocent way.

"Being restrained. Losing her voice. Having no choices. Suffering abuse." Cecilia took a breath. "You wouldn't know anything about any of it, Mel. Your life is perfect."

Mel looked as if she was about to cry. Cecilia wondered if it was for what Monique had to endure or if she had hurt her southern sensibilities. "I'm sorry, Ceecee. I guess...I don't understand a lot."

Cecilia reached for Mel's soft hands, noting the pink-polished nails. "Nothing to be sorry for, love. I have no doubt Monique will come back. No doubt. By the way, Ella and I are going to Chicago next month for Lanei's birthday. We're sure going to miss Moe."

A couple hours later, the friends hugged. "Happy Valentine's Day, Ceecee. You should be going on a hot date tonight," Mel declared.

Mel made her way to a husband and daughter who were waiting for her. No one was waiting for Cecilia. Not even a dog. She drove to the mall to buy a new outfit for tonight. She was going on a first date with the new neighbor on the second floor. She hadn't told Mel because she wanted to know more about the man first. Just in case.

Or maybe she just loved to keep secrets.

43
Lanei

For the past couple years, Lanei had marked time by the number of weeks Maria did not require a trip to the emergency room, how often Kevin made Lanei laugh, and how he nurtured their daughter. She monitored his medications, making sure the refills came in the mail on time and that he never missed an appointment with his psychiatrist. These medications had given Lanei frequent reprieve from the nightly sexual assaults Kevin called love-making. Kevin brought Fred over once a week for dinner, and the older man showed Lanei a side of Kevin that had been hidden. She had opened the oven door and was basting the pot roast, golden potatoes, and carrots when she felt the cold March air coming in through the front door.

"Smells good, hon," Kevin said, kissing her forehead. "You sure know your way to a man's heart."

Three-year-old Maria jumped up and down. Kevin scooped up the toddler and tossed her in the air, pretending to let her fall. She giggled.

Lanei smiled. "Maria, I need Daddy to help me hang the new curtains. Remember?"

"Daddy, my aunties are coming for Mommy's birthday," Maria said.

Kevin stopped on his way down the hall and turned to Lanei. "What... what is she talkin' about?"

Lanei had planned to tell Kevin after dinner. Usually, she could get him to agree to her ideas better on a full stomach. She cleared her throat. "Oh, Ceecee and Elle are coming to spend my birthday with me this weekend. I can't believe we're turning twenty-five this year." She shook her head. "We haven't seen each other since the graduation. I—"

"We ain't got room, and I'm in no mood for company."

She wanted to say they weren't coming for him, but instead she took a deep breath. "They're staying at a hotel in town. They want me to stay with them overnight." Lanei took a sip of water from the glass on the counter to moisten her dry mouth. "Um...I'll leave Maria with Peggy. We're having brunch here on Sunday for my birthday, and I'll have Peggy and...oh, please invite Fred. I—"

"So now we got money for dinner parties." He drummed his knuckles on the table. "I was gonna take you to that seafood buffet place you like." He bared his teeth in a grin, eyes flashing. "Guess you had other plans."

She walked up to him and ran her hand down his arm. "Go take your shower. Your pot roast dinner will be on the table when you finish."

Maria wrapped her arms around his legs. "Daddy, Uncle Nate gave me a pretty book today at the library. Want to see it?"

Lanei's stomach seized. She stared at Kevin. He closed his eyes. When he opened them, his lips stretched flat against his teeth. He tousled Maria's curls. "Daddy will see the book after his shower." He turned to Lanei. "I'm glad your friends are coming. I know you miss them. I'll keep Maria for the weekend."

Lanei said nothing, but she would never leave her daughter alone with Kevin. His anger periodically broke through the chemical barrier of the medications, the way it had when he had seen Nate at the hospital a couple years ago. They hadn't talked about it much since then, but Nate was coming to brunch this weekend. The relationship with Edith hadn't worked out, but he dated on and off. He came to the library once a month to see Maria, but otherwise he kept his distance. She peeled the cellophane off the yellow candles and placed them in the glass holders on the dinette table. The bright yellow print on the throw pillows camouflaged the shabbiness of the dark gray couch. The matching valance in the bay window brought early spring into her apartment.

When the doorbell rang the following day, Lanei fluffed her hair and ran her palm over her green cable-knit sweater and her black corduroy slacks before opening the door and falling into Cecilia's and Ella's arms with tears of joy. They all started talking at the same time.

"Come in, come in." Lanei closed the door behind them. "Look at my sisters. Oh, how I missed you. This is going to be my best birthday ever."

"Lan, the place looks beautiful. Like an indoor spring garden. You've always loved yellow," Cecilia said. "Where's Maria?"

"It smells good too," Ella added, sniffing the air. "Is that breadfruit and coconut I smell?" Lanei noticed the fullness of Ella's body.

"Yep! I found breadfruit at an Asian market here." Lanei said, turning to Cecilia. "Peggy came and got Maria earlier. You'll see her Sunday at the brunch. I wish you guys were staying longer than two nights." She pouted.

"Sister, I've never seen ice on streets before," Ella said, pushing her glasses up over her nose. "Where I come from, ice belongs in drinks or on dead bodies. It's too damn cold for this Haitian sister. *Brrrrr*!"

Lanei and Cecilia laughed. "You get used to it, Elle," Lanei said. "Anyway, let's eat lunch and let the fun begin." She wanted to leave in case Kevin decided to come home early from work and cause trouble.

After lunch, they drove to downtown Chicago and parked Cecilia's rental car. Their first stop was at the Sears Tower, which provided a spectacular view of the city. Cecilia pulled out her camera and snapped pictures of everything. "We need pictures of ourselves to send to Moe," Lanei said, swallowing the sadness that left a constant heaviness in her heart. They asked a man in a trench coat to take a picture of them. Standing in a tight circle, they pulled down their coat sleeves to reveal their gold bracelets. They linked their arms and turned their faces to the man who narrowed his eyes. "Go ahead," Lanei said. The man hit the button and moved the lever to chamber another frame and snapped several more shots. "Thank you, sir," they all said and giggled.

"I'll mail copies to you, Lan, when I develop the film back home," Cecilia said. "And I'll send some to Moe."

"I'd like that," Lanei said. "I'm so happy, but I miss Moe."

"It's not the same without her," Ella said. "Maybe I can take the photos to her. I need to go to Haiti for some answers."

"To what, Elle?" Lanei asked.

"Not sure, but I'll know when I get there," Ella replied.

It was late afternoon when they walked into the Renaissance Hotel on Michigan Avenue for dinner. Cecilia ordered a bottle of wine. The place smelled expensive. When Lanei saw the prices on the menu, she leaned forward on the silk upholstered seat and whispered, "Um…I only have like twenty dollars on me, Ceecee. I—"

Cecilia reached over and covered Lanei's hand. "Don't, sweetheart. I'm good for it. I have no kids, no…not even a dog. I should be allowed to spoil my sister on her birthday. Right?"

Lanei's old secret envy of Cecilia's success dimmed like the glow of the amber lamp on the table. Lanei had Maria, Mama, Peggy, Kevin, and even

Nate. Yesterday, Nate had given Maria the book and left, barely making eye contact with Lanei. The excitement of having him over to her place made her dizzy. Surely Kevin would behave. Safety in numbers.

By the time they made it to the hotel suite, Lanei felt the years of stress melt away to reveal the teenager she was before she met Kevin. The teenager her island sisters had allowed her to be from time to time. Cecilia ordered drinks and snacks from room service, and they settled into plush cushions in their suite.

Lanei sipped her white wine and shook her head. "Elle, you're more likely to understand what Moe is facing in Haiti. Please, tell us."

Ella poured vodka over the ice in her glass, splashed in some 7UP, and stirred with her finger. "Well, ladies, I don't know how else to explain the difference between Monique's social rank in Haitian society and mine," Ella said. "Moe is being persecuted because her family is *very* wealthy and *very* mulatto. Mine is invisible because we are *not*."

Lanei blinked several times and stared at Cecilia who shrugged. "What does it all mean?"

"It means"—Ella gulped a mouthful of her drink—"that you ladies need to read up on what a dictatorship looks like and the class struggle in Haiti that started even before we gained our independence in 1804 from the French colonizers. The same French colonizers who left their imprint on Monique's lineage. My family is more closely related to the slaves who fought for freedom. I guess we're still fighting."

Lanei frowned and made a mental note to search for books in the library about Haiti's history. "How's Bernard? I'm glad he lets you...I mean that he was okay with you coming here."

Ella sucked her teeth. "I don't need Bernard's permission to move my body from one place to the next," she said, her eyes bulging behind her glasses. "He's preparing to run for city council. That man is ambitious and a bit...selfish. But we made a pact!"

"Remember what Freda said at our meeting last week?" Cecilia said. "We're responsible for our own destiny. A marriage is a partnership not a bondage."

"Well, Miss Single Professional, a marriage demands sacrifices and compromises," Ella said, glaring at Cecilia before filling up her glass again. Lanei squinted at Cecilia. "Freda helped me see how Bernard likes to be in control. But he's an island man. It's...more cultural than anything else."

"You don't believe that—" Cecilia stopped when Lanei stood in the middle of the room like a referee.

Since Monique had involuntarily joined Lanei and Ella's rank of married women dealing with "marital issues," Cecilia had become the face of success and envy. Lanei hid her envy within her weekly confessions, but Ella never could. Ella smiled at Cecilia and said, "Sorry, Ceecee. I'm being a bitch again."

"But maybe…you're right, Elle," Cecilia said. "I've never been in a relationship, so I…shouldn't—"

Lanei stopped Cecilia by raising her hand and said, "Elle, do you still go to church, honey? You need to take the kids and yourself. God will help. You have to believe."

"I know," Ella said. "I go on my Sundays off."

"Good! Let's get ready to have a bit of fun downstairs," Lanei said. "I want to dance with abandon tonight. I can't remember the last time I did."

At the club Lanei let the music carry her to the center of the dance floor. With her eyes closed, she danced until tears escaped from under her eyelids. The look of confusion on Cecilia's face made Lanei smile. She took her friends' hands, and they formed a circle on the dance floor. "Happy tears," Lanei said. "I'm glad you two are here."

The last time Lanei had danced with such recklessness was her thirteenth birthday, and the night had ended in tragedy. She blamed herself.

It had taken Lanei a whole year to talk Mama into celebrating her "sweet thirteenth" birthday. She'd never had a party before. Her birthday reminded Mama of her father's rejection. When the day finally dawned, Lanei slipped on the yellow organza dress she had sinfully coveted in the window of a local store.

At the church hall with her choir friends and her classmates, she had danced and wanted the night to never end. But a few hours later, it had ended. She'd opened the back door with her hip, her arms laden with gift boxes, and bumped into someone.

"Hap…py thirteenth birthday, Lan," her father said. Lanei dropped the boxes and clamped her hands over her mouth to stifle a scream.

"Oh!" she said, peering through the dark night at the face that looked like hers.

"I'm…sorry, honey." They both stared at the boxes on the ground.

"Wha…what are you doing here?" She found her voice. "I haven't seen you in…many years. Not since you got married and had your *better* children."

He leaned on the door. "Lan, I'm weak and I made the wrong choice. But for the love of God, please forgive me."

"You're drunk." She pushed him away from the door. "I don't need you anymore. I won't ever forgive you."

The next morning Father Arnoldo told Lanei that her father had gone home, closed the garage door, and hooked up a hose to the exhaust pipe of his car. He had gone to eternal sleep in hell.

All these years Lanei had believed her forgiveness would have saved her father's life. She had confessed for that sin ever since. But why? She was a child. He was asking her to restore his manhood, his conscience. She no longer wanted to carry the guilt of her father's suicide, Maria's illness, Nate's love, and Kevin's abuse. On her twenty-fifth birthday, Lanei was on a quest to understand her faith, restore her self-esteem, and live in joy.

On Sunday morning she left Cecilia and Ella asleep at the hotel and took a cab to church for the early service before going home to cook her birthday brunch. As soon as she hung up the phone with her mother, it rang again. "Kevin, please answer the phone," she yelled from the kitchen. "I have to wash my hands."

The two nights she had spent at the hotel with Cecilia and Ella had not only brought joy to her life, but the time away from Maria had given her a glimpse of the possibility that they both could return to the outside world one day. But when she'd checked the bottles of medication earlier, she had noticed Kevin had not been taking his pills. That discovery slammed her back into a world of fear and caution. She inhaled deeply and let the breath out slowly through her lips. She was going to enjoy the time with her friends today. She would pray about the medication issue later.

"It's for you!" Kevin said. Lanei wiped her hands on a dishrag and hurried to the living room. Kevin handed the receiver to her and said, "It's the kidnapped one." He laughed. "I'll be back."

Lanei covered the mouthpiece with her hand and said, "The guests will be here at one. It's twelve—"

"I can tell time, for Christ's sake." He slammed the door.

She sat on the couch and cradled the phone between her head and shoulder while she massaged her right foot. "Hey, Moe. How're you doing, honey?"

"He called me 'the kidnapped one.' What a jerk!" Monique said. "I'm okay. Happy birthday, love."

"Thank you, sister. We really missed you the past two nights. We had a great time. Even the weather cooperated, which is a miracle for Chicago in March. The sun has been out for days."

"Mmm!" Monique said. "I can almost taste your breadfruit dish from here."

"Moe, I'll make you all the breadfruit you want the next time we're together. I pray it'll be soon. I love you."

"Speaking of love…how's Nate? Still waiting for Jesus to give you the green light?" Monique laughed. "You know, one day he might be gone for good."

Lanei could always count on Monique for a dose of reality. She had been thinking about Nate marrying somebody. Lately, he looked at her with more regret than longing. "That's why I miss you, crazy girl," Lanei said. "Well, if Jesus wants me to have Nate, he'll show me the way. I pray Brian is waiting for you in Miami."

"Get real, girl. I don't expect him to," Monique said. "But you know, the first time I meet a man who disturbs my heart in a good way, I get yanked away from him." Monique sighed. "Is that corny or what?"

"Not at all," Lanei said, thinking of how being around Nate made her feel alive. "Not at all, sister-friend."

"I'll see you one day, Lan. That's a promise." Lanei heard the clink of the bracelet on the phone. She clinked hers before hanging up.

A few minutes later, she let Cecilia and Ella into the apartment. "Moe called," Lanei said. "That sister never loses sight of her dream. She ends every call with—"

"I will see you one day. That's a promise," Cecilia and Ella recited in unison.

Before she locked the door, Peggy walked in with an excited Maria. "Mommy, Mommy, are they my aunties?"

Lanei scooped up her daughter and brushed the hair out of her green eyes. "Yes, they are, sweetie." She put Maria down on the floor. "Give them hugs and kisses."

"You're so beautiful, Maria," Cecilia said. "I want to take you home with me."

Maria shook her head. "No, I can't leave my daddy. He said he needs me."

Lanei smiled. She had always wanted her children to have the daddy she was denied. The smell of the pineapple cake, bacon, and curry infused the apartment with joy. Lanei filled up the glasses with wine. When the bell rang again, Maria ran and yanked the door open. Nate stood behind a giant bouquet of yellow roses. "Come in, come in. Nate, you always remember my favorite color. I—" Lanei stopped when she saw the woman behind him.

"Cecilia and Ella, right?" Nate said, walking into the room and shaking the women's hands. "So nice of you to come celebrate Lane's birthday with her." He pulled the woman who had entered with him forward. "Everybody, this is Becky, my girlfriend," Nate said, gazing into Lanei's eyes.

A chorus of "nice to meet you" made the round of the living room. Lanei caught her hand right before it reached her mouth. Cecilia stared at her and cocked one eyebrow. "Let's all sit down," Lanei said, keeping a smile on her face while her heart raged with anger. How could she be angry? She had no right.

She filled two glasses with wine and served the new arrivals. Kevin walked in the door with six red roses clasped in his hand as he pushed Fred's wheelchair into the apartment. After almost ten years, he still didn't know that yellow was Lanei's favorite color. But the man with the new girlfriend had known all along.

"I'm so happy you could make it, Fred," Lanei said, kissing his leathery forehead. "I'll get you some coffee."

Fred took her hand and kissed it. "Happy Birthday, my dear. Couldn't have made it without my friend helping me get ready today."

Kevin parked the wheelchair by the window and tucked the blanket around Fred's remaining leg. Kevin tapped Fred's shoulder and said, "Let me know if you need anything, buddy." Kevin turned and Lanei saw the softness in his eyes. "I'll get the coffee, Lan."

After everyone had a drink and small talk and laughter filled the room, Lanei escaped into her bedroom and closed the door. Sitting on the bed, she reached for her rosary under her pillow and whispered, "God, what do you want me to do?"

She waited as if she expected an answer to appear in the clouds swirling outside the bedroom window.

44
Ella

~~~

The night before the brunch at Lanei's, Ella had locked herself in the hotel bathroom to change into her sleepwear. After seeing Cecilia's taut physique in her bra and panties as she stripped out of her clothes in the middle of the room, Ella hated that she couldn't control the expansion of her treasonous body. But she'd given birth to two children, while Cecilia for all they knew was still a virgin. Nobody had thumped, squeezed, and bit into her flesh like ripe summer mangoes.

Ella had scrubbed her face hard to remove her makeup, hoping to erase the signs of constant frowning and doubt. She wished the pleats around her mouth were from laughter instead of the way she had learned to gather her lips to keep bad words from spilling out. Leaning into the mirror, she'd parted her hair to reveal several strands of gray. Gray hair at twenty-five? Every strand carried the many ways she'd tried to plan her return to school while taking care of two children, working to pay bills, and fighting Bernard to keep her dream alive. She would have been a fourth-year medical student now if she hadn't had the children. But what kind of mother thought like that? Bernard had accused her of being selfish. Selfish!

Bernard had started graduate school when Ella was pregnant with their daughter. By the time she gave birth and was ready to start school, he'd sworn that his employer would pay his tuition only if he completed his degree in the next three years. He would support her decision to go back to school full-time once he was done.

Last week she'd asked Bernard to help Alex with his homework and his bath while she was doing the dishes.

"I'm busy," he'd said. "I have homework and community events to plan. Besides, the kids prefer when you do it anyway."

"Because you've never done it," she'd yelled. "I work a full-time job too. Do you have any idea how much work it takes to manage a household with two kids?"

"Unlike mine, your job is practically brainless. And what kind of mother complains about taking care of her children? You're selfish, Ella. These kids need you *now*, not when they're adults."

She had walked from the kitchen and stood in front of him, shaking with anger. "First of all, that was a very hurtful thing to say about my job. We have one year, Bernard, to set up a schedule that will work for all of us *when* I go back to school."

"Elle, this is America. You can go to school anytime. Enjoy your kids. Besides I'm applying for citizenship for us soon. It only takes a couple years. Citizenship will give you access to more resources for school."

"What?" Just then, six-year-old Alex, trailed by two-year-old Perrine, had run into the family room. They were both crying, and each held the end of a tattered Winnie the Pooh. "Mommy, I had it first," Alex said.

Ella had yanked the stuffed toy from both kids and yelled, "You two go to your rooms and stop fighting." They stared at her in fear. "I have a goddamn headache, and I'm tired." She glared at Bernard. "*Merde*! Can you help me here instead of plotting ways to keep me from school? You wanted the children. Remember? I don't want to go to school *anytime*, Bernard. I'm going next year. Be ready to enjoy *your* kids."

Lanei had knocked on the bathroom door. "Elle, are you okay in there? You're talking to yourself."

"I'll be right out," she'd said, rubbing Vaseline on her face until the worry lines disappeared into the grease.

At breakfast this morning, Ella marveled at the fact that she didn't miss her children as much as she'd thought she would. This was the first time she'd been away from them overnight. She knew they were safe with Bernard. Lanei had called to check on Maria from the pay phone at the Sears Tower gift shop yesterday, from the restaurant last night, and from the hotel room early this morning. But Ella's children were healthy. Bernard only had to feed them and make sure they didn't kill each other. She smiled.

"Elle, that is the fifth teaspoon of sugar you've stirred into that cup of coffee," Lanei said, as Ella read the breakfast menu at the diner around the corner from their hotel. It was a crisp, sunny March day. Mounds of dirty snow blocked the sidewalks. People walked with purpose. It was too cold for strolling.

"Lan, I'm Haitian," Ella said. "I love sugar, rice, and bread. I used to be a bean pole, remember? I haven't been able to lose the weight since Perrine was born two years ago. I eat when I'm stressed. Been doing a lot of eating lately. That's why I'm fat."

"You're not...fat," Cecilia said. "Good thing you're tall. You carry the... extra pounds well. What's going on? I'm going to have plenty of free time when I finish grad school in June. I can babysit. I want to help in any way you need me."

"Thank you, Ceecee. I'm up three sizes, and I can't seem to find the time or motivation to do something about it. Lately, Bernard is not even...you know, the way he used to chase me around the bedroom." Ella sighed.

"Maybe it's not your weight," Lanei said.

Ella closed the menu and stared at Lanei. "What are you implying?"

"Well, I can tell when Kevin is cheating. He...loses interest, which in my case is a blessing. I've long tolerated Kevin touching me because...at least he uses a condom *religiously*. He never wanted children," Lanei said. "Sometimes it saddens me that I may spend the rest of my life...never enjoying, you know...intimacy, let alone experiencing the big O."

Cecilia cleared her throat. "And you all want me to find a man. Moe has been kidnapped by one. Lan lives with a cheater and abuser, and Elle, well—"

"But Bernard and I love each other," Ella said. "I'm fitted with an IUD. I just need to lose weight, and everything will be like before."

Lanei and Cecilia exchanged a quick look before examining their menus once more. "I'm cooking a lot of food later for brunch," Lanei said. "So we can have a light breakfast."

"Look, Bernard is not perfect," Ella said, not ready to let this go, "but he followed me to Port-au-Prince and to Miami because he wants to be with me even though my family...hates him. You guys don't know him like I do."

"Have you ever questioned why your family...you know, hates him so much that they *exiled* you to keep you away from him? Once from your village to Port-au-Prince and then to Miami?" Cecilia asked.

Ella opened her mouth to answer, then closed it. Bernard had convinced her that her family had fabricated rumors to keep them apart. Nobody knew her husband the way she did. Or did she? He had convinced her that Western

Union had made a mistake. He had never sent money to anyone in Haiti. She'd believed him. But who was Martha Antoine? Ella stared at the menu as if it was a Ouija board. She would go to Haiti for answers.

When the waitress came, she ordered enough breakfast to feed a regiment. After all, who started a diet while on vacation?

45

Monique

❧

Monique sat in the passenger seat of Julien's car in the driveway. Dressed in a Cleopatra costume for a *bal masqué* at the home of one of Julien's friends, she pasted a smile on her face, and hoped it would last through the evening. She rolled down the car window and inhaled the smell of ylang-ylang on the summer breeze. Maybe she'd make more connections for her cause. In the two and half years she had been in Haiti, she and Tina had started "Pass-It-Along," a program that sponsored young women to get into universities, elite secondary schools, and government and private sector jobs using Monique's unwanted clout as *Madame Etienne* to open doors that otherwise would have been closed to these women. It gave her life purpose while she waited for her chance to escape. Confident in his power to keep Monique in Haiti, Julien let her roam free, so long as she was home before him in the evening.

"I gotta get my watch. Be right back," Julien said as he was about to step into the car.

"Oh, get my shawl," Monique yelled to his retreating back. "The red one. It's in my top dresser drawer."

Several minutes later, she walked back into the house and bounded upstairs. "Asshole probably can't find the shawl," she muttered, sucking her teeth like Ella and smiling. Seated on her side of the bed, Julien held the bag of birth control pills Chantal had been sending to her, and tears dripped down his face. The nightstand drawer was open; loose pills scattered on the bedspread and the parquet floor.

She rushed to him. "I said the shawl was in the *dresser* drawer." She grabbed the bag from his hand. "Give me my—"

The punch sent her hurtling against the armoire. It knocked the wind out of her, but she straightened up and pounced on him, her long nails leaving bloody tracks on his face. "I will not bear your bad seeds. You will have to kill me first. I hate this place. I hate you. I—"

Julien slapped her twice on the same side of her face. Her ear rang like a church bell. He managed to restrain her hands and got on top of her on the floor. "Monique...*Monique*." He shook her shoulders. "Stop screaming." His low, calm voice penetrated her fury. "I don't want to hit you again, so don't say another fucking word," he whispered. "For over two years my father...I mean, I've been waiting. You lied. You're right. I may have to kill you, but you're going to have *my* child!"

He released her hands and walked out of the room, clutching the bag of pills in his hand. Monique grabbed the pillow from the bed and screamed into it until her throat burned. When she couldn't scream anymore, she went to the bathroom to examine her face. As she smeared a layer of makeup on her bruised face, she thought of Lanei. In the dining room she caught Anita staring at her face. "Oh, I slipped...um...in the shower and hit my face," Monique said.

Anita squinted. "Be careful, madame. It can be slippery around here, especially for someone like you."

"Oh, Anita." Monique blinked rapidly. The bruised side of her face throbbed.

"We need you to be safe here, madame, so we can continue to have high pay and days off," Anita whispered. "Be patient."

Monique peered into Anita's keen eyes. "Patience is not one of my virtues."

"I told you I'll do anything I can to help you, madame." Anita looked over her shoulder.

"Thank you. I still wish you'd call me Monique."

Anita shook her head. Her chuckles hid sobs in their echo. "Monsieur Etienne...would not approve. *Bonne nuit.*"

Monique pulled a suitcase from under the bed and started throwing clothes in it, then stopped. Esther and Solange had homes in the Dominican Republic, but her parents had no passports to leave the country. How could she escape, knowing they would hurt her mother, her family? She might have her issues with Papa and Solange, but she wanted them safe. Julien did not come home that night.

The next morning, Julien burst into the bedroom and stood over her. The bloody zigzag lines looked like mud tracks on his face. He seized the back of her neck and brought her face to his. Their noses touched. "Look what you did to my face," he said with a growl, spraying her face with spittle. "I trusted you. Do you have any idea what my father can unleash on you and your *bourgeois* family?" She did not move. She counted. "You look down on my family. You may not disrespect me. *I should be good enough for you.*"

"Julien—" she said as the pressure increased on her neck.

"Don't speak! In this house I rule!" He shook her head back-and-forth, then threw it on the pillow. "This is not America. You live in Haiti! You're a *Haitian* woman. You're going to give me a child."

She tried once more. "Julien, you have the power to stop this insanity. Let me go. Why do you want me?"

"You know, last night I thought about letting you go," he said, staring at her with what might be a twinge of compassion. "But after talking to my father this morning, I realized Papa lets me *keep* you. You have it good with me. Trust me." Julien left the room.

Monique shivered. She looked at the four walls of the bedroom and opened her arms wide as if to keep them from closing in on her.

In September, she missed a period.

Six months later, a swift kick from the baby forced her to rub her stomach. She stepped out of the car in front of the obstetrician's office. It was a beautiful March day. Cecilia and Ella would be in Chicago with Lanei to celebrate her twenty-fifth birthday. She shaded her eyes and looked at the sky. The sun warmed the bracelet around her wrist. Monique wondered if her island sisters were looking at the same blazing sun in Chicago. She entered the office with new resolve, prepared to execute her plan to deliver her baby in Miami in three months.

46
Cecilia

◦─◦

Cecilia slammed her apartment door, wanting to shatter something to mitigate her anger. She had planned to finally invite her neighbor over last night for a nightcap after their third date. But before dessert had arrived, the man had slid a document toward her and had asked her to cosign on a car note with him. Good thing she hadn't told anybody about him yet. That was why she kept secrets—to avoid shame. She threw her work bag on the table with the tests she had to grade tonight and hit play on her answering machine. She picked up the phone. Someone needed her. She could embrace somebody else's disappointment instead of her own.

"Hey," Cecilia said when Larry answered. "I just got home from class. Is everything okay with—"

"Yes, yes," Larry said, cutting her off. "I wanted to share the good news. The test result shows my wife's tumor is shrinking. She had a good day today, so I had a great day today."

Larry wanted to share joy, not pain. Who could she share her pain with tonight? The pettiness of her thought in light of what Larry's family was going through mortified her. "I'm so happy to hear that, Larry," she said, meaning it. "Listen, let me know if I can take the boys out again…to give you guys some free time."

"You're a beautiful person. The boys want to go from kindergarten straight to high school to be your students." He laughed. "I'll take you up on that offer. Good night."

Cecilia had always wanted children, so she could be the mother she'd wanted but never had. Mel's and Ella's children filled her with joy even though their smells, their softness, and their kisses bruised her lonely heart. But she had enough love in that heart to nurture her friends' children. It felt good.

After work the following day, Cecilia opened the side door of the high school auditorium and stepped into a puddle of water. "Where did that rain come from?" she muttered. "The forecast lied." Her car was being serviced, so she hailed a cab.

The driver came out and opened the door for her, holding a big red umbrella over her head. She took in his lean physique and noted that his beige shirt matched his skin as if he was nude. A gold chain disappeared in the curly chest hair peeking out of his open collar. Their hands touched the door handle at the same time. Her fingers tingled. As she slid into the cab, her skirt rode up her legs. His eyes roamed over her body and bore into hers before he closed her door and climbed behind the wheel.

"Where the pretty lady going?" he asked, a smile playing on his wide lips. Raindrops glistened on his short black hair like crystals. His island accent pulled her closer to the partition between them. They were a couple of blocks from the school.

"Oh, I'm sorry," she said, giving him her address.

"No need to apologize. I take you wherever you wanna go." He winked, his light brown eyes crinkling in the corners. "I'm Orson, Orson Matthews, at your service."

"Nice to meet you, Orson, Orson Matthews." They laughed. "I'm Cecilia, Cecilia Peterson."

"Well, Cecilia Peterson, the afternoon is slow. How 'bout some hot tea to chase away the late March chill?" The way he said "hot" while looking at her through the rearview mirror tickled her tummy. She didn't look away.

"Thank you. But I need to get home. I have…um…papers to grade."

"Come on, pretty lady. Just some tea. Me cold in Miami." At the red light, he turned and looked at her. "Please."

There was a coffee shop a block away from her building. She could use the tea. *What am I afraid of? It's just tea in the afternoon, not a nightcap. Me cold too.*

"What's so funny, pretty lady?" he asked. Cecilia didn't realize she had laughed out loud.

"Oh, nothing. I'll have some tea. Thank you."

After their third cup, the waitress asked if they wanted to see a menu. Wedged in a corner of the small café, their table faced the street. The rain turned into a downpour. People walked fast, making their way home to husbands, wives, children, and pets.

"How old were you when you left Saint Thomas, pretty lady? You don't have much of an island accent."

She pulled her gaze from the window and focused on his eyes. "Why do you keep calling me 'pretty lady'? I told you my name."

"Isn't it obvious?" He stared at her, almost daring her to argue a fact.

Cecilia patted her afro, looking everywhere except at those lips. "I noticed you switch from colloquial to grammatical speech?"

"Ever the schoolteacher." He smiled. "You sound like my mom. She's a retired English teacher. I dropped out of college after two years. Couldn't figure out what I wanted to be when I grew up. I guess at thirty, I'm still waiting."

"You look much younger than thirty."

"Do you say that to all the guys?" Orson batted his long eyelashes with a wicked grin.

"Never. There's no…um…other guy." Her face heated up.

"Never 'no other guy'?" Orson raised one eyebrow, staring at her with intensity.

"Never…um…no other guy." She looked away. *Why did I say that? But it's the truth.*

"It's okay, pretty lady. Did you always know you wanted to be a teacher?"

"Yes." She perked up. "My second grade teacher in Saint Thomas inspired me. I worked hard to lose the accent. Kids teased me."

"You worked hard, period. You've accomplished a lot before your twenty-fifth birthday. I was fifteen when my family came here from Trinidad. I had a hard time too. It's been so long, but I still miss home sometimes. Life was… simpler."

"I know. So where do you live now?"

"Oh, I stay with my folks. I'm saving money to buy my own place."

"How ambitious! I'm doing the same thing. I need a house, so I can have a dog. I miss Friendy."

"Tell me about Friendy." Orson sat back, folding his hands behind his head and listening to her as if there was no one else in the world.

After a dinner of white rice and black bean soup, pulled pork, green salad, and three hours of conversation, Orson walked her to the front door of her building. He took the key ring from her and unlocked the door, holding it open for her. When she reached for the keys, he held her hand for the briefest second.

"I'd like to see you again. May I have your number, please?" he asked.

"Well, only because you asked so properly," she said in her teacher voice as she scribbled her number on the piece of paper he proffered. "And I'm not signing on any loans for you." She was already wondering what Orson would need from her tomorrow or next week. She would never give any man her hard-earned paycheck despite what her mother thought.

"Excuse me?" he said, squinting at her. "I don't understand."

"Never mind. It was a—" She waved. "Good night, Orson, Orson Matthews."

He smiled. "Good night, pretty lady."

As soon as she locked the door behind her, she ran for the phone, wishing she could see Monique right now. She dialed. *Be home, Elle… Be home…* The machine answered. She dialed another number. *Be home, Mel…*

"Hey, Mel, I met this gorgeous guy this afternoon. His name is Orson and—"

"Wait a second. Who's this? You sound like my friend Ceecee, but that can't be." Mel laughed. "Ceecee doesn't talk about *gorgeous* guys."

"Very funny, Melissa Anne. Listen—"

"I was beginning to think you were preparing to join a convent. Pray tell, girl. Don't leave anything out."

"Not much to tell…but I gave him my number."

Why was she eager to tell her friends about this man she just met? She'd never done that before. Orson was an island man. They shared similar history. Why had she said "never no other guy" earlier? He might think she was a virgin. But wasn't she a virgin? She had never given herself to a man. Regardless of what might happen with Orson, tonight Cecilia felt special. He called her "pretty lady." Would she still be pretty to him if he learned about her ugly secret?

47
Lanei

L anei rolled the rosary beads until the pads of her fingers hurt. Since her birthday a couple weeks ago, she had been coming to daily morning mass again. Nate appeared to have moved on. She'd been waiting for God's signal, but so far, he was silent.

Last week Nate had stopped by the library after lunch, and Lanei's heart had bloomed open with joy and hope. Hope for what?

"Hi, Lane," he'd said, waving to her. "I brought something special for my girl." He pulled a pink unicorn from the bag in his hand. Maria squealed, pulling down on his white coat. He picked her up and groaned. "You're getting big." He tried to put her down.

Maria wrapped her legs around his waist, refusing to go down. "I'll be four in July," Maria said. "I miss you, Uncle Nate."

Nate held Maria, but his eyes never left Lanei's. Did she see regret or was she projecting her own feelings? She wanted him to be happy. It didn't make sense for them both to suffer. She needed time to let him go as if he'd been hers. In her heart he was, and it had made life with Kevin bearable. "Uncle Nate is busy…at work," he'd said. "I miss you…a lot."

After mass she put the rosary in her purse before slipping her coat on and wrapping the wool scarf around her neck. The last snowfall had melted into black puddles, but the air bit like it had teeth. She dashed the couple blocks to Peggy's house and let herself in. Since Kevin had stopped taking his medications, life had returned to a game of survival with Lanei being the prey.

"Did you walk from church?" Peggy asked. "It's cold today."

She kissed Peggy's face. Her keen green eyes searched Lanei's. Her natural blonde hair had turned snow white. "I made chicken soup. Why don't I fix you some?" Peggy said. "Maria is napping."

Lanei saw Peggy's lips move but did not register the message. "Huh? What did you say about the soup? I'm sorry—"

"Is everything okay? You've been distracted lately." Peggy sat on the chair next to Lanei in the warm kitchen and took Lanei's hands in hers, rubbing them to bring blood to her fingers. "I know life with my son hasn't been easy, but you're a good Christian and a great mother. Kevin is lucky to have you as a wife."

Lanei scowled. "What am I lucky to have, Peg?" She regretted the words as soon as they were out. "I'm sorry—"

"Stop being sorry. You should have gotten more from life than a father who rejected you, a sick child, and stalled professional dreams. I believe in my heart that God wants his children to be happy, Lan."

Like the happiness Nate had brought into her life by being there, by loving her even when she couldn't love him back in the way that he needed. She loved Nate. Lanei swiped the tears with the back of her hand. "What... what do you mean? I'm...so confused. Kevin is your son...but...he has pushed the love out of my heart with every blow until there was none left, Peg. Leaving my heart open for—" She stopped. Peggy gave her a knowing look. "What am I supposed to do?"

"I know you respect your church doctrines, but I'm Methodist so I don't understand. I love you, and you have to raise my granddaughter. Kevin—" Peggy shook her head, stood, and poured coffee for them.

Lanei wrapped both hands around the mug, feeling the warmth thaw the coldness in her heart. "You know he stopped taking his medications. Life is... hard. Kevin is so angry."

"That boy was born angry, and Vietnam didn't help. You know, his daddy was a traveling jazz musician who put his saxophone before his son. Kevin struggled with his biracial identity. I think Fred became the father he never had. Helping the vets makes him forget about his own struggles."

"He doesn't talk much about his childhood or the war," Lanei said. "Maybe you can talk to him when he comes for dinner about going back to treatment."

"I'll try. But remember that Jesus already died for our sins, so we don't have to."

Lanei hung on to those words. Maria bounced into the kitchen, clutching the unicorn, and said, "Grandma, look what Uncle Nate gave me. I love it with all my heart."

"Sweetie, go wash your hands." Lanei stole a look at Peggy. "We're going to help Grandma cook Daddy's birthday dinner before he comes by after work."

Lanei stood and opened the fridge, pulling stuff out. She would have to decipher the words Peggy had spoken later. Her words contradicted what Father Abbott had been saying to her all these years.

She loved Peggy's words. They could bring her salvation and freedom.

48
Ella

Ella scrubbed the kitchen floor until her eyes stung with the sweat running from her scalp to her face. The weather in Miami was unusually hot for March. The air-conditioning in the house had broken down, and while she waited for the repairman, she started to clean. A clean house always seemed to lessen her anxiety, as if she could throw it away along with the grime of daily living.

Out of shape and out of breath, Ella dragged the trash can to the curb, praying no loitering neighbor would see the flesh bulging from her too-tight shorts and midriff top. She hoped the sweat would wash away the stubborn fat that clung to her like a second skin.

Last night Bernard had reached across the bed and run his hand through her hair, massaging her scalp in the way that made her forget she was mad at him for all his hurtful digs. She'd moaned as he pulled her cotton nightgown over her head. Her hungry hand explored the toned surfaces of his body. Then he'd flicked on the bedside lamp and stared at the rolls of flesh around her middle. She had pulled the sheet up to cover herself. "Elle, I told you that IUD was going to make you *fat*." He'd thrown the words like a punch. His face had registered his disgust in the flattening of his lips. He'd switched off the lamp and turned his back to her. She'd put the pillow over her head to quell her sobs.

Ella huffed her way back into the kitchen with the empty trash can, thinking about how Bernard never hit with his fists, but his words hollowed her out. After putting a new bag in the can, she washed her hands. Her stomach growled. She filled a bowl with the rest of the spaghetti she had made for the kids earlier and sat at the dining room table. The salad she'd eaten earlier was long gone, leaving an empty space inside. She yearned for Bernard to fill it with his love, his support, his presence. Holes needed to be filled. She smiled, thinking of Monique.

Wiping her mouth with the back of her hand, she reached for the letters on top of the pile and read them again. Her admission back to school for the next spring semester and the scholarship from the hospital guaranteed her return to school. She had started out in the class of 1980, and now she'd be in the class of 1988. But nothing could stop her now. She pushed the bowl away. Her academic goals filled her like the food that had been her comfort. She'd left home to be a doctor and that was what she was going to be.

It had been over seven years since she'd left Haiti, and it would take her a decade to complete her medical education. Would her papa live that long? She thought the craving for her father's acceptance had died, but just like her yet unrealized professional dreams, it simmered. Her mind made up about making the trip home, she took the spray bottle and the sponge and made her way to the master bathroom, avoiding looking at her face in the mirror.

When Bernard got home from work, she put a dinner plate in front of him and said, "I'm going to Haiti next month. I'll only be gone a weekend. Jan is in Jamaica, but Lois will keep the kids."

Bernard raised his head and punctured the air with the fork. "I'm not paying for you to go to Haiti. I told you to wait to buy a car. Now we have two car notes. These women, even the ones that are far away, fill your head with stupid ideas."

She turned from the stove, the spoon dripping gravy on the floor. "What are you talking about? Ceecee taught me to drive to relieve the stress of the commute. You've never cared to ask me how I managed with transportation since we moved here almost three years ago. I've worked for years, damn it. I can buy a round-trip ticket to go see my father."

"Your father doesn't give a shit about you, Ella. Remember?" His eyes hardened like small black marbles.

"Your mouth is like a weapon, Bernard." She threw the serving spoon in the sink. A glass shattered. "I'm going to see my father."

Bernard blinked. Alex slid off his chair and walked to Ella, reaching for her hand. "Daddy, you make Mommy sad. You're mean," the six-year-old said.

Bernard stood from his chair and walked toward them, balling his hands. "Don't be fresh, boy," he said, pulling Alex away from Ella and shoving him toward the corridor. "Go to your room." Alex tripped over a toy, turned, and looked at Bernard with hurt in his eyes as he rubbed his upper arm.

Ella rushed to her son and pulled him onto her lap on a kitchen chair. "Don't you ever *touch* my children like that, Bernard." She shook with anger. "How would it look to your Haitian *haute societé* if you go to jail for child abuse? Huh? Keep your hands to yourself around here."

Bernard stared at her. The corner of his mouth twitched. The coldness in his eyes chilled her. "If I ever raise my hand, Ella, you will *never* be able to call the police after." Something in his low voice sped up her heartbeat. "You better not go to Haiti." He took his car keys off the kitchen table and left.

The following week, her sister called. "Hello…Therese," Ella said. "You didn't write last month. Is everything okay?"

"*Oui, petite soeur*, but we…I miss you. Please come for a visit."

"I know. I've been thinking about it. But I have the kids. Bernard works long hours. Something is always breaking down in the house. The bills—" Ella stopped. "I'm going to try to come before I start school."

"Elle, Papa is happy you're going back to school. I told him last week when I got your letter. How's life…with Bernard? Are you happy?"

Ella was glad her sister could not see the confusion that must be on her face. "Bernard provides for us. You know, being in a marriage is like being in a constant state of negotiations, Têtê," Ella addressed her sister by the fond nickname she'd given Therese when she was a little girl.

"Well, I've never been married, Elle, but I sure know when I'm happy or not."

"Why did the family oppose my relationship with Bernard? You never answer that question. Why? I'll keep asking."

The deafening silence made Ella stand from the chair. Therese sighed loudly. "I had hoped to never have to tell you."

Ella swallowed something bitter in her throat. "What…what is it?"

"Come home as soon as you're able. Maybe we won't have to talk about it. After all, Bernard is your husband."

"But…but…I need—" The dial tone punched her eardrums. She had to go to Haiti to find the truth. Ella wished she could afford to take the kids with her, but they would need passports as well as tickets. She wanted to tell her father she loved him before it was too late. But what did Bernard mean by his threats? She reached for the phone and dialed.

"Hello, it's Freda. May I help you?"

"Freda, I need to see you, but I have the kids. I'm scared. I don't know what to do."

"I'll come over, Ella."

The band around her heart began to slacken.

49
Monique

In late March Monique walked into her obstetrician's office and closed the door. "Is everything okay?" the doctor asked. "I heard you wanted to talk to me before your next scheduled appointment."

She placed her folded hands on top of the mahogany desk. Her gold bracelet glinted under the fluorescent lights as if her friends were in the room urging her on. "Paul, I need to give birth to this child in Miami," Monique whispered. "That's part of my escape plan. Please help me!"

Monique had learned from Maman that Paul's sister had barely escaped to Canada with her life several years ago after her husband had been thrown in prison never to be seen again. Paul's family had been friends of the Magloires for generations. Paul looked toward the closed door, then at Monique. "You know Julien chose me to attend to you because I trained in the US and specialize in high-risk pregnancies." Paul stared at her. "So far, your first two trimesters have been…uncomplicated."

She wiped her eyes with a ball of tissue she pulled from her purse. "It's time for some complications, Paul." Monique reached for his hands. "I appreciate the danger, but you have to send me to a colleague in Miami. You understand. *Please.*"

"Monique, I have a family to protect. I can't—" He stopped and closed his eyes for several seconds. She held her breath. When he opened them, he picked up his pen and started writing in her chart. He lowered his voice. "I'll fudge some results. Whether Julien lets you go"—Paul shrugged—"that's out of my hands."

Monique drove past Julien's house and stopped several blocks away in front of a two-story house up the hill. The gate was open, and there were no cars in the driveway. She exhaled and climbed out of her car.

"What a pleasant surprise, Monique," Amelie Etienne exclaimed. She was dressed in a gray pleated skirt and a black silk short-sleeve blouse that showed off her keen hazel eyes. Her black heels echoed on the marble floor. "Follow me to the sunroom. I was having a drink. I missed you at dinner last month."

"I'm sorry to barge in on you like this, Amelie, but I need your help," Monique said, lowering herself onto a chaise. The ceiling fan lifted her hair around her face.

Amelie poured a glass of orange juice and placed it next to Monique on a glass-topped table. "I should be glad Julien is having a child, but I don't condone the way he went about it." She sipped her drink and stared at a point over Monique's head. "Of my three sons, Julien and I had the closest relationship. In his teens I spent a year in France with him taking art classes, visiting museums, and teaching him about the world beyond Haiti. Hector and his older brothers teased him mercilessly." Amelie closed her eyes, her skin crinkling like tissue paper, and Monique thought she'd fallen asleep. "I guess he had to show his father that he could be as ruthless as they are. Julien confided to me that he wanted to let you go. He knows that you'll never be the wife he wants, but I think he's afraid of Hector. Please don't tell anyone what I'm about to tell you." She lowered her voice even though no one was around. "I wouldn't have ever married a man like Hector, but I got caught in his web because of my late father's political views. Hector told me once that your father humiliated him in front of his men when he went to Magloire Enterprise to shake them up. He holds grudges forever, Monique."

Monique placed the glass back on the table and sat up. "But I met Julien randomly at a party. I almost didn't go."

"The hostess told Hector your mother was coming and that you were flying in that day and would be at the party too. Nothing random about it, *ma petite*. Hector was waiting for the right punishment for your father. He could have done a number of things to your family, but in Haiti making a *sex slave* out of someone's daughter is the ultimate defilement. Especially a girl with your pedigree and ambition." Amelie fiddled with the pleats on her skirt. "Julien broke my heart."

Numb from this revelation, Monique saw Julien for the weakling that he was. He could let her go and deal with his father's taunts. He could stand for something. "Thank you, Amelie. I know this wasn't easy for you."

Amelie dabbed at her eyes with a dainty hanky and said, "I'm sorry. I got carried away. You mentioned you needed my help?"

When Monique finished talking, Amelie reached for her hand and they both cried. "Haiti is full of pitfalls for idealistic women like us," the older woman said. "When the time comes, rest assured that I'll talk to Julien about doing the right thing for once."

Three months later, Monique peered through the window of the plane, her hand stroking her huge belly to thank her baby for this miracle. The June heat filled the cabin as if it too wanted to escape Haiti. Her spirit had made this journey daily for the past three years, but this time her body was free to follow. Julien's voice intruded into her happiness.

"Monique, I'm letting you go because I want my son to get the best care if needed," he'd said. "I hope the tests are wrong about his heart."

In less than two hours, the plane taxied to the gate in Miami. The baby kicked hard. Monique patted her tummy and said, "Hang in there, baby. I still have a couple weeks. I need to spend time with my tribe before your arrival."

She climbed into Chantal's car, and they made their way to the hospital. Cecilia and Ella would be there. They thought they were meeting Chantal at the cafeteria to hear important news about Monique. Before Monique reached the table, Cecilia turned, and screams erupted, followed by gasps, tears, and laughter. Heads turned toward the group that rushed Monique and enveloped her in an embrace.

"*Oh mon Dieu*," Ella said, "Moe, you're here. How—"

Monique dropped her bulk onto a cafeteria chair. "I'm here," she said simply and started crying with relief.

Through her friends' tears, she was bathed in love, companionship, and compassion.

"We've missed you so much," Cecilia said. "Oh, you'll have to meet Orson—the guy I've been telling you about."

Monique squeezed Cecilia's hand. "Can't wait. Now you all stop crying. This is a goddamn celebration. I only wish Lan was here."

"Moe's back," Ella sang. "Now tell us how you managed to get here. I can't believe Julien let you leave Haiti."

"My obstetrician helped," Monique said. "Julien wants his *son* to have the best."

It seemed they would never run out of words to say. They hung out every night at Cecilia's. Monique peered longingly at the den which was supposed to have been her bedroom. Three days later, on their way to see Freda, Monique made a detour to the hospital. She gave birth to a healthy baby girl on June 23, 1983. She named her Odile Marie. Julien, who'd expected a son, canceled his flight. He dodged the arrest for her 1980 rape in Miami. But she would never give up.

She settled into one of the guest bedrooms in her family home. The house smelled like Pine-Sol and lemon. The Haitian couple who took care of the property had prepared it for Monique's arrival. Cecilia fluffed the pillow behind Monique's head and tickled the baby's foot. "Odile looks just like you. She's beautiful," Cecilia said. "I'm so glad I'm on summer break, although Orson wants to spend every minute with me." The glow on Cecilia's face showcased her beauty.

"I can't wait to meet him," Monique said. "He's a lucky guy. I hope he knows that."

"He's fine-looking too." Ella winked, her big eyes disappearing into her pudgy face behind her glasses. "Brian will die if you don't let him see you soon. He looked all over the hospital for you."

"That's why I picked another hospital," Monique said. "He has called and we have talked every night since I've been here. I want to see him, but I'm afraid." She looked at Cecilia and Ella. "Why is he still single?"

Ella glanced at Cecilia and said, "Well, we didn't tell you since the wedding didn't take place, but…about six months ago his fiancée called off the wedding less than two months before the date."

"Oh," Monique said, feeling happy and wretched at the same time.

The following day, Monique left Odile with Ella's sitter Lois. She walked into Freda's office. They embraced for a long time as Monique sobbed. "Remember me, Freda?"

"Of course! You're memorable, my dear." Freda smiled, pointing at Cecilia and Ella seated next to Monique on the couch. "Your tribe here told me what happened to you over the years. I'm so sorry."

"I can't begin to tell you what I have endured. I fear the hatred for Julien will corrode my insides."

"Yet, you've survived," Freda said. "This man can break your spirit only if you allow him to."

Monique nodded. "I have a daughter who I wasn't sure I was going to like. Now I think I love her. She will need me to protect her."

"She has a lioness for a mother," Freda said, shifting her weight in the leather chair and facing the women. "You know, in all the years I've been counseling abused women, I've seen broken bones, broken spirits, broken families, and broken dreams." Freda squinted. The three women leaned forward. "I'm no scientist, but I believe our *island* culture predisposed us to accept inequality, injustice, and oppression as a condition of having been born female. Know your worth, ladies."

They nodded, listened, cried, and talked. When they finished, Monique said, "Thank you, Freda. There were so many days in Haiti I wished I could talk to you."

The weeks flew by. Julien called every morning. Monique delayed seeing Brian, although every fiber of her body screamed to be held by him. Flowers perfumed the bedroom. Their nightly talks lulled her to sleep.

"The flowers are beautiful, but you need to stop," Monique had said the night before. "It's beginning to look like a funeral home in here."

"I wish I could bring them myself," Brian had said. "I'd like to see you and meet your daughter."

"Well, there's a six-week-old lady who'd like to meet you, and her maman wouldn't mind saying hello either," Monique said. "Are you free tomorrow afternoon?"

"Really?" Brian had asked excitedly. "I'll be there even if I have to cancel God's surgery. But I don't think he's on my schedule tomorrow." Monique had let out a throaty laugh that sounded unfamiliar to her ears before going to sleep.

Now the smell of food welcomed her into the house from the garage. Her stomach growled. She hadn't eaten since breakfast, and it was past four. She peeked into the kitchen and got a glimpse of the Haitian spread prepared by the restaurant that had catered the dinner. She greeted the server and kissed a sleeping Odile in the bassinet next to the babysitter.

After a quick shower, she ripped the price tag off a teal blue spaghetti strap dress and pulled it over her head. The ruffles at the hem stopped above her knees and swirled when she moved. The gold chain with the entwined hearts pendant Brian had sent the week before was nestled in her cleavage. This chain would never come off her body. Like her bracelet, it would connect her to Brian forever. She stepped into a pair of four-inch slide-in heels. As she walked out of the bedroom, the doorbell rang. Her legs shook on her way to open the door. She stared at Brian until it looked like she was seeing him through a clear wet plastic. Then he folded her into the cocoon of his chest.

"You look beautiful," he whispered, clearing his throat.

She reached up, ran her palm over his short hair, and said, "You cut your locks. Now I can see your tamarind eyes." They walked into the dining room. Brian reached into the bassinet, took Odile in his arms, and kissed her forehead. "Whoa! She looks just like you, Moe."

They talked all through dinner, filling in almost three years of absences. After dessert she led Brian to the living room with Odile cradled in his arms. Soon the baby whimpered. Monique said, "I have to feed her."

With Odile nestled in the crook of her elbow, she reached for Brian's hand and turned toward the hallway. Brian hesitated on the threshold of the bedroom. She pulled him inside and closed the door. Seated on a chaise, Monique slid her finger under the strap of her dress and pushed it off her right shoulder. She drew her breast from the strapless bra, placed her engorged nipple in her baby's mouth, and raised her head. Their eyes locked. She smiled. Brian blew air through his lips. The wet sounds of Odile's sucking broke the silence.

A bead of sweat collected on Brian's upper lip. His tongue slithered out, and he sucked it back into his mouth. Seconds ticked by. Their breathing spiked. He shifted his weight from foot to foot and let out a low growl as a wet stain spread on the front of his khaki pants. Monique breathed through her parted lips. Her red-painted toes curled in her shoes.

"Monique," he whispered. "What are we going to do?"

The telephone sounded loud in the silence of the house. She handed Odile to Brian, and they walked to the family room.

"How did your postnatal exam go today?" Julien asked. "Can't wait to see you and meet my daughter. I want us to start over, Monique. We're a real family now."

Monique frowned. She pulled the receiver from her ear and stared at it as if Julien could see her with Brian as he held Julien's daughter. "Checkup was fine," Monique replied.

"I booked your flight for tomorrow."

"But I want to do some shopping. I—"

"Monique, please come home. My father can't wait to see his granddaughter. You understand." He hung up.

"Moe, is everything going to be okay?" Brian asked.

"I hope so. I'm counting on Julien's mother to help me. She has some influence on him." Monique sat next to him on the couch, his presence disturbing every molecule in her body. "I'm not going back. I'm safe here, but my family in Haiti is not. Amelie promised to help."

"Are you okay if I leave? I have to make rounds."

"I'm fine. Thank you for coming." She blushed. He smiled. "I mean...I enjoyed your company for dinner."

He placed his finger on her lips. "Good night. Enjoy your day tomorrow with the island sisters."

The man listens.

Monique called Julien the next morning. "I can't come back today. Odile has a fever. I want to take her to her pediatrician on Monday." She needed to buy time. She hadn't heard from Amelie or Tina.

"Monique, you're playing a dangerous game." The trill in his voice doused her with terror.

He hung up.

Monique wished she knew how to pray to something or somebody as she dialed. "Tina, please tell me you talked to Amelie today. I don't want to call her house."

"One of Amelie's servants told me she went to the Dominican Republic unexpectedly last week to see her sick sister and is scheduled to return later today," Tina said. "I'll be waiting for her at the airport. Go have fun with your friends. I'll be in touch."

"Okay, *mon amie*," Monique said. "Lanei's coming today. They surprised me. I'm so happy."

Monique dropped off Odile at Chantal's house before the trio headed to the airport. They made a circle. "Lan, you're here!" Monique kissed the frown lines on Lanei's forehead like she wanted to iron them out. Anger and regret can crater the skin into fault lines that could one day open and let your essence leak out like sap. Monique would die fighting for her and now her daughter's freedom from oppression. "Where are we going, Ceecee?" Monique asked as they all climbed back into Cecilia's new Ford sedan.

"Nice car," Lanei said.

"Ladies, we're going to spend the day at the Oasis Spa," Cecilia said. "We'll get manicures, pedicures, massages, and eat cucumber sandwiches. My treat."

Ella sighed and said, "I need to *only* eat cucumber for the rest of the year. Maybe then I'll lose this weight."

"Elle, you look like you've lost a…few from when I saw you in March," Lanei said. "Don't you think so, Ceecee?"

Before Cecilia could answer, Monique said, "Girl, you are *fat*. You're embracing your Haitian womanhood!"

"Moe, that's insensitive," Cecilia said. "Elle is trying."

Ella laughed. "Ladies, in our culture that's a compliment. Haitian men like their women with plenty of meat on their bones. Except now Bernard is very *American*, if you know what I mean."

Monique said, "What exactly are you saying, Elle?"

"Not now, Moe," Ella replied.

At the spa Monique surrendered to the ministrations of the staff, feeling the stress leave her body through the vapors of the sauna. In the Jacuzzi she threw a handful of fragrant suds at Cecilia, and a water fight ensued, accompanied by giggles. Ella's glasses fell, and they all plunged their faces below the water to look for them. Monique couldn't recall ever being happier than she was in this moment.

"Lan, wait till you meet *Orson*," Monique said. "It's no wonder Ceecee is so happy. That man is *fine*. Bet he knows how to take care of business." They all stared at Cecilia.

"Don't you all look at me like that," Cecilia said. "I wouldn't know how he takes care of business because I'm not ready for *that*. It's only been three months since we met."

"Are you kidding me?" Monique said, licking her lips. "I wanted to rip the clothes off Brian last night. I was so horny I couldn't sleep until I found my sweet spot."

"Moe, that's a sin," Lanei said, blushing. "Besides, Ceecee is doing the right thing. Sex is not the most important part of a relationship. It's the communion of the spirits."

Ella rolled her eyes. Monique snickered.

"Really, Lanei, don't you want to fuck Nate?" Monique said. "Oh, excuse me! I mean have *communion* with Nate." Her laughter echoed in the large room, and the other women joined in. Lanei leaned over and kissed Monique's wet cheek. "I missed you, sister."

The rest of the day Monique was filled with hope through the friendship that had sustained her even when miles separated them. When Cecilia dropped her at home later that afternoon, Monique said, "I'm looking forward to seeing Mel and Mike at dinner tomorrow, Ceecee. Love y'all!" She waved, walking into the house with Odile in her arms.

After recounting the day to Brian during their phone call, sleep teased Monique's body as she basked in her new freedom. "Sweet dreams, Brian," she whispered.

"I'll dream about you," he said. She surrendered to a peaceful slumber.

A loud noise coming from somewhere in the house woke her up. She fumbled with the receiver. There was no sound. She turned on the lamp and listened before running to the front door. "Who's it?" Fear doused her awake.

"Open up!" Chantal said. Monique yanked the door open. "Esther called me. Your line is busy." Monique blinked as if to wake up from a nightmare. "They set your parents' house on fire. Auntie Lucia is in the hospital with burns. They arrested Uncle Marcel again. While Esther and her husband were in the hospital with Auntie, they took Rodrigue out of bed." Chantal blew her nose.

Monique dropped to her knees. "*Oh, mon Dieu!* What have I done now?" she said, moaning. "Rodrigue is just a little boy. My poor nephew. All I wanted was to live a normal life and raise my daughter in safety. I wanted to escape the abuse, Chantal." Monique beat the tile floor with her palms until pain shot through her shoulders. "Amelie was supposed to stop Julien."

Chantal helped her up from the floor. "Let's call Esther."

Monique picked up the phone and realized she hadn't hung it up properly after talking to Brian earlier. What if Amelie had called her? Well, it was too late now. She dialed. "Julien, I'm going to the airport soon, and I'll be on the first flight to Haiti. Please…bring Rodrigue back. Please," Monique begged. "He's just a boy."

"Now you're begging." He slammed the phone down.

Monique made several calls. None of them to Brian. She had to go back to the lion's den to keep her family safe. They had burned her mother. She retched into the toilet bowl, clutching at her stomach to ease the pain. Julien would pay one day for his wickedness. Monique hung on to that as she went back to the last place on earth she wanted to be.

50
Cecilia

$\sim$

Cecilia drove to the beach with Orson after dropping the women at home after the spa. Orson loved the outdoors. Cecilia breathed in the smell of the ocean. The warm breeze caressed her skin, and she fit her small hand into his, feeling his heartbeat thrumming on his fingertips. After the day at the spa, she wanted to crawl into bed with Orson and see if he could "take care of business." She giggled nervously. But Cecilia had no prior sexual experience for comparison. Except for the rape. A violent act that left her still afraid.

"What's so funny, pretty lady," Orson asked, looking down at her from his great height. The sunset cast a golden glow over his square face. She fought the urge to bring his wide mouth down to hers.

"Oh…something Moe said." She squeezed his hand. "That girl is funny. Now I wish Lanei could move back here too. We had so much fun today. It's like we were freshmen again."

She walked faster, kicking the sand with her bare toes as she tried to keep up with Orson's strides. The subtle hints he sent her did not help her anxiety about letting a man see and touch her body. Was she ready for that? She needed to be sure that he would be there after he learned the truth about her past. It had only taken three months to feel as if Orson had always been part of her life. He was patient, nurturing, and smart. "So what's on the menu for tomorrow, chef?" she asked. "I bragged about your cooking to everybody who's going to be there."

"Patience, love. I'm glad Bernard and Mike are coming. The four of you *and* Mel…whoa!" He laughed.

She elbowed his ribs. "Hey, don't make fun of my tribe." She smiled. "Oh, I invited Larry and his wife too. Make extra food so they can take some home."

"You have such a big heart. Larry is lucky to have you as a friend. If he didn't have a wife, I'd be jealous."

"Larry is a good man. I hope his wife beats her cancer." She sighed. "I'm starving. The cucumber sandwiches at the spa were fresh, but I need real food now."

Back at the apartment, she opened the fridge and pulled out two cold cans of soda. She planned to get booze for tomorrow. Orson did not drink alcohol or smoke. The man was like a saint. "I just had a brilliant idea, Orson. How about you go to culinary school? You're a natural."

"I have a better idea." Orson took the can from her hand and placed it on the counter. He pulled her to him, kissing her deeply. She closed her eyes, feeling her body move. When she opened them, Orson was on top of her on the couch, licking the salt off her body.

Suddenly, she couldn't breathe. She pushed him off. Feelings of lust, disgust, and fear mingled in her brain. "Orson, stop!" He stopped. "I'm sorry, but…I'm not ready." She sat up.

"It's okay, honey. Take all the time you need." Orson brushed her bare shoulder with his warm lips. "I'm not going anywhere."

She showered and changed into a loose housedress. They ate in silence with Beethoven playing on the stereo. The day they'd met she had told him she had never been with a man. She didn't want to lose him. What should she do? Was this the perfect time to tell him why she wasn't ready? How she may never be ready? But the words could not pass her lips. She had survived by never talking about her rape. It was her secret. No man needed to ever know about it. They cleaned the kitchen and put away the leftovers. They snuggled on the couch to watch old movies in the living room when the phone rang. They looked at each other and frowned. It was late. "Hello," she said. "Moe! Is everything… What? No!" She dropped the phone and stood.

Orson placed the receiver on the base and asked, "What is it?"

"Monique has to go back to Haiti on the first flight this morning. Her husband—" She shook her head. "I'm going over there."

"I'm sorry she has to go so soon. But what can you do? You need your rest. We have guests coming later for dinner."

Cecilia glared at him. "There won't be any dinner. It was to celebrate Moe's return. You don't understand anything," she yelled, shocking herself.

Orson stood from the couch and turned off the television. "I don't understand because you won't tell me anything. These women have lives and families outside of you. What about your life? Do you have to stand guard over everybody? Don't you ever want a man of your own? I—"

"Orson, please leave," she said in a calm voice when she really wanted to scream until all her angst was poured out, leaving her with peace. "Maybe I don't want a man. They all seem to come attached to pain."

He reached for her. "I'm sorry, pretty lady."

"Don't touch me," she said, stepping out of his reach. "*Go!*"

After Orson left, she dressed quickly, and locked the door behind her. She closed her eyes before starting the car. What had she done? Would Orson come back to her? But Monique needed her. Cecilia had survived on her own. She was too angry and afraid for Monique to care about ruining her relationship with Orson.

51

Lanei

anei and Ella climbed into Cecilia's car in the early morning. No one said a word. Periodic sniffling, nose blowing, and sighing broke the silence. Earlier, Monique's apparent escape had given Lanei hope that she too could one day be free. She looked at Cecilia driving next to her and wondered why she had tears running down her face. Unlike the three of them, Cecilia had no tormentor. Lanei hoped this man Orson would be worthy of this successful and beautiful sister, and that Cecilia knew her worth.

They found Monique pacing the family room after Chantal let them in. Dark circles ringed Monique's eyes, keeping the fear trapped inside them. Lanei knew fear. They were constant companions. She pulled Monique into the middle of the circle of women. "Thank you for coming, sisters," Monique said. "I don't know when I'm going to see you again, but I know that I will. When I come back, it will be to stay."

"It's hard to fight one man, Moe," Lanei said. "How do you fight a regime, especially now that you have a child?"

Monique pulled them down to the couch. "When I found out I was pregnant, I wanted to rip this thing out of my body. But I love my daughter. I'll protect her with my life. Tina and I have a group of young militants in Pass-It-Along. I'm fighting the regime in my own way, Lan. We use education as a weapon. We take self-defense classes. We're preparing to fight for what we deserve."

Lanei shook her head as she listened to Monique, a new understanding dawning. To live in happiness required struggle. The night before this trip, Kevin had reached under her nightgown in the bed. "Kevin, please stop. I have…my cycle," she'd said.

"Oh, so I let you go to Miami and I get what?" His nails had dug into the soft flesh of her inner thighs with malice.

When Kevin was done, she had taken a long shower, gotten dressed, and waited for daylight to go to the airport. *It was rape.* Cecilia and Ella might not understand what Monique's life was like living with someone intent on having total control of your body. Lanei did.

"Kevin rapes me," Lanei said with a new certainty. Three pairs of eyes stared at her.

"Julien rapes me," Monique said.

"Bernard doesn't ever force himself on me," Ella said smugly. "He just thinks I can't be…a doctor. But I'll show him. I would have left him long ago if he'd abused me."

"Being disrespectful is abuse, Elle," Monique said.

A look of horror smeared Cecilia's face. "Why…why do we attract men who would do this to us? I need to understand before I commit myself to *any* man. I'll be damned if I'm going to let a man abuse me after my own mother nearly destroyed me."

"Ceecee, you have accomplished your professional goals," Lanei said. "You don't need a man to take care of you. Remember when I said that we all had holes to fill?" She looked at Monique who just stared at the wall. "You have filled all of yours."

"Not really, Lan," Cecilia said. "I have wounds that still need healing." Lanei saw Monique nod at Cecilia. Those two shared a secret Lanei and Ella did not know about. "But I'm grateful to be where I am today."

"I'm going to Haiti soon to see my father. My sister claims she has information about Bernard that I need to know and can use as leverage. Bernard can't stop me. I have a scholarship. I'm going to be a doctor," Ella said.

"Don't lose that drive, Elle," Lanei said. "Kevin *wants* me to become a pharmacist to take care of him. But I will do it for me. I want to. I need to." She fingered her rosary in her pocket.

"Meanwhile, we stay and get raped daily," Monique said, kicking the coffee table with her foot. "I would kill Julien in a heartbeat, and I would not lose one second of sleep over it. That asshole will pay for what he's putting me and my family through."

As the sun broke through the early morning mist, Lanei stood up from the love seat and stretched. Her neck hurt. She shook the others awake. "Time to go."

They waited with Monique at the gate until her flight was called. They clinked their bracelets and hugged. Monique disappeared down the corridor with Odile as if she was being swallowed by a giant mouth. Lanei believed Monique would find her way back to freedom.

But could Lanei ever leave her marriage, go back to school, love another man, and keep her faith?

52
Ella

Ella closed her eyes, but Lanei's crying since they had dropped Monique off at the airport needled her migraine. She turned from the front seat of the car and patted Lanei's hand to calm her down. "Let's go to my house for some breakfast," Ella said. "Ceecee, do you want to invite Orson?"

"Elle, I don't know if he's going to see me again. I practically kicked him out of the apartment last night. Orson doesn't understand…our friendship," Cecilia said. "You know, since we started seeing each other, I haven't met any of his friends."

"Bernard never brings anybody to the house," Ella said. "Sometimes I have to explain…*us* to him. Orson will call you if he's smart. Men don't always understand female friendships."

The quiet house soothed Ella's nerves. She flipped the light switch for the fan in the kitchen. The sun peeked through the picture window over the sink and chased the gloom from Ella's heart.

"Elle, can you make that New Year's Day soup?" Lanei said. "I miss it."

"I think I have all the ingredients, but it takes time," Ella replied.

"Well, we have all day," Lanei said. "Right, Ceecee?"

"Sure. I'm sorry about canceling the dinner party but—" Cecilia stopped.

"Nobody is in the mood for that…without Moe," Ella said. "Oh man, she loves my soup. Remember the first year I made it? It was New Year's Day, 1977. I was pregnant with Alex, and it was my nineteenth birthday." Ella swallowed, overcome with nostalgia.

"I remember," Lanei said. "We were so young." She stood from the kitchen stool and filled the coffee maker.

Cecilia smiled. "Lan, we're still young at twenty-five. Plenty of time to make changes, learn new things. Life is a journey. We ride the peaks, aiming higher, and we swim the lows, keeping our heads above water."

Ella squinted behind her glasses at Cecilia. "Now you sound like Freda." She pulled pots, bowls, and cutting boards from their hiding places inside the cupboards. Ella heard Perrine coughing in her room. "I'll be back," Ella said, turning toward the sound. "Start peeling the vegetables, Ceecee. Lan, start breakfast."

They worked in silence to avoid waking up the household. The smell of the Haitian coffee filled the house. It always reminded Ella of where she and Bernard had started from. She turned from the fridge and saw him standing in the doorway dressed in a white polo shirt and new brown pleated dress pants. His perfume competed with the coffee and won.

"What's going on here?" he asked, in lieu of greeting the women.

Ella stared at him hard. "What does it look like, Bernard? You don't even greet guests in our house." Ella cut her eyes at him. "Where are you going? It's Sunday."

"I'm having breakfast at the country club with Monsieur Meridien." He puffed up his chest like a rooster. "We have business to discuss after golf."

He poured himself a cup of coffee and turned to leave. Lanei cleared her throat and said, "Congratulations on completing your graduate degree, Bernard. It makes it so much easier when you have support. I'm so happy Elle is going back to school in January."

"Yeah," he said, his lips flattening into a smile, but his eyes were opaque black and narrowed. He stared at Ella, and she stared back, knowing he could see the conviction in her eyes. She had the scholarship from the hospital, an IUD, and the passion. He took his keys off the table and left.

Ella looked up from stirring the pot when she heard the door open again. "Did you forget something?" she asked, raising her eyebrows. "Like your expensive golf clubs?" She snickered.

Bernard tsk-tsked. "I have an idea, *mon amour*. Let's meet in town for a movie later. I'll call you with the details." He pulled the door closed behind him.

"How nice," Lanei said. "Kevin and I don't go anywhere together. He says we have no money. In his free time, he drives vets to appointments."

"So is Nate still dating what's-her-name?" Ella asked. "We met her and Fred in March at your birthday party. You should have seen your face when he pulled her from behind him. Kind of mousy-looking though. No competition, Lan." Ella winked.

Lanei's face heated up. "Becky was very…nice. But…I think my friendship with Nate intimidated her even though Nate stayed away. They broke up last month. I feel sorry for Nate."

"Do you really now?" Ella said, thinking Lanei was a lousy liar.

"Nate deserves to be with someone who can give him what he wants," Lanei said. "I feel…responsible."

Alex and Perrine bounced into the kitchen, and the women turned their attention to the children's adorable faces. The women ate soup, drank coffee and booze, and cried about Monique's departure.

Later that afternoon, Ella hugged Lanei and Cecilia hard. They were leaving so she could get ready for the movie. "Hang tough, Elle. You will succeed," Lanei said. "I love you, sister."

"Love you too," Ella said. "Remember, no soldier will be left on the battlefield. Moe said so."

After packing overnight bags for her children to stay with Lois, Ella walked into her bedroom and opened her closet door. About an hour later, she looked at the pile of clothes on the floor that no longer fit and cringed. No popcorn or soda at the movie tonight. She was starting today. Bernard had not taken her to any social functions since the debacle last year. She was too fat. The shame still stung.

On Haitian Flag Day last May, Ella had stared at a woman dressed in a black sequined gown with ruby studded jewels, representing the colors of the Haitian flag. A tiara was perched on the woman's golden hair. Her light gray eyes stopped on Bernard. It was the woman Ella had seen with him on the poster. Ella wanted to disappear into the black polyester pants she had managed to stuff herself into and the white long-sleeved blouse that hid her jiggly arms. She blended well with the waitstaff in her flat black shoes. Ella moved from under the giant chandelier, feeling like a specimen under a microscope. A Haitian flag stood behind the podium with about a dozen chairs lined against the wall with names pinned on the backrests. She adjusted her glasses and saw Bernard's name next to Representative Meridien. It was as if the elite of Haiti had congregated in the room. People covered in gold and perfume milled about, speaking French and sipping probably expensive wine.

The woman waltzed toward Ella and Bernard in the hotel lobby. Ella reached for Bernard's hand.

"*Bienvenue, bienvenue*, Bernie. Come! I want you to meet our Haitian lobbyist in DC," She said, kissing Bernard on both cheeks. She waved her red-lacquered fingers at Ella. "You must be the *wife*."

"I'm Ella. Nice to meet you—"

"*Representative* Meridien," the woman said slowly as if Ella was dim-witted. She looped her arm through Bernard's, pulling him with her and leaving Ella in their wake. "Bernie," Representative Meridien said, leaning close to his ear and whispering something Ella could not hear. Bernard laughed.

Ella grabbed a glass of red wine from a passing waiter and hurried after them. A light-skinned man with jet-black hair wearing a black suit with a red tie waved his arms as he spoke in French to a group of well-attired people. "And I hate Haitians who try to pass in the US for what they were never part of back home in Haiti," the man said. Ella bristled and drained half her glass, staring at Bernard who pouted as if he knew such people.

"Oh, I hate the imposters," Representative Meridien said, pinching her long nose as if to block an unpleasant odor. "America brings the riffraff from the bowels of our country into our midst. They steal. They lie. They plot against those of us with pedigree. I have more respect for someone who kills for honor than a thief." She patted Bernard's hand. "Errol," she said to the light-skinned man. "This is *the* Bernard Antoine I've been telling you about. Bernard has won many academic and professional awards for his success at the university and his community involvement. He understands *our* cause. Bernie was born and educated in Port-au-Prince, but his family hails from our proud North like us."

Ella spat the red wine back into her glass and stammered, "Wha...what's she talking—" She whimpered when Bernard squeezed her fingers. He extended his hand across Ella's chest to shake the lobbyist's hand and knocked her wine glass, spilling its contents all over her white blouse. "Oh, I'm sorry," Bernard said, shaking his head like she was a naughty child. "Now we must leave. Obviously, I can't take you anywhere, Ella."

"Don't leave, Bernie," Representative Meridien said with a pout. "I have clothes in my suite. Surely, we can find something *she* can fit into."

"Come on, *ma chère*." Bernard snorted. "Nothing of yours would fit *her*."

In the car Bernard had looked straight at the road. His face a mask. Who was that man? Did she even know her husband? "Why did you lie about where you came from, Bernard?" she'd asked, turning from the passenger seat to look at him. "You don't think they'll find out the truth about your origins if they go to Haiti."

"Ella, you bury your head in those outdated medical books as if you were really going to be a doctor." His laughter stabbed all her pudgy parts. "You need to educate yourself about the world around you. *Ces gens sont des exilés politiques.* They will never go back to Haiti as long as the dictatorial regime is in power. Ask your *sister* Monique what the regime is like. They can keep you in, and they can keep you out. I need the Meridiens and their entourage now to get to where I want to go. Then one day they will need *me*."

"Where do you want to go, Bernard? Is there room for me and the children in your plan?"

His face relaxed into an expansive smile. "Always, Elle. You'll always be in my plan."

Ella had cried all the way home.

But tonight her husband was taking her to the movies. Ella hadn't seen Representative Meridien since that disastrous night. Now she applied a light coat of makeup, remembering his white polo shirt. She pulled her hair into a tight French braid that made her face look thinner. She wished he had come back to pick her up, but they would cuddle when they returned home and hopefully make love anywhere in the house since the kids were spending the night with Lois. Her future was on track. Bernard wasn't the perfect husband, but was there ever such a thing?

Dressed in a long black gathered skirt with an elastic waistband and a green cotton sleeveless blouse, Ella draped a colorful satin shawl over her arms, locked her car door, and made her way into the movie theater looking for the concierge sign where Bernard had said he'd be waiting.

She froze in her tracks. Standing under the sign was her husband in the arms of Representative Meridien. His hand cupped her chin, and his mouth covered hers. Ella gasped. Bernard looked up and his eyes locked on hers. Like a robot she trotted toward them, the ground shifting under her feet like quicksand. "What's she doing here, *mon amour*?" Representative Meridien said, looking back-and-forth between her and Bernard. "I thought you were *separated.*"

"Don't worry, *ma belle*." Bernard kissed the tip of the woman's nose. "It ends tonight." He sneered at Ella, disdain coating his face. "Now you're following me. I'm leaving you."

Their laughter inundated Ella's brain with panic and confusion. She bolted for the door. The drizzling rain felt like an outward expression of her weeping heart. She put the car in reverse and accelerated out of the parking lot. Bernard had wanted her to see this. Why? He could have just left. At a red light Ella pulled down the rearview mirror and stared at her haunted face. Anger seeped into every pore of her body. "I live with a monster."

The rain pounded on the roof of the car. The whooshing sound of the wipers seemed to clear her head of the cobwebs Bernard had stuffed it with over the years. She couldn't let him get away with treating her this way. She needed to tell *Ms.* Meridien who Bernard Antoine really was. At the next light, she made a sharp U-turn. By the time she saw the headlights and braked, her car fishtailed, and the sound of crashing metal seared into her brain as she disappeared into darkness.

53

Monique

❧

Julien took Odile from Monique's arms and whispered, "I'm your Papa, pretty girl." He kissed the baby with a tenderness that surprised Monique. She stole glances at Julien while he drove her back to her prison from the airport. Her hand rubbed the pendant around her neck as if it could grant her a wish. To be in Miami.

"Julien, where are Papa and Rod—"

"Don't say a word, Monique, or you may never see them again."

She closed her eyes when the front door shut behind her. Anita was waiting in the bedroom upstairs. "Welcome back, madame," Anita said as she took the baby from Monique. "Look at that pretty girl. She favors you."

Julien walked into the bedroom. Anita lowered her head and left with the infant. He closed the door behind Anita and turned to Monique. "Do you have any idea how weak and impotent you make me look in front of my father? He came here to see Odile last night."

"Julien—" Monique said, drying her sweaty palms on her skirt.

He lunged at her. "I didn't ask you a question." He unbuckled and removed his leather belt as if in slow motion. "If you fight me today, Monique, I swear you'll never see your nephew again."

He threw her face down on the bed, bunched her skirt up around her waist, and pulled off her underwear. The spanking seemed to last an eternity. Slaps and punches made Monique feel like a warrior, but a spanking reduced her to a slave. When she came to, Anita was ministering to the lacerations on her back and buttocks. Monique screamed.

"Shh. It's going to be all right now, madame," Anita whispered. "Your sister called and said your father and nephew are home. Bide your time. God is watching."

"Anita, please don't mention God to me. He must be a fucking Haitian dictator. We're all in hell. Can't you see that?"

"But God is all I have," Anita said with hurt in her voice.

"I'm sorry." Monique took the small woman in her arms. "Please forgive me."

In the weeks that followed, Monique lost herself in caring for Odile and plotting in her head the different ways she could kill Julien. When Esther walked into her bedroom one afternoon, Monique was running her fingers through her matted hair. "I had to come today to check on you," Esther said. "You won't answer the phone. I know things must be hard but—"

"You have no idea what my life is like, Esther." Monique cut her off. "Does Serge ever beat you? Does he rape you every night? Julien says I ruined him. Can't get it up with anybody else." Her laughter sounded demented in her own ears. "*What a fucking privilege!*"

"Sweetheart, I came in peace." Esther raised her hands palms up. "Maman asks for you every day. She's been staying with me since she left the hospital last week. Papa is fixing the house." Esther rocked Monique in her arms. "Moe, there are some good Haitian men. It's important that you know that. Serge has never raised his hand to me, nor does he cheat. He values and respects our family. Men like Julien and his father can do what they do because of the regime. They're cowards. You'll see them run one day."

Monique clutched Esther like a lifeline. "I'm sorry...for all the pain I've caused the family. Papa doesn't talk to me. Solange—" Monique shrugged. "It'll break my heart to see Maman. Esther, what have I done? Poor Rodrigue. Amelie was supposed to help, but she couldn't come back from the Dominican Republic. I have since learned that her sister died in surgery. Forgive me."

"Nothing to forgive. You were trying to save yourself. As for the family, everyone is scared. I admire your strength and conviction. I would leave with my family so you could escape, but Papa can't."

"I know." Monique pulled away from Esther and blew her nose. "I don't know what I'm going to do."

Monique stood in the doorway of the nursery that night and watched the back of Julien's head as he read to Odile and cradled her in his arms like he did every night. "I love you, Ode. You're my angel," he said, kissing her cheek as he placed the sleeping infant in the crib. He turned and saw Monique. He smiled and said, "Thank you. We're a family."

She turned her back and walked out of the room.

Five months after returning from Miami, Monique was pregnant again. "But I'm still breastfeeding," she said to her obstetrician.

"Breastfeeding is not a contraceptive, Monique," Paul said. "I could have prescribed something for you if you'd asked."

"I can't buy anything like that here. Julien would know. Please, I can't have this baby, Paul. I swear I will not have any more children by Julien. *Never!*"

"I want to help, but I can't do a procedure like this…in secret." He lowered his voice. "There's a nurse here who's married to a militia man. She spies on me because of what happened to my sister's family. I can't fire her. I'm sorry, Monique."

"You've done a lot to help me already. Thank you, Paul."

Monique cried all the way to Tina's office. There were spies everywhere. She closed the office door behind her and whispered, "I'm pregnant and I'm not having this child." She sat in the chair. "What can I do? Where can I go? I don't trust anyone here but you."

"Who else knows?" Tina asked calmly.

"Paul. He won't tell anyone. He's as scared as I am."

"We have an ob-gyn friend in our sponsorship group. Pass-It-Along helped his sister get into our alma mater on a full scholarship. His clinic is in Carrefour. Come back here Friday."

It was two long sleepless days before Monique stood in front of the squat blue building across from the ocean at the entrance to Carrefour. The cool November breeze smelled like salt and freedom. She looked up the road and saw the beginning of a large city. The houses sat close together as if they needed to lean on each other to stay up. People walked in groups. The colorfully outfitted pickup trucks called *tap-tap* zipped by them, messages to God stenciled all over their frames. People and baggage spilled from them and clung to their flanks like mountain climbers. Tina pulled Monique inside the clinic and closed the door. The procedure took place in total silence. The diminutive doctor never told Monique his name, but his movements conveyed trust and compassion.

Monique got home about a half hour before Julien with a year's supply of pills in her big purse and a promise for more from the doctor. Tina drove Monique's car from her office where they had left it earlier, and Francois, Tina's boyfriend, followed in his. They hustled away as soon as they delivered her to Anita who escorted Monique upstairs.

"I'm glad you're here, Anita," Monique said, trying to fight off the drowsiness. "Look in my bag, take the package with the pills, and go put it in your room. I'll tell you what we're going to do with it later."

"*Oui*, madame." Anita put the bag under her apron and left the room.

Julien burst into the bedroom as soon as he got home. "What's going on?" he asked. "It seems like you're always in bed lately. I heard you threw up the other morning. Are you pregnant?"

Monique willed herself to breathe slowly. She clasped the entwined hearts pendant and felt calmer. "That's why I went to see Paul a couple days ago, because my cycle has been so irregular. I thought I was pregnant, but it was a bug. As a matter of fact, I got my period today while shopping. I felt so ill Tina had to drive my car back."

Julien squinted at her. "I was waiting to see when you were going to tell me why you saw Paul this week. We need to resolve this issue with your period soon. I want a boy to carry my father's name," Julien said with a whine, as if Monique had failed him when she showed up six months ago with a girl. He pulled an envelope from his back pocket and threw it on the bed. "You give me a son, and you'll get more in your weekly allowance."

She welcomed the pain twisting her insides, knowing that she would never have to accept more money from Julien for a son. But for now, the money he doled out like a ransom served her cause. She stashed it in the duffel bag hidden in the storage room with the rest of her luggage.

Monique had registered her daughter with the American embassy as soon as she had returned to Haiti. Every night she swallowed the pill Anita left in a teacup inside the china cabinet in the dining room. This was all part of her plan.

A week later, with a bag full of Julien's money, Monique drove to her weekly Pass-It-Along meeting at Tina's church. Everything cost money in Haiti. Especially a rebellion.

54
Cecilia

Days had crawled into weeks and months since Cecilia had driven Monique to the airport after kicking Orson out of her apartment in August. She missed Monique daily, but she saw Orson in every cab, every store, every dream. What had he done wrong that night except try to understand? She hadn't given him a chance.

Then one afternoon in November, she found Orson outside her apartment. She knew she would not push him away again. She had waited for him to return, confident that he would. She would conquer her fears and give the relationship she sought a chance to bloom. She ran into his open arms. He kissed the top of her head. Then they started apologizing at the same time. Cecilia placed her index finger on his lips.

"What are you doing here?" she asked, wanting to be sure.

"I…I needed time to think about what I want," he said, "and it's you, Ceecee. I'm sorry for failing to understand the depth of your friendship with your island sisters. I promise to listen and learn."

"That's all I ask. It's a package deal." She smiled. "Let's go inside."

They talked for hours while Orson fixed dinner as if he had never left. "Well, I have an idea," Orson said. "I want to take you and your friends out to dinner. Get to know them."

"Orson, that's so thoughtful. It'd be nice for you to spend time with Elle and Mel and their husbands. They're an important part of my life. And I have no doubt Moe and Lan will return one day."

"How about this weekend? I'm a man on a mission." He kissed her forehead.

They settled in to watch a movie after she'd finished grading homework and he'd read the paper. He left a few hours later after kissing her cheek in the doorway. He waited for her every afternoon that week. They talked, they laughed, and they relaxed into their comfortable companionship, recapturing the four months they'd dated before the breakup.

Cecilia kissed Mel and Mike in greeting at the restaurant that weekend.

"I'm so sorry about Elle," Mel said.

Cecilia nodded and let Orson guide her into the brocade-upholstered booth. He slid in next to her just as the waiter approached. "Excuse me, ladies. May I please take your drink orders?"

"I'll have a glass of red," Cecilia said. "Cabernet sauvignon."

Orson placed his hand on her upper arm. "The pretty lady will have a *virgin* piña colada," Orson said with a smile on his clean-shaven face. "I'll have club soda with lime." He turned to Mel. "What do you want, dear?"

The women exchanged a look while Mike ordered a cognac and Mel asked for a glass of chardonnay. Cecilia sat up straighter and stared at Orson, her eyebrows almost touching her hairline. He stroked her arm and kissed her dimple. The moment passed.

The laughter, good food, and Orson's musky aftershave pushed Cecilia deep into the backrest and relaxed her shoulders. After devouring his French dessert of *choux a la crème,* Orson stood and got down on one knee. He took Cecilia's left hand and reached into his jacket pocket. Cecilia blinked, her body tensing with fear and excitement. "What…wh—"

"Pretty lady, will you marry me?" He held a ring between his index finger and his thumb.

Cecilia's head swiveled toward her friend. Mel looked away. She was on her own. "Orson, I don't know what to say," she said. "It's so… It's too soon."

"I love you Cecilia, Cecilia Peterson," Orson said, smiling. "Let's not waste precious time. I've never wanted anything more in my life."

With tears running down her face, she said, "Yes, yes. I will marry you, Orson, Orson Matthews."

Mike and Mel looked at each other and frowned. "Inside joke," Cecilia said, missing her sisters at this important moment in her life. The moment her mother had said would never happen for her.

The patrons who were close enough to witness the exchange started clapping. Mel and Mike clapped, but the quizzical look on Mel's face planted doubt into the spot in Cecilia's heart where happiness had just taken root. Orson talked nonstop on the way home, but Cecilia couldn't follow the conversation. She wished she hadn't quit smoking. She could use a cigarette now. She leaned her forehead on the car window and stared at the pedestrians strolling in the sultry November night on Key Biscayne. What should a newly engaged woman do? Would Orson expect her to invite him into her bedroom tonight? She wanted him, but she was scared.

"You're home, pretty lady. A penny for your thoughts?"

"Why did you order me a nonalcoholic drink when I wanted wine? I respect that you don't care for alcohol, but I enjoy a drink sometimes."

Orson reached across the seat and took her hand. "I'm sorry. It's just... that alcohol is not good for your health. We don't need it to have a great time."

"I don't ever want a man making decisions for me. I've been taking care of myself my whole life."

"Forgive me, Ceecee. I didn't mean to upset you."

She yawned. "It's been a long day. I'm tired."

Kissing her ring finger, Orson said, "It's okay, love. Let's get married next week. I want to be with you."

He placed her hand on his lap. She pulled her hand away from his erection. She opened the car door and stepped outside. Orson followed her. "Orson, how can I plan a wedding on such a short notice?"

"We'll make it work. I promise." He leaned into her against the car door and kissed her deep and long.

"Orson," she said when he let go of her face. "I have to tell you something."

He put his finger on her lips. "Don't worry about anything, pretty lady. You go in and get some rest." He opened her apartment door, kissed her forehead, and left.

Cecilia locked her door and placed her left hand on her beating heart. It wanted to follow Orson on the road to happiness. She called Mel.

"Mel, I'm sorry to call so late."

"It's okay, sugar. Didn't expect your call though. Where's Orson? Shouldn't you two be, you know...*celebrating*."

"Mel, he wants to get married *soon*. What should I do? I've missed him all these months. I want to be with him."

"Well, let's plan a wedding, darling. I wish you'd been with him a bit longer though. What was that with the drinks tonight?"

"Orson doesn't drink or smoke. It's okay. We talked about it tonight. Thanks, Mel. Good night, *sistah*."

The following weekend Cecilia married Orson in a small ceremony in Mel's backyard. Uncle Paul and his family came from Saint Thomas. Freda, Larry, and Helen, Orson's mother, joined the couple. Cecilia missed her daddy today. She missed her tribe. It wasn't how she had envisioned her wedding day. Her three sisters were supposed to be her maids of honor on the happiest day of her life.

"Thank you for being here, Uncle Paul." Cecilia hugged him hard.

"I'm sorry about your mother," Uncle Paul said. "She should be here."

"I don't need her. Today, I start my own family." She fanned her face with her hand and blew air out of her mouth. "You look so much like Daddy," Cecilia said to her uncle. She rested her hand on her young cousin's head. "Betty, you were the best flower girl ever." Cecilia kissed her doughy face.

"You're so pretty, Ceecee." Betty said with a lisp. "I want to come to high school here. I love Miami."

"That would be great, Betty." Cecilia patted her head. "My door is open, sweetheart."

Helen took her new daughter-in-law's hand in hers. She noted the fine wrinkles around light brown eyes in a square face like Orson's. "Cecilia, my dear, I've heard so much about you from Orson. We're so happy to welcome you into our family. My late husband would have loved you."

"Thank you, Helen. I wish I'd met you before today," Cecilia said. "Orson looks a lot like you."

"Please come over Monday for a cookout. It's a school holiday," Helen said before leaving. "My son Benjamin and his family are flying in today from Africa."

As the last guest left, Cecilia's anxiety increased. "It was a beautiful wedding, pretty lady," Orson said, closing his car door. "Let's go home, baby."

When they reached the threshold of her apartment, Orson put the gift boxes down by the door and picked her up and deposited her on the sofa.

"Don't move," he whispered, kissing her lips.

Cecilia sat upright when she heard the water running in the tub. She took off her white sandals. The white eyelet sundress clung to her damp body. Orson led her to the bathroom. Scented candles cast a soft glow in the small room. Pink rose petals floated on the water in the tub. Orson turned her around and unzipped her dress, stopping to kiss her back until he pulled the dress over her head and threw it on the floor. Her strapless bra and white lace panties followed. His soft touches over her skin blazed a trail that ended between her legs, then snaked its way inside. She closed her eyes and leaned her head against the wall for support. When Orson stopped to take off his clothes, she shivered in the warm bathroom.

Her body responded to Orson's hunger with its own famine demanding to be fed. He took her hands, and together they stepped into the warm, sudsy water. With her back to him, he never took his hands or his mouth off her body. She closed her eyes and relaxed into him. When the suds disappeared and the water turned cold, Orson gnawed her earlobe and murmured, "Let's go to bed."

She stepped onto the bath rug and whispered, "Orson, there's something I...need to—"

He swallowed her words with a kiss as he wrapped her in a towel and carried her to the bedroom. "It can wait, my love." He laid her down on the blue satin sheet and kissed his way down her neck, her breasts, and her stomach. He stopped at the junction between her legs; she stifled a scream and sucked in her bottom lip.

"I'm going to make you happy, pretty lady. I've been waiting for months."

He climbed on top of her and pried her legs open with his knee. "Open your eyes, Ceecee," he said, his voice shaking.

"I can't...I have to tell you what happened first... I was—"

His skin burned hot against hers. He kept kissing her trembling lips, chopping the hard words away as he guided his penis into her.

"Orson—" Her heart thundered like a tempest. Orson was all the way inside and stopped. She opened her eyes and looked at him with tears running down her temples. Orson's face contorted in a grimace. He thrust into her as if he was seeking a promised treasure, and she screamed from the pain. Within seconds, he groaned.

"Some virgin you are!" he yelled, pulling out. "Why did you let me believe you've never been with a man?" He put his boxers back on and stood at the foot of the bed.

"Orson, I've been trying to tell you. I was...raped. I—" She covered her face with her hands. She rolled off the bed and reached for his hand. He pushed her hard. She fell and hit her head on the edge of the nightstand. She stayed on the floor.

"Shut up! You wouldn't give me any for months, keeping it hidden like the holy grail! *You are a liar!*"

He stormed out of the bedroom. Her face stung with shame. After a long shower, she slipped into a nightgown. On her way back to the bedroom, she peered into the quiet living room. Orson was on the couch, drinking from a bottle of cognac with a crushed gift box at his feet. Visions of Monique, Lanei, and Ella kept her company all night. If that was love, Cecilia wanted none of it. She would be the one that got away before it was too late.

The next morning the smell of bacon wafted under the bedroom door. She limped to the bathroom, the soreness between her legs stirring painful memories.

"Come out for breakfast, pretty lady. It's getting cold." Orson poked his head through the door.

He pulled out the chair for her and placed a cup of hot coffee in front of her followed by a vegetable omelet and her favorite homemade biscuits. Orson fell on his knees. "Ceecee, I really don't quite remember what happened last night, but I know I hurt you. Please forgive me. It will never happen again. I promise."

She pushed the plate away. "Why can't you remember what you did last night?" She looked at his clean-shaven face and tearful eyes. "I want you to leave today. We can annul this marriage."

"What? Ceecee, honey." He took her hands. "You could have told me the truth. You know what my expectations were. We're both wrong. Let's start over, please."

She stared at him and blinked back her own tears. "I tried to tell you… before and last night. I was ashamed of what happened to me, but I'm not *wrong*."

"It's okay." He stroked her face. "It doesn't matter. I love you, pretty lady."

Orson held her until her sobs subsided. He kissed her eyes, her mouth, her neck. When he reached to unbutton her shorts, she grabbed his hand and squeezed hard. "Stop," she said.

He stopped. "Okay, sweetheart. Take as long as you need. I'll be here. I love you."

Cecilia met Orson's brother at the cookout the following day. "It was so nice to meet you today, Cecilia," Benjamin said after the other guests left. "I heard you're a math and science teacher. Orson dropped out of MIT. Did he tell you? He's undoubtedly very smart, but—"

"Hey, Mr. CPA," Orson said to his older brother. "What lies are you filling my pretty wife with?" He smiled, but his eyes were hard.

"Benjamin was telling me you went to MIT," Cecilia said.

"And how I threw it all away to drive a cab instead, right?" Orson replied. "It's getting late, honey. We have work tomorrow."

Had Cecilia decided to stay in her marriage when she agreed to meet the rest of his family? Everything seemed so normal. The love Helen expressed for her children was deep. Cecilia wanted to love her own family like that one day. "Why did you drop out of MIT?" she asked, as the car approached their street. "You never told me."

"Long story." Orson sighed.

"Well, we have all night. There seems to be a lot I don't know about you."

"What you see is what you get, baby. Orson, the happy cab driver. Maybe one day I'll make you proud of me with some titles." He reached for her left hand and kissed her palm.

It was a week filled with firsts for Cecilia. The first week of her new identity. The first week of sharing her space with Orson. He cooked, cleaned, and held her in his arms at night. And he waited while she debated whether she could turn off her feelings. She loved this man. He loved her the way no man ever had. It was her fault. She should have told him. Everything was going to be fine. She had no more secrets.

When Cecilia got home on Saturday afternoon after her weekly lunch with Mel, Orson was humming while he cooked. "It smells good. What are you making?" she said, walking into the kitchen.

"I caught some snapper today. It'll be ready soon. Today is our one-week anniversary, pretty lady."

Cecilia stood on her tiptoes to kiss Orson on the mouth. He smelled of fresh soap and ginger.

"Ceecee, don't start anything you don't want to finish," he said, holding her waist.

She took his hand and led him into the bedroom. Feeling in control aroused her. She stood naked in front of him, and it felt right. Their lovemaking was slow, patient, and unselfish. Orson explored her body like he was searching for a treasure, bringing her to her first orgasm.

The perfect end of a week of firsts.

55
Lanei

A fter Fred's sudden death from a heart attack in October, Kevin lost the well-paid job at the mills that provided insurance for the family. He went back into the boxing ring to earn a living. Lanei's illusion of peace evaporated with every fight he lost.

She'd bought a small mortar and pestle at the local drugstore and had crushed the pills to put in his food. These pills had afforded her a couple of years of relative peace in her marriage. The sex then was perhaps what other couples would call normal, but Lanei wouldn't know. Since the first time in Talofofo Falls, sex with Kevin had always left her feeling dirty yet wanting. Like there should be more to it than what he was doing to her body and her soul. In the end she could not mix the powdered pills in his food. Father Abbott said it was a sin.

Lanei drew strength from the three women she was exiled from, but whose tribal optimism infused her with hope even in the face of all their own troubles. She buried her anger for not being able to go to Cecilia's wedding. There was no room to nudge Kevin without fallout. Father Abbott helped her maintain her faith in the church she had begun to question.

Last week she had asked the old priest. "Why does God want me to suffer so?"

"My child, he gave us Jesus, his only son, who died to redeem us," Father Abbott had answered. "God has united you and Kevin, and only he can separate you. Remember your vows, Lanei."

"Yes, Father." Lanei had knelt at the pew inside the chapel and breathed the anger out of her body. For the first time, she had been unable to pray.

It was a cold November night even for Chicago. Lanei kissed her daughter after reading her favorite story three times and smiled, pulling the blanket over Maria before turning on the night-light. She made her way to the couch, spread the throw over her feet, opened her book, and dove into Jane's world in *Persuasion*. She had no idea how much time had passed when a gust of cold air blew into the apartment. She looked up from the book, closed it, and stood from the couch.

"Oh my God, Kevin, what happened?" Dark blood stained his face, and his left eye was swollen shut. As she walked by him to close the front door, he pushed her. She staggered backward, hitting her shin on the leg of the coatrack.

"What the fuck do you think happened?" he yelled. "I lost the fuckin' fight. I'm tired. Don't know how much longer I can do this shit."

Lanei wrapped the sweater tighter around her torso as if it could make her smaller. "Kevin, you're over forty. Maybe…um…you should get another type of work."

"What kind of job is gonna pay the kind of money I make getting my teeth kicked in, huh? You'd be done with school and making good money by now if you didn't have that fuckin' kid. I told you to get rid of it."

Lanei flinched, the words searing her heart like a hot poker stick. "How dare you say something like this to me! My education was the one thing I could claim as mine. Now it's my fault you don't get to live off my back?" Lanei was now too angry to be frightened. "I live with the guilt that the stress you create in my life caused my daughter's health issues. You need to get back on your medications."

"Oh, you want that, bitch? Bet you fucked Nate when I couldn't get it up for you." The smell of alcohol filled the air. "He dumped the girlfriend 'cause it made you sad." He pushed his bottom lip out in a mock pout. "Y'all think I'm stupid cause I ain't had no college."

"Nate is my friend," Lanei said, feeling her anger unspool. "That's all it is, *a friendship*. I respect my marriage, Kevin. You can't say that, can you? You're *degenerate*."

"Daddy, you have a boo-boo on your face," Maria said, standing on the threshold of her bedroom rubbing her eyes.

Before Lanei could reach her daughter, Kevin lunged at the girl, picked her up, and threw her on her bed. "Stay there," he screamed.

Maria yelled, and Lanei rushed to the room. "Mommy, my head hurts." Maria rubbed the spot. "The wall hit me."

Lanei laid her daughter back on the pillow and charged at Kevin. It was as if she had become a giant and Kevin was a roach she wanted to crush. "You hurt my child." Lanei pushed him away from Maria's bedroom door. "I will *never* let you hurt Maria. I'm calling the po—"

"Is that right?" Kevin grabbed Lanei's hair, dragged her to their bedroom, and locked the door. "Oh, you're gonna get it now."

Several hours later, the pain and swelling in her left arm had not eased with ice packs and aspirin. It was after midnight. Unable to sit or lie down, she called Nate. They dropped Maria off at Peggy's and drove to the emergency room. Kevin had left the apartment after the attack. "If you call the police, I swear I'll kill you and the kid," he had said before slamming the door.

"Mrs. Williams, my name is Shirley, and I'm a social worker," the woman said. Lanei looked at Nate sitting in a corner of the room. His face was pinched as if he was in pain. She closed her eyes. "What happened to you last night, Mrs. Williams?"

"I...I fell," Lanei said, staring at the cast that covered her arm from her wrist to her elbow.

Shirley stared at her, her face blank. No judgment. "I can only help if you tell me the truth, Lanei."

"Ma'am, may I speak with my friend for a minute, please?" Nate said, standing by the bed.

"Of course, I'll be on the floor when she's ready." She left, pulling the door behind her.

"Lanei, for once you're going to tell the truth," Nate said. "If you don't, *I will*." He touched her hand. "I saw Maria this morning. She has a huge lump on the back of her head. You could lose custody of your daughter. You know he'll hurt her again, and I cannot watch this abuse continue and do *nothing*."

Lanei shifted on the bed and winced. "Kevin will go to jail if I tell the truth. You don't understand. I'm scared. He threatened—"

"You deserve better." Nate wouldn't let her look away. "Please do this for you, for Maria. Give her a chance to grow up with healthier memories."

She tried to sit up and gasped. "What is it?" Nate asked. "Do you need something for the pain?"

"No medication, Nate." He stared at her and frowned. Lanei knew he could see the new resolution in her eyes, but what he could not see was the tear in her rectum that had caused her to gasp. "Nate, get the social worker. I'll talk to her."

In the morning Lanei opened her eyes to find Kevin staring down at her in the hospital bed. "Lan, please forgive me. I promise to go back on the medications. I don't want to ever hurt you like that again."

Lanei slid her hand under the sheet and pressed the call button for the nurse. "You will never hurt me again, Kevin. My faith may have kept me married to you, but you crossed the line when you hurt Maria and sodomized me. They're coming for you."

Kevin lifted the telephone and shoved it toward her. "Call the police now and tell them it was a mistake."

"Get away from me, devil," she screamed. "*Now.*"

"I ain't going, bitch. You—" Before he finished the sentence, two police officers rushed into the room, read him his rights, and handcuffed him.

"You'll never get away from me," Kevin said, his green eyes browning like the approach of a Guam typhoon.

Flanked by the two officers, Kevin was dragged out of her room. God had just given her the first sign that he could take Kevin out of her life.

56
Ella

Last night, the noise from the machine recording Ella's vital signs had sounded like it was coming from inside her head. As she'd tried to turn her body toward muffled voices, a wave of nausea had forced her to close her eyes and breathe through her mouth.

"How are you feeling, Ella?" The question had come from a stout man in a white coat. He held a thin chart against his chest. "I'm Dr. Berger, a psychiatrist."

In Haitian Creole, she'd said, "*Mwen pa konpren ou. Kimoun ki Ella'w?*"

The man had pointed to the door, said some words, and left. He'd returned shortly with a middle-aged woman with cornrowed hair who introduced herself as Tercia, a Haitian translator with the hospital. Tercia explained what had happened to Ella and who the older man was.

"A psychiatrist! Am I crazy?" Ella tried to sit up. "I'm hurt!"

Tercia translated.

"Ella, your right leg is broken." The doctor read from the chart. "Your pelvis has a hairline fracture, and both shoulders were dislocated. You sustained a severe concussion and lacerations on the back of your head. You've been in a coma for almost three weeks. Now it seems you have amnesia." He'd paused to let Tercia translate. "Your body will heal in time, but I'm concerned about your mind. I can send your husband in for a short visit. Your children can't come in yet."

"Husband? Children?" Ella had fought the fogginess swirling inside her head. "*O bondie!* What's going on? I want my sister. What's her name? Please help me, Tercia." She grabbed Tercia's arm. "Ter...*Therese!*" Ella said triumphantly.

"Where's Therese, Ella?" the doctor had asked, patting her hand to calm her down.

"I don't know." She sobbed. "But she loves me."

Now, she pulled her gaze from the sunny window and followed the doctor's gaze as he glanced at a man through the cubicle's glass wall. She stared at the man and pushed her brain hard to place him. His face opened in a wide grin as he walked toward her bed. Fear gripping her, she scrambled backward until her head hit the IV pole.

"Mr. Antoine," Dr. Berger said. "Your wife came out of her coma last night. You're aware of her physical injuries. My job is to find out why she attempted suicide." Tercia pursed her lips, stealing a look at Mr. Antoine before turning her attention to Ella.

"Suicide?" Ella cried. "Why would I want to do that? I don't understand. I need to go to class. What day is it?"

"Today is Sunday, September 11, 1983," the doctor said. "Based on site evidence, the police have concluded that you turned into the path of an eighteen-wheeler."

"Doctor, my wife has been…acting strange lately," Mr. Antoine said. "I'm sorry I didn't intervene before this tragedy." He pulled a white hanky from inside his blazer and patted his dry eyes. "Shouldn't she be in the psychiatry unit?"

The doctor said, "Mr. Antoine, I make the decisions here. Ella has what I hope is anterograde amnesia. It has more of a temporary nature. Hopefully, she'll be able to tell us soon what really happened after she left the movie theater. She doesn't remember having a family, but she asked for her sister Therese."

Ella tried to focus on the conversation, looking back-and-forth between the three people. Mr. Antoine raised his eyebrows and said to Tercia in Creole, "You can leave. I'll tell my wife what's going on."

She whispered something to the doctor. "No. Tercia, I prefer to have you tell Ella what we're discussing," the doctor said, turning to the man. "Who's Therese, Mr. Antoine?"

"Therese is Ella's sister in Haiti," Mr. Antoine said with a snort. "Why would she ask for her?"

"I don't know yet, but she remembers Therese loves her," the doctor said. "Ella, your friend Cecilia has come every afternoon to sit with you. I thought you'd want to know that."

"*Cecilia, Therese,*" Ella whispered, clinging to the names. A face, a smile, and a good feeling hovered above her, trying to pierce the darkness.

"Ella needs rest," Dr. Berger said. "Tercia will stay with her."

A petite woman in a powder blue dress walked toward her bed later that afternoon. Ella smiled. Everything about the woman soothed Ella's anxiety. She greeted Tercia, then bent down and kissed Ella's forehead. Her eyes swam with tears. "I heard the good news from the nurse's station. You're awake. Girl, you scared the hell out of me, out of *us*."

"You must be my friend Cecilia." Ella said in Creole.

A look of hurt flickered on Cecilia's face but disappeared when Tercia explained everything. "Call me *Ceecee*," Cecilia said. "I'll be right back." When Cecilia returned, she was holding a gold bangle bracelet in her hand, and she banged it over and over against the identical one on her wrist while looking into Ella's eyes.

Ella was afraid to blink so she wouldn't lose that spark of recognition. The bracelet meant a lot to her, but she wasn't sure what. She pulled her arm from under the sheet and extended it to Cecilia who fastened the bracelet on her wrist. "*Ceecee*," Ella said, trying the name on her dry tongue. "There are others?"

Cecilia nodded. "Yes. *Monique* and *Lanei*. We are the island sisters."

"*Monique, Lanei, Ceecee*," Ella repeated like a lullaby. Cecilia's face froze between a smile and a cry.

Two weeks after waking up from her coma, Ella went home with bits of memories like pieces of a puzzle she needed to put together. Her maternal instinct kicked in, and she embraced her children even though she'd forgotten segments of their lives. During her weekly visits with the psychiatrist, she tried to remember her past.

By the end of October, she didn't need Tercia to communicate with the doctor. Her big clothes told her she'd lost a lot of weight in three months. Life with Bernard was a new experience. In his presence her emotions were jumbled, filling her full of panic and joy like a seesaw.

One night while watching television, a political ad for Representative Meridien jolted Ella's head from Bernard's shoulder. Her heart pounded in her chest. She pointed at the screen. "I...I know her, Bernard. Why do I *know* her?" She shook her head from side to side.

He took her head between his hands and stared into her eyes. "Elle, honey, where would you know her from?" He frowned. "You see that's why I'm afraid to leave the kids with you. I think they should have kept you in the hospital until you remembered why you tried to kill yourself."

"I did not! Stop saying that. I told you it must have been an accident. I'm afraid." Ella sobbed, moving away from him on the couch. "Why?"

Bernard cradled her until she fell asleep in his arms, already forgetting why she was so scared of him.

As the weeks flew by, she remembered slivers of her past but not what had happened at the movie theater. Bernard assured her that she had never made it to the theater to meet him. That she was depressed and sad before she attempted suicide. She remembered always being hopeful about going to school. Sometimes he made her feel good and beautiful. Other times she cringed when he came near.

One afternoon Ella found her scholarship letter from the hospital as she was dusting the bedroom furniture. Cecilia had told her she had wanted to be a doctor. Ella swallowed a sob. She couldn't even be a nurse's aide. The hospital had let her go when she couldn't remember her tasks. She'd lost the scholarship. The doorbell rang.

"Oh, Ceecee," she said, hugging her friend hard.

Cecilia hugged her back. "Let's go for our walk. Orson's cooking is dangerous for my figure."

Ella swatted the air and leaned on her cane. "You glow with happiness," Ella said. "You're beautiful." She waved to a neighbor. "Ceecee, you know last night I remembered making the U-turn because I was very angry about something, but I can't put my finger on it yet. I'm trying."

"I never believed the suicide theory. You were meeting Bernard at the movies, but the police said your car was driving in the opposite direction, as if you'd been there and were going back home."

Ella stopped walking and stared at her friend, trying to understand, but nothing came. "Bernard said I was depressed and believed...I wanted to die."

Cecilia rested her hand on top of Ella's on the cane. "Elle, you're the most driven and upbeat of all of us. I think it's because of the huge financial sacrifices your family made to send you here. I don't know why he wants you to believe that lie."

Ella squeezed her friend's hand, and they walked in silence while her brain sprinted in a loop. Cecilia filled in many of the blanks in Ella's life on their walks. Cecilia had brought an album with pictures of the four island sisters that replayed happy memories in Ella's mind.

Later that evening, she sat on the couch working on the assignment Dr. Berger had given her earlier while a Christmas jingle played on the TV in the other room. It had been about five months since her accident.

"Mommy, the phone," six-year-old Alex yelled from the family room where he was watching television with Perrine.

"*Petite soeur*," Therese said. "How are you?"

"Têtê, my body is fine, but I still forget things I want to remember and remember things I want to forget." Hysteria coated her laughter over the static on the line. "How's Papa?"

"He's ill. He asks for *you*. You were coming before your accident. Remember?"

Ella held her head to rein in the migraines that had plagued her since she left the hospital. She breathed to stop the nausea. Suddenly, she remembered Bernard's anger about her going to Haiti. But why? "Therese, was there something else I needed in Haiti besides seeing my father? I can't—"

"I promised to tell you something about Bernard. You need to come, Elle."

Ella's eyes opened wide. *A secret.*

A week had passed since Therese's call. She waited for Bernard to leave for his weekly weekend business trip. "Please give Moe hugs and kisses," Cecilia said the day before Ella left while they walked. "I wish I was in town this weekend to keep the kids, but Orson is taking me away. We haven't had a honeymoon yet."

"Go have fun, sister. Lois will keep the kids. I love you, Ceecee. I don't know what I'd have done without you."

"What are sisters for, Elle?" Cecilia squeezed her arm.

Three weeks before Christmas, Ella dropped her children at Lois's house. Times like these, she wished Janet hadn't moved back to Jamaica, but her daughter Lois had been a great substitute.

"Lois, Bernard doesn't know I'm leaving," Ella said. "Hopefully, he won't come home during my absence. He said something about extra work out of town. Remember, I'll be back in three days."

"Go," Lois said, hugging her and closing the door. Ella heard the dead bolt click.

She let out her breath and climbed back into the taxi to go to the airport. She'd left Haiti seven years ago to pursue a dream. But what and who had she left behind? And why? This journey would either heal or destroy her.

57

Monique

M onique stared out the open window of her parents' large living room. The sun slid behind the tall mountains as it pushed the darkness forward to cover its disappearance. The acrid smell of charcoal wafted through the window. Plumes of smoke snaked across the last yellow swath of sunset. The glittering lights from the colored bulbs of the tall Christmas tree claimed a spot on the picture window to create a false sense of happiness inside the house.

She turned from the window to look at her family. Esther and her husband Serge, sat on a settee holding hands and laughing with each other. Drunk as always, Solange glared at everybody. Her husband looked at her with droopy eyes and a blankness that made Monique wonder if he even remembered Solange's name. Papa sat so far away from Maman he might need to put his glasses on to locate her against the backdrop of the floral fabric on the sofa across the room.

Solange suddenly stood from a wing chair and opened her arms like a bird to balance her hefty derriere on her skinny high heels before stumbling toward Monique. The amber liquid in her glass sloshed over her hand. She licked her fingers. Monique stepped back from Solange's sour breath, holding the back of Odile's head. "What are you staring at, Monique?" Solange said, the words colliding in her mouth. Monique counted.

"Solange, I think you've had enough to drink for the night," Esther said. "Let's all have a nice meal together for once. It's the week before Christmas. Please."

"You always take her side, Esther," Solange said with a screech. "What's so special about *her?*"

"That's enough, you two," Papa bellowed from his seat. "Monique, don't start trouble again. Leave Solange alone."

"What did I do?" Monique exploded like an uncorked bottle. "I'm not responsible for her miserable life here." She pointed to Papa. "*You are.*"

Papa walked toward Monique with his hand raised. "Take a look at what your *husband* did to your mother. Don't you wish I'd picked yours?"

"Don't you dare," Monique said, baring her teeth. She placed six-month-old Odile on the love seat behind her. She marched toward him, taking a judo stance that she had been learning in self-defense class with Tina's group. "You're never going to beat me again." Monique rubbed the scar on her elbow and glared at her father, memories flooding her with thoughts of revenge.

Ten-year-old Monique had stood in front of Papa in the living room and said, "I see women driving. Why can't Maman drive?"

"Monique, that's why we have a chauffeur." He'd blown the smoke from his pipe into her face.

"He needs time off with his family. He has six children, and he's always here. Why—"

Papa had grabbed her ear and smacked her legs hard several times with his open hand. He pushed her toward the stairs. "You'll learn to keep your opinions to yourself if I have to beat it into you." She'd fallen on her elbows trying to break her fall and scraped her knees. Blood had oozed from her cuts, and she wasn't allowed to come down for dinner that night.

A wail came from where Maman sat across the room. Papa lowered his arm. Monique picked up Odile, ran to Maman, and walked her upstairs. She then placed Odile next to her grandmère and knelt on the floor. She lay her head down on their joined hands and sobbed. "I'm sorry for everything, Maman. I never paid attention to the regime growing up… Now I hurt everyone."

"I know you didn't mean to hurt us, Moe," Solange said from the bedroom doorway. Monique turned to look at her sister, blinking. "But you always got to do whatever you wanted when Papa never let me and Esther choose. It's not fair."

Monique stood and embraced Solange, the sister she'd thought hated her. They cried. "Sol, you're right. It's not fair. But I'm not the enemy. We're on the same side of this war."

Solange nodded and wiped her face. "I'm sorry, about…all of this." She pointed at Maman and Odile sleeping next to her. "I don't hate you, but I envy your strength. I was jealous."

Solange kissed Maman's cheek and left the room. Maman took Monique's hand with a force that surprised her. "*Bébé*, I can die happy now. When you become a lawyer, fight to free others but make room for life, love, and laughter." She sighed. "Be patient in all you do, Moe. Armor protects the body but may crush the spirit. Let your big heart be your beacon. I'll be there even when you can't see me." She stroked Monique's tear-stained face. "You make me proud."

Monique sat in her car for a long time that night, surrounded by the quiet darkness. It was as if the night creatures bowed silently to honor her pain. Maman might never see her become an attorney, but her spirit would push Monique on its wings toward freedom. She would only take her armor off after she dealt with Julien. She'd missed the opportunity to get to know Brian. Would he propose to another woman again? Could she escape before he met the next one? She put her head down on the steering wheel and roared as if to release the beast within.

58
Cecilia

Cecilia scoured the stores in South Florida looking for Christmas decorations with island motifs. She bought balls painted with blue oceans, white clouds, pine trees, and red berries. She wanted her first end-of-the-year holidays with Orson to be memorable. The past weeks with him had been what Cecilia had always imagined being married would feel like. Orson paid attention to her every need. Cecilia hummed a Christmas carol as she climbed inside her car and placed the wrapped gift on the passenger seat. She hadn't seen Freda since the wedding. She had no crisis in her life. Or was it that she couldn't tell Freda what had happened on her wedding night? But he would never hurt her again. Orson was gentle and compassionate.

"Look what the cat dragged in," Freda said, smiling as she stood to hug Cecilia.

She squeezed Freda and inhaled her island smell of Cashmere Bouquet and bergamot pomade. "I miss you," Cecilia said. "I've been busy with adjusting to having a husband and in-laws and staying in contact with my dispersed tribe." She handed the gift to Freda. "A small token of my great appreciation for having you in my life. I'm able to handle my marriage because of what you've taught me."

Freda put the box aside and stared at her without blinking. "One does not *handle* a marriage, Ceecee. One grows, adjusts, enjoys, and lives a marriage. Is your marriage what you expected it to be?"

Cecilia pushed her chair back. It scraped the cement floor, making her teeth gnash. "I'm very happy. You know it's only been a little over a month, so it's a period of adjustment. Orson loves me. I love him."

"Good. I'm glad to hear that. I know the day before the wedding you still hadn't told him about your rape. It sounds like you needn't be as anxious as you were." Freda clasped her hands together over the desk.

Cecilia stared into Freda's kind eyes, and she knew she had to tell her the truth. She would no longer hold secrets that tormented her spirit and set her tormentors free. Besides Freda knew. Cecilia could tell.

She took a deep breath. "Orson said some vile things to me on our wedding night. He called me a liar and pushed me. I hit my head." Cecilia looked down at the grungy floor. "He drank a lot of alcohol after and could not remember what happened. But I should have told him before."

"*Stop*, Cecilia," Freda stared at her with disappointment in her eyes. "There's never any reason why it's ever okay for a man to abuse you. Why was he drunk? I though he didn't drink. Is he an alcoholic?"

"No, he was upset, and the liquor was a gift. I haven't seen him drink since then."

As she said that, it occurred to her that Helen never served alcohol at her house and Orson had asked Cecilia to not keep alcohol in their apartment. What did this all mean?

"Ceecee, I'm glad you're happy. I hope you'll continue to come to counseling. I've never been married, but I've heard it can be a very fluid state of being. People change. Circumstances change. I'll always be here for all of you. Thank you for the gift."

Cecilia arrived home to find it quiet as a tomb. She flipped lights on in the kitchen, the bedroom, and the den before she plugged in the Christmas tree. She took a deep breath as if the darkness had settled on her chest. On the kitchen table was a note.

Hi Pretty Lady,

My boss asked me to work a night shift. Making money toward buying our house. I'll be home in the morning. Have a good night.

Love you,
O

Cecilia walked around the apartment, feeling the loneliness follow her from room to room. She stopped in front of the fridge and opened the door. "Dammit, I need a drink." She slammed the fridge door, and the picnic basket Orson kept on top of it tumbled over her head. Among the stuff that spilled onto the kitchen floor were two empty flat bottles with whiskey labels. There was still a drop of gold liquid at the bottom of one.

Cecilia sat on the floor, staring at the bottles as if they could speak their secrets to her. Where had they come from? Why was Orson drinking in secret? Cecilia wasn't sure she could live with alcoholism once more. She threw the bottles in the trash can. A few minutes later, she fished them out and placed them on the counter. She would confront him in the morning. No secrets.

Unable to sleep, she got out of bed and buried the bottles at the bottom of the trash can. Drinking wasn't a crime. She would not make a federal case out of it. He'd been a model husband. They laughed, and they made love often as they were trying to start their family. So he drank some whiskey, but he never even raised his voice at her. Everything was perfect.

Yet she held her head between her hands in the bed, closed her eyes, and sobbed.

59
Lanei

Kevin's two-year sentence brought Lanei peace and space to plan. The weekly home visits from the Baptist social worker came with Bible study that showed Lanei a more flexible side of God. Not receiving communion would not condemn her soul to hell if she served him with good deeds. Spending weekends with Peggy gave her and Maria an escape from the humdrum of homeschooling and the confines of the apartment. They baked, cooked, played board games, and watched old movies. Lanei hadn't been this happy and uncoiled since before she'd married Kevin.

Nate joined the trio for dinner most Saturdays and brought Maria's favorite double chocolate ice cream for dessert. Lanei wanted to give herself to Nate to love, but she could not. Not while she was still married to Kevin. Weekly confessions scoured her soul clean, but her body screamed to be touched by him.

One Saturday night after Nate left, Lanei was putting the monopoly pieces away in the box and she said, "Peg, I never said it before, but I'm not sorry Kevin is in prison. I know he's your son, but he…hurt me a lot."

"Honey, you did him a favor. He's getting counseling from the prison chaplain." Peggy reached into her canvas bag, pulled out a sealed envelope, and handed it to Lanei. "He sent this when I visited him this week."

"Thank you," Lanei said, taking the envelope. "Maria and I are blessed to have you in our lives." She kissed Peggy's cheek.

Later that night, she tore up the unread letter, and flushed the pieces down the toilet. She had not answered any of his letters or accepted his collect calls. Lanei needed more time between herself and the pain Kevin had delivered to come to a decision she could live with.

When she heard her cousin Carlina's voice on the telephone the following day, she reached for her rosary. It was the middle of the night in Guam. "*Hafa*

Adai, Lan," Carlina said. "Sweetie, your mama had a stroke. She keeps asking for you."

"Oh, no!" Lanei sat on the living room floor. Her hands shook. "Is she going to be okay, Car?" Lanei asked, her guilt and regret for not bringing Mama to live with her like she should have punched her insides like Kevin's fists on her body.

Carlina blew air through the receiver. "I hope so. Is Kevin home, Lan? You shouldn't be alone."

"He's—" She stopped. "Thank you for being there for Mama. Please tell her I love her. I'll call tomorrow."

Nate came over that afternoon to take Maria to a father-daughter Christmas dance sponsored by the children's program at the library. "Why the long face?" he asked. "Wanna go to the dance with us?" He chuckled. He had cut his afro, sporting a close-cropped hairstyle that showed off his strong features.

"Mama had a stroke. I haven't seen her in…seven years. I need to go to her, but I don't know how. I—"

Nate halted his steps toward Maria's room, turned, and sat next to her on the couch. "Lane, pack your bags. We're going to Guam."

Lanei stood and paced. "Nate, I can't let you do that. Do you have any idea how much this trip will cost?"

He took her in his arms. "I'm sorry about your mom, but I have a trust fund and I'm…single. Please let me do this for you. We could all use a vacation. Don't you agree?"

She could only put her head on his chest and sob. After he left with an impatient Maria, Lanei reached for the telephone and called Cecilia and Ella.

Three weeks before Christmas, a weary Lanei arrived in Guam with Maria and Nate after almost twenty hours of flying time on three flights. In the rental car, she awakened Maria so she could see the palm trees that lined Marine Corps Drive, the thoroughfare that ran along the coast. Maria's eyes opened wide. Sunbathers lay on the grass next to the picnic shelters along the water's edge. Christmas decorations adorned the city, cars, and people. They had left snow on the ground in Chicago. Lanei rolled down the window, and the smell of grilled meats mingled with sea air invaded the car.

She asked Nate to wait with Maria outside her mother's room at the hospital and walked in. Mama stared at her, and a smile broke on the left side of her face. "I'm so sorry, Mama. I'm so sorry," she whispered in Mama's ear, holding her tight. "I wanted to bring you to me but—"

"Hush, baby. I'm glad you're here. Let's not waste precious time talking about the past." Mama kissed her wet cheeks. "Where's my grandbaby?"

Maria bounded into the room pulling Nate behind her. "*Hafa Adai*, Grandma," Maria said. "I'm four." Nate picked up Maria, so she could kiss Mama's sunken cheek. "This is Uncle Nate."

"*Hafa Adai*, Ms. Perez," Nate said, kissing Mama's hand.

Mama nodded. "Lan said you're a great friend, Nate. Thank you."

"Nate, take Maria with you, please," Lanei said. "I'll see you two later."

Lanei held Mama's hand, afraid to break physical contact. "Lan, I'm happy...you never left the church. You can serve God and be happy too." Mama's voice was so low, Lanei put her head on the pillow next to hers. "I learned that too late, baby."

"I listen to God, Mama. He's pointing the way. I will follow."

"God rewarded you with a beautiful daughter for being a good servant. He's merciful. He wants us to be happy, Lan."

"Yes, Mama. He does." Peggy had said the same words.

Lanei joined her relatives in the courtyard in Dededo at night, while Nate settled into a hotel on the beach. Watching Maria play with the children in the courtyard reminded Lanei of her childhood. Despite missing her father, Lanei had been a happy kid. Mama had poured all the love she had in her heart into her only child.

She buried her mother a week later. Two days before she left Guam, Lanei stared at the ocean while she and her cousin waited for the waiter to bring menus. The smell of chicken kelaguen and red rice anchored her home. The sound of the waves crashing against the rocks below the restaurant soothed her longing. She watched Nate running across the very beach where she'd met Kevin almost ten years ago. Maria was straddling his neck, her arms open like bird wings.

"Lan, you shouldn't be in Chicago when Kevin gets out," Carlina said. "Why did you stay so long?" Lanei opened her mouth. Carlina raised her hand and said, "I know. Your faith."

Lanei wiped her tears. Doubt was ever lurking in her mind like a shadow. "Car, I don't want to end up like Mama. Living alone. Dying alone. Plagued by guilt because she loved my father and gave herself to him. I always felt like the *sin* that had condemned Mama to a life of loneliness and regret. She said God is merciful, but she didn't allow his mercy to bring her redemption. This trip... has opened my eyes. She was only forty-three years old." A sob escaped Lanei's pressed lips. "Would God have wanted Mama to suffer like that? She was his faithful servant."

"I kinda fell out of favor with the church a long time ago," Carlina said, with her high-pitched laughter erupting from her red lips. "I'm not married. I have three kids with two fathers, but I'm happy. I think God is smiling because I'm so damned happy. What you think, Lan?" Carlina cocked her shaved eyebrow with the razor-thin pencil line.

Lanei smiled. "You have no idea how much sense you make, cousin."

On New Year's Eve, the day she was to return to Chicago, Peggy called. Kevin would be released early for good behavior. Tomorrow was the first day of 1984. A perfect time to set new goals. Lanei knew exactly what her first resolution was going to be.

60

Ella

When Ella stepped off the plane in Port-au-Prince, no one was waiting for her. She made her way to the station for the bus that would take her south to her past and hopefully, her future. She peered out the bus window a few hours later, and the decay on the buildings reminded her of her stalled dreams. The bright yellow paint of the cathedral had faded to a dirty white. A missing stained-glass pane below the steeple gaped like a missing tooth. The branches of the flamboyant tree in front of the weather-beaten high school, where she and Bernard had planned their lives years ago, swayed as if to welcome her back.

"*Bernard was born and educated in Port-au-Prince. His family hails from our proud North like you.*" This phrase popped into Ella's head. It had come from the woman with the golden hair on the television. Why hadn't Bernard corrected her mistake? Lurking under Ella's wide-eyed joy at being home was the shame of facing her family, but she needed to hear her father say, "*I asked for you. I love you, daughter.*"

At the final stop, she took her small bag from under her seat and stepped off the bus. The smell of burning charcoal, kerosene, and ripe fruit mingled with the dust that covered everything. It was a short distance to her sister's house. Dusk followed her like a shadow as she walked. Her heartbeat accelerated, but her legs slowed. It had been fourteen hours since Ella had left Miami. Unable to sleep, drink, or eat during the over-six-hour bus ride, she felt parched and cored.

A group of people was singing with bowed heads in her sister's front yard. A hush fell over the praying crowd as Ella sprinted toward the open front door. Before she crossed the threshold, a howl cascaded down the stairs and slammed into her like a physical blow. She bolted the rest of the way upstairs.

Seated on the edge of the bed, her sister Miriam cradled their father's lifeless body. Ella gripped her chest as if she could pull her aching heart out to stop the pain. She keened. Her six siblings turned and stared at her. Just like that she remembered all their names. *Miriam, Sarah, Therese, Emile, Joseph, and Vincent.* No one moved. Unable to remain standing, she crumpled on the old parquet floor, clamping both hands over her mouth to keep the screams from escaping her dusty throat.

"Elle, you came," Therese said. "Papa passed only seconds ago." She sat on the floor and held Ella until the last sob escaped her cracked lips. Her father had taken to his grave the love Ella craved and the acknowledgement of her existence she sought.

After the funeral the following day, the family gathered around Miriam's dining room table. Ella coughed to dislodge the lump in her throat. "I can't find words right now to apologize to all of you for my betrayal in helping Bernard follow me to Port-au-Prince, then to Miami, and marrying him in secret," Ella said. "But we have two beautiful children. I'll pay back the money Papa spent as soon as I can one day." She wiped tears from her eyes and looked at her oldest sister. "Please forgive me, Miriam."

Miriam's face knotted like the bows she used to tie to Ella's braids. "I will never forgive you. *Papa did not ask for you.* We sacrificed a lot to give you many opportunities, and you wasted them all. You had great potential, and you threw it away on a man who doesn't deserve it. You're nothing but a liar, Ella." Miriam pushed her chair back and stood. "You broke Papa's heart. You killed him—"

"*Stop it!*" Therese shouted, standing up and moving behind Ella's chair. Her hands shook as she rubbed Ella's back. "Miriam, you go to church every Sunday, yet you carry this much hatred in your heart for someone you claimed you once loved. Ella is not responsible for anybody's death."

Ella stared into the eyes of every one of her siblings as if to commit them to her fragile mind. She walked upstairs and came down with her bag. She could not let Miriam's hatred and her father's unbending heart destroy her. He took the love she had thought she needed to his grave. This trip had showed her that her life was in Miami with her family and her friends, and she could get her memory back. Her head held high, she walked out the door.

"Elle, where are you going?" Therese asked. "It's the middle of the night."

"I'm going to wait at the depot for the next bus to Port-au-Prince. I'm going home, Têtê,"

"You can't spend the night at the station. It's not safe. Come! I need to tell you something." Therese handed a blanket to Ella and wrapped herself in another one.

"Something about Bernard," Ella said slowly, remembering.

The sisters settled on two rockers on the front porch, and Therese began.

"Bernard was seventeen when Papa asked Miriam to take him in to give him a chance to learn a trade at the missionary school in town. His father worked for us and died in an accident on our farm. As the oldest of eight, Papa wanted Bernard to be able to help his mother financially. They're very poor. But clearly Bernard had other plans."

Ella stopped rocking. The letter from Western Union about the transfer popped into her mind. "Who's Martha Antoine?"

Therese peered at her in the dimness of the streetlight across the street. "Martha is Bernard's mother. He didn't tell you about his family?"

"No, but he sent money to her. Maybe often."

"Hmm." Therese nodded her head. "Bernard may have some redeeming qualities."

"But...why did the family oppose our union? Being poor is not a crime. Bernard is very smart."

"I want to be honest with you, Elle. We felt you could do better than him. He followed you to Port-au-Prince. When we sent you to Miami, unbeknownst to us, he decided to find you at any price. About four months after you left for Miami, Emile took the harvest money to Port-au-Prince for deposit and to buy stuff we needed. Bernard ambushed our brother and beat him badly. But he didn't count on an eyewitness following him to the boarding house where he was staying. When the police found the half-empty sack with our farm name on it and his bloody clothes, Bernard admitted to the crime and signed the confession." Ella ran her palms over her face. Fear tightened her throat. Would she remember all this? "His father was a good man," Therese continued. "In honor of his father's years of service to us, Papa chose not to press charges and let Bernard keep the money on the condition that he never contacted you and he took care of his family. Bernard took the money, and said he was going to the Dominican Republic to work. He swore he'd never go near you."

Her mind was a jumble of running thoughts. Ella whispered, "That's why he got so mad when I told you we were married years ago."

Ella and Therese sat in silence for a while as Ella absorbed what she had just learned. Ella's fatigue left her body as understanding replaced it. "*Oh mon Dieu*, do you have the signed confession?" Ella asked, when it seemed like Therese had fallen asleep. "Why didn't the family tell me before?"

"You mean before you married him?" Therese asked with reproach lacing her words. "You didn't tell me until months later. Remember? We thought he was in the Dominican Republic. Once our father learned you were pregnant, he said to leave it alone. Bernard was your family now." Therese pulled the blanket to her chin. "Your child would bear his name. A father's sin of *thievery* would mark a son forever in our culture. You know that."

Ella said nothing. Soon sleep carried her away.

Dawn seeped under Ella's closed lids as she stretched the kinks from her joints. She stood and shook Therese awake. Therese pressed Ella's head to her bosom. "Please take care, Elle. Our siblings are upset. Give them time." She handed a sealed envelope to Ella. "Use this proof as you wish. But know that once you put it out, you can't put it back. *Mwen renmen'w.*"

"I love you too, Têtê." Ella clutched the envelope in her hand as if her fingernails had grown into talons. She now knew why Bernard was still with her.

At the airport in Port-au-Prince, she craned her neck, scanning the throng of people. She smiled when she spied Monique pushing through people to get to her. After a long embrace and enough tears to fill a cistern in her village, Monique said, "How are you, Elle? Your accident really scared me. It was an accident, right?"

"Yes, it was. I have no reason to kill myself. I have two beautiful children I adore, great friends, a future—" A gurgling noise escaped from her mouth, sounding like a sob and a laugh. "My father died before I got there. But I remember a lot."

"I'm sorry about your father. I'm slowly learning that I may actually care about Papa more than I allow myself to feel."

"We spent too much time hating. We need more time healing. How's your maman, Moe?"

"Maman suffers so much from her burns. Her pain keeps me alert." A flash of anger crossed Monique's face. "Self-defense classes are a great outlet for me. I fight every day. Go back and fight for *you*. But please be careful!"

The Christmas decorations at the airport made Ella long to go home and decorate the house with her children. They talked for hours until Ella's flight was boarding. "See you soon," Ella said, hugging Monique tight as if she wanted to fold her into her carry-on. She leaned over and whispered into Monique's ear, "I wish 1984 brings the change you need to escape. *Joyeux Noel et Bonne Année, ma soeur.*"

Ella wished her desire to hold her children would make the plane go faster. When the jet landed in Miami, she pushed people out of the aisle to exit the cabin. She needed her children's hugs, smells, and touches to help her feel the earth under her feet again.

At Lois's, she kept her finger on the doorbell until the door finally opened. "Oh, Lois, I'm sorry I didn't call while I was in Haiti but—"

"Honey, come inside." Lois led her to the sofa.

Ella picked up the stuffed purple elephant Perrine carried everywhere and sprung up from the couch like a windup toy. "Lois, where are my children?"

"I'm sorry, Elle. Bernard took them yesterday." Lois handed an envelope to her. "He left this for you."

Ella ripped open the envelope and read the words that swam in her tears. *My lawyer called your actions "child abandonment." I have my children. I know I shouldn't trust you with their safety. You are crazy and suicidal. I'll be in touch.*

She felt something like a tear in her stomach, and she ran to the bathroom to retch. She lay on the cold tile floor curled up in a fetal position, whimpering. Lois banged on the door. "Elle, open the door. Let's talk, sweetie."

"*Talk*," Ella said, jumping to her feet. "Talk, talk, talk." She opened the bathroom door. "Lois, please take me home. Bernard might call the house and want to *talk*."

When she got home, she inhaled the scent of the purple elephant, and the sweet smell of her daughter comforted her. She rummaged through the hamper for Alex's shirt and climbed into bed with the objects. The empty house enveloped her like a tomb that swallowed her further. She prayed her children would be home before Christmas. Cecilia came over every day after work.

Ella decorated the house and waited for her children to return. A week later, Bernard strutted back in, whistling a tune. Ella turned from the stove. "Mommy, Mommy, where were you?" three-year-old Perrine cried, hugging her legs. Ella sat on the kitchen floor and gathered her children onto her lap, kissing them with hunger. Bernard stood in the doorway, his sinister smile mocking her tears.

"I think you've finally lost your mind," he said. "I'm starting a PhD program in the fall. I will be a *doctor.*" He paused as if to let his poisonous words seep into her pores. "Look at you. So, did your family fill your crazy head with lies about me?" He snorted. His voice rose to a crescendo. "I'm leaving you. You will never be a doctor. Don't you forget that!"

Ella recoiled. And just like that she could see clearly through the veil Bernard had used to hide his true feelings all these years. And she had loved this man. She'd made lots of sacrifices for this monster. She pulled the confession letter from the pocket of her slacks and shook it like an exhibit. "You can keep this copy. I have the original," she said, throwing it on the floor. "I will make you eat your hurtful words while I wipe that pretentious smirk off your face. I'll tell the high-society Haitians of this community who Bernard Antoine really is. *Don't you forget that!*"

For the first time, she saw the confidence slip off Bernard's face when he picked up the paper off the floor. "Your father promised to destroy this."

"I guess Papa cared about me after all. He must have known that I'd need this one day. I'll call you when I'm ready to talk. Now *get out!*"

She followed him to the front door with one arm around her daughter and the other hand on top of her son's head. With a heavy dose of power, Ella slammed the door behind him. It was time for her to formulate her list of demands.

61
Monique

The days following her mother's death had plunged Monique into the darkest place in her mind. A place she had thought only Julien dwelled. Except now she hunkered in there with her guilt. The child Monique had not wanted brought rays of light with a soft touch on her unwashed hair, a *ba* on her wet cheek. She wondered where she would find the courage to attend Maman's funeral the following day. She couldn't remember ever feeling more alone. She put the pillow over her head in the darkened room and let the tears soak into the mattress, hoping sleep would take her away for a spell.

A voice penetrated her slumber. "Monique Hazel Magloire." She was dreaming about Cecilia. She turned and faced the wall. "Moe! *Moe*! I'm here."

She tossed the pillow on the floor and switched on the lamp. Her eyes opened wide and then wider. She shook her head as if a perverse dream was playing a sadistic game with her raw emotions.

"Ceecee, is that you?" Monique said, squinting. "Oh dear! Chantal." She kicked the sheet off her legs and hurried to the door, pulling the women inside and closing it. She fell into their arms, and sobs traveled through them like waves.

The door flew open a few minutes later, and Julien stood on the threshold with a smiling Odile in his arms. "Oh, you have company," he said. "Ode and I wanted you to join us in the garden for some fresh air."

"No," Monique said, reaching for her daughter. Odile turned sideways and threw her arm around her father's neck.

"By the way, you never gave me the information for the funeral tomorrow," he said, kissing Odile's forehead.

Monique pushed the women behind her as if to protect them and stood in front of Julien. She poked his chest hard with her middle finger. "I don't want you or any of your family members near Maman's funeral." The simmering rage erupted like vomit from her mouth. "Stay away! You murderer! *You killed her.*"

Julien backed away as she pushed the door closed behind him. Monique dropped down on the floor and held her head in her hands, rocking back-and-forth. The women sat on either side of her, their bodies bookending her in place in the silence of friendship and love.

Seated between Cecilia and Chantal at the church, Monique found the courage to pay homage to her mother. The funeral director walked toward the open casket and, as if in slow motion, lowered the lid over Maman's peaceful face. With raw pain squeezing her heart, Monique's mind flew to the many times she had seen Maman seated in the pew that bore their family name. She turned her gaze down the long bench and nodded at Esther, Solange, and Papa. They would forever be a family.

The clicking of the casket lid sounded like a message from Maman for Monique to take flight. After the reception on that clear December day, she filled a basket with food items, a bottle of rum, wine, and blankets. She drove away from the city with Cecilia and Chantal. The streets were crowded with people who seemed to be performing a choreographed dance with the bundles on their heads, under their arms, and on their backs—burdens as ever-present as the oppression they lived under. A small crowd carried protest signs against injustice, poverty, and hunger. "Are these people demonstrating, Moe?" Chantal asked. "I'm surprised to see that here."

"The countryside has always been where it starts," Monique said. "There are sporadic killings, but the people are determined. That's why our Pass-It-Along group is preparing for our *D-Day*."

"Please be careful," Cecilia said. "I know this place must be dangerous if they can keep *you* here."

"You know it, Ceecee," Monique said. "Many women here have no idea they had rights and an obligation to arm themselves with knowledge. We have a small army spread across the countryside planting seeds in fertile minds." She chuckled. "Hopefully 1984 will be the year!"

She stopped in Leogane, and they settled down in a grove of coconut trees. The expanse of the sea made Monique long to swim away.

"This is beautiful," Cecilia said. "It reminds me of home."

"I had no idea such splendor existed in Haiti," Chantal said. "My parents stopped bringing me here when you started coming to Miami every summer, Moe. You were about eight or so."

"Don't let the beauty fool you. Haiti's politics are a cancer that rots the country from the inside, while the outside looks pretty. Anyway, Ceecee, tell me about Orson. He makes you happy?" Monique said.

Cecilia leaned on an elbow and raised her head to look at her friend, pushing the sunglasses on top of her head. "You know, the beginning was a bit... rocky. I had to get used to making space for someone to be so close to me. Orson is...considerate. I love him. We're making things work."

"I don't want to sound too sinister, but keep your eyes open for signs," Monique said. "I spoke with Lan. I can't believe what Kevin did to her. And I saw Ella here on her way back to Miami a couple weeks ago. But you and I have always known Bernard was... How did you describe him, Ceecee?"

"Opaque," Cecilia said. "But you know, sometimes when you live close to it, you don't see it. You plunge into the murkiness as if you can see the other side." Cecilia shook her head. The sunglasses fell on the blanket. "Love is complicated, Moe."

"I think about Brian *all* the time," Monique said. "Love is complicated."

"Oh, Brian sent a package," Chantal said.

"What?" Monique said. "Now you tell me. Where is it?"

"I didn't want to bring it to your house, so it's at Esther's," said Chantal.

"Good idea," Monique said.

But what was in the package? Her heart skipped a few beats. They ate, drank, talked, and napped. Monique hated to leave, but she had to go back to her daughter, the package, and her plan. After the women settled into two of the guest bedrooms, she walked into her room, sat on the bed, and ripped the brown paper from the package they'd picked up earlier. She frowned when she saw the title. *Love Story*. Who hadn't read that book? She opened the cover and saw a pink envelope taped to the inside. A whiff of a familiar scent rose to her nostrils. With shaking hands, she opened the envelope and pulled out a sympathy card.

December 1983

Dear Moe,
Please accept my condolences. I'm sorry about your deep loss.

I love you always,
Brian

Monique smelled the card, searching for the man she had lost but never had. She inhaled the faint smell of Brian's aftershave and felt a stirring that brought a flood of tears. What did he mean by *always*? Why had he sent her a copy of *Love Story*? Chantal had said he had a girlfriend.

When Julien burst into the bedroom, she lowered her hands and slipped the envelope back inside the book on her lap. He walked over and sat on her side of the bed. "I took Odile to see my parents. They're as much in love with her as I am. It hurts that you wouldn't let me comfort you."

"I don't need you, Julien, and I never will."

"You're upset. I understand." His hand trailed the skin of her thigh. She cringed.

"Don't touch me," she yelled. "I buried my mother today. I need room to grieve. *Can I please have that?*"

For the first time since she had been condemned to share that house with Julien, he took his pillow off the bed. "I'll give you a couple of days, Monique." He left the weekly envelope with her allowance on the bed. "I don't need your fucking money," she screamed at the empty room. "I need my passport!"

Early the next morning, she dropped Cecilia and Chantal off at the airport. "I'll see you all soon," she said, hugging them.

"When...when are you coming?" Cecilia asked, hope brightening her eyes.

"I need a passport first since Julien seized mine when I returned from Miami with Odile," Monique said. "It'll be soon, Ceecee. Soon. That's a promise."

Monique drove by the front of the passport office twice. She knew enough high-placed people who could get her a passport, but she couldn't trust anyone. She hoped that an office employee would not recognize her maiden name, and she could get a passport without alerting Julien. Men with guns and dark glasses loitered around the entrance. She parked her car several blocks away and walked toward freedom or solitary confinement. She was already in prison.

62

Cecilia

C ecilia and Orson settled into a comfortable routine after they bought a three-bedroom house in the suburbs in the spring of 1984. Cecilia had confronted him the previous December about her suspicions. He'd confessed to his addiction to alcohol. Unlike her mother, Orson loved her. He wanted to stay sober. He called her pretty. He started going to AA meetings. Cecilia decorated their new home with wicker furniture, pastel artwork, and filmy blue-and-beige drapery. Now she could have a dog. But her heart ached for her long-gone Friendy. The day after they'd closed on their house, they'd attended the funeral for Larry's wife. Cecilia felt like she had lost a friend. She had gotten to know the woman through her boys and her husband. His daily calls pulled Cecilia into the depth of his loss.

"Did you eat today?" Cecilia asked Larry before hanging up the phone. "The boys need you to be healthy."

"Thank you for the shepherd's pie. The twins wanted to eat the whole thing in one sitting." He chuckled. "Going back to work is the best medicine for me."

"I know what you mean. I love my job too." She tried to stifle a yawn.

"Sorry. You sound tired. Where's Orson? He doesn't mind me keeping you from him this long?"

"Oh, he's not home yet. He's still driving the cab in the evening. Good night, Larry."

She hung up and turned on the TV. But her mind kept drifting to Orson. She was concerned about his safety at night, but he came through with his share of the down payment for the house and the monthly bills they shared. Cecilia felt shame for the seed of doubt and unease that prickled her mind like a grain of sand in a shoe. Just as she reached to turn off the lamp, she heard the creaking sound of the back door. She sat up in the bed and yelled, "Honey, I'm still awake."

Because she was a heavy sleeper, Cecilia had missed Orson coming home in the wee hours for several days. She was up and out of the house by six in the morning while he slept. They needed to synchronize their schedules, so they could have a couple of nights a week to be together. Orson had fallen off the proverbial wagon a month before. He went to rehab and met his sponsor frequently. He was trying.

"Okay, I'll be right in," he said. "I have a surprise for you."

With a big smile on his face, Orson walked into the bedroom and offered her a puppy sitting on his hands like a platter. It looked like Friendy. He was a light chocolate Yorkie with a white underbelly. She jumped off the bed and threw her arms around Orson's neck, the puppy yelping between them.

"Oh my God, Orson! How did you know?" Happy tears poured down her face as she reached for the puppy and held him to her chest.

"I found an old picture of your dog. That's why it took so long. It was hard to find *Friendy*, pretty lady."

"You are undoubtedly the best husband on the planet. I love you."

Cecilia had become obsessed with filling the rooms with babies. But after five months of marriage, she sought professional help. Orson had held her hand at the fertility clinic the week before. The pictures of newborns covered half a wall in the doctor's office and pulled her eyes to the beauty of this gift she wanted. The doctor walked in, and the look on her face tanked Cecilia's hope. She squeezed the *Many Causes of Infertility* flyer she'd been reading and stared at the woman.

The doctor shook their hands before sitting behind her desk and riffling through a chart. "I'm sorry, Mrs. Matthews, but you have pelvic inflammatory disease from an untreated infection you would have contracted when you were raped, based on your medical history. If it had been treated early, it wouldn't have caused infertility," the doctor had said, shaking her head. "We're going to treat the disease now, but there are other options to create a family."

Cecilia had stood from the chair, pulling Orson with her. The devastating news had left her hollow again. She'd always sensed that these men had taken more from her that day, but she hadn't known how much more. Orson had taken her in his arms in the parking lot until her body-shaking sobs had turned to a soft whimper. "It's okay, pretty lady. We're a family with or without children." He'd kissed her wet cheek. "I love you."

Now she hugged the puppy until she felt his little heart flutter. "My Friendy," she murmured, kissing the dog. "*My baby*."

Orson kissed her lips, and the strong smell of the Juicy Fruit gum he chewed invaded her nostrils. But another odor hid underneath the scent, or did it? Cecilia sniffed, placing the puppy on a pillow. She pulled him down next to her and kissed his neck, his lips. "I love you, Orson Mathews. Thank you."

She pulled the T-shirt over his head, feeling a hunger. "Go take a shower," she said. "I'll be waiting." Her hand stopped over his head. His hair was still wet and smelled like a lemony shampoo they did not have in the house. She stared at Orson, urging him to make her believe what he was about to say.

"Um…I stopped by Mom's earlier and grabbed a shower," he said, pulling her nightwear off in a frenzy. "I was…grimy."

Orson reached over to turn off the lamp on her side of the bed. Cecilia lost her appetite for sex. "Let's go to sleep," she said. "It's late."

"Oh, no," he said, climbing on top of her. "You started this."

"Stop it," she said, and he did. She reached for Friendy in the dark, her hand stroking his fur and rising up and down with the dog's fast breathing that matched hers.

63

Lanei

anei yanked Kevin's clothes off hangers and threw them in a pile in the middle of the bedroom. His shoes, boxing gloves, and toiletries joined the clothes. She felt a release, a space in her mind and her heart where she could be fearless. She only wished she could pour gasoline on his belongings and set them ablaze, but it would be a sin. Wouldn't it? Since her return from Guam in January, she had been planning her move to Miami.

The telephone stopped her movement as she shoved his effects into the big trash bag. With the receiver nestled between her shoulder and her neck, Lanei listened. "Lan, have you booked your flight yet?" Cecilia asked. "We can't wait to see you and Maria."

"Yeah! Ceecee and I need you down here," Ella said. "It seems the four of us can never be together at the same time."

"But I believe Moe is coming back soon," Cecilia said. "When I went to her mom's funeral with Chantal, I sensed—"

"Speaking of death," Ella said, cutting Cecilia off. "I felt like an orphan when I lost my father, and I wasn't even close to him the way you and your mama were, Lan."

"Ella, may I finish a sentence before you jump in?" Cecilia said.

"Ceecee, I'm thinking about how odd it is that my father, Lan's mama, and Moe's maman died all around the same time. What's the message?" Ella continued as if Cecilia hadn't spoken. "Is the universe trying to tell us something?"

"Life is telling us that we are mortals," Cecilia said. "Our time will come. We don't know when, so we need to make the best of today. Right, Lan?"

"Where are you guys?" Lanei asked, a smile teasing her lips.

"At my new house," Cecilia said. "I'm on the bedroom phone. Elle is in the kitchen. We wanted to talk to you together."

"God listens," Lanei said. "He may not answer as fast as we would like, but he does respond. He answered me. I'm coming back to Miami on Saturday."

Lanei had to pull the phone away from her ears. The women screamed and started banging their bracelets against the phone. "I'm glad it's before Kevin's release," Cecilia said. "You can stay with me until you find a place."

"No! She should stay with me. Maria needs playmates," Ella said. "I have the kids. Oh, sorry, Ceecee. I didn't mean—"

"It's all right, Elle," Cecilia said. "Lan, do you need help with moving expenses?"

"Sisters, sisters," Lanei said, raising her voice and feeling happy. She needed that heavy dose of love to keep on moving forward. "Mama left me some money. I had no idea she'd saved that much. She never wanted anything for herself. She lived a very deprived life." Lanei wiped tears from her eyes. "You know, as I watched Mama's shriveled body on her deathbed, I realized God could not have wanted her to stop living because she bore a child out of wedlock. Mama died a little every day after I was born."

After mass the following day, Lanei went to the church office. "Where's Father Abbott?" she asked the young priest who had officiated the service now sitting behind the desk.

"I'm Father O'Malley," the priest said. "Please sit down. Father Abbott is in the hospital. How may I help you?"

"Oh! It's such a long story, and Father Abbott knows all of it." Lanei tightened the scarf around her neck. The hissing heat from the radiator could not chase the late March air seeping into her core.

"I have some time," the priest said.

When she stopped talking, Father O'Malley took a quick look at the clock on the wall. Lanei followed his gaze.

"I'm sorry. I told you it was a long story. I refuse to believe that God would want me to sacrifice my life to uphold vows from his church. I try to be good in my heart and in my actions." Lanei stared at the priest. "Isn't that what God sees and judges us by, not by reading words in a book and chasing them with bad deeds?"

He nodded, the corner of his mouth twitching into a smile. "You took the words out of my mouth, Lanei."

Light entered her heart. Father Abbott and Father Arnoldo had always told her to honor the vows she made in the church. "But, Father, what does *till death do us part* really mean?" Lanei asked.

"It means you try hard to honor your God-sanctioned marriage, and you have done that. God doesn't ask us to sacrifice our lives to please him." Father O'Malley shook his head. "It would be suicide!" Lanei leaned over the desk, as if she wanted the words to give her wings. "You already understand what you need to do, my dear. Go serve God with happiness in your heart, Lanei, not resentment and fear."

She stood to leave, trying to control the impulse to hug the priest. "Thank you, Father."

Nate deposited a sleeping Maria on her twin bed that afternoon and looked around the almost empty apartment. "Maria ran around that playground nonstop. She's healthy, Lane." He plopped down on the couch next to her and rubbed his eyes with both fists like a little boy. Nate's biceps stretched the sleeves of his sweater. "Did you finish packing?"

She reached for his hands and Nate sat up. She touched his face. "I'll miss you, Nate." She needed to say that.

Nate's fingers glided over her wet cheeks like silk ribbons. "I will go to Miami with you. You must know that."

"Nate...I need time and space to seek therapy. I was sixteen when I met Kevin. I want to know myself first. I need to learn to take care of my family. Maria and I will go to school and start new chapters."

For a brief moment, Nate's face clouded over. He nodded, kissed her forehead, and left.

Alone and happy, she pulled a suitcase into the middle of the bedroom to finish packing. She hummed a song as she worked. It was "My God Is Good."

64
Ella

B ernard left the evening Ella gave him the copy of his confession letter in December. He had been gone for a couple of months. Ella needed the time to figure out what she wanted to do. The trauma of losing her father and almost losing her children had set her back. With Freda's guidance, she sifted through the mountain of sorrow and loss to find herself again, so she could see the self-sufficient woman she knew she could be one day.

After putting her children to bed that night, she used a knife to pry the lock open on the two-drawer file cabinet Bernard kept in a corner of a closet in the hallway. She sat on the floor and read the bank statements with only his name, the joint mortgage documents, their immigration papers, and the children's birth certificates. She pulled out a fat manila envelope stashed in the back of the bottom drawer, opened it, and gasped. Inside were years of monthly Western Union receipts for funds Bernard had sent to Martha Antoine, his mother, starting in 1977 when he was only tutoring students for a living. There were several messages with the receipts. They all said pretty much the same thing. *Please make sure the kids go to school. Be patient. I'll bring all of you to America when I'm a citizen. You will be proud of me. Papa will not die in vain. They will pay. I love you.*

"Oh my God," Ella said, holding her head. "What does he mean? Therese said his father died on our farm. How?"

She needed more information.

The following day, she walked into the room at the back of the hospital and stopped when she saw the Women Talk group. She wanted to talk to Freda alone. "Come on in, Ella," Freda said. "We'll talk after the group meeting."

Ella listened and marveled at the fact that these women had endured so much pain from life. She identified with many of the situations, except Bernard had never raised his hand to her. How could women stay in relationships where men beat up on them like drums? She would have left if he'd done that. Or would she? How far could a woman go with no money, no degree, and no tools to help her stand on her feet? Bernard had cheated on her. He'd controlled her financial freedom. He'd sabotaged her academic plans. She tried not to stare at the petite red-haired woman with the patchy bruises all over her face and neck. This woman lived with a monster.

At the end of the meeting, Freda walked everyone to the door before coming back and sitting across from Ella with the desk between them. "How is the memory?" Freda asked.

"Well, I remember to come here once a week." Ella smiled. "I remember to speak English, although I have to search for words sometimes. I remember I wanted to be a doctor. I remember Bernard never hit me." Ella pulled a wad of tissue from the box. She could feel the tears forming in her eyes. She told Freda about the money transfers and the messages. She remembered more than she'd thought or perhaps was ready to admit.

"Ella, you said your husband never hit you, but abuse is not always physical. You heard the stories today of exploitation and isolation. Abuse in any form strips you of your confidence, your potential, and sometimes, your life. A member of our group was murdered last week by her fiancée when she called off the wedding. Bernard's actions are calculated. He's a *planner*. That makes him very dangerous. Don't justify his actions by any measure. Bernard was bad from the word *go*."

"But I believed he loved me. I love…loved him, Freda. How do I turn that off?"

"Perhaps you did love him or still do. You'll have to sort that out for yourself. But could it also be that you hung on because you had to prove to your family and to yourself that you made the right choice so long ago?"

Ella nodded. "Freda, I want Bernard out of my life legally, but first I will get everything I deserve. He's not waltzing into the sunset, leaving me trapped with two kids, no job, and no degree. That will be his punishment. The prick!"

"Ella," Freda said, staring into her eyes, "I want you to be clear about the real reason you want your husband around. There are resources available to help you get on your feet. Remember, when you make a pact with the devil, you may not like your share of the bargain in the end."

"As soon as I get what I want, Bernard will be free to go. Not until *then*."

Later that afternoon, she called Bernard at work. She was ready to negoti-ate. Besides, she couldn't let him walk away to become a *doctor* as if she'd never mattered. Bernard would soon learn what it felt like to make sacrifices.

After tucking her kids into bed, she pulled out the chair across from him in the kitchen where he sat nonchalantly waiting for her. She threw the bag with the money transfer receipts on the table. He sat up straighter.

"Why did you lie about sending money to your family? And what do these messages mean?" He pulled the bag toward him, glaring at her. "There are a lot of details I still don't remember since my accident, but I resented my family because they didn't want us to be together. It turned out that wasn't the whole truth though." Ella shook her head and took a sip of water. She'd love a stiff drink now, but she needed a clear head. "You almost killed my brother to come to Miami. Now I know why." She stared at him with disgust in her heart. "You want to rub my family's noses in my failures. They wanted to help you, so you could help your mother." Ella spoke fast before she forgot all she wanted to say. "Why, Bernard? I've never done anything but love you."

Bernard lifted his head and stared at Ella; his face was closed. "Your family killed my father by overworking him like a donkey because we were poor. They buried him on the farm like a dead dog. I don't even know where to put a tombstone to mark his life and death. They wanted me to be a shoemaker. One night, before they sent you to Port-au-Prince, Miriam squatted on the floor where I slept on a straw mat and said she'd throw me out on the street if I even talked to you. I was traumatized—"

"You're still a criminal and a *thief*." Ella leveled the words like a hammer. "You can't justify what you did, Bernard. *No!*"

He reached for her hand. She pushed his away. "Elle, I hated your whole family for their sanctimonious handouts," he said in a low voice, "but I didn't mean to hurt Emile. I needed the money to join you here in Miami. I missed you. I wanted—"

Ella raised her hand to stop him. "It's not going to work anymore, Bernard. You lied. You cheated. I'm going to show people who you really are."

Fear danced in his eyes. "Please don't tell anyone *here*," he begged. "The Meridiens and the Haitian community can never know about this. I have aspi-rations, Ella. I—"

"Uh-uh." She stopped him. "You should ask me what I deserve for supporting you all these years. What do I want for my silence?"

Like a chameleon, his face brightened, and he smiled. "Elle, I'm sorry. I'm willing to do anything to help you. I was wrong about a lot...but never doubt that I love—"

"Don't, Bernard. You kidnapped our children. You planned my pregnancies. You withheld financial support for my school. You belittled me at every opportunity." Ella took a deep breath and stood. "My psychiatrist believes I'll be ready to go back to school next year. When the time comes, you're going to pay for *all* of it. In exchange, I'll keep your ugly secret from the Haitian community and the *Meridiens.*"

He stood, and before she could step away, he cupped her chin in his hand and leaned toward her lips. Like a lightning flash, she saw Bernard cupping Representative Meridien's chin at the movie theater, and the words he had uttered slapped her harder than his fist ever could. She pulled back so fast the chair clattered on the tile floor. "Don't touch me," she screamed. "*Don't ever touch me.*" She held her stomach to stop the nausea rising from its pit. "*O mon Dieu!* You are an evil, *evil* man. That night at the movie theater, you wanted me to see you with her. You wanted me to die."

"Elle, please let me explain. I—"

"*Non, non, non!*" She pushed him away. "Representative Meridien thinks you have pedigree like her." Ella glared at him. "You know how much she hates thieves and liars. Now, get away from me before I change my demand."

"I would always help you, Elle." His voice shook. "We're a team, remember?"

Ella sucked her teeth so hard, her ears popped when she swallowed her saliva. "Please leave." She locked the front door behind him and made her way to the bedroom. "Now it's my turn," she said out loud before turning off the bedside lamp.

Sleep would not come. *When you make a deal with the devil...*

65
Monique

Monique removed her wedding ring and stuffed it in her jeans pocket before climbing the steps leading to the passport office. She needed to be prepared to leave when the regime fell. She believed it would happen soon.

She walked inside the office with her birth certificate and her *carte d'identité* bearing her maiden name. *Monique Magloire.* She fixed a smile on her face and nodded at the heavily armed gendarme in the lobby. Her heels echoed against the floor, and she saw giant pictures of the late Papa Doc Duvalier and Baby Doc, his son, covering most of the wall. People stopped and stared at the pictures as if they were about to genuflect and make the sign of the cross. Monique focused on keeping her eyes from rolling back in her head.

She approached the reception desk. "Bonjour, mademoiselle," Monique said. "I lost my passport, and I need to apply for another one. Please."

"Bonjour, Mademoiselle Magloire," the receptionist said, reading the name on the documents Monique placed on the desk in front of her. She gave Monique a clipboard with an application. "Bring it back when you finish."

"*Merci,*" Monique said, feeling more air reach her lungs. She sat in a metal chair against the opposite wall and kept her face down as people came and went at a rapid pace.

As soon as the guard stepped outside, shaking a pack of Comme Il Faut cigarettes in his hand, the receptionist motioned for Monique to approach her desk. Monique pointed down with the pen, indicating that she wasn't done yet. The woman waved frantically. She approached the desk. "You need to leave now, Monique," the receptionist whispered. "I'll drop the passport off at Tina's office in a couple days." Monique blinked. "I'm one of the first beneficiaries of Pass-It-Along. You changed my life."

"Laurette Moïse," Monique whispered, recognition dawning. "*Mesi anpil.*"

Julien turned to her in the bed that night and asked, "What did you go to the passport office for today?"

She inhaled deeply but quietly, and as casually as she could, she said, "Oh, I wanted to get a new *carte d'identité*. I can't find my old one."

He narrowed his hooded eyes until they looked closed, but she knew he was staring at her. "You better not try to leave Haiti with my daughter. I'm not letting either one of you go. We're family."

Monique pulled the light blanket over her head, but the chill came from inside her body. She counted. Julien rolled out of bed, and she could hear him pulling open drawers in the dining room downstairs. Her stomach clinched.

Part Three

66
Cecilia

C ecilia answered the phone in the kitchen, hoping it was good news for a change. Orson had spent the month of May in rehab again. Cecilia was grateful for Friendy and that Lanei and Ella were nearby. Mel and Michael had gone to Europe on vacation the first week of June. She raised the receiver to her ear and tried to spice her voice with a pinch of joy she wasn't really feeling.

"Hello," she said. "Oh, Uncle Paul! Is everything—"

"Hey, Ceecee." She registered the levity in his voice. She relaxed. "Everything is great, sweetheart. I'm calling because Betty really wants to come to Miami for high school in the fall. I want to know if she can board with you."

"I'd be thrilled. I have plenty room," she said, feeling the space in her heart that needed someone to nurture. "Betty told me at my wedding that she wanted to." She looked around the quiet house as empty as her womb. Friendy was snoring on the kitchen mat. Orson was working late again. "I can't believe Betty is fifteen already. She looked so young at my wedding barely two years ago."

"She skipped a grade. She'll be fourteen in September. I can bring her in a couple weeks for the summer. Don't you need to talk to Orson about this?"

"Oh, no. He'll be fine with it. Can't wait to see you both."

A few weeks later, Betty's presence and Friendy's unconditional love brought a much-needed liveliness to the house. The teen settled in as if she had always lived with Cecilia and Orson. One week after Betty's arrival, she'd overheard Orson and Betty talking. "Betty, I'm so glad you're here. You bring diversion to Ceecee's routine. She needed a child," Orson had said.

"I'm not a child, Uncle Orson," Betty had replied. "I'm going to high school."

Cecilia had smiled. Soon Betty became Mel and Mike's favorite babysitter.

One day in August, right before school started, Betty baked all afternoon. "Uncle Orson, I saved you a piece of the sweet potato pie I baked today," she said to him as he rubbed sleep from his eyes. "Would you like some coffee with it? I can make some."

Shy and precocious Betty reminded Cecilia of herself at that age, but Cecilia had never had to battle a weight problem. "Betty, you're an angel," Orson said. "Skip the coffee 'cause I gotta sleep a bit, but bring on the pie, sweetheart."

"I made a pie for Larry's boys, Ceecee," Betty said. "We can drop it off later."

"Oh, that was so thoughtful," Cecilia said, before going back to paying bills at the dining table. Friendy planted his front paws on her thigh and stared at her. She laughed before picking him up. "We'll go for a walk soon." She kissed his head. "You're spoiled rotten."

"Jeez, why is everybody feeding Larry and holding his hand?" Orson said, staring at Cecilia. His bloodshot eyes drilled into her. "He depends on you a... lot, Ceecee."

"If I didn't know better, I'd say you're jealous, Orson," Cecilia said. "Don't be. I'm not the cheating type."

Orson looked away.

A few weeks later, Cecilia hurried her steps when she saw Orson's car in their driveway. Her meeting with Freda tonight had been particularly revealing. Cecilia had sat across from the counselor, her arms crossed tightly around her middle as if the words would tumble out on their own if she didn't hold them in. "My mother was an alcoholic who hated me way before she started to drink. I—" Cecilia had paused. "The truth is, I'm married to an alcoholic who I want to support. He has a disease. Would I abandon him if he had diabetes? He's been out of rehab for a couple months, and I'm making myself sick thinking I can control his sobriety. He's not bringing in as much money from the cab now, yet he's gone long hours. Could he be cheating? I don't know, but I can't seem to bring it up with him. It would require that I take action. Right?"

Cecilia sobbed. Freda walked over to her and gently pried her hands away from her face. "Look at me, Ceecee. Your husband has the disease of alcoholism and perhaps suffers from other types of addictions. He will have to want to be sober for him, not for you. If he had diabetes, you couldn't make him accept treatment if he didn't want to be healthy. You need to face a problem in order to fix it, right?"

Cecilia nodded, took a tissue from the giant box on the desk and blew her nose. She hugged the counselor who always knew what to say to get Cecilia thinking with her head.

Now she pulled inside the garage, fighting the urge to go snoop inside Orson's car. She hastened her steps, hoping that Betty and Orson were still up. They could spend some time together. It had been weeks since they were all home at the same time. She had given up trying to convince him not to drive a cab at night. His reassurance of his safety left no room for argument. Could it be that he was dealing with more than alcohol addiction? What was he doing with his money? Did he gamble?

The hairs on her arms stood up when she walked into the quiet house. She stubbed her right toe on the leg of a stool. She pulled her lips in and let the pain subside. She turned on the kitchen light and walked toward Betty's bedroom door. It was locked. She frowned. Friendy scratched and yelped from inside Betty's bedroom, wanting to come out. No movement came from the teen. Frowning deeper, Cecilia peeked into their bedroom. Sprawled in the middle of the bed, Orson snored. She changed into her sleepwear in the bathroom. The darkness weighed down on her as if it had a physical presence. She tossed and turned before sleep pulled her into a nightmare where a monster dressed in Orson's clothes chased her into a black hole.

"You're quiet this morning," Cecilia said to Betty. "You slept well?"

"I...I have a headache," Betty muttered.

"Friendy wanted to come out last night." Cecilia stroked the dog's head on her lap. "Why did you lock your bedroom door?"

"Um...no reason." Betty shrugged.

"Well, we're on our own for breakfast. I didn't even see Orson this morning. He must have left early. Hopefully, he went to an AA meeting."

"I'm not hungry," Betty said, with her back to Cecilia as she walked to her room.

On their way to the garage, she heard Betty sniffle behind her. Cecilia turned and saw tears in the teen's eyes. "Must be a bad migraine, Betty. I'll get you some aspirin before we leave for school."

That afternoon, Cecilia found Betty leaning on her car in the teacher's parking lot. "You're still here? I thought you went home with Susan's mom," Cecilia said. "I told you I had a staff meeting."

"Susan was out today. I…wanted to wait for you." Betty opened the car door and sat inside.

Cecilia slid behind the wheel and turned to her cousin. "How's the headache?"

Betty shrugged and stared ahead.

"I know," Cecilia said. "Let's stop for your favorite. Chinese food." She smiled. Betty crossed her arms over her chest and mumbled something. "Betty, honey, are you okay? Are kids…bothering you? You'd tell me if someone was… upsetting you at school?"

Betty nodded but said nothing.

One week later, Cecilia woke up and found Orson sleeping in his dirty clothes on the couch in the spare bedroom. Shaking him awake, she felt something hard in his pocket. She pulled it out and screamed, dropping it on the floor.

"Orson…*Orson*." His bloodshot eyes blinked several times before focusing on her. "What are you doing with a gun? What's going on?"

He swung his legs off the couch and planted them on the floor. "I drive a cab at night. I need to protect myself."

Cecilia squinted at him, trying to understand. The small gray gun sat between them like a chasm. "Orson, I don't want a gun in my house. Why do you have to drive a cab at night anyway?"

"Told you I make more money."

"How so? And where's the money? You haven't given me your share of the bills this month yet. Why are you sleeping in here? Are you drinking again? Are you going to answer me?" Cecilia fired the questions like darts.

"Take a breath, woman." Orson cleared his phlegmy throat. "I didn't wanna wake you this morning, so I crashed in here. Why aren't you at work?"

"Today is Columbus Day," Cecilia said, sniffing the pungent air in the room. "I'm not going to go through another round of rehab with you. It costs too damn much in dollars and emotion. We need to talk. You've been avoiding me for weeks."

"Ceecee, I'm not drinking. Why do you always have to accuse me like I'm a criminal?" Orson stood from the couch and almost jogged to the front door. "I'm going to a…meeting." He left.

Cecilia paced the length of the house, trying to corral her thoughts. Something was very wrong. She grabbed her car keys, her handbag, and Friendy. The little dog licked her face as if to take her worries away. She smiled. When she turned the corner to Helen's house, she realized that was where she intended to go.

"Is everything okay?" Helen asked, ushering Cecilia inside.

"No. I think Orson is drinking again…but I'm not sure. I don't know how many times I can go through this." Cecilia sat on a stool in the kitchen, stroking Friendy on her lap. The warmth coming from his body soothed her nerves. "I have my limits, Helen. What else is wrong with your son?"

"Ceecee, I'm so sorry. Please let me help with the money for his rehab if he needs it. Addiction is not curable, but with your support and your love, Orson will stay…sober."

"I couldn't accept your money, Helen. You were so generous with the gifts for the house."

"Oh, Orson told you about the down payment for the house?" Helen asked, placing her palm over her chest. "See, he's trying to be honest."

"Wait! What do you mean?" Cecilia asked slowly. "I was talking about the open house gifts last year. You know, the blue porcelain set and the paintings." She narrowed her eyes, shrinking Helen to a shadow. "You gave him his share of the down payment? Oh my God!" When she'd married Orson, she'd wanted to be sure that he wasn't more interested in her *paycheck* than her, so they'd kept separate accounts and shared the expenses. "You give him money for the monthly bills too, don't you?"

Helen twisted her hands like a kid who had just broken something. "Please think of it as his early inheritance," Helen said. "We help our children with school and—"

"No," Cecilia stopped her. "You've hidden a lot from me. You led me to believe Orson was only dealing with alcoholism. Now I know he must be addicted to other…vices. Tell me the truth. Is he on drugs? Does he gamble? What am I dealing with, Helen?"

Helen covered her mouth with the back of her hand. "Ceecee, give him a chance. He loves you."

Cecilia got off the stool with Friendy in one hand, and she took her handbag off the counter and left. She climbed back in her car, put Friendy on the passenger seat, pulled down the rearview mirror, and stared at her face. "I need to give *me* a chance," she said to her reflection. "I'm pretty not because Orson says it, but because *I am*."

67

Lanei

After moving back to Miami, Lanei had settled near the university. Two weeks before his release in April of the previous year, Kevin had stabbed an inmate and gotten two years added to his sentence. Lanei had lit several candles at the church to thank the Virgin Mary for the reprieve, but she knew the day would come when she'd have to face her fears in the presence of Kevin. She appreciated every extra day to strengthen herself.

Remembering the advice of the young priest in Chicago, Lanei had followed Cecilia's suggestion to meet with Freda. The day she met the middle-aged therapist all her unease had disappeared.

"Welcome to Women Talk. I'm Freda. The group will start in an hour. We can talk until then," she'd said.

"Thank you, Freda." Lanei had fidgeted on the chair. "I've only ever talked to my priests."

"Well, I can't give you penance to absolve you of any real or perceived sins,"—Freda had pointed to the tissue box on her desk—"but I've been told I'm a pretty good listener."

Lanei had talked about her mother's sacrifices, her father's rejection and suicide, Nate's love, and her dreams. How the abuse she endured in her marriage had shaken her Catholic foundation, because her faith had shackled her to a man who used her body sinfully. "Why did God let this happen to me, Freda? No priest has ever answered this question to my satisfaction."

Freda had pulled her chair closer to the desk and leaned toward her. "Have you ever questioned the role of your free will? If God created you, didn't he or she also give you the gift of self-preservation? Have you ever noticed how men use the Word of God to keep women bound and tethered, while they seem to have a direct path to God for their own redemption?"

Lanei could only weep. When Cecilia and Ella came later for the group meeting, they sat together. They'd listened as women representing many other segments of society talked about the many faces of abuse. Lanei saw pain and resolve merge to build strength and a path to wholeness.

Standing in the parking lot with Cecilia and Ella after that meeting, Lanei had said, "Moe was right. It feels as though I've known Freda forever. She seems to know how I feel before I even open my mouth."

"She's an *islander*," Cecilia said. The women nodded as if that explained everything.

❧

A year after Lanei moved back to Miami, Nate settled into a condo on Biscayne Boulevard. Lanei enrolled in school while working part-time at the pharmacy where she'd met Nate as a freshman nine years ago. After being out of school since the fall of 1978, she was back in the fall of 1985, and she felt like she never left. Her physical and financial independence had given her the room to sort out her feelings and make choices based on what she wanted. Her love for Nate brought good feelings that Lanei no longer felt guilty about.

Lanei closed her chemistry textbook in the quiet kitchen, and even though she missed Maria, she reveled in her daughter's good health that allowed her to go to school with Alex and Perrine and enjoy sleepovers at Auntie Ella's. She pulled the pile of mail toward her, sorting it by category until she got to the last one. She turned the envelope in her hands for several minutes. Kevin couldn't hurt her anymore. She'd gotten away. She ripped it open and read the letter that had come in the mail that day.

October 13, 1985

Bitch, I got divorce papers yesterday. I won't be locked up forever. I'll never let you go.

Your husband, Kevin.

Lanei walked to her bedroom, knelt in front of her bed, and reached for her rosary under her pillow. She prayed until joy replaced the fear that had lassoed her body. She could hear the priest in Chicago. *Serve God with love, not resentment and fear.*

She stood and rubbed her knees before picking up the phone. "What's wrong, Lane?" Nate asked.

"I filed for divorce a year ago," she said. "It's final. I received an…upsetting letter from Kevin today."

"Why didn't you tell me you filed for divorce?" Nate said with a tremor in his voice. "You shouldn't be alone. Didn't Maria go over to Ella's for a sleepover?"

"Yes." Lanei swallowed. She took a deep breath as if she was about to plunge into an icy lake and whispered, "Please come, Nate."

She opened the door a few minutes later and walked into Nate's open arms. "Is it okay, Lane?" he asked, his eyes widening with understanding.

She buried her face in his neck and whispered, "Yes."

He kissed her with a hunger that demanded to be satiated. She took his hand and walked into the bathroom where yellow candles scented the air. Her need frightened her. They peeled each other's clothes off with a slowness that fueled her longing. Nate's eyes fingered her naked body. He turned her to face the shower wall and poured shampoo over her hair. He massaged her scalp while his wet lips sucked on the skin of her neck until she grabbed the soap tray to stay upright. After he rinsed her hair, she soaped his body with tentative strokes, touching his pulsing penis.

"Lane, I've waited for this moment for a long time," he gasped. "I need to have you now."

She nodded, unable to form words. Her breath struggled to escape her chest. He lifted her right leg and entered her. Her breath stopped. She fought to regain it. The sensation wrapped around her like mummy sheets. Nate thrust into her with reverence and urgency. Her screams when she came for the first time released her pain, her regrets, and all of her confusion. They stood against the wall connected in body and spirit until the water turned cold. "Let's go to bed, Nate. I want more," she said against his chest.

Lanei drifted to sleep in Nate's arms feeling blessed by God. Kevin could no longer touch her physically or emotionally. Lanei was a warrior in God's army. She could not lose.

But she would have to face Kevin one day.

68
Ella

For the first time, Ella swept away the emotional debris of her life—her father's indifference, Miriam's resentment, and Bernard's betrayal—and focused on self-healing. Time flew when life had purpose, and Ella's was full with her children, her friends, and her school. Two years before, the car accident had almost killed her. Years of therapy had given her the wings to fly solo, but debris had a way of being stirred around by the wind.

Bernard had manipulated her twice to follow her—first to Port-au-Prince, then to Miami—because he claimed he couldn't be apart from her. Well, he had his wish now. He was bound to pay for her therapy, for a roof over her head, and most importantly, for her school since she'd lost the scholarship that had come with her job at the hospital. He had to take a second job teaching night school at a community college to keep up with the family's financial needs. Ella rejoiced when Bernard dropped out of his doctorate program because he couldn't fit it into his busy work schedule. Served him right. *The prick.* Meanwhile, with Bernard out of her daily life, Ella could finally move on unimpeded with her academic plan.

When Lois flew to Jamaica in early October to tend to her mother, Ella wished she could have gone as well. Janet loved her like a mother would.

"Hey, baby girl," Janet had said in a strong voice that belied how ill Lois said she was. "So nice to hear your voice, darlin'. How's school?"

Swallowing her tears, Ella had said, "Jan, I'm twenty-seven, and I just started my second semester of *freshman year.*" A smile had bloomed on her face as if Janet could see it. "I'll forever be grateful for your love, your—"

"Stay in school, child," Janet had said, cutting her off. "The devil will always try to take you on the wrong path. Be strong. I'm glad your friends are with you."

"Oh, yes! I couldn't do it without them. Monique will make her way back. I have no doubt. Lan is in school too. They help a lot with the kids, especially Ceecee. The kids love Auntie Ceecee. She spoils them, you know." Ella had smiled. "Jan, I did buy a cast-iron skillet for cooking, but Bernard better never give me another use for it."

Janet had laughed until a coughing spell stopped her. "My work is done, sugar. I can go in peace now. Please be careful. *Never* trust that man, Elle. You hear me?"

"I love you, Jan," Ella had said, before hanging up the phone.

Janet passed away two days later, leaving Ella with more tools in her armor.

Later that day, the women met with Freda before the group session. Ella spoke first. "It's painful to accept that Bernard never loved me." Cecilia and Lanei exchanged glances. "I don't understand why he thought seeking revenge and sabotaging my dreams…would keep his secret hidden."

"By *abusing* you," Freda said. "Call it by its name."

"But—" Ella stopped.

Cecilia touched her hand and said, "Men like our husbands are driven by impulses greater than their sense of morality."

Lanei nodded. "Elle, I don't understand why Bernard agreed to your terms because he doesn't want people here to know he stole some money and beat up your brother years ago. Who would care about that in Miami?" Lanei frowned.

Ella scooted to the edge of the couch to make eye contact with them. "You see, Representative Meridien believes Bernard is somebody he's not. He *wants* her." Ella swallowed bitter saliva. "She'd never be with him if she knew the truth. The Meridiens don't tolerate thieves." The women nodded. Ella continued, "Bernard needs her *kind* and the Haitian community to launch his local political career. And if I publish his confession letter in the local Haitian paper, he'd have to move away from here and leave all he's built behind." Ella inhaled deeply to find the last shred of resolve she needed. "I met with your lawyer, Lan. I'm filing for divorce. She said I'll get alimony, child support, and basically everything I need until I finish school. Bernard owes me big. I'll let him climb the social ladder for now. The higher he gets, the harder he'll fall. But I *will* destroy him with that letter when I finish school, no matter how long it takes. *He knows that.* He's boxed in, ladies."

"Caged animals bite," Freda said.

"He stays over at her penthouse," Ella said, sucking her teeth. "She's in town a lot working on a new real estate development. Bernard only comes to the house to get the bills."

That night, Ella heard a noise coming from under her bedroom window. She ran to the kitchen and grabbed the butcher knife. Her heart racing like the second hand of a clock, she peeked through the blind and saw a raccoon climbing inside the dumpster. She laughed and put the knife back. But she couldn't fall asleep. There was an edge to her breathing. She slid out of bed and checked on her children. Then she fixed herself a cup of cinnamon tea, opened her biology book, and stared into the darkness through the kitchen window. She mentally counted the number of years Bernard would have to support her until she earned her degree.

She was on her slow journey to becoming a doctor.

69

Monique

T he Pass-It-Along meeting had lasted longer than usual. Monique pulled the car into the circular driveway and jumped out. Julien was home. She took a deep breath and filled her lungs with the smell of burnt tires on the streets of the city. The smell of rebellion. She walked into the house.

"Where the hell have you been?" Julien said before she was fully inside. Two-year-old Odile trailed behind her father with a new doll Monique hadn't seen before. "Do you know how crazy it is on the streets now with these demonstrators? They're burning people, Monique, not just tires." His usually hooded eyes were opened wide with agitation. He picked up Odile and hugged her as if to calm himself down.

"I was at Tina's. I'm not as afraid of the streets as you should be."

"Is that right?" He steadied his eyes to spear her with his gaze. "From now on, you stay in the house. It's almost Christmas, and you haven't decorated the house for Odile. I'm having a New Year's Eve party. We're bringing in 1986 with *fanfare*. These demonstrations will be crushed as always."

Except this time the demonstrators were students, parents, teachers, farmers, intellectuals, the unemployed, and the illiterate. After almost thirty years of the Duvaliers' oppressive regime, Haitians were ready for change.

On Christmas Eve, Monique snuck out of the house to attend a celebration at Tina's church. Pass-It-Along had helped over two hundred women since Monique and Tina had started it in 1981. When she arrived, the hall vibrated with murmurs and emotion. Almost everyone in the room knew someone who had been shot, beaten, or imprisoned. Yet hope and determination blanketed the attendees like rain. There was no longer any room for fear. Some shared their concern for Monique because of her involuntary association with the regime. She raised her fist in the air and the room grew silent. "*Merci*," Monique said. "I want you all to know that no matter where I go, I will always be with you.

I'm very proud of all of you. *Joyeux Noel et Bonne Année.*" Monique pumped her fist. "*A ba Duvalier.*"

A chorus of "Down with Duvalier" reverberated in the hall. The escalation of unrest infused Monique with hope. People denounced, they looted, and they burned.

That night, Anita came into the bedroom. "Madame, be prepared to leave with your daughter," she whispered. "I was at a meeting last night in my neighborhood. It's happening this time. People are literally dying for change, and change is finally coming. I'll stay here to protect you as best as I can, but you should leave soon."

"I have a plan." Monique looked at Odile playing next to her on the floor. She hugged Anita. "Thank you, my friend. Will you and the staff be safe?"

"Don't worry, madame. *We are the people.*" Anita smiled.

Monique packed and waited.

In late January, Julien barged into the bedroom where Monique was sitting with Anita, keeping vigil until daylight.

"Monique, the city is on fire!" His voice trembled. "They torched my office tonight. My father is in hiding, and my brothers are missing. They're burning everything. Are we packed? We have to leave."

"We're leaving tomorrow," Monique said.

"Good, we're going to the Dominican Republic." He walked into the closet to pack, Odile following him. Monique said nothing.

"Pappi, Pappi," Odile babbled, raising her arms. "Up. Up."

Julien scooped up his daughter and placed her on the back of his neck, twirling around the room with her. She giggled, beating his bald head like a drum. A touch of sadness tapped at Monique's heart for her daughter. One day, Odile would know the ugly truth about her father.

The next morning, a caravan from the American embassy came to take them to the airport. Julien held Odile in his arms. Monique walked up to the older man who seemed to be in charge and spoke in French loud enough for Julien to hear. "Sir, I want to leave with my *American* daughter. I'm a legal resident of the US. I don't want my husband to come with us. He has abused and persecuted me and my family for over five years."

"Ma'am, we have orders to evacuate one American child and her parents. We can't forcibly take her from him if he objects." He shrugged. "I'm sorry."

Julien snorted and climbed inside the car with Odile in his arms. The sound of a horn tooting made Monique turn. Papa shuffled out from the back of his car. They stared at each other until he cleared his throat and said, "Monique, I'm sorry. I want to say thank you for the sacrifices you made to keep our family safe." He looked away briefly. "Do you need anything? I can—"

"I don't need anything, Papa," Monique said. "Thank you for coming."

Esther and Solange stepped out from the back of the car and rushed her. "Moe, I'll miss you, but I promise to come visit," Esther said, hugging her tight. "Go live your dreams, *bébé*."

Solange extended her arm like an olive branch. Monique pulled her to her chest. "I'm sorry, Moe. I've been horrible to you since you were little. I thought you got everything that should have been mine. But now I see there was always plenty for all of us. Forgive me."

"Nothing to forgive, Sol. I haven't exactly been the easiest little sister." They smiled.

The American driver blew the horn. Monique stared at her father before folding her body inside his shaking arms like she had never done before. He kissed her cheek, and a tear escaped from his closed lid and landed on her face. Monique watched him limp behind her sisters toward his car, and empathy replaced the anger that had dwelled in her heart for this man. Maybe one day love would take root there. A breeze lifted her bangs and deposited them back on her forehead like one of Maman's soft kisses. Monique turned to Anita and hugged the small woman in a bear hug. "Remember, you can reach me through Tina whenever you want to. Please be safe and thank you for your friendship." Monique picked up the duffel bag next to her feet and handed it to Anita.

Anita opened the bag and gasped. "*O bondie!* I've never seen so much green money in my life. Won't you need it over there, madame?" Anita asked.

"No! This money belongs to you and all the people on the street. Share it with the staff," Monique said. "I'll be okay. I'll miss you, *zanmi*."

Anita wiped her face with the back of her gnarled hand. "I'll miss you too, mada…*Monique*."

"*Finally*, Anita." They laughed through their tears.

The ride to the airport was bittersweet for Monique. She hated leaving Tina, Anita, and the women she had worked with over the years. Their resilience in the face of daily hardships had bolstered her determination to never give up. She looked out the window and saw a mob with signs demanding justice from three decades of tyranny.

The smell of burnt flesh got stronger as the car stopped at a roadblock. A pair of legs dressed in the dark blue uniform of the *Tonton Macoutes* twitched inside a ring of fire as people chanted. Julien's eyes bulged. She would have opened the car door and thrown him onto the burning pile if she weren't concerned about being mistaken for the enemy and jeopardizing her daughter's life. Fear rearranged Julien's features as if he could read her mind.

When they reached the airport, the mob was screening people for evaders—people trying to escape overdue justice. It took three well-armed Marines to get Monique and her family inside the terminal. As they were about to board a helicopter, Julien turned to the man in charge and said, "I demand to go to the Dominican Republic with my family." He glared at Monique.

"Sir, this chopper is heading to Miami to evacuate an American citizen to American soil. You can stay here if you wish, or you can go to the Dominican Republic from Miami. What'll it be? We have to leave now," the man said.

The chain-link fence separating the mob from the travelers groaned as people pushed and growled like hungry pit bulls. The posts shook. Like a cornered animal, Julien scanned the scene before climbing into the chopper. His shoulders slumped.

The chopper lifted off on its way to Miami. Monique let out her breath, and a smile lifted the corner of her lips. Everything happened exactly the way she had planned it.

70
Cecilia

Cecilia walked into her classroom and wrote the date on the blackboard like she did every morning. This time she changed every segment of it including the year. *Monday, January 6, 1986.* She'd made a resolution on New Year's Day. She was prepared to be alone because she knew her worth. She could no longer live her life on that emotional roller coaster with Orson and his vices. Her appointment with a divorce attorney later in the month had launched her resolution. Perhaps she would never understand the depth of Helen's love for her son, since Cecilia would never be a mother, but she had listened to the anguished woman.

Orson had gone back to rehab after Halloween. Helen had paid an investigator to search for him since no one had seen him for days. Cecilia had nothing left to care for Orson, but she had Betty and Friendy to nurture and love.

"Ceecee, I have no right to ask," Helen had said, shifting on Cecilia's blue sofa, "but Orson wants to come home for Christmas when he's discharged. He—"

"Helen, please." Cecilia had stopped her. "I'm filing for divorce. I should have done it sooner, but I thought I could cure Orson. I deserve better."

"You're right. I'm...so sorry, but—" The raw pain on Helen's face made Cecilia uncomfortable and sad. "I will make it easy for you to get out by giving you Orson's share of the house. He agrees." Helen pushed. "In return, please let him come home for the holidays. That's all he talks about when I visit. I'm looking for a condo for him. He doesn't want to live with me, and I don't want him on the street."

"No, I can't. I don't need a husband. I don't need a man. I don't even know why he'd want to come here. It's over and I'm okay."

The first week of school after the holidays grounded Cecilia in a familiar physical and emotional place. Betty rushed out of her room on Sunday afternoon, buttoning her blouse. "Ceecee, are you going somewhere?"

"Yeah, I'm meeting Mel. Is everything okay, sweetie?"

"Orson was waiting around the corner yesterday when I came back from the mall."

Cecilia gasped. "Why didn't you tell me last night? Did he talk to you?"

"He waved," Betty said, her voice shaking. "I ran all the way to the house."

"I don't want him loitering around here. That's why I filed a restraining order. Don't talk to him and don't ever let him inside the house." Betty nodded. Cecilia kissed her cousin's forehead and said, "Have fun tonight. You've been moody lately. Sourpuss." She pinched Betty's cheek. "I'll bring you that dessert you like."

The next morning, Cecilia knocked on Betty's door. "Betty, I went to the movies with Ella and Lanei last night thinking you'd be out. Susan and her mom are in the hospital. A van ran into them on the way to get you last night. I didn't want to wake you when I got home. I'm so glad they hadn't picked you up yet."

"I wish I'd been in the car with them, and I was dead," Betty said in a flat tone.

Cecilia gasped. "I know Susan is your best friend, but why would you say something like that?"

Betty ran to her room. Cecilia followed her. "Honey, you're upset about the accident." She sat on the edge of the bed. "They'll be fine though."

Two days later, Betty poked her head from her bedroom. "Ceecee, the cramps are bad today. I'm staying home."

"Poor baby. Must be a family thing. I used to have them bad when I was your age. They get better. I'll get you some hot tea."

Cecilia stroked Betty's cheek with the back of her hand after placing a cup of herbal tea on the side table. "Do you want to stay with Mel? It'll take your mind off the pain."

"No, I have to study for a couple of tests. You changed the lock when Orson left, right?"

"Of course. But he won't come here. He knows I filed a restraining order against him."

"I hope so." Betty sipped the hot tea.

"Betty, is there something you need to tell me about Orson? Is he bothering you in any way? Please tell me."

"Um...it's nothing. I'm glad he's gone. I'm sorry you may be sad."

Cecilia hugged her cousin and smiled. "I'm not sad. More disappointed. I love myself"—she tickled Betty's neck—"and I love you, little cousin."

Betty giggled. "Love you too."

"Call the school if you need me."

Later that day, Cecilia got a substitute to cover her last two periods, bought Betty's favorite Chinese food, and hurried home. She would check the paper for a movie they could see if Betty felt better. When she got home, she threw her keys on the kitchen counter, placed the food cartons down, and knocked on Betty's bedroom door.

"Betty, I brought Chinese food."

There was no answer. Cecilia paused. Betty slept like the dead. She'd let her rest, and they could eat later. Cecilia turned to walk down the hall to her room to change. She heard a muffled sound, then a crash. She rushed toward the bedroom and knocked with both fists on the door.

"Ceecee, please help me. He—" Betty shouted.

Cecilia reared back and kicked the door handle with her foot. Her heel broke. The door flew open and splinters rained down on the tile. She winced at the throbbing in her big toe, but the scene in front of her assaulted all her senses. Her eyes misted. A scream caught in her throat. Her ears filled with a buzz, and the smell of fear and something foul lurked in the room. Betty pulled her torn blouse to cover her exposed breasts, cowering against the headboard. Standing by the window, Orson fumbled with the latches. Cecilia had put special locks on all her doors and windows for their safety.

"Betty, what...what happened in here?" Cecilia screamed as she rushed to the teen and grabbed her shoulders, lifting her head to look into her eyes. "Did Orson...did he? Oh my God."

Cecilia lunged at Orson by the window and pummeled him with her fists. Spittle flew from her mouth. "You're a monster. You're going to prison where you belong."

Orson tried to push her away. "I didn't do anything to her. I was just talking—"

"He has been trying to touch me for months, Ceecee," Betty said with a sob. "I was ashamed and scared. I thought it was Susan at the door. He pushed his way in and followed me in here as I tried to lock my door. He didn't... I fought him."

Cecilia picked up a T-shirt from the chair by the window and threw it to Betty. Orson's bloodshot eyes followed her like a light beam. "I'm calling the police," she said as she made her way to the kitchen.

Orson followed her. "If you send me to prison, you better not be in this country when I get out."

Cecilia grabbed a knife from the butcher block on the counter and pounced on him. He twisted her arm. The knife clattered to the floor. He pulled her face close to his mouth. His breath smelled like something had died in there. "Don't try me, woman."

He let go of her head, and she fell onto a stool. Orson scooped up Friendy off the floor and opened the front door. He turned. "I almost got my virgin," he hissed and slammed the door.

"Oh no—" Cecilia said as she ran to the kitchen sink and vomited. She leaned on the counter to steady herself. Friendy's bark faded as if life itself was slipping out of her body. After rinsing her mouth, she called the police.

After the police officers left, Cecilia cleaned the house, wiping away the fingerprint powder left behind. She wanted to erase every trace of Orson in her space and in her life. She peeked into Betty's room. She'd given Betty some Midol and ginger tea earlier and tucked her into bed.

"Oh, you're up, sweetie. How are you feeling?"

Betty sat up and stretched her arms over her head. "My stomach is better. Ceecee, please don't tell anyone. I want to go home."

Cecilia reached for her cousin. With her arms around her neck, she stared into Betty's puffy eyes. "We never ever hide the vile sins committed against us by men and carry their shame." She shook Betty's shoulders as if to stuff the words deeper. "Orson is going to pay for what he's done."

Cecilia crawled into Betty's bed with her. She had failed her cousin. If she hadn't come home early, Betty would have suffered the same fate she had. How could she have been so blind? She would make Orson pay. A wave of pain knifed her stomach like a scalpel incising a tumor. The tumor had grown from her mother's hatred, from the men who had violated her twelve-year-old body, and from the husband who had betrayed her. "Get dressed. I need to find Friendy. We'll grab dinner. That Chinese food is jelly now."

"I don't feel like going out, and I'm not hungry, Ceecee."

Cecilia tried to extricate herself from Betty's embrace. "I'll go and bring some pizza back."

Betty held her with such force, Cecilia leaned into her to slacken the pull on her neck. "Please, Ceecee, don't leave me alone here. What if…what if he comes back?" she asked, sobbing.

"Okay. It's okay, baby." Cecilia kissed her forehead. "It's going to be all right."

When Betty's snoring reached a crescendo, Cecilia tiptoed to the door and closed it. In the bathroom, she splashed cold water on her face and peered into the mirror as if seeing her face for the first time. Her daddy's princess, the professional woman, and the beloved friend stared back at her in the face of an attractive woman. A pretty woman. Ugly secrets had concealed her beauty from her until all she could see was despair. She would house secrets no longer.

Early the next morning, Cecilia dropped Betty off at school. When she reached Helen's house, the maid was leaving, adjusting her purse strap over her shoulder before pulling the front door closed behind her. "Mrs. Matthews is at Jackson Memorial Hospital, ma'am," the maid said. "She left me a note."

"What happened to her?" Cecilia asked, her concern for her mother-in-law diluting her anger toward Helen's son.

"I don't know." The woman shrugged. "I have to go catch the bus."

Cecilia hoped she would not get a speeding ticket. She decided to go directly to the hospital.

Helen buried her face behind her hands when she saw Cecilia in the doorway. "Orson was already here when the police tracked him down," Helen said. Two police officers stood guard by the hospital room door.

"I'm sorry, Helen. I couldn't let Orson hurt me or anybody else again."

"Do you want to see him?" Helen asked, crying silent tears. "My son is clinging to life after a heroin overdose. He's on life support. It—"

"No! I don't ever want to see Orson again." She touched Helen's shoulder. "Please, do you know where Friendy is?"

"Orson loves that little dog."

"He can't have him, Helen. I'm prepared to fight—"

"That won't be necessary, Ceecee. You can pick him up now. He's at my next-door neighbor's house. I'm sorry." Cecilia rushed out of the hospital to pick up Friendy.

A week later, Cecilia filed for divorce. Afterward, she gathered with Lanei, Ella, and Mel for lunch at Ella's. Cecilia told them about her rape in Boston.

"Oh, Ceecee, why didn't you tell us years ago?" Lanei said. "You helped all of us. We could have helped you."

"But you are strong despite all of it," Ella said. "You inspired me even when I was jealous of your success."

"I don't have a bracelet to clink," Mel said, raising a glass of mimosa. "To my best friend and sistah. You enrich our lives, Ceecee."

Cecilia raised her glass and said, "To all of you and to Moe, who's on her way."

"To Monique," they all said, clinking glasses and bracelets.

As she drove home, Cecilia thought about how far she'd come in her life. She was many things. A friend. A teacher. A mentor. An island sister. Every loving relationship required the ability to forgive, thus she would forgive herself so she could continue on her journey of self-love. When she crawled into bed that night, Friendy licked her face, wagging his tail as if to say he agreed. She scratched behind his ears and smiled. Her future was full of adventures, but her present was great. She was in the driver's seat of her destiny.

71

Lanei

At the Spring Fair in the church parking lot, Lanei rode almost all the rides. She giggled louder than Maria. The book she always carried had stayed in the car. The January breeze ruffled her hair, blowing it across her face, and the sun browned her skin.

With Freda's help, Lanei had evicted Kevin from her mind. She refused to be paralyzed by his imminent release. Life was to be lived in happiness. Maria got off the pony ride and ran to Nate, jumping into his arms. "Are you ready for the movie?" he said.

Lanei and Nate stared at each other and smiled. They walked hand in hand to the car with Maria in the middle. After the movie ended, Lanei woke up to find her head on Nate's shoulder, a sleeping Maria curled up in his arms. Nate drove them home, and Lanei yawned as she stepped out of his car in front of her building. Nate opened the back door and scooped Maria up. Lanei threw her right arm around his neck as she hummed the tune from the movie they'd just seen, and they made their way toward the lobby of her apartment building.

A figure shot out of the shadows from the side of the building and blocked their path. Nate stopped. Lanei's mouth opened but no sound came out.

"Get your grabby hands off my daughter!" Kevin said with a growl as he reached for Maria. Nate stepped back. "You been fucking my wife, college boy? Huh?" Kevin bared his teeth like a rabid dog.

"Get away from us!" Nate yelled, trying to hand Maria to Lanei. "Take her, Lane."

She ignored Nate. This was her fight. "Kevin, let go of my daughter," Lanei said in a voice that made Kevin stop long enough to blink and then squint at her. Standing tall and strong in front of her abuser, Lanei felt no fear.

"We'll go to court and settle visitation one day, but tonight I'm taking Maria upstairs to bed. Now, go!"

Kevin let go of Maria's arm and raised his hand. "*Don't you dare!*" Lanei said, the words coming out of her gritted teeth with sharp edges to them. She grabbed the front of his shirt and pushed him back. "Get away from me, you devil!"

Nate tried to put Maria down, but she clung to his neck, whimpering. A tenant walked by, looked at Kevin, and said, "I'm calling the police."

Kevin walked backward to his car. "You can't get away, *cunt*," he yelled as he drove away.

Shaken up, Lanei prayed while Nate put Maria to bed. A few hours later, Lanei received word that Kevin had been arrested at the Miami airport before he'd boarded a plane back to Chicago.

The following night, at the Women Talk meeting, Lanei told the group about Kevin's surprise visit the night before. "These assholes think they own us," a petite redhead said while Cecilia stroked Lanei's back. "He crossed state lines and violated his probation. He'll be in the slammer for a lot longer this time. I'm a paralegal."

"It will never be long enough," Lanei said, "but I'll have to deal with that one day."

"Are you okay otherwise?" Freda asked.

"I'm fine," Lanei said. "I'm happy and I will not let Kevin pollute that." She smiled, touching Ella's and Cecilia's hands. "I have my tribe."

"I heard Monique is on her way," Freda said. "The tribe will be complete."

The three women clinked their bracelets in response.

When the phone rang that night, Lanei was rubbing her knees after she'd finished praying before going to bed. It was her lawyer. "Lanei, are you sitting down?" the woman asked.

Lanei's stomach seized. "What? What is it?" she said, wishing she'd let Nate stay tonight like he'd wanted to, but Lanei never wanted to rely on a man for anything ever again.

"I just got a call from the prosecutor's office. Kevin assaulted a guard today because he wouldn't mail a letter to you. Kevin put the man in a coma. The guard may not survive. Kevin is looking at a *very* long time, Lanei."

"How long?" she asked, feeling sadness for Peggy.

"If the guard dies, Kevin will get the chair. This is Florida," the lawyer said. "You moved to the right state."

Kevin was out of her life in all the important ways. Lanei got back down on her knees and prayed fervently to her merciful God. He was making miracles in her life every day. She did not want the guard to die, but God would know best.

72
Ella

E lla fed her children dinner, cleaned the kitchen, and hunkered down with
her homework. What had happened to Lanei with Kevin a couple days
ago terrified her. She got up and walked into Perrine's bedroom. She pulled
open the dresser drawer and shoved her hand in until she touched the envelope
she'd stashed there a few days ago. She sighed and went back to the kitchen
to continue studying. One day, she'd have a great laugh about the envelope's
contents. Not today. She was going to meet with the lawyer who'd handled
Lanei's divorce tomorrow. She wanted a clean slate. Tears blurred her vision,
and one drop fell on her book. She was crying for the many losses in her life,
but the future was hers to shape.

Later in the evening, Bernard walked into the kitchen where Ella was
studying along with eight-year-old Alex. Perrine was coloring in her book.
Neither of the kids acknowledged his presence. That saddened Ella. He opened
envelopes from the pile on the baker's rack. "Why the hell is the electric bill so
high, Ella?" Bernard snapped. "Are you doing it on purpose?" He pointed to
the lit hallway. "See what I'm talking about."

Ella raised her head from her book and stared at him. The simmering fury
in his eyes registered on her brain like a stamp. She pushed a sheet of paper and
a pen toward him, wiping her palms on the legs of her pants.

"Bernard, please write the address where I can mail the bills to you. I don't
want you coming here anymore. Our lawyers will set up visitation if you care."
She shrugged. "Now please leave. I have a lot of homework."

"I work fourteen goddamn hours a day, Ella, and now I tutor every extra
hour I have." He stood next to her chair. "I have no social life. I hardly have
time to sleep." He cleared his throat. "Speaking of sleep, I'm staying here
tonight."

"Oh no. You're not. Why don't you go back to *Representative Meridien?*"

His eyes clouded over. Ella pushed her chair away from him and adjusted her glasses on her sweaty nose.

"She…she broke up with me because I don't have time for *her*. She wants me to come back when I *rearrange* my schedule." He made jerky air quotations with his fingers. "I don't know how much longer I can keep this up. I'm tired." He punched the cabinet door. Alex looked at his mother with alarm in his eyes, holding his pencil like a sword. Ella patted his hand.

She stared into Bernard's eyes and held their content away from her heart. How dare he complain to her about his love life? The prick. "Only eight more years. That's how much longer, *Bernie*," she said, imitating Representative Meridien's whiny voice. Ella stood and walked toward the bedroom to get her chemistry book. "Now leave and lock the door behind you." She would change the lock tomorrow.

His footfalls came fast as she started to turn. Bernard threw her on the bed and straddled her chest, his hands closing around her neck. Her glasses flew off her face. His features shifted in the dim light of the bedside lamp. She kicked her legs hard on the bed and scraped his face until a black void started to pull her under. *But Bernard has never raised his hands to me.* That thought played on a loop in her oxygen-deprived brain. The last thing she heard was Alex's distant voice. "I called 911 like you told me to do, Mommy."

Tired of fighting since the day she'd come into the world, Ella surrendered to the welcoming calm that summoned her to stop struggling, to rest, to sleep, to let go.

73
Monique

It was early afternoon when Monique arrived at her family house in Miami after the evacuation from Haiti. The Haitian couple who took care of it had left her a welcoming meal. Papa had called them. Another knot loosened in her heart. She tucked her daughter into bed for a nap and returned to the foyer where a dazed Julien sat on the floor as if his legs could not hold him up. The armed driver brought the last piece of luggage inside the house and stood by the door.

"Monique, why isn't he bringing my belongings into the house?" Julien said in Creole.

Monique controlled her impulse to crush him under her shoe like a roach. "You think you're staying here? You raped me in this house. I filed a police report, remember? You're going to pay for everything you've done to me and my family. You have no place to hide."

Julien tilted his head back to look into her eyes. "*You bitch*! You planned all of this." He nodded his head up-and-down like a puppet. He sprung up from the floor. "You think you can get rid of me like that." He snapped his fingers, heading to the bedroom. "I'm taking my daughter."

"No, you're not. You can wait for the police outside. I called them."

Julien turned and sprinted to the front door. "I'll be back. Count on it."

He pulled the door closed behind him.

"Are you going to be okay?" the driver asked.

She nodded. "I'll be fine. Thank you."

Monique took a quick shower, got dressed, and called Cecilia. "What? Elle... Oh shit, Ceecee! Why didn't you call me?"

"We tried many times," Cecilia said. "Couldn't get through."

"I know. Things are crazy in Haiti right now. Come get me, Ceecee."

She hung up and screamed, beating the pillow on the couch with her fists. She paced the length of the room. Fear crowded her brain. Now she wished she could pray, but what could she say? What kind of God let a man do this to a woman? Why wasn't Bernard struck down by a bolt of lightning when he raised his hand? The doorbell rang. She ran to the door and fell into Cecilia's arms. Sobs racked their bodies.

"Moe, I'm so glad you're here. I don't think Lan and I could have gone through this without you. It's horrible."

"Where are the kids? Poor Alex and Per. I knew in my bones Bernard was bad news. Where's that asshole now? I need to get my hands on him, Ceecee. I want to do worse to him than he did to my sister."

"The kids are staying with me, but I left them with my friend Larry. Bernard is in jail where he belongs. Lanei is with Elle. One of us stays with her at all times."

They dropped Odile off at Chantal's house. Monique rolled down the window and let the cool January breeze dry her flowing tears. She wanted to shred Bernard the way Ella had taught her to shred the cabbage to make *pikliz*.

The hissing sound of the machines at the hospital filled the room with hope and despair. Ella's relaxed face betrayed the struggles she had fought. Lanei stood from her kneeling position on the floor with her rosary and hugged Monique hard. "Welcome back, Moe," Lanei whispered.

Monique kissed Lanei's cheek and took Ella's cool hand in hers and squeezed. "Elle, you have to fight now, sister. Please."

Cecilia touched her shoulder. "Moe, I found an envelope at the bottom of Perrine's dresser drawer. It says *TRIBE*. It's at the house. We'll open it later."

Monique nodded. When she saw the bracelet on Ella's wrist, Monique's sobs came from a place she had protected all her life because she thought she had to be infallible to be strong. Now in the company of her island sisters, she opened the gate to let it all out. As she wept, she felt her pride break loose, making room for healing.

"I wouldn't let them take her bracelet off," Lanei said, blowing her nose on a shredded tissue. "Brian has been so helpful. He listed us as family to allow us to be with her."

They stood at the foot of the bed, holding hands like three sentinels blocking an opponent they could not see.

Monique smelled his aftershave before she turned and fell against Brian's chest. Her heart knocked against her ribs as if it wanted to escape its confines and touch his. "Oh, Brian," she said, stroking his face hard with her palm to feel his flesh against hers before pulling away from him.

"You're really here," Brian said. "I'm so glad you're safe."

"Brian, is Elle going to be okay?" Monique asked, pulling the lapel of his white coat. The soft light of the ICU cubicle and their whispering voices pricked Monique's brain like needles.

"Only time will tell, Moe," he said, looking at Cecilia and Lanei. "She's getting the best care here. After all, she's an *island sister*."

Monique sniffled. "You know the right thing to say to welcome a girl home, Brian."

His pager beeped. "Welcome back," he said. "I have to go. May I see Odile later?"

Monique followed him to the hallway. "Come by tomorrow instead. I'm staying with Ceecee tonight."

"Good! You shouldn't be alone in that house. You saw what happened—"

She squeezed his hand and pushed him down the corridor. "I'll be fine."

Later that evening, the women tucked Alex and Perrine in bed after their bath. They sat on Cecilia's couch as she opened the sealed envelope. Heads almost touching, they read the letter Ella had written only a couple weeks before her attack.

January 1, 1986—my twenty-eighth birthday!

My sisters, if you're reading this letter, it means something bad happened to me and Bernard most likely did it! I was never as strong as the three of you, but you have carried me this far. Give my bracelet to Perrine on her thirteenth birthday. Maybe she'll start her own tribe with Maria and Odile. Ceecee, I'd like you to raise my children along with Auntie Moe and Auntie Lan. I hope to read this letter with all of you after my graduation. We'll have a great laugh, won't we? Live your life with joy.

Elle

They all nodded as Cecilia folded the letter. They sat in silence, twirling their bracelets around their wrists as they cried. The phone rang. Monique became alert.

"It's Larry," Cecilia said before picking up the receiver. "Hello. We just got home. Uh-huh." She listened, shaking her head. "No change. Okay, we'll talk tomorrow."

"Larry sounds like a great friend," Monique said.

"He is," Cecilia said, her dimples tunneling deeper into her beautiful face with her quiet smile.

When Monique stood to leave, Lanei said, "You should stay with me. Don't be in that house alone with Julien around. We have enough to worry—"

"Brian is coming by later. He'll stay in one of the guest rooms," Monique said, ashamed of how easy it had become for her to lie. "I won't be alone."

Lanei dropped Monique off at home. Monique made herself a strong cup of Haitian coffee, pulled her hair into a tight bun, and changed into loose pajamas. She lay on the couch in the dark, recapping the last five years. She believed Julien loved his daughter. She also believed that his father was responsible for the carnage against her family. But Julien had abused her daily by forcing her to stay in Haiti. He could have stopped what his father started.

She'd been waiting for hours when she finally heard it. The noise came from the kitchen. She rolled to her feet. She flipped the light switch on the kitchen wall and came face-to-face with Julien. She took deep breaths to slow down her heart just the way she had practiced in self-defense class. "Welcome back," she said, looking at the broken window and clucking her tongue.

"Monique, please listen. My father was captured on the border of the Dominican Republic. They threw a burning tire around his neck." He blew his nose on the tail end of the same shirt he'd been wearing when they'd left Haiti the day before. The stale odor of alcohol mingled with sweat floated toward her. "I'm sorry about everything. Please give me a chance to make it up to you. We're leaving today for the Dominican Republic. Where's my baby?" Julien threw what looked like airline tickets on the table between them and pointed a knife at Monique's chest. "What? Cat got your tongue now? Go get Odile." He waved the knife toward the hallway. "I want my daughter. I've lost everything. I'm not losing her." Tears flowed down his unshaven face.

Monique breathed, pushing the fear down deeper. "You need a weapon to make me go with you now?" Monique smiled, grateful that Julien could not see her heart racing inside her chest. She closed her right hand around the neck of one of the bottles on the table. She had filled up a few with bleach earlier and placed them around the house. Her eyes never left his. "Why, Julien, you're scared of me *here*!"

He jabbed the space between them with the knife. "I'm not sca—"

She flung the bottle at Julien's face. The loose cap flew off the bottle, and the thump of the glass hitting bone filled the room along with the smell of bleach. He screamed, grabbing at his nose and face, but he remained standing. She dove over the table, closed the distance between them, and brought her right knee to his groin. She felt a crunch. Julien groaned as he grabbed his crotch with both hands. Blood dripped from his nose. Monique kicked the knife from his hand with her foot, connecting with his chest. The weapon skittered on the floor and disappeared underneath the pantry door.

"Damn it, Monique, why do you always have to push me to hurt you?" he said, panting as he knocked a chair out of his way and reached for her.

Monique ducked to evade him, throwing herself in a slide across the tile floor. She crossed her legs around Julien's ankle like a pair of scissors and pulled, bringing him down hard. He sat up and lunged at her, trying to grab her neck. She bobbed her head from side to side and raked his face with her long nails. When she connected with one eyeball, she pulled and heard a pop. Julien howled and threw himself on top of her on the floor, throwing a flurry of punches that she dodged, except for a couple that she let land in the right spots. She raised her torso off the floor, clamped her teeth on his right earlobe, and pulled. With his left eye swollen shut and his skin blistered from the bleach, he screamed, reaching blindly for her face. She scooted out from under him and delivered a karate chop to his neck that struck his carotid artery dead-on. His right eye stared blankly at the ceiling as he went still. Monique kicked his face with her foot. His head rolled to one side and stopped.

"We'll see about that, asshole," she said, pulling her hair into a tighter bun as she made her way toward the kitchen phone to call the police.

Sirens competed with a loud knock on the front door before she'd finished dialing 911. Monique ran down the hallway and collided with two police officers when she opened the door.

"Ma'am, are you okay?" one of the officers asked, looking at her ripped pajama top while the other officer rushed inside with his gun drawn. "A neighbor called."

"My husband tried to kill me," she said. "His knife is in the pantry."

"You have a cut on your cheek and bruises on your face and chest," said the paramedic who'd followed the cops inside. "We need to take you to the hospital." Monique had gotten Julien where she wanted him. Attempted murder, aggravated assault, and rape.

Later that day, Monique sat across from Brian at a table in the hospital cafeteria where she'd sat with Ella and the others over the years. "Monique, you lied to me about staying over at Ceecee's," Brian said with hurt in his voice. "You could have gotten yourself killed. I can help with a place—"

"I'm sorry about the lie. As a friend, I will never lie to you again, but I *needed* to do this. Now I can put my armor down." Maman's voice echoed in her head. "As for where I'm gonna stay, I'm getting my job back at the women's shelter and living in a transitional apartment. I need to do this on my own. My whole life men have taken care of me. *No more!*"

"I respect your decision. But Julien will be released one day." Worry lines mapped Brian's forehead.

Monique shrugged. "My time is too precious to spend on that." Monique speared a piece of tomato from her salad with the fork. Halfway to her mouth, her hand stopped. "So, I heard you have a girlfriend. You look happy." She grinned but it wasn't a smile.

"I *had*." He stared into her eyes. "She joined a practice in Boston late last year. We tried to make it work, but I wouldn't leave Florida." He shrugged, then smiled. "I'm a southern boy."

Monique's feet stopped tapping the floor. She felt a lightness as she chewed on the tomato, never breaking eye contact with the man she had thought about daily for almost six years. Whatever happened with Brian in the future, Monique was glad to have felt the romance of her love for him.

A week later, Monique put Odile down on the tile floor of their new two-bedroom furnished unit at the transitional housing complex. She emptied the grocery bags into the small fridge and the pantry, saving the coupons she hadn't used and her loose change in the tin box where she kept them. She turned in a circle around the small living room, feeling like Mary Tyler Moore and wishing she had a beret to throw up in the air. She smiled. She had put her armor down as Maman had asked, but her freedom would never be negotiable.

That night, perched on the edge of Odile's twin bed, Monique closed the picture book and kissed her daughter.

"Pappi," Odile said, fighting sleep. "Want Pappi."

Monique's heart ached for her daughter, but she was grateful Odile was only two years old. One day, they would talk about Haiti.

In therapy she was learning to unravel the threads that had bound her to Papa, who had thought beating her into submission would protect her, and to Julien, who'd been hell-bent on destroying her. As her nightmares subsided, she allowed herself to dream of Brian again.

Yesterday, he'd reached for her hand on the table at the hospital cafeteria and said, "Moe, you look happy and…self-assured. I'm glad therapy is helping you deal with the trauma you endured."

"It was a war. I think Odile helped me make less reckless choices because I had to protect her."

He squeezed her fingers. Monique wanted to touch him everywhere. She shifted in the booth.

"I want you to know that I'm here."

"Brian, I never asked you to wait. I have a marriage to dissolve and a child. I have baggage."

"Don't you think I know that?" His eyes drilled into her, searching for the feelings she knew she couldn't hide. "You never asked me, but nevertheless"—he shrugged—"I'm here."

A couple weeks after her return to Miami, Monique climbed into the passenger seat of Brian's Camaro convertible with the top down. Puffs of white cloud floated above them, revealing the clear, blue sky. The wind whipped Monique's hair straight behind her like a kite. She stuck her right hand out, splaying her fingers, while the breeze tickled her palm. She squealed like a little girl. She caught Brian stealing glances at her.

"Keep your eyes on the road, boy. How far are we going anyway? In case—"

Brian touched her hand. "I left instructions. The hospital will page me."

It was after seven, and they had been on the road for a couple of hours. The Friday afternoon traffic crawled alongside the desire that invaded every pore of her fevered skin. The late sunset splashed the sky with a bucketful of red and yellow streaks. When Brian pulled onto the redbrick driveway, her eyes opened wide. The heart-shaped sign on the colonial two-story structure read: *At Last Bed & Breakfast, Naples, Florida.*

"Stay in the car," he said, running inside. He came back shortly, opened the passenger door, scooped her up in his arms, and bounded up the stairs.

"Brian…honey, you can put me down now."

"Not until I get you in the bed," he whispered. "I've been waiting for five years, four months and—"

She pulled his head down and folded the words within her kiss. "And twelve days," she murmured against his lips.

He pushed the unlocked door open with his hip and deposited her on top of the bed. She watched as Brian lit candles around the room. She felt their flames as they mimicked the burning inside her body. He walked back to the bed where she was struggling to get out of her dress. "Please, let me." He turned her on her stomach.

He fingered the tiny buttons on the back of the dress, freeing each one with his teeth. His wet tongue branded her skin.

"Hurry," she said, moaning.

"Patience, *ma chérie*," Brian drawled in his southern accent. "We have the whole weekend."

He pulled the dress down over her legs. His fingers teased the elastic band of her cream satin panties as he gnawed at the skin of her buttocks. She bit into the thick white duvet to keep from screaming. He raked his fingers through her hair. Monique closed her eyes and let the sensation transport her to a place she had never been with a man before. "Oh, Brian, fuck me already. Please."

He turned her on her back and stared into her eyes, smiling. At that moment, she opened her heart and let him see her secrets. Everything she had endured in Haiti, all that she was, and all she would become. The fighter, the survivor, the mother, the friend. The attorney she wanted to be. He ran his hand up the soft flesh of her inner thighs and opened her legs. She reached down between them and guided him into her. She closed her eyes and concentrated on his touch, letting the sensation search for all her battle scars and sand them smooth. "*Je t'aime*, Monique," he said, touching the entwined heart pendant on her chest with tears shining in his eyes.

Hours later, exhausted and happy, Monique laid her head on Brian's chest. The *thump-thump* of his heart spoke to her. She looked into his eyes and whispered, "*Je t'aime*, Brian."

On their way back on Sunday, Brian's pager beeped. "It's the hospital," he said. Monique breathed in deep and exhaled slowly, trying to slow her racing heart. He pulled over to call. She followed him into the phone booth.

"We're about a half hour away," he said. "Be there soon." He hung up. "Ella had another stroke."

Monique kicked the car tire until Brian crushed her to his chest. She pushed Brian away and climbed back into the car, trying to remember the prayer words Maman had taught her when she was a little girl. They wouldn't come. Monique did not believe they would help anyway.

74
Cecilia

Cecilia kissed the top of Ella's head before leaning over the bed and whispering, "Monique is on her way, Elle. She had an escapade with Brian. You'd agree she earned it, right?" Cecilia smiled, and Lanei gave her hand a reassuring squeeze. "Hang in there. Your babies need you. We need you." She inhaled, trying to dislodge the weight crushing her heart. She stroked Ella's hand. "You're going to be okay, sweetie."

Monique rushed into the room a few minutes later. Cecilia could see Brian talking to the nurse assigned to Ella. He wiped his face with his palm and hung his head before turning his gaze toward the cubicle and locking eyes with Cecilia. With their arms wound around each other's necks, the three women watched Ella's labored breathing. Lanei rolled her rosary, her lips moving as if she thought Ella would stop fighting if she stopped praying.

Soon the room filled with medical personnel. Suddenly Ella opened her eyes. The three friends walked closer to the bed as one unit. "Hi, Elle. Honey, we're here," Monique said. "Please—"

A breath escaped Ella's open mouth. They waited. It was her last.

Cecilia bit her lip to stifle her screams. She could not fall apart now. She stared into Ella's lifeless eyes and silently asked her for the strength to care for her children. Monique rushed toward the bed. She cradled Ella's head and screamed, "No, no, no!"

Brian reached for her and tried to dislodge her from Ella's body. "I'm so sorry, Moe," he said. "We've tried our best. I can assure you—"

Monique pushed him away. Her hands balled in front of her face in a fighting stance. "Your best wasn't goddamn good enough," she yelled, kicking everything in her path as another man helped Brian pull her outside. "I want to kill the bastard."

Cecilia fished her car keys from her bag. She needed to get away from Ella's body and embrace her children. She hoped to hold on to her late friend through the children she'd gifted her.

Lanei wrapped her rosary around Ella's wrist and removed her bangle bracelet. "Her body is gone, sisters, but she's in God's kingdom now. No one can hurt her there."

Cecilia had no idea where her dad had gone when he had passed, so how could she know where Ella was now? She only wished they were here with her. Monique turned to Lanei from the doorway. "No one should have hurt like this *here*, Lan."

Later that afternoon, the women sat on the couch at Cecilia's house in silence. Ella's bracelet lay on the coffee table. Larry had the kids. The muted TV flashed pictures of happy people laughing and couples kissing. Cecilia hugged a pillow to her stomach to stop the nausea that threatened to expel yesterday's meal.

She leaned over from where she sat at the end of the couch to look at Lanei and Monique and said, "We have to make funeral arrangements."

Monique stood and the tea mug that had been resting on her lap shattered on the tile floor. "I'm not ready to talk about planting Ella in the ground, Ceecee. She just died."

Lanei cleared her throat. "Ceecee is right, Moe. Prolonging it will not make it any less real."

"I'm going to haunt the prosecutor until they bury Bernard in prison," Monique said, "and I'll be cheering when his ass is strapped to the fucking electric chair."

Monique and Lanei left with their children. After Larry brought them home, Cecilia tucked Alex and Perrine into bed, unable to tell them that she was their new mommy now. She crawled into her bed and pummeled Orson's old pillow until feathers filled the room like confetti at a parade.

She reached for the blank journal from her nightstand drawer and started to put her new pain into words to lessen its impact on her heart.

75

Lanei

L anei found Nate waiting for her at her apartment. She put Maria to bed and asked him to pray with her. They knelt on the rug in front of her bed, and she reached for her rosary under her pillow. She recited the prayers that had always comforted her when she'd thought she had no escape from her woes. Now she needed God to show her how to deal with losing Ella. She prayed that Monique would make room in her heart for God to lighten her pain.

Lanei let the tears she had been holding flow. Nate took her in his arms, and seated on the floor, they rocked. Sobs shook her body. "Shh…shh, I'm sorry, Lane," Nate whispered, kissing her forehead. "So sorry, my love."

Lanei pulled away from Nate and stood. "Nate—"

"I should stay with you tonight. I'll sleep on the couch."

She shook her head, afraid screams might come out instead of prayers. "Okay, Lane. Call if you need me."

Lanei locked the door behind him, sat on the couch, and opened her Bible. She stared into the lamp on the side table. Had God rewarded her with going back to school, Maria's good health, Kevin's incarceration, and Nate's love because she served him with all her heart? What had Ella believed? But Ella, Monique, and Cecilia were good, decent, moral women. Just like Lanei they had fallen in love or crossed paths with the wrong men. No one deserved to die because of that. Lanei had no doubt Kevin would have eventually killed her. Would that have made her a bad person? She paged through her Bible and found the readings she needed. Anger escaped with every breath until her pain became a dull ache.

76

Monique

M onique slammed the apartment door, startling Odile awake. The toddler whined, then closed her eyes. "You have to wake up, baby. Mommy has to go to a meeting." She wondered who the guest speaker was tonight. It better not be some priest or pastor. God knew Lanei had given her enough Jesus to last a lifetime.

The phone rang. She placed Odile down on the couch and stared at the loud instrument. A vision of Julien flashed through her brain, delivering another dose of anger.

"Hello," she said, holding the receiver so hard her fingers cramped.

"Moe, I'm glad you made it home okay," Brian said. "Words can't express how sorry I am about Ella."

She lowered her body into one of the two chairs around the dinette table and ran her fingers through her tangled hair. While she'd been having sex with Brian, Ella had been dying. Why had she gone away when she'd needed to be by Ella's bedside? Could she blame Brian for pressuring her to go? "I should have stayed by her, Brian," she said, blowing her sore nose. "You didn't tell me she was going to die."

"Moe, how could I have known? Elle had been in a coma for several days. You shouldn't feel guilty about—"

"No!" she screamed. "You don't get to tell me how to *feel.*" She slammed the receiver down, loosening the base from the wall.

She sat on the plaid couch that had come with the transitional apartment. It smelled like Lysol and freedom. She picked up her daughter and inhaled her smell of innocence before making her way to the residents' mandatory weekly meeting downstairs. "You will never know your Auntie Ella," Monique whispered to the sleeping child, "but her memory will not die. Ever."

She locked the door behind her and hefted Odile to her shoulder. In the brightly lit meeting room, she sat in the circle on a plastic chair next to the woman who lived in the unit next to hers with her two teenage sons.

"Hi, Monique," the woman said, peering into her face. "You okay?"

Monique dried her eyes with the back of her hand. "My friend died today. Her husband killed her."

"Oh, dear, I'm so sorry." The woman squeezed Monique's arm. "I hope they got him. You know last week we had a financial planner, but tonight's guest speaker is this female attorney who's a killer in the courtroom. She's a strong advocate for women like...us."

Monique looked at the popcorn ceiling as if she could see the sky. Maybe there was a God, and maybe that God tried to make it up to believers and non-believers when he screwed up.

She pulled her notebook and a pen from her bag to record information. Bernard would die for what he'd done. That was her new mission.

77

The Sisters

Three days later, Monique, Cecilia, and Lanei sat across from Freda in the booth of a diner in Aventura. The specter of death after Ella's funeral had followed them from the cemetery. None of them wanted to go home and be alone with their dark thoughts.

Freda banged the table with her fist. Water spilled on the red-and-white checkered tablecloth. Monique pinched the skin between her eyes to staunch her tears. Cecilia puffed her cheeks in and out to slow her heart. Lanei prayed over their food.

"It could have been any one of us in the ground today," Cecilia said, wiping her face with a napkin.

Freda looked each one of them in the eye. "You have all managed to put your abusers behind bars, even Ella. You have to be vigilant in your future relationships, in cultivating self-love, in raising your children, in advocating for other women, and for the day these monsters may walk among you again."

"We are ready," the trio said in unison, nodding their heads at the same tempo.

Hours later, they parted ways, each remembering Ella's advice to live with purpose, joy, and passion.

In the weeks and months to come, Cecilia learned to be the best mother she could for Alex and Perrine. Her suppressed maternal instinct blossomed under the guidance of Monique and Lanei. With Freda's help she let go of the guilt and opened her heart to love Ella's children with gratitude.

Lanei accepted Ella's death. Although she missed her daily, Lanei believed she would see her sister again one day.

Monique threw herself into rebuilding her life alone with her daughter. She advocated for the women in her complex by becoming a liaison with the prosecutor's office. Bernard's conviction became her obsession.

The following year, Lanei graduated with her pharmacy degree, sporting the heart-shaped diamond ring Nate had proposed with the previous Christmas. Cecilia settled into her new role as a mother and maintained a comfortable friendship with Larry. Friendy was always by her side.

With student loans and her part-time job at the women's center, Monique had started law school in the fall. She'd never been happier living with so little money but so much gratitude and pride. When Brian proposed on her twenty-ninth birthday that October, she asked him to wait until she graduated with her law degree to propose again. She wanted no strings. He could wait or not.

Every Thursday night the trio alternated meeting at each other's homes for food, laughter, gossip, and solidarity.

One night at Cecilia's house, they heard Perrine suck her teeth the way Ella used to at something Maria said. They looked at each other and smiled with wet eyes while staring at Ella's bracelet sitting in the velvet box on the coffee table.

On a beautiful December day, Monique and Cecilia dressed in identical yellow chiffon gowns walked down the aisle between rows of white garden chairs in the courtyard of the hotel as Lanei's maids of honor. Six-year-old Perrine, a replica of Ella, walked in front of them, carrying a white satin pillow with Ella's gold bracelet nestled in the middle. Brian stood beside a beaming Nate. Alex and Freda sat next to Larry and the twins in the front row.

When Lanei reached them, the three women stood in a tight circle. Lanei smiled and raised her wrist with the bangle bracelet that had linked them for over a decade. Perrine walked up to them and lifted her mother's bracelet. They clinked four times. Freda and Mel stood and clapped.

The crowd applauded.

Author's Note

This novel is based on the lives and deaths of many women I have met over the years. Some were friends. Some were relatives. Some were clients.

Monique, Cecilia, Lanei and Ella are not mere strangers on a page. They are our mothers, daughters, sisters, aunties, nieces, cousins, friends, neighbors, co-workers. The women who inspired me to write this book did not live in a vacuum. They were surrounded by family and friends, yet no one helped. It was not because they did not care but because domestic violence, in many parts of the world, is considered a private and personal matter, not the heinous crime it really is.

When celebrities' acts of violence toward their partners make the news, we talk about abuse against women with the right amount of indignation, until the next news cycle brings more tantalizing stories.

Domestic violence against women destabilizes our society. Abused women and their children tend to lag their counterparts in health, economic, educational and social upward mobility.

Today there are many organizations that aid battered women. They do an excellent job in equipping women with the tools to become independent and live free of abuse. Yet, many still suffer in silence and in shame as if they are responsible for their abusers' actions. They hide in plain sight. No one sees them.

The statistics are staggering. One in three women will experience violence by a partner. We need to raise boys and girls with the same expectations, and respect for each other. Girls need to learn at an early age that they *matter*. Boys need to learn that their physical advantage is not a weapon to abuse and intimidate girls but rather a tool to nurture and protect all the women in their lives. The more we educate ourselves and each other, the more we can help stop this cycle of abuse. Thank you so much for reading this book.

Psst! Tell someone else about it.

Acknowledgments

First, I want to thank all the women who have spoken to me about their abuse because I listened. Without these women, there wouldn't be this work of fiction about domestic violence. I have never experienced it, but my Haitian culture did expose me to it at an early age.

I am grateful to have had the privilege of living in Guam and St. Thomas for a few months. The climate reminded me of home. The people reminded me of my people. They were warm and welcoming. They are islanders. I chose these beautiful countries as settings for the book. Cecilia's and Lanei's stories are universal and do not represent specific characteristics of these islands and their cultures.

I want to thank Anthony (Toni) J. Ramirez, a proud Guamanian who drove me around Guam and proudly explained its rich history. To the librarians from both islands, who pointed me to the right materials for my research.

To the Tarpon Springs critique group for listening to me read from this manuscript for a couple of years and their valuable feedback. To Bill Frederick for reading the whole thing and being honest with his comments.

I met Illinois State University Professor Susan Kalter via email through an acquaintance. She read my manuscript and offered generous feedback. So, the next time I was in Chicago, we met for dinner, and it was as if we'd known each other for a long time.

Gratitude to my family for believing that I could do this. Writers may write alone, but our stories come from living with and being around people. As the middle child of seven, I've always had a built-in tribe. My sister Marlene is my top cheerleader. Since she read the very first draft (which was not really that good) she declared it a bestseller.

To my daughters who, since their births, have given me more reasons to fight for women. You make me a proud Maman.

To my husband, my first beta reader for his unwavering support in everything I write and in everything I do. You are my champion, the wind beneath my wings, my *poto mitan*. You have been on this journey with me since the beginning, and we will ride it together until the end.

And of course, a book without readers is a long journal entry. I thank all my readers for making this a book. As I wrote it, I envisioned the conversations that would take place around kitchen tables, in coffee shops, everywhere, because we all likely know somebody who has been abused in at least one of its many facets. I wanted women to know they were not alone. That help is available. More importantly, that they *matter*.

About the Author

Micki Berthelot Morency was born in Haiti and emigrated to the US with her family in the seventies. A graduate of Northeastern University, Micki had a career in finance before she found her calling in social services as an advocate for women and children. A mother of daughters, she lives in St. Petersburg, Florida with her husband.

Printed in the USA
CPSIA information can be obtained
at www.ICGtesting.com
LVHW090847101123
PP17960900001B/1